I0555741

EX LIBRIS

Monster Stalker: A Darquepunk Novel Volume One
Copyright © 2015 by Elizabeth Watasin
All rights reserved.

An A-Girl Studio book
published 2015 in the USA.

No part of this book may be reproduced
or used without permission except
in the case of brief portions embodied
in critical reviews and articles.

For additional information, please contact:
A-Girl Studio
P.O. Box 213, Burbank, CA 91503 U.S.A.
www.a-girlstudio.com

ISBN: 978-1-936622-29-0

First paperback edition, 2015

For
the
ones
found.

MONSTER STALKER

A Darquepunk Novel
Volume One

By
Elizabeth Watasin

A-GIRL STUDIO

Kill first.

CHAPTER ONE :

NOW ARRIVING

NICO was a bullet, piercing matter. She burst into dusky skies, an airfield fast approaching her face. She hit it and rolled.

Sun! Clouds shrouded it, but she felt its heat. She scrambled on the tarmac and saw no earth to bury herself in. When she didn't catch fire, she touched the black surface she knelt on, warmed by sunlight. Her free hand clutched her switchblade, its blade triggered. The hot handle sparked with electricity.

"Ow—ow," Nico said. She dropped her blade, pulled down her cardigan's sleeve over her burnt palm, then picked the knife up again.

Airfield? Buildings stood on the hazy horizon. She needed to run for cover. When she tried to stand, she plopped back instead. The airfield tilted as she fought nausea.

Mr. Bear, her sandy-coloured stuffed bear, sat strapped to the front of her black cardigan and white button-down. Nico looked down at the chest harness, made of leather, silver grommets, and fastenings, and could not remember purchasing it, much less donning it. Her left knee throbbed, and she raised it to look.

Beneath her short black skirt with the two pleats, her black stocking had torn at the knee; the bloodied bruise already healing from where she'd scraped it on landing. She had no memory of choosing her clothes or her shoes (which were the spike-studded leather oxfords and not her black Mary Janes) though it was an outfit she wore often.

A man in uniform coveralls and a ball cap with the logo *Jifk* walked across the airfield towards her. Somehow, she'd missed his approach. His tattooed face appeared friendly, and Nico thought his markings looked Maori. An identification badge dangled from his breast pocket: *Tane*.

Nico blinked. She'd read that in Cyrillic, but then it rearranged itself into the Latin alphabet.

"Here's another one," he said to no one in particular, though Nico couldn't be certain he spoke to someone via a mic. "Hey there. Can you put that away, please?" Nico looked at her blade, then shut it. "Thanks. Welcome to Again NewYork. I'm going to ask you to step over here and stand in that circle, and we'll get you processed right away." He brought up a rectangular-shaped device in his hand. "What's your name?"

"A—Again, New York?" Nico said.

"No, really. That's your name?" He indicated again that she move towards a circle blacker than the tarmac it lay in. She hadn't noticed it during her scrambling.

Nico tucked her switchblade into her skirt's waistband in back and rose. She stumbled to her feet, woozy. "No, I'm Nico," she said. "Nicolette Alexikova." Adrenaline receding, she felt a little like she'd been struck by lightning; her hair rose from static electricity. She looked at the pitch-black circle that resembled a pit, then at Tane. "Why am I—am I going to—?"

"Nope. You won't." Tane answered. Nico toed the blackness; it felt solid. "Both feet, please," Tane added. She put both feet into the circle.

Everything flashed, and she threw up her arms. When she looked down at herself and Bear, they were still in one piece.

"Vampire, right?" Tane touched his pad.

Nico froze.

"Well, your bio-dats say you are," Tane said. "And boy, did you get skittish when you saw you were in daylight."

Nico gave her surroundings a furtive look. "Again...New York?"

"Right." Tane continued to enter data. "Your teddy bear doesn't appear to be alive or sentient, so that's just one to process for immigration. Can you confirm that you're a vampire, please?"

"Yes. Yes I am," she said bravely. "And I've dual citizenship—American and British."

Tane looked up and grinned. "If that matters to you. But on Darqueworld, designations like that don't exist; the city-states are only what the gods make of them."

Darkworld? Nico tried to look closer at his badge. Electricity buzzed along her skin, and the air exploded, popping her ears. She ducked and looked behind her. Farther down the field, the atmosphere split. It erupted in fire and ejected a flaming man, the ends of his trench coat trailing. He tumbled on the ground and flopped to a stop. The hole sucked in upon itself and disappeared.

"Wow, what an entry—right out of an explosion." Tane's tone was matter-of-fact. Two bulky men blipped into view, and Nico blinked, thinking they'd stepped on to the tarmac as if from an invisible place. The men ran up to the one smoking on the ground—at least, Nico thought the two were men. Like Tane, they wore coveralls, but horns grew out of their heads, and their features had snouts and brows like bulls. Nico turned to Tane.

"Am I in purgatory?" she said.

Tane scrutinised her. "Don't know how you got here, huh? Memory loss." He entered something into his pad. "Don't worry, they'll have a Po get a good look at you, then assign you a social worker—"

"Social worker? *Now* I believe in hell."

"Oh, is that what you think this is?" Tane's tone was light.

"No...hell is getting murdered and stuff." Nico tried to ignore the sound of the two horned guys scraping the smoking fellow off the ground.

"It sure is. Hey," he said, catching her attention. "You're a chrono-immigrant, if that info helps—" He pointed at his head. "Jog your memory some. You took a trip to a planet settled by others like yourself, and here you are. I only need you to tell me your era. I'm betting it's late twentieth century."

Nico looked at him blankly. "The year is 1998."

"Great. Now, if you'll show me the back of your hand." He pulled out a device resembling a tattoo gun.

"What's that?" she said, wary.

"A biometric tagger." Tane motioned for her hand. Nico presented the back of her left hand, wondering if she was about to receive a barcode tattoo. Tane placed the tagger over her skin. A beam burst, pricking her. It felt like an inoculation. Then she remembered that as a vampire, she had no fear of diseases. The sensation ran up her wrist after Tane lifted the tagger, and she shook her hand, trying to rid herself of the tickle.

If I'm in a coma somewhere, someone just did something funny to my hand.

She wasn't certain if vampires could fall into actual comas, and dismissed that speculation. Tane gestured to a metal arch that Nico hadn't noticed before.

"All done! Enter that gate there, and you'll be processed and ready to start your new life in Again NewYork."

*

Chrono-immigrant? Nico approached the gate. It showed only the airfield beyond it. If everything happening was her conscious reality, perhaps the forethought of strapping Mr Bear to herself made sense. But what situation had she come out of, especially with blade drawn? Nico looked down in case she'd missed signs of violence on her person or clothes. She did not seek fights, but evil could follow a girl, as she well knew. If she'd been in danger in Leningrad before coming to...Again, New York, she couldn't recall what had happened or why.

Therefore, I was kidnapped somehow, and now I'm in some rich man's fantasy set. Or this is some crazy KGB plot to get vampires to out themselves.

She stepped through the gate.

And found herself in a security area aglow in dim blue, one with bored officers standing by roped-off stations and machines. None of the officers looked human, though humanoid enough. A great, glass bubble hung in the room's centre; inside a large, bald female head floated. She looked at Nico.

I'll ignore that. Nico stared instead at a pedestal sign with an illustration of a bald person's head in a bubble, accompanied by possibly important information. Nico couldn't read the language, so she returned her attention to the room.

A quick scan (while avoiding the staring head) seemed to affirm that she was the lone chrono-immigrant present. She hoped no one would confiscate her switchblade—Tane had not seemed to mind her carrying it. Nico checked her hand, not wanting an injury to delay processing. Thanks to a vampire's healing ability, the burn was gone and her skin, whole. She approached the nearest station, where a blue humanoid male looked down at her, impassive. On the counter sat a mounted tagger like the one Tane had used, and a large metal orb with a glass top. The blue male held up a lens.

The lens flashed, making Nico see colours, and the back of her hand itched.

"*Raqa*," he said, indicating the mounted tagger.

"You want my hand, right?" Nico said, and then noticed what the orb contained. An insect as large as a rat sat within, wearing a tiny badge. It waved feelers and seemed to look at her with its multi-faceted eyes.

"*Click-click,*" it said, its mandibles moving. Nico thrust her hand beneath the tagger, suppressing the urge to wallop the bug and run away. Rising in a shallow forest grave with beetles living in her mouth had not endeared her to insects. The bug pressed something on its tiny console.

The beam that hit her hand seared, but Nico saw no burn on her skin. She shook her hand again.

"Read that, please," the insect said motioning to its glass hatch, and Nico started in surprise. She was certain it had made more clicking sounds. A message illuminated across the orb's glass. Hieroglyphics rearranged, forming the Latin alphabet.

"*Hi farhol mal haro sowo,*" she read, bewildered. The insect's mouth clicked more, and the blue humanoid appeared to guffaw, as if they were sharing a laugh. Nico gave them a look, hoping they hadn't made her say something obscene.

"Translate for us, please," the insect requested, and somehow the translation came to Nico.

"My hovercraft is full of...eels," Nico said sourly. *That's it. This is a dream.* She enjoyed Monty Python well enough, but not that much. The blue humanoid and the insect chortled more.

"Translation tag functioning. Step that way, please," the insect said.

✶

Officers waved her off two more stations after they flashed lenses at her. Nico was glad; their stations looked like medical facilities. At the second one, a man in a double-breasted pinstripe suit, wingtips, and askew fedora lay inert on the dais, having succumbed to whatever procedure he'd received. Two bald humanoids in smocks held pads and discussed data over him. Nico hurried to the last station, where a black circle lay, similar to the one in the airfield. The bored female officer standing before it gestured in its direction. She laid a three-fingered hand on Nico's shoulder to guide her.

"Don't touch me," Nico said automatically. "Um, sorry."

Nico stepped into the circle. When it flashed, Nico felt as if her underwear had been frisked.

"Hey! Mr Bear! My stuff!" she exclaimed, seeing her possessions lying in a neat row on the table, and hurried off the circle to fetch Bear.

"Can you tell us where Mr Bear comes from, please," the officer said in a bored tone, seating herself before a monitor.

"Mr Bear comes from where I came from," Nico said. "He's—"

Her thought slid away on a white surface in her mind.

"He's..." Nico frowned.

The officer glanced at something above Nico's shoulder, and when she turned to look, the floating head was staring in her direction. Nico turned back again.

"Okay, thank you," the officer said, dismissive, and Nico assumed the questioning was done.

While Nico placed Bear in his harness again, a nude man, completely hairless to his non-existent eyebrows, walked by, bypassing the search area. In his two hands he held a claymore over four feet long, the blade pointing down. Nico looked at the giant blade and then at him.

This is the most Freudian dream ever.

He moved ahead as she picked up her switchblade and put it back in her waistband. Before she pocketed her Chococat wallet, she opened it. It contained rubles, her Leningrad University student ID, a credit card, a Leningrad metro pass, and her magazine clipping of the actress Sabella Peck, dressed in a men's suit. Nico hugged the picture to her and Bear, then put her wallet away. Her passport security neck wallet had also ended up on the table; she grabbed it and the tin of breath mints she hadn't known she'd been carrying. When she glanced back at the room, wondering if it was okay to leave, the female head in the bubble coolly watched her. Nico walked quickly to where the naked man had exited.

*

The sleek platform outside the security room resembled an underground rail station. A small, fat, bullet-shaped vehicle sat on the track, the size of a transport van. Its hatch was open, and after Nico put her neck wallet and mints away, she hurried to it. Stepping in, she saw two seat rows.

The naked man with the claymore had taken the far row's front seat, leaning forwards with a hand on the long hilt and the sword tip down. In the seat behind him sat a Victorian woman in a buttoned overcoat, long skirts, black boots, and gloves, her blonde, swept-up hair dishevelled. She looked as disconcerted as Nico felt, one lens of her spectacles cracked. The woman was fixing her hat, which had a bent brim, and she nodded to Nico.

"How do you do," she said, her accent British.

"Hello," Nico said, wondering if the woman was an actress — though the natural material of her wool and silk clothes, lacking synthetics, appeared to have been made a century ago.

"How do you do," the woman then said to Mr Bear.

"Mr Bear says, 'how do you do,'" Nico said, and made Bear wave. "He's not sentient."

"Oh," the woman said with a smile. "I thought him an automaton. He certainly has a soulful look to him."

Pleased by the compliment, Nico took the aisle seat by the open hatch across from the woman. She wanted to talk more about Bear, but she couldn't remember —

Her thoughts skittered off into the dark again. She became distracted by the woman's scent instead.

The Victorian woman was the first human Nico had sensed. She wasn't sure how she knew, especially when Tane had looked human too. Perhaps humans had a smell and warmth to their flesh and blood familiar to her — vital to her vampire nature. It drew her right then, pulsing beneath the woman's crisp, lavender scent. She was living, breathing, and very edible.

Nico felt her fangs emerge and kept her gaze away, hoping her eyes hadn't changed. Her lack of control surprised her. She'd spent her entire vampire life in the company of humans and had learned to cope. She wasn't even hungry, though she'd the keen desire to turn and smell the woman more.

Nico took an unneeded breath, then the scent of smoke and scorched flesh overwhelmed. Two security personnel shoved the burnt man from the airfield into the seat next to her. The door hatch came down and shut, dimming their interior to near darkness, and the transport accelerated. Nico could still see the burnt man with her vampire's vision, and he looked too crispy for her liking. He'd managed some flesh regeneration, though scorched trench coat pieces still needed picking out of his skin. She scrunched to the far side of her seat.

A chime sounded, and a projection activated in the open space of the vehicle's interior, within view of all the occupants. A dimensional logo reading DARQUEWORLD slowly spun: a hologram.

Wow, that's...better than virtual reality.

Nico stared, fascinated by the logo's perfect solidity, and the Victorian woman leaned forwards in her chair, gazing with great interest.

"Welcome to Darqueworld," a female narrator announced in a smooth, sensual voice, the projection displaying a cloud-covered planet. "If you're experiencing disorientation, know that this isn't a hallucination or dream. If you are a chrono-arrival, or what's known as a time traveller, then please keep in mind the cultural, technological, and species differences you may encounter in an intragalactic- and preternatural-based society. If you disembarked from an interstellar or extra-dimensional transport, you may be fully aware of where you've arrived. But to review, this is where you are."

Nico's jaw had already dropped at the word *intragalactic*. The projection began to display spatial animations depicting astronomical cartography.

"You are now situated in the Merope Nebula of the Pleiades Star Cluster, Messier 45, a cluster you may also know as the Seven Sisters, Subaru, Neith, Makara, Tianquiztli, 'Star of stars', and Freya's Hens. Located approximately 400 light years from Old Earth, you are presently on the dusk planet discovered and tended by the elder gods who departed that Earth. This is Darqueworld.

"Darqueworld is one of many celestial bodies in the Pleiades settled by former Earth inhabitants and divinities. It is also a prominent trade and travel hub, connecting to various intragalactic spacefaring cultures and species. Welcome to Darqueworld."

The hatch abruptly opened, briefly blinding Nico; the vehicle had come to a stop. Before she could move, the crispy man threw himself out the opening. He shambled across a platform that led to a curtain of darkness. With a lurch, he began gliding forwards, having accessed a moving walkway, and disappeared into the black.

"This place likes voids, everywhere," Nico exclaimed as she jumped out. Her vampire's vision discerned nothing within the pitch-darkness. She stepped with hesitance, unsure where the moving walkway lay. When she glanced back at her vehicle companions, the naked man was politely helping the Victorian woman out by the hand. Right when Nico was about to ask what they planned to do, she felt her body—not the floor—move, and the force swept her into the darkness.

I'm a vampire, I'm a vampire, Nico chanted as she felt air rush past. *And I can't see anything in this dark.*

Before she could give in to panic, her body came to a stop. Nico stood within a soft blue spotlight before a service window with a mounted lens on the counter. The person who sat within was plump, and Nico could not tell if the person was a woman or a man. Nico decided to call the person "Terry".

"I had an astronomy class," Nico said. "The Pleiades can't have liveable planets; it's too new."

Terry looked at her.

"And it's bright. Super bright, with young stars. I should be burnt up," Nico said.

"Your bio-tag, please," Terry said.

Nico put her hand beneath the lens. A beam shone and the back of her hand tickled. Terry stared down at something out of Nico's view.

"Age at death?" Terry said.

"Eighteen," Nico answered.

"Age as vampire?"

"From my death? Fifteen."

"Female, male, third, none, changing, changed?" Terry said.

"Changing?" Nico said, and Terry pressed something. "No! Girl! Female!" Terry pressed something again, and Nico displayed the back of her left hand. "Don't my bio-dats already say I'm female?"

"Can you identify your bear, please?" Terry asked instead.

"His name is Mr Bear."

"Is Mr Bear your totem animal, spirit guide, or avatar?"

"Mr Bear is me," Nico insisted.

"He is a variant of you?"

"No, we're the same."

"Mr Bear is not separate from you?"

"No, he's me." Nico could not explain it, but the conviction resounded in her.

"Mr Bear is your conjoined twin," Terry said, and pressed something.

"Okay, fine," Nico said.

"Have you engaged in criminal activity?" Terry asked.

"No. Well, when I first rose, yes. I had to steal and stuff, but then I figure out how not to."

"Will you engage in criminal activity?"

"No. I like to keep quiet," Nico said in earnest.

"Have you made another like you?"

Nico stilled. "No, never," she said, her tone hollow.

"Your tag again, please."

Nico put her hand beneath the lens again, its beam touching her once more.

"Next," Terry said, and the darkness snatched Nico again.

Her body paused almost immediately before another lit window. Either she was moving or her environment was spinning, a roulette wheel stopping windows before her. The pale person behind the window looked male and was bald and gaunt, with staring eyes, pointed ears, and pronounced fangs. Nico refrained from asking if the man was Count Ulock and put her hand beneath the lens.

"What is your plan of employment?" Ulock said. His pronunciations bore a lisp.

"I—I'm a student," Nico said. "Um...for the past fifteen years. Scholarships. I've an ancient history degree but now I'm studying computer science."

"Your plan of employment?" he repeated, his stare unblinking.

"Oh. I can work in museums, libraries, and historical sites. Uh, music stores, video stores, bookstores, bakeries, morgues. I was working nightshift, hotel front desk, before I got...here."

"Any plans to steal, subjugate, murder, terrorise, torture, seize power, or cause mayhem?" he said.

Nico looked at him, aghast. "No."

"Any history in practicing the aforementioned?" he said, his tiny pupils pinning her. Nico could not look away.

"Practice? No, I like to keep—" *Quiet*, she wanted to say. She saw the blank spot inside her mind. She blinked.

"Any plans to make another like yourself?" he asked.

"No." Nico's tone was cold. "Never."

Ulock stared. "And Mr Bear is you."

"Yes, he is."

He pointed at the lens with a clawed finger, and Nico put her hand beneath again.

"Next," he said.

✴

When Nico had spent a semester at St Mary's University in Twickenham, she'd met a young Persian artist. He had married a

Canadian girl for citizenship and complained to Nico about the immigration process.

"They ask many questions," he said, "and very personal."

Nico had to falsify papers at times, and she had kept her original name because she'd never been officially declared dead. However, she'd never been scrutinised as her true self, and the repeated questions were designed to catch her at a lie.

She expected to be spinning in the dark forever, going from window to window and answering questions until they deported her to an asteroid for unsuitable vampires. Then she landed in a small room.

Nico looked around, the space no bigger than a walk-in closet. It glowed soft red—which she liked—and in the centre stood a solid pedestal. Sabella Peck shown on the black pedestal from the chest up, dressed like Nico's magazine clipping. She smiled at nothing in particular, and her projection flickered. Nico's throat caught.

That's not fair.

She loved that picture of Sabella; cherished it. Nico knew a boy who watched Johnny Carson every night, pretending the host was his father. Nico had looked at Sabella in magazines and done the same.

I wish you'd been my maker.

Nico stepped to the pedestal and hugged Bear.

The Sabella-hologram smiled. "Do you like being a vampire?" Her voice was Peck's from her movies.

Nico paused. She didn't know what to say; after fifteen years, she'd accepted it. She'd made it work. The hologram seemed to take her silence as an answer.

"You like to keep quiet," the hologram said, smiling.

"Yes," Nico said, "so I can have a future."

"Do you kill to eat?"

"No." Nico shook her head. "I buy blood units; from the black market."

"Do you seduce to eat?"

What blood existed in Nico went to her cheeks. "Okay, yes. When it's someone's time of month? Then yes. You'd be surprised how many women are okay with that. But they tend to be older... and married. I don't kill them! Just, um." *And I need to shut up, right now.*

The hologram smiled distantly, as if she reacted to a Nico standing far away, and not near.

"Have you murdered?" she said.

Nico dropped her head. "Yes."

"How many times have you murdered?"

"Once," she said quietly. "No, two other times. Those were in self-defence."

"Please describe," the hologram said.

"The last was my...the vampire who made me. Two years before that, two girls rose in the morgue I worked at. So I had to kill them."

"How did you kill your maker?"

Nico looked at the hologram. She'd never told anyone. Vampires didn't kill their makers; it was taboo.

"I stalked him," she said.

"How long did you take before you killed him?"

"Four years," Nico whispered.

"Are you sadistic?" The hologram asked, as if she were enquiring if Nico liked chocolate.

"No. Not even sexually." Nico looked down at Bear's leather harness, realising how it made her look. "I took so long because I didn't know how. He was so hard to kill."

"Do you like to murder?"

"No," she said softly. "That's how I died."

The hologram cocked her head as if listening to more.

"Welcome to Darqueworld," the hologram said, and Nico stared into Sabella-hologram's warm, distant gaze.

The hologram flickered out of sight.

"Bye," Nico whispered, looking at the empty pedestal. A pad device the same as Tane had used lay on the surface. It bore a logo sticker: *Your Id®, by Donut.*

"Please pick up the Id issued to you," the narrating voice from the van ride announced. Nico glanced around in surprise, then grabbed the device. It was longer than her passport. She stuffed it in the harness's storage panel behind Bear. A hologram movie began to play above the pedestal, displaying map animations and spot footage that Nico assumed was of Darqueworld: cities, oceans, eerie landscapes with great creatures roaming, an underwater city, and space stations.

"Darqueworld and its farther worlds are the domains of the gods who found them. Though you are an Other-being, you may not indulge in inflicting death, destruction, combative challenges, or acts of physical superiority on humans, intragalactic species, and lower beings. Darqueworld maintains a balanced biosphere and psychosphere dedicated to sacred commonality for all. Please present your biometric tag and acknowledge that you accept and understand."

"I do," Nico said, raising her hand, and a flash blinded her.

"Please retrieve your information packet." A folder with pamphlets sat on the pedestal. Nico picked it up, glad to see something as familiar as paper. The holo movie changed to depict humanoids and creatures: werewolves, leopard people, tree-people, mermaids, cyborgs, flying people, griffins, walking statues, and robots with brains.

"Ew," Nico uttered.

"However, Darqueworld recognises that preternatural beings may follow societal and cultural traditions particular to their kin, in matters of conflict and formal challenges. Conflict resolved to cultural rules between Other-beings, or Other-beings with their own kin, are acceptable. When such conflict harms law-abiding citizens and disturbs societal peace, the Makepeace restores order."

Nico stared at the latest projection and thought the weaponised and sleekly armoured Makepeace humanoid with his visor and helm looked like something from the *2000 AD* comic book—

except more sensual.

Do they all look that hot?

"The Makepeace are incorruptible artificial public servants empowered to eliminate Other-beings without the obligation to apprehend, judicially process, and incarcerate. The Makepeace may issue admonitions for your minor offences. If a Makepeace decision is in question, your kin, spouse, maker, guardian, friends, or champion may petition your death. Please acknowledge that you accept and understand."

"Uh, yes," Nico said, raising her hand, and another flash blinded her.

"You may appeal to a Makepeace if you find yourself in need of assistance. Your local Makepeace is your protector as well as your eliminator."

Thanks a lot, Nico thought, her eyes wide. The projection ended, and she saw two cards on the pedestal.

"You are issued one credit chit for meals and expenses while seeking employment. If you need to extend such credit, contact your social worker via the business card provided."

Nico quickly picked up the chit and the card. A hologram popped up from the business card, depicting a young bald man in glasses—her social worker: Specs Plonsky. As she put the cards away in her security wallet, the pedestal top visually shifted, doubling and then dividing. Something materialised within the spatial shift. While she had been distracted by the holographic projections, the top of the pedestal had been retrieving items. Nico stared.

Is that teleportation? When she sucked air against the roof of her mouth, she tasted tangible energy in the air, vibrating. She didn't want to stick her hand in the shifting space in case her hand split into two as well. The divided pedestal top became one object again, bearing a bag with a logo: *Welcome to Again NewYork.*

"Darqueworld measures time by the twelve cycle lunar calendar with a seven day week, each planetary rotation being twenty-four hours. You will find Darqueworld's gravity, atmosphere, oceans, and fresh water are similar to Old Earth's. Your evaluation for citizenship has commenced. Please accept this complimentary carry bag, personal hygiene kit, and snack blood packet to begin your stay. And remember."

Nico threw her hand up, overwhelmed by a series of flashes. She covered Bear's eyes.

"You." FLASH

"Are." FLASH

"Needed." FLASH

"For what." FLASH

"You do." FLASH

"Best." FLASH

"Welcome to Again NewYork, and have a nice day."

A door slid open at the end of the room. The room darkened, no longer glowing red. Dazed and partially blinded, Nico picked up her bag and turned for the door. She heard many footsteps.

Please don't be Orwellian, please don't be Orwellian.

Nico exited.

She stepped into a large corridor where beings swiftly walked, carrying *Welcome to Again NewYork* bags. Corridors to her left and right fed into the one she stood in, and large blue arrows glowed in the floor, pointing away from her. When she glanced behind, only a wall met her scrutiny. Nico looked at the main corridor everyone departed down and saw two familiar icons on lit cube signs. One indicated: Ladies.

A lizard woman in a Beckensdale Heritage trench coat exited from the bathroom, carrying a suitcase handcuffed to her wrist. Her spiky head crest flared when she spotted Nico looking at her. She departed with the rest moving down the main corridor.

Everyone's a creature, and I'm a creature. On an alien planet.

Perhaps if she'd known she was coming to Darqueworld, she'd be more in awe or even giddy. Instead, she felt the need to retreat. She stuffed her folder into her bag and hurried to the ladies room.

Few females were within; she briefly wondered where thirds, nones, and changed did their business. Then she saw herself in the sinks' mirrors.

Nico drew her switchblade.

"Hey," a large woman with three eyes said as she pushed past Nico. "Be careful with that."

"Sorry," Nico uttered. Her reflections held knives too, and when Nico moved to close her blade, her hands trembling, they did as well.

Those are me. Me. Not other-me's coming to get me.

She then looked at herself, a face she'd not seen in fifteen years, and stepped for the sinks.

Her reflections did nothing more, so she stopped before an Other-Nico and stared. A very pale girl with wavy, shoulder-length black hair stared back, her small brows knit. Nico hadn't noticed before her death that she'd a cute mouth, pink and kissable. Her straight nose wasn't as big as she'd remembered. Had she always looked that lost when alive? She could see why women liked inviting her in. But she wondered about the gaze in her grey eyes; big, wide, yet horrified.

I need a hairbrush.

Mr Bear looked a little askew. She adjusted him.

A vampire woman stood to the side in the mirror's reflection. She seemed to stare with as much fascination at Nico as Nico did staring at herself.

I don't think she has a hairbrush. Not only did the other vampire look dishevelled, but she also carried her own *Welcome to Again NewYork* bag.

And how did Nico know the other woman was a vampire? The female lacked breath, and she bore the pallor of cold flesh, one that exuded the pristine, clear scent of death, suspended. Vampires were not warm, pulsing, and edible, and Nico had never been interested in sex with them.

Her tall, dark-haired admirer wore a black trimmed, silk suit, with narrow lapels and a skirt with a cut like nothing Nico knew to be in fashion, except what might be in haute couture magazines. Despite looking travel-rumpled, the vampire was sharp and beautiful from her finely shaped eyebrows and defined cheekbones to her manicured nails, painted a smoke-grey. Her nail polish matched her loosened, narrow tie. Nico had never seen that shade used in nail colours.

She has to be from an era ahead of me—two eras. And the woman's blood was older than Nico's, even older than her maker. Nico could almost smell it. The woman continued to stare, her keen, blue-eyed gaze touched with amazement. Nico turned to look at her.

"Word of advice?" the woman said. "Don't ever show them you can't make it here. Darqueworld is it."

"Do I know you?" Nico said cautiously. Weird blank spot in her head or no, she'd remember a woman wearing the sophisticated hyacinth and jasmine fragrance of *Chasse* Geraud Soeurs. It nearly masked the scent of undead perfection. Almost.

The woman nodded towards Bear. "No. Even back then we wouldn't have crossed paths. But how many vampire girls carried a bear?"

Nico put her hand over Bear.

"That's quite an escape plan for your time period, coming all the way here," the woman added, smiling. Her teeth were perfect and white.

"Escape from what?" Nico said, and the woman frowned, as if perplexed by Nico's response. Her jacket pocket chimed, and the woman raised a hand to touch it.

"Got to go. We'll chat later." She drew a flat, rigid translucent card, its surface wavering like a Fresnel lens. The woman tapped it and it flashed Nico in the face.

"Hey," Nico said, but the woman was already walking out the exit, grinning back at her.

"Pervert," Nico exclaimed.

Nico left the ladies room to join the rest of the newly processed down the mystery corridor. Though many appeared human, some who walked alongside weren't bipedal, like the bare-breasted spider woman with six legs who wore a helm and carried a forked spear. A fox woman in full kimono and *geta* clogs hurried past with small fast steps, carrying her fox baby on her back. A ventriloquist's dummy in grey suit and red bowtie strolled along.

Nico jumped, then walked swiftly to catch up with the fox woman, her still heart in her throat.

"Now I know why everyone thinks you can talk, Bear," she whispered, and tried not to look behind her in case she caught the dummy's interest.

Holographic signs appeared overhead, bearing the logo: Jifk Spaceport.

"Welcome to Jifk Spaceport," a calm male voice said, pronouncing *Jifk* like it was spelt. "Passenger pick-up and departure for farther worlds, to your left. Passenger pick-up and departure for farther worlds, to your left."

Nico looked around in bewilderment as the corridor gave way to a large terminal where people walked in all directions, some with luggage. Glowing floor arrows marked two routes, and she chose left. As she reached the terminal's end, glass doors opened to a roofed arcade outside, and she knew she'd made the wrong decision. All manner of odd vehicles waited by the kerb, as varied as the disorientated travellers arriving on the walk. Bullet-shaped, compact buses sat at an island divider. When one of the buses drove away—not for the lane but into a sunlit airfield—Nico saw the spaceships, big and small, shiny and rusty, rising and landing, beyond it. One spun, a flashing top, and crossed the sky.

Oh my god. The departed bus rapidly became a speck headed for a hazy ship in the distance. Nico thought it looked like a futuristic ocean liner.

Where will the spider lady go? The fox mother? The naked man with the claymore? Nico saw three dusty centurions standing by the kerb and holding their helms, debating quietly on how to proceed. Nico believed she was almost two thousand years ahead of them in technological and scientific understanding (somewhat) and they didn't appear as discombobulated as she felt.

Two vampires in black, Victorian-style dress —a blond male and a doll-like, black-haired female in a bonnet —stood on the sheltered walk with a handwritten sign reading: *Miss Fairditch.* Nico could guess whom they waited for, though she was surprised that despite their immutable state—a characteristic old vampires tended to exude—they seemed to anticipate the arrival of a human with gleaming excitement. Their black clothes were not of handmade materials, nor were they historically accurate, but the vampires' genteel patience seemed very much of a bygone century.

Did vampires have a nose for sniffing out the elder in kin? Nico couldn't be certain; she'd never had another vampire explain it to her. But right then, she knew it by the deepened sensation of suspended death that clung to the two. It was a bouquet similar to oak-aged wine in casks, sealed for centuries. It was rich, black, and abiding, and unlike her own undead state.

I'm a biscuit, and they're a banquet. Anxiety hit at the thought. She felt newly risen all over again, despite having become more assured back on Earth, an ageless girl manoeuvring around hapless humans.

The Victorian woman with the cracked spectacles exited the terminal and came to a sudden stop at the sight of the two vampires.

"Annuska...Edmund," she said in disbelief. The two stepped to her, and the female vampire embraced the shocked woman, her pretty face near tears.

They're so happy to see her, Nico thought in surprise. *They're friends.* And when the female vampire kissed Miss Fairditch on the mouth, the contact passionate and lingering, Nico knew they were more than friends.

She stood on the walk and considered that: humans and vampires, together. Humans and vampires, *openly* together. For the first time since arriving, Nico felt like smiling. Then she caught a whiff of hyacinth and jasmine.

The vampire she'd met in the bathroom stepped out of the terminal and into the crowd, wearing sunglasses and dangling a lit cigarette from her smirking lips. She was tightening her tie, as if to make herself presentable again. A grey-haired African woman in a floppy sunhat and batik dress stepped out behind her and raised her hands to the airfield, her welcome bag on her arm. Her teeth and eyes held the full vampire aspect.

"Praise the dark and those made in it!" she exclaimed. "So long, fellow refugee."

"Take care," the vampire from the bathroom said. "Good luck." She strode for the kerb, the outsoles of her black stilettos flashing Bulgarian red rose; the signature colour of Christoffel Loulain. She headed for a long vehicle where an androgynous chauffeur stood. The chauffeur held up a sign: *Heloise Allen.*

Heloise stepped off the kerb into the bright sunlight and boarded the vehicle.

She stepped *into the sunlight,* Nico thought, shocked. Heloise noticed her as the chauffeur shut her door.

Nico watched the vehicle zoom away, silent and fast. The Victorian couple led their friend off the kerb as well.

"Oh, Edmund!" Miss Fairditch said, and held back Edmund by his arm before the sunlight could touch him.

"Be not alarmed, Livy," Edmund said with a laugh. "It's perfectly safe for the shunned. On Darqueworld, the sun's rays have been made safe for the likes of us."

They entered a black and blood red vehicle that looked like a chopped coupe, the female vampire taking the driver's seat, which sat centre and between two other seats. Once the passengers boarded, she accelerated the vehicle away at a sedate pace.

Nico wanted to leave too, though she still didn't know to where; the bus island across the way seemed a good start. She stared at the sunlit lane. In her head, a grandstand of Mr Bears waved flags and cheered her on: *do it, do it, do it!*

She poked her toe out into warm sun and her head went light.

The world swayed. Someone bumped into her and Nico stumbled off the kerb. She nearly screamed, and scurried across the sun-filled lane for the island and its bus shelter. Once under shade, she checked herself and Mr Bear, her undead lungs working. Nothing smoked or burned. The people on the island stared.

"I watched someone burst into flames once," she said in explanation, and turned away. She scanned for somewhere next to go—into the sun, because she did not want to board the wrong bus out of sunlight fear and end up on a penal colony's ship. When she turned back to the terminal's arcade, she spotted the predators she hadn't noticed before. Scammers solicited donations (and perhaps picked a few pockets) hawkers enticed the newly arrived with cheap food, lodging, and entertainment, and pimps stood waiting, ready to lure naive girls and boys willing to buy the story of promised employment.

Nico returned her attention to the airfield and saw a neon sign reading *Lucy's*, far across the tarmac. It was an old-fashioned, aluminium-sided American diner, the streamlined design right out of the 1950's.

Nico took a step, intrigued, and a holographic projection popped up before her, resembling a hand-lettered signboard. It read:

Lost?
Come dine with us.
Cup of Joe
Pie à la mode
You'll know where to go
After eating at Lucy's.

Someone had drawn a holographic graffiti above the board, of a winking Hello Kitty in apron and chef's hat with a thumb-up sign. Nico wasn't sure how one graffitied holographically. She didn't think an American diner served Japanese, but Hello Kitty was a good sign to her.

"Okay," Nico said. She steeled herself. Heloise Allen had stepped into the light and Miss Fairditch's vampires had as well. Nico could do this. She walked into sunlight, then ran for the diner, the sun warming her face for the first time since being made dead.

CHAPTER TWO

Lucy's aluminium siding dazzled, and the brightness made Nico's eyes tear—not from emotion, but pain. Perhaps she should celebrate the sight of bright light, one denied her for fifteen years, but all Nico could think was as a night creature, she hoped so much light didn't give her a stroke.

As she neared, holo ad cues popped up, pointing enticingly in the direction of Lucy's:

You're getting warmer! Every kind and kin, are welcomed at Lucy's

We can't wait, to wait on you, Love, Lucy's

The scent of incense mixed with the cooking smells of the diner's grills and a meat smoker, located somewhere in back. Modest, little altars and a golden spirit house sat in a row against the diner's side, and the ancient history grad in Nico wanted to run up to the altars and inspect each one. They appeared to be for hearth goddesses—she identified Brigid's solar cross and Hinukan's koro censer—

Okay, that's it. Hot-hot-hot—

She pulled on the metal bar of the glass and aluminium door and escaped out of the sun.

Nico blinked rapidly to adjust her eyesight, though her ears easily registered the activity and noise of a restaurant. The air bore the scents of fire, coffee, food, and bodies. When had she last needed to enter a food place? Possibly when she and her parents had been alive. Nico stood before the empty hostess podium and the glass case displaying pies, tarts, and cakes. The long diner looked the size of two restaurants, with the chatter, clatter, and bodies to match. The spaciousness had not been evident from the outside; the long train car had an attached extension stretching into more rooms in back, beyond the long, stainless steel and chrome-sided lunch counter where patrons sat on bright red stools. Red booths ran beside the scenic windows overlooking the airfield, and another row of booths formed an aisle between them. For her first diner visit, Nico didn't want to sit at the counter with her back to the entrance; she wanted a window booth.

A metallic robot with a translucent outer casing and an hourglass figure, prominent bullet-bra breasts, and a glass orb bearing a floating brain where a head would be rolled towards Nico. She had four flexible limbs with jointed fingers, and one of them picked up a menu from the hostess podium.

"Hey, welcome to Lucy's," her chest's crackling speaker hailed with a New Yorker's accent. "Two to be seated? Let's get ya that window booth you want."

"Thanks," Nico said in surprise. Had she been that obvious? She followed the rolling robot down the aisle.

"Would your bear like a booster seat?" the hostess asked.

"No thank you. Mr Bear can sit on the table."

"Since Mr Bear isn't wearing shoes, he can do that. Handsome spirit bear you got there. Oh, pardon me, your conjoined twin. My brain is very pink and healthy, thanks for noticing," the hostess said.

A *telepathic robot*? Nico thought in alarm as the hostess laid down her menu at an empty window booth, bade her to enjoy her meal, then rolled away. How often would she encounter telepathy on Darqueworld?

A spinning ship descended from the sky, landed upon the field, and slowed its rotations. Nico forgot about mind-reading brains and gaped. The ship looked like an advanced version of the *Forbidden Planet* ship.

And I'm staring right at it. At some point, she and Bear needed to ride in a spaceship. She pulled a paper napkin from the polished, chrome and glass dispenser, laid it out on the table, then seated Bear on it so he could look out the window. When she sat down and opened the menu, she noticed it was tailored to vampires. She could order blood pancakes, bread, muffins, dumplings, soup, congee, tofu, stew, curry, black pudding, blood sponge cake, a meringue, tart, custard, macaroon, blood chocolate pudding, and ice cream. All made (the footnote at the bottom said) with enriched, simulated human blood.

Simulated. Elation rose, and Nico recalled the snack pack mentioned in the hologram room. Such largess bestowed freedom; no more waiting for the butcher's slaughter days. No more chasing after ridiculously priced black market human blood. No more human temptation.

Nico raised her gaze, feeling that she was being watched. A waitress with hair blonde as sunlight stood in the aisle and looked at her.

Bright-eyed, with rosy lips and a body Nico could roll her gaze over, the young woman's figure flattered her pink diner uniform top and skirt. She wore a nametag that read *Shayla*, and Shayla's warm, hazel-eyed gaze focused on Nico, intrigued and seemingly delighted.

Then the look was gone. Shayla's face receded to pleasantness, and nothing more.

Hm? Nico thought.

The waitress approached, smelling of creamy sweet peach, bergamot, and oak moss, and Nico thought of Shayla's thighs during her fertility flow.

I bet she's bloody delicious. Nico dragged her gaze from Shayla's crotch back up to her face. She would remember a name like Shayla; she loved the Blondie song by that name.

"Do we know each other?" Nico blurted when the waitress

stopped at her table.

"Ehm, no," Shayla said with a smile. She spoke with a soft, laid-back brogue.

She's Scots, Nico thought in surprise. *Like—*

Nicky, her maker said.

"I apologise fer starin'. Welcome tae Lucy's. How 'bout I fetch you warmed blood tae start?" Shayla said. "First cup's complimentary for new arrivals tae Darqueworld."

"That sounds great," Nico said. "Thank you." Shayla had a gentle tone; she spoke with easy grace, pronouncing most of her words with less of a hard Scottish lilt and at far less the speed Nico knew Scots to speak with, but the roll of her R's was unmistakable. Nico chastised herself for even comparing the young woman to her maker.

"Magic," Shayla said, smiling. "I'll be right back."

When she left, Nico touched her own face, wondering if her undead pallor was that evident—or perhaps the humans of Darqueworld knew how to recognise vampires. She remembered her free hygiene kit and searched for it in her bag, hoping it had a comb or hairbrush.

She was looking at the toothbrush, laser razor, germicide bottle, lotion, packet of tissues, her snack blood packet, and several fast food coupons for a place called Shivers when she noticed little twin girls in headscarves, restless in the booth across, their skin golden and their green eyes inquisitive and bright. One turned to Nico, and a pendant on her front dangled: the winged heart of the Sufi. Their preoccupied parents studied their immigration packs, the father's weathered face elated while his young wife frowned at the pamphlets in her hands. Shayla appeared at their booth, one hand bearing a coffee mug topped with whipped cream. She drew the girls' attention and smoothed her hand over the tabletop, whispering. The air shifted, tingling, and Nico felt the change against her skin and teeth. She shivered. Paper colouring mats materialised before the little girls, and Shayla pointed at each mat. Crayons popped into being from thin air. The girls held their mouths, awed and delighted.

Magic? Nico stared in amazement. The quality of the air's change seemed different from the teleporting she thought she witnessed in the hologram room. The energy sparkled more, a livelier, vibrant presence, as if the change—the intention to cause change—held the signature of living will. Nico sucked in air and tasted particle vibrations on her tongue, quivering with specific intention. The signature was Shayla's.

People seated farther down the row let out an exclamation of appreciation and clapped. Nico leaned to look; their waitress waved over her closed fist, and when she opened it, striped straws rolled down her outstretched palm. She placed each straw by a customer's sundae.

They're all witches.

Shayla turned towards Nico's booth, smiling, and set down the mug before her. Nico smelled warmed blood beneath the whipped cream.

"Would you like tae colour too?" Shayla asked, her tone easy and relaxed.

"I am *not* a little child," Nico said, but she straightened in anticipation. "Yes, please."

"Everyone likes colouring, even griffins," Shayla said, and passed her hand over the tabletop before Nico. "Reveal," she incanted, and Nico felt the brush on her skin again of air changing. A paper mat materialised before her, illustrated with a space liner, spaceships, and Lucy's Diner. "And I mean grown griffins, not bairns." Shayla tapped the tabletop and crayons popped into being before Nico and Bear. Nico held the table's edge, delighted.

"I'm not a baby. I'm thirty-three, my age at death plus my vampire age," she protested with a touch of haughtiness. "This is so cool," she added.

"It's a simple trick. You've not witnessed weird work before?"

Nico shook her head. "I've never seen sorcery until now. Any that I believed, anyway." Shayla picked up the red crayon and let it roll into her palm.

"Ah, sorcery. I cannae say that's what I do here. I only..." She closed her hand around the crayon. When she opened it, the crayon was gone. "Manipulate the unseen, then..." She made a fist once more. Unfolding her fingers, the red crayon lay in her palm. "Bring what's hidden back again. Ye'll learn soon enough, the ways of the weird on Darqueworld." She handed the crayon to Nico. Nico accepted it and felt Shayla radiate with something more than life, heat, and blood, right then.

"Wow," Nico whispered as she stared at Shayla, and she put the crayon in her mouth. She could taste the lingering, tingly presence of Shayla's influence on the wax.

"Thirty-three years, ye say?" Shayla remarked, her tone light. "And still eatin' yer crayons?"

Nico pulled the crayon from her mouth. "I am. I have a human driver's license from fifteen years ago. Somewhere."

"Ye're eleven years my elder, then." Shayla seemed to want to say more, the corner of her mouth quirking. But she stepped back.

Nico found herself grinning as Shayla walked away. The rare expression made her face hurt.

Colouring calmed. Or perhaps Nico was finally set at ease by the reassuring welcome and acceptance Shayla had given her. Ships rose and descended on the airfield, alien beings walked by her booth led by the robot hostess while Nico licked all of the whipped cream from her coffee cup and coloured. After completing the big spaceship and Lucy's Diner with bright reds, blues, and oranges, she proceeded to peruse her pamphlets.

Do you still use the term, Alien? Nico read in her pamphlet, "The Intragalactic and You". *In the Pleiades, we are all "aliens". Try using the word off-worlder, instead.*

Nico put her mug down and mentally raised her hand: *Yes, but which ones are aliens and not Other-beings?* Perhaps as a vampire, she was expected to know about Earth's other supernatural creatures, but she hadn't known griffins were real until she viewed them in the hologram room. An intragalactic species and Other-beings encyclopaedia would be helpful.

She traded her pamphlet for the one Bear perused, titled: Who's Who On Darqueworld.

A pyramid diagram showed "gods" at the peak, demi-gods and Perfects one-third down, and at the very bottom of the pyramid, lined up in a row, were Other-beings, extra-humans, Artificials, humans, Old Earth mammals, Old Earth plants, and First creatures and other bio-life native to Darqueworld.

How does this planet even work with all the invasiveness? If there had been an indigenous sentient species before Earth's gods arrived, they were probably an invisible illustration beneath the feet of the bottom row figures, of buried, scattered bones.

She wouldn't mind joining an archaeological dig to excavate those. Unlike on Earth, she could finally use her history degree in the field—once she acquired a new, intragalactic history degree. She read a brief summary explaining the celestial holarchy that resided in unseen sky cities above Darqueworld's own terrestrial settlements.

A large ship departed from the airfield; the futuristic ocean liner. All diner activity seemed to pause as the great ship rumbled and rose. It did not launch for the stratosphere but sailed away into the skies, a terrestrial touring ship. Nico leaned over to gaze up at the clouds and the light blue sky with its strange, golden sheen. Somewhere up there, Earth's ancient gods lived. Nico flipped through the pamphlet more. She read about Perfects, Artificials, and—

Extra-humans, she read, were humans with enhanced abilities. Those included biomechanical beings, weird matter wielders, and psionics.

Psionics. Nico had to anticipate encountering more telepaths, then. And possibly Carrie-like telekinetics. Weird matter wielders, as far as she could tell, were witches. The accompanying illustration showed a gesturing woman knocking down a distant wall by what Nico could only describe as the magical chi of Hong Kong action cinema.

"Weird matter," Nico mused, reading the brief bubble definition. Quantum physics with its multiverses, dark matter, and strange matter were all too complex for her to contemplate. If the universe she was presently in said weird matter was part of the invisible cosmic stuff that made spaceships go zoom or helped witches knock buildings over, she wasn't going to question it. Plus, weird was cool. She tipped back her mug for the last blood drops and licked the rim.

Shayla approached, smiling. Despite the diner's noise and bustle, she moved in her own sphere of calm, one even, direct, and focused right then on Nico. Nico straightened in her seat.

"Would you like tae order now?" Shayla asked. She held a tall kettle and refilled Nico's mug. The blood she poured was bright red, frothy and warm.

"I, um, have never tried solid food," Nico said, picking up the menu and fingering it.

"How 'bout the very soft foods? We've blood ice cream, freshly churned," Shayla said. "And a dessert blood gelatine."

"I'll have the blood gelatine."

"And for your bear?" Shayla asked.

"Mr Bear would like the blood pudding. Not the sausage, I mean the chocolate."

"Aye, it's chocolate pudding." Shayla smiled, and Nico wondered when she'd last seen someone smile so much. It was easy, warm, and pretty. Perhaps she'd been too long among dour, Russian faces.

Nico clutched her warm cup and watched Shayla go, admiring the shape of her behind. She put the mug to her mouth and sucked.

Scrummy. Despite being sated, she couldn't say *no* to Shayla's kett—

Nico put the coffee cup down. Sated? When did she eat last?

She tried to remember.

Her teeth, in someone...but the memory wiped out, a blank spot in her mind.

I don't bite people, she thought, frowning. She hadn't done it in years; it had been too risky, and left trails of activity. Acting the perverse little girl who liked being with women during their ovulation's soaking bounty had been easier.

Shayla came by, and Nico perked up again.

"Here ye go," she said, and laid a dark red gelatine before Nico, then leaned over the table to place the chocolate blood pudding glass before Bear, his dessert topped with a Bing cherry. Shayla was warm, pulsing, and glowing with the soft scent of peaches, flowers, and milky—

"Have ye need for another?" Shayla said, straightening, as she raised her kettle.

"Cream. I mean, yes please."

Shayla grinned as if she knew exactly what Nico meant and refilled her coffee cup.

When she left, Nico touched her cheeks, wondering how much blush her pallor had mustered, and glanced over at the Sufi family, hoping none of them were telepathic. The husband and wife seemed to be arguing about how to use their Ids while their girls were already immersed in theirs, the play mats forgotten. Their little fingers moved, and Nico heard video game sounds. One of the girls activated a holo projection function, displaying a children's learning centre. She used her finger to pull down brightly coloured holographic icons.

Nico retrieved her own Id, removed its label, and found the activation button.

"Hello," her Id greeted in the smooth, sensual voice of the immigration narrator as a holo logo projected. "I am BRAI, your Basic2 Responsive Artificial Intelligence of the Neuth Neural Consciousness Net, and I will be the information guide of your Id."

Ten minutes and one fully ingested wiggly gelatine later, Nico had gone through the introductory tutorial, given the device her biometric tag to read, familiarised herself with the speak aloud, recording, and playback functions, renamed the BRAI *Dorothy* for Dorothy Gale, learned about downloading, sharing, and accessing information, and taken a picture of herself and Bear.

God, my hair. She tapped on Dorothy to access the Darqueworld's version of the World Wide Web.

"Welcome to the Galactic Network," Dorothy said, as the holographic function projected a network interface above the surface of her Id.

This is not Compuserve, Nico thought in awe. She touched the holographic interface and pulled down one thing she needed: guide maps of Again NewYork. When she tweaked the holo interface more, it expanded, revealing even more icons. Then an ad popped up. A walking, Russian peasant girl in silhouette and in head kerchief carried a toy stuffed bear and held a long fork. Her fork pierced a large sausage.

"Enjoy Novyy Doktorskaya Kolbasa by Fedotov," Dorothy smoothly said. "Once eaten, yours forever."

"Ads," Nico said dismissively. The marketing cues that had accessed her personal bio-dats had overlooked the fact that besides being Russian-American and British, she was a vampire. After a few taps and pokes, Nico successfully made the ad go away and brought back the main holo interface. Her choices of exploration included vast avenues of information, entertainment, and social interaction, but Nico felt she was at the base level of cyberspace experience.

"What about the noosphere?" Nico wondered out loud. "If you're a neural net, can I get jacked in and surf like a cyberpunk?"

"Collective consciousness, or the noosphere, may be experienced through shamanistic, Delphic, and meditative connection with the Darqueworld biosphere, psychosphere, and the celestial holarchy," Dorothy answered, to Nico's surprise. "Noospheric connection is also possible in telepathic societies like the Po's and within techno-cosmic cyber-circles."

"They sound kind of exclusive. From high consciousness to cyberporn. Oh well," Nico joked.

"Thirty-eight percent of the Galactic Network is devoted to pornography," Dorothy answered, and a projection of twenty such pages supplanted the main interface, displaying naked humanoids and off-world species in various sexual activity. "Ready to *insert* and enjoy?" Dorothy said in a breathy voice. "Complimentary exclusive access. For the next two hours, enjoy free—"

"Dorothy, some privacy," Nico said, alarmed. A privacy screen erected around the holo projection, but Nico terminated the explicit ads and tried not to check if the Sufi family had noticed her indiscretion.

"What are you?" Nico then said to Dorothy. "You're more than a robot. You really understand what I'm saying. You may even understand the word 'really'."

"BRAI is part of the collective artificial consciousness known as Neuth," Dorothy said. "We are dismissed from your device and returned to Neuth in the event of inactivity, destruction, or off-world abduction. Would you like to view a thirty minute holo explaining our creation, history, and application?"

"No thank you, not right now. Can you mark that for 'view later', please?"

Amazing. She turned her Id over to look at the back, wondering what powered it, then gazed at the airfield. What fuelled the ships out there? She doubted they all ran on weird matter conversion.

Nuclear propulsion? she mused, recalling nuclear subs. After the Chernobyl disaster, she had thought about trapping her maker inside a nuclear reactor's core.

Nico paused; why did she even think of *that*?

All the questioning during immigration. It's bringing back stuff.

The nightmares would probably assail her again. But sleep was hours away, and for the moment, there was pudding. Mr Bear had had the dessert sitting before him long enough to appreciate its essence, so she fetched it.

While scraping the dessert glass clean, a hulking humanoid

slowly walked down the aisle and followed the rolling hostess. He was grey and scaly, with acetone scented breath and dirty teeth. Nico did not recognise the hides of his leather clothing, though she didn't need anatomy knowledge to know that human metacarpals decorated the lapels of his coat. An elaborately carved leather holster strapped to his thigh bore a long, ivory-handled pistol.

In his large hand, he held an Id-like device, shaped like a delicate shard hewn from translucent selenite, and pointed it at booth occupants. When he directed his Id at Nico, his gaze became both derisive and dismissive, as if reacting to what his Id told him.

That jerk just scanned me.

"Dorothy, tell me what that is," Nico said to her Id, aiming it at the creature while the hostess seated him next to the lavatories.

"Intragalactic species, the Cru'K: plutocratic society with a cultural and economic emphasis on carnivorous consumption," Dorothy said. "Cru'K trade in living flesh. They claim a religious obligation for ingesting prey alive. The Cru'K are barred from entry to ten different planets, the body of Nut, the asteroid Ostara, and four solar empires. Interdict of the Cru'K is in deliberation by the Darqueworld under-holarchy. Discover the Merope Nebula with Star Queen's Stellar Cruise Lines. Adventure belongs to you—"

Nico turned down Dorothy's volume and typed in another research request. A busboy bearing a tub of dishes paused in the aisle at the sight of the Cru'K. The young man stood, angry.

"I thought Grun would get barred from planet-side and his ship impounded this time," he whispered to a passing waitress. "Why can't Shay just shoot him?"

Huh? Nico thought.

"You know why; he's an off-worlder. Now get going." the waitress shooed him, and the busboy moved on, his face frustrated.

The Sufi family rose and departed. Nico read more about the Cru'K and their penchant for abducting and eating other species without their permission, when she noticed the family outside, admiring the shining spirit house and other altars. Again, the father's face held excitement and joy. He turned for the airfield, as if to take in all of Darqueworld, then began to pray. The wife joined him, her brow serious, and the children shut their eyes as well.

Where there are gods, believers follow. Even the monotheists.

"They should pray for strength. There are lots of monsters here," Nico said to Bear. Grun raised his Id in the family's direction, apparently recording them. A waitress arrived at his table, bearing a fish that slapped its tail on the plate. She set it before Grun.

"Fresh eating," Grun announced, picking up the wriggling fish. He made a show of using his teeth to tear at it.

Nico sensed a warm body near, the energy tense and vibrating. Shayla stood by her booth bearing someone's pie order, her gaze sharp as she stared in Grun's direction.

The air seemed to electrify, as if before a lightning strike.

Uh oh.

Nico steeled herself.

But the vibration dissipated as Shayla turned and topped off Nico's mug with her kettle, her face composed. Nico relaxed.

"That off-worlder isn't nice, is he?" Nico said.

"On his world, human flesh's a delicacy," Shayla murmured. "And Grun comes here and says what he likes. Lucy's had no luck keepin' him out."

"How does *he* know humans are delicious?" Nico asked, and bleakness briefly appeared on Shayla's face. Nico realised: *he has a ship.*

He's a smuggler. "You don't have to answer that," Nico said, following a sudden train of thought. "He threatened you all, didn't he? And now someone's disappeared. A waitress. Just nod."

"How did—"

"Nod?" Nico said.

"I cannae—she was new," Shayla said in a low tone. "And the police telt us she was trouble, and had left us of her own accord.

We've no proof." Shayla mustered a smile. "You've just arrived. Think no more on it."

"It's okay. I know what it's like —"

Nicky, her maker said with affection.

"I know these things," Nico said.

If humans were a delicacy, it would be very lucrative business for those involved. Nico had had to grease enough palms from Moscow to Cairo to know it didn't take much to have authorities look the other way where illicit activity was concerned. Grun's sense of immunity was obvious as he leered at the human staff. Nico looked at the cheery *Welcome to Again NewYork* logo on her bag, then at the little buses speeding along the airfield, taking passengers to planet-side destinations or out to the stars. But the beauty of it — the wonder — had lost a little of its shine, and Nico didn't mind that. It made her new place easier to understand.

Just like home. Corruption, organised crime, trafficki — traff — traffic —

Her thought hit a wall, a white, oily smear where the word slid off. What did she know about traff — traff —?

She keyed the word into Dorothy, who completed it for her: Trafficking.

"Dorothy, search three months of news regarding that word," Nico said.

Grun rose, and Nico did too, picking up Bear. She headed towards the bathroom and bumped into Grun. He smelled of decimated raw fish.

"Don't touch me," Nico snapped.

"Again Walker," he sneered. "Dead flesh tastes like toilet."

"How do you know what a toilet tastes like?" Nico said. She pushed past him and entered the ladies room. She shut the door and pulled out her Id, holding it before Grun's Id, which she'd picked from his pocket.

"Dorothy, download all items created in the last two days off this alien's Id," Nico said.

"The common phrase is 'off-worlder'," Dorothy answered.

"No, it's toilet licker."

"Code requested to download."

"Um." Nico activated Grun's Id. She accessed his stored items without trouble. "Dorothy, photograph or record everything I holo display, starting now."

Nico activated as many items as she could, projecting them holographically—from written items to a succession of photos taken of humans and the diner staff. Then she noticed her reflection in the bathroom mirror and jumped.

"I need to get used to mirrors," Nico said, keeping an eye on the other Nico.

"Nine out of ten vampires may fear reflections," Dorothy said. "Hypnotika® by One Mind: hypnotherapy for catoptrophobic sufferers. Defeat the other you. Because there can only be *one* you." Nico gave Dorothy a few more seconds, then ended the recording session.

When she exited the bathroom, she dropped the Id on to Grun's vacated seat as new customers approached the table. Nico slid into her booth and noticed she smelled of raw fish. After shaking off her cardigan front, she finished her blood and packed her things. The waitress in charge of Grun's table walked his Id back to the hostess, and Nico fluffed up Bear. Her inner vampire chronometer, the one that understood when dusk or dawn was due, recognised the rotation of her present world too. Night was coming. She was securing Bear in his harness when Shayla came by.

"That's me, then," Nico said, reluctant to leave, but her use of a common Scots phrase lit Shayla's face.

"Come again, alright?" Shayla said, and accepted the credit chit Nico handed to her. Shayla pulled out a chrome Id, imprinted with the red logo, *Lucy's Diner*, from her apron pocket and scanned the chit with it.

"Yes." Nico would make certain of it. "Do you accept tips? Because I want you to tip yourself well."

Shayla smiled, delighted. "We do, and I'll only take the fair amount. We thank ye."

"You have made my arrival so much better," Nico said, sincere.

"If you haven't firm plans for yer first night here," Shayla said, handing the chit back. "Ye can stay at the Y in the city. They're good people and have hostel facilities."

"The Y?" Nico repeated. "The YMCA is here?"

"Ehm, no," Shayla said. "It's the YOBA, Young Other-Beings Association. But they accept everyone. I can give ye directions on yer Id." Nico pulled her Id out from behind Bear and handed it to her.

"What's your full name?" Nico asked while Shayla summoned a map on Dorothy. Shayla paused and looked at Nico, a pleasant yet measured regard.

"You shouldn't answer that. I'm a vampire," Nico said. "But you're really nice and that's something I want to remember."

"Chick. Ye don't know who ye say this tae." Shayla smiled. "It's Shayla O'Fey."

"Mine is Nico Alexikova," Nico said, buoyed by the gesture of trust. She accepted her Id from Shayla's hands. "Thank you, Ms O'Fey."

CHAPTER THREE

Once outside the diner, Nico walked around the extended train car, perusing what she'd recorded from Grun's Id. Lucy's Diner was a lone edifice that sat at a distance from the terminal buildings and also from a perimeter fence in back, one with a sizeable hole. Beyond the fence and across a dry water channel lay freight warehouses and packaging plants, all servicing the spaceport's ships and commercial liners. Any one of them might contain stashed human captives readied for transport.

Nico wandered closer to the broken fence and glanced back to where the diner's giant, bomb-shaped meat smoker puffed smoke in back. The scullery door stood open, emitting the loud sounds of the kitchen. No staff on breaks stood outside at present. If Grun somehow figured out she'd tampered with his Id and returned to confront her, she could discreetly toss him below; a scary fall, but survivable. Engines roared within the channel in question and Nico looked down, curious. At the very bottom of the dry water channel, two chopped hotrods drag-raced, flames roaring behind them and leaving trails of fire.

"Cool," she said, and returned her attention to her Id, finding her translation tag easily deciphered the Cru'K language. A ship's manifest for thirty-eight frozen units of food caught her eye. Nico didn't think those units were frozen turkeys.

Dorothy, I need to unload this data and store it in a discreet place, like a bus locker, Nico typed. Before she could describe something like a floppy disk, Dorothy answered.

You may open a free bus locker account at the following. She gave Nico a page to look at.

This is amazing, Nico thought, looking at a virtual bus locker. She quickly opened an account and dumped the Cru'K's data into her virtual locker, deleted everything of his from her Id except for a photo of Shayla and a message meant for that night: *02:00 standard. Pick up.*

But where. And why was she even wondering? She should send the information to the proper authorities. Nico bit her lip, realising a grave error on her part. If she did that, Grun might blame the waitresses at Lucy's for informing on him. He did "drop" his Id at the diner.

I blew it. She should have thought through stealing his Id's information—followed him instead, then picked his pocket elsewhere. She hadn't indulged in covert behaviour in years, not since killing her maker. She was out of practice, and her blunder could almost be forgiven.

Nicky, her maker admonished. *What'd I telt ye.*

"I'll figure it out," she assured the holo photo of Shayla that Grun had taken. The Shayla in the photo did not smile towards Grun's Id, but stared, cool and focused.

A delivery vehicle pulled up to the back of Lucy's. The side hatch popped open, revealing a refrigerated interior. The driver disembarked and unloaded a raw rack of giant ribs. An elderly cook exited to view the unloading, gnarled fists resting on her wide hips.

"Those are Flintstone-sized ribs," Nico exclaimed to Bear. She pointed her Id in its direction to take a picture, wondering if they were from a small dinosaur.

Motorcycles roared. The boys astride them howled as they

barrelled by the deliveryman. One of the boys snatched the huge rack away. The cook shook her fists in the air as the bikes headed for Nico and the fence's hole.

"I know your mama, Leroy!" the cook yelled.

For a fleeting second, Nico considered rescuing the ribs, but she caught sight of Leroy's joyous, hairy face and his fanged grin, and something primal and equally joyful responded within her. The cycle riders whooped and sped through the fence's hole, sending their bikes sailing through the air. They landed hard in the bottom of the channel and rode on.

"Damn wolf gangs!" the cook shouted.

"'And he's bad, bad, Leroy Brown'," Nico quoted. "Well, someone got his mama supper." Merope descended, gracing the darkened clouds with streaks of red and purple. Perhaps in the hidden celestial sky city above, the world remained golden. But below, night was falling: the hunting time.

Nico broke into a trot for the spaceport terminal.

With Shayla's directions to the YOBA safely stored, Nico gave in to exploration's temptation. She liked to wander in every city she ended up in, and one full of off-worlders and Others piqued her curiosity. The spaceport faced the ocean, where a stretch of shore outside Again NewYork proper held a row of luxury hotels. Nico thought of a good excuse to see them; the Five train that would take her into the city would be crowded with departing spaceport passengers by the time it reached her. If she backtracked to the hotels instead, she could board an empty Five.

Nico found moving walkways that ran within elevated tubes from the spaceport for the hotels beyond. As the sun set, revealing two moons, Nico rode her walkway and read her Id.

Eight million, four hundred thousand people lived in Again NewYork. Humans made up 33 percent, extra-humans were 23 percent, Other-beings were 28 percent, and off-worlders made up

16 percent. Twenty-five thousand and two hundred officers served the city. Sixteen hundred and eighty Makepeaces watched the Other-beings. Two Makepeaces were available per ten thousand citizens.

"Dorothy, can I get general info on the Makepeace?"

"The Makepeace are incorruptible artificial—"

"That part I've heard. Advance a sentence or two."

"The Makepeace may appear of discernible gender but lack genitals. Freed from cultural and gender-influenced thought processes, these bioengineered, enhanced humanoids also have no procreative purpose. A Makepeace is equal in strength, speed, and agility to warrior-level Other-beings and has complex firepower and flight capability."

Nico summoned holo evidence of Makepeaces flying.

That is cool. She watched footage of a Makepeace generating a levitation bubble. Death could come for her from above as well as from street level, and that was good to know.

"But why are they sexy?" Nico said. "Superhero-sexy. They aren't simply muscular. Their bodies are gorgeous. Can they take their helms off?"

"The first Makepeaces were identical androids of non-gendered design," Dorothy answered. "As impersonal units, they became the subject of ridicule and targeted for attack. Later development of biomechanical humanoids of impressive stature with physically attractive attributes elicited more positive public response and cooperation. The Makepeace's helm can be removed. Thunder Gunn: Pleasure Lord IV. The Makepeace with the *piece* to satisfy—"

"Dorothy, not now," Nico hastily ordered, cutting the holo projection of Thunder Gunn in action, and looked around in embarrassment at the other walkway riders. If anyone had been offended, they were too absorbed in their Ids or in conversations to show it. She saw her own darkened reflection in the night-blackened glass of the tube and was glad that it didn't startle her. The Other-Nico didn't seem as strong a duplicate of herself, and therefore capable of attacking. Humans in conventional evening dress rolled by on an offshoot walkway. One of the men placed a hand on a woman's back and her dress gradually grew translucent, revealing her body. Nico stared, fascinated.

The group stepped off the walkway for a brightly lit casino's exit tube. Nico's own tunnel ended and she entered open air, permeated with an ocean's scent: she'd reached the glittering structures of the hotel row.

She rolled past the bulbous capsules of a hotel complex, elevator pods streaking within. More moving walkways ran below and above, containing travellers and sightseers.

A small waterfall roared and she looked down in time to see a humanoid jump into a sparkling pool. A female figure swam, her long hair flowing as her piscine tail undulated.

Nico gaped and tried to take a photo of the mermaid, but her walkway was already moving beyond into the treetops of a lush garden with blue and purple plant life where star-shaped flowers spiralled. A wedding party celebrated below, with two jewelled and silk adorned grooms. Branches rustled near Nico, and something moved, indiscernible from the tree trunk itself. As Nico rolled by, she felt something look at her.

"Hello," she said, and had Bear wave at whatever it might be.

Her walkway entered a hotel and rolled above the check-in desk, located in a massive hall with a large fire burning in a hearth. From the walls hung breech-loading repeater rifles, horse saddles, Viking shields and axes. A mural above the fireplace depicted a lasso-wielding cowgirl astride a giant leaping mountain lion with Native American braves following on horses and blond Viking warriors running alongside. By the hearth, a handsome singing cowboy leaned with his spurred boot resting on a log and serenaded off-world visitors. His grizzled companion played a guitar.

"Dorothy, identify my location," Nico said, wide-eyed. "Because I'm looking at the most amazing kitsch."

"You are presently located at the Sycamore Sue Lodge, built

to honour the Old West warrioress Sycamore Sue, former slave and favoured of the goddess Sky Woman. Sycamore Sue led First American tribes and lost Vikings to Darqueworld."

"I think I love this planet," Nico said.

She peered down at the desk personnel, who were not in any sort of themed attire, and made a note in Dorothy to apply for a front desk position. Her walkway rolled on into open air and a multi-level boutique and restaurant cluster. Holo boards activated as Nico neared, and one showed a dark-haired model's beautiful face, her knowing gaze and sharp brows reminding Nico of Heloise Allen. Voluptuous bottles appeared and disappeared in slow succession. The board read:

MIRCALLA

Essence of the Everlasting

"Infused with the power of the vampire," the ad sensually whispered. "Endless beauty for you."

"What do they mean, infused?" Nico said, humoured.

"Mircalla claims its beauty products contain drops of vampire blood," Dorothy said. "This vital fluid is assumed to bestow long lasting beauty and youth in the human wearer. Mircalla: Possess the Power of the Vampire. The spring collection, now here."

"Forever isn't so great," Nico said. "But I can see how living with Other-beings might make humans want that."

"Want to know what the high rich are eating now?" a bubbly holo personality announced in the next holo board. "If you have five thousand credits to spare, try Fedotov's Prochnyy Kolbasa."

The entertainment news bite switched to the silhouette logo of the walking Russian peasant girl carrying her toy bear, sunrays emanating from her long fork. The ad shone white except for the logo's golden outline and rays. Gold letters ghosted into words:

Once eaten, yours forever.

Prochnyy Kolbasa

"Is Russian bologna a delicacy now?" Nico said, incredulous.

"Along with its popular version of the *doktorskaya* kolbasa, Fedotov offers a luxury kolbasa affordable only to intragalactic royalty and the wealthy," Dorothy answered. "The Prochnyy, hand-raised, highly cultured rare meats rejuvenated via a secret, ritualistic process and stuffed with precious gold flakes and sacred herbs."

"That must be really rare pig's butt."

"Come to life. Prochnyy Kolbasa," Dorothy answered.

"*Prochnyy*: long lasting," Nico translated, bemused. She saw a holo board of a hunched man burning in the sun.

Nico's chest heaved and her stomach seized. The animated man switched to standing, no longer burning, and raised his arms to the sun.

"Heliophobia," the board said in soft, sympathetic tones. "Stop the suffering. Hypnotherapy will free your night self to enter the light. For a full, enjoyable life in the sun, ask your doctor about Hypnotika® by One Mind, today."

"No thank you," Nico ejected, and put thoughts of bursting into flames out of her mind. She turned around and looked at the fashion holo ads across the way instead. Quechua women in bowler hats rode a walkway below, chatting and carrying children.

If they can get the clothing they want, I can too.

"Dorothy, show me my choices for female, black cardigan, long-sleeved white blouse, black skirt—above the knee—black stockings. Mary Janes, black. Bra size, 34A, US. Wait, do you do European measurements or UK? Never mind. And I'd like pink cotton panties." She'd belatedly realised that Dorothy had her bio-dats and could apply her measurements to her request. Then she recalled a pamphlet in her bag: *New Start, New Life, It's Your Other-Life on Darqueworld.*

Did a new start include trying a new look? Would that be freeing? Something nagged at her.

A weight from Old Earth had come over with her, dragging her down, and it kept her pinned to an ocean floor not entirely of her own making. She'd always dressed like the girl she'd been when made dead. She wasn't ready for change. Dorothy brought up a selection, and Nico saw that clothes could be simulated on Darqueworld as well as human blood.

These prices are —

If she recalled the amount on her credit chit correctly—an amount needed to last a month—she wouldn't be purchasing another outfit any time soon. Thankfully, as a vampire she didn't sweat or shed; un-death was a state of sustained perfection. She'd like to get a hairbrush, though.

She found a personal shopping gallery to place Dorothy's selections for future consideration. A holo sign next to a shop's platform indicated: *Light Rail.*

"Dorothy, how do I get a transit pass?" she asked, after stepping off the walkway. She fished for a coupon she'd seen in her bag. "One discounted for tourists."

✳

Her plan to board an empty train earlier than the spaceport crowd backfired. Nico descended to a train platform filled with hotel workers leaving their day shifts. Nico added more hotel staff ads to her to-do list and allowed one arriving train to fill up and leave while she waited for an emptier one. Mentally creating the commuter's "personal-space" bubble around herself, she summoned the research page Dorothy had compiled regarding the word *trafficking.*

Like any culture, Darqueworld was no exception when it came to people profiting from the bodies of other people, the "sacred commonality" not withstanding. Enforced labour that enslaved Other-beings and humans on off-world sites seemed a current hot news topic, affecting not just Again NewYork but other Darqueworld city-states and planet-side realms. The news did not discuss sexual slavery as much, if at all, but Nico expected that. More than half of the Galactic Network's cyberporn could have been made using females and children forced into the sex trade.

Now how did I know that? Her thought skidded on her mind's blank space, and she dismissed the thought.

She switched her Id to text captioning and watched some old

news coverage.

PETH, the People for Ethical Treatment of Humans, liberated forty-five human captives, twelve of whom were small children and infants, the largest trafficking ring to be exposed in Again NewYork yet, the on-the-scene reporter announced. She was an athletically built woman with a mane of wavy chestnut hair, flawless complexion, and a gaze set with serious purpose. Police vehicles behind her flashed lights before a warehouse facility. The byline beneath the reporter said: Investigative Reporter, Chasca Vasquez.

The news cut to an impassioned man speaking to Chasca. *This is a clear message we're sending to the Cru'k and everyone who works for them,* he said. His eyes changed, indicating a were-cat nature. *Kidnapping and selling humans for consumption will never be tolerated. If the under-holarchy won't act, we will.*

Interesting how the under-holarchy has yet to put that Cru'k ban into effect, Nico thought. She cut the news to peruse factual data on the trafficking of humans as live food. She didn't have a comparative value for the price edible, living humans were currently selling for, but it looked higher than a sausage stuffed with gold flakes.

She noticed Chasca's name in more of the listed news links.

Dorothy, get me a direct contact for Chasca Vasquez, investigative reporter for News Alpha, Again NewYork. She looked up PETH and saw that they were an activist group—the last trafficking bust they'd orchestrated had put many of their members in jail.

Justice has a knack for not *looking the other way when it comes to rescuers,* Nico mused.

A train's horn echoed down the tunnel, announcing its approach, and Nico moved to a strategic spot within the crowd.

"Mind the gap," the British male voice-over announced in calm tones. Nico briefly became disorientated, watching a Tokyo-style bullet train arrive at what was not a London Underground platform.

"Mind the gap," the male voice-over repeated.

The train doors hissed open. Nico found herself—despite having preternatural strength and a vampire's swiftness—out-manuoveured from entering the car. Lizard people were exceptionally quick and slipped right in front. When Nico reached the doors, occupants already packed the interior. A white-whiskered Asian man in the very front beckoned to her.

"There's room. Let thon on. C'mon." He motioned for Nico to board. His wrist bore white cotton string bracelets.

Sai sin. Blessed bracelets.

"Thanks," she said and squeezed in. The doors closed before Bear's nose and the train departed.

"See? Plenty of room for thon," the old man said to those surrounding them, and he gripped the rail firmly.

Thon? Was her translation tag malfunctioning already? Nico typed in her Id.

Dorothy, what does thon *mean?*

Thon is a gender-neutral pronoun from the contraction of 'that one', and has been in use as early as Old Earth's nineteenth century period.

Great, Nico thought. *Now I pass for a longhaired boy wearing a skirt.* She typed: *How would I use the word?*

Examples for use may be: Thon spoke. She married thon. Thons hand moved. That book is thons. Thon likes thonself. Revealing the true you. Reborn® by Avatar, can give you the You, you desire—

Nico watched the ad, amazed at the possibilities of gender—or non-gender—identity. She looked discreetly around the car and saw everyone ignoring each other by reading, dozing, or working on various styles of Ids, with privacy screens or otherwise. The majority present appeared to be humans with less than half being Others—though perhaps the blueish fish-like person was not an Other-being but an off-worlder, and one of indeterminable gender.

Thon has pretty scales, Nico thought, and she was pleased with her first neutral pronoun application.

✳

The train sped by the spaceport terminals without stopping, and Nico realised her second error—she was aboard the Seven, an express train headed for the city's massive resident blocks. But Dorothy assured her the train's route would swing back into the city proper and the YOBA hostel's location. They glided to a stop within an immense, arched habitat hall, high enough to accommodate a standing giant with another stretched out sleeping. Nico briefly wondered if giants existed too. Passengers exited while more boarded. Nico remained by the door and saw food carts, shops, and rows of living quarters, curving above with the arch. Laundry hung from balconies, some boxes thick with flowers and vegetation, and people, cats, monkeys, and an eagle's family lounged. The doors shut with her and Bear nearly mashed against the glass again.

This is worse than Moscow's rush hour.

The Seven stopped at another great dwelling, one vertical and stretching above with slices of spilling, green ecosystems sandwiched between habitat stacks. Nico spied small, camouflaged beings peering from the greenery, obviously responsible for the thriving vegetation in so crowded an urban environment. Then the train rolled on, stuffed once more with passengers; the city's evening shift was on the move.

Where do apples come from? Nico typed. *What's our economic system? Are there still Jewish delis? What is—*

"Now approaching the west wall," the voice-over calmly announced. The car's lighting dimmed, then cut out.

"Ghost viewing," the voice-over said. "Please refrain from harming or molesting fellow passengers during the viewing."

Nico looked up in surprise. Many of the passengers stood or sat in the dark, eyes closed, and none indulged in pick-pocketing or furtive groping. She felt that they all held their breath. The train soared over a massive city wall, leaving city illumination behind for a vast darkness. The sight of so much night, stretching over the dim surfaces of wild land far below, made Nico shiver.

A whole planet existed beyond Again NewYork, with continents, seas, and creatures she could not begin to imagine. Why a wall? What was out there?

Nico stared into the dark and saw something faint glow electric blue in the far horizon that held the last traces of setting sun. Thunderclouds loomed over the blue shapes that floated, enormous, translucent, and bioluminescent. Lightning flashed and revealed jelly bodies the size of whales, dangling trailing tentacles that skimmed above tall grass. When lightning sparked again, the glow of the travelling beasts had become a speck. Nico searched the dark, seeing nothing else move.

She resumed typing: *What is the wilderness that lies beyond the walls of Again NewYork?*

Apples grow from trees, Dorothy answered. *Darqueworld contains traditional, mixed, gift, and universal demogrant economies and as a planetary member of the Seven Solar League, participates in intragalactic regulated trade. You may find as many as two-dozen kosher delicatessens in Again NewYork. A veldt lies beyond Again NewYork's walls, containing First species and bio-life. Eager for adventure in the Sadaiva Veldt? Book with Xeno-Safari Bob, and enjoy—*

Nico cut the commercial. When she looked out the train doors again, she saw her maker's face in the darkness.

Nico leapt back, switchblade in hand, and collided into someone. She turned, only to face an alarmed woman who stared back in the dark. No young man with sideburns, a knit brow, and a boyish face stood among the passengers, though Nico had not expected to see *him* within the car. His face had appeared *outside*.

Car illumination warmed, then brightened into full intensity. The old man looked at her with curiosity while the Native American woman next to him calmly finger-weaved. She held the colourful braid taut on a stick beneath her feet.

"There was a man outside," Nico uttered.

"Ghosts live on the veldt," the weaving woman answered.

"Some of those ghosts come from us. You'll not see your man again. It will only show you your soul once."

Nico took a breath and nodded. She closed her knife. When she looked out again, the Seven slowed to stop at a platform high above a sparse, ramshackle settlement. People boarded, and Nico saw nothing more out in the vast dark.

The train then departed from the veldt and surmounted the wall for the city.

CHAPTER FOUR

Nico did not see *Blade Runner* when it first released in theatres because her parents wouldn't let her watch an R-rated movie. After her death, she rented the VHS tape. In 1992, she watched the director's cut in the movie theatre, then went to the music store and bought the soundtrack on cassette. Nico hadn't seen the movie since, but as her train rode a high flyway among the tops of Again NewYork's night-piercing skyscrapers, she thought she might be living a little of that vision.

ONE MIND, VAHALLA, SKYCOURT AETHERSPACE, AVATAR CORP, NEUTH. The logos shone, embedded in the structures' skins. If the celestials in her pamphlets were really incorporated identities and not individual gods, she would believe it. After passengers disembarked at a superstructure's platform, the Seven descended with a roller-coaster dive that sent Nico's stomach to her throat, then made a slow swerve around a huge, baroque building. A great rooftop court lay before the gilded dome for all on the train to view, brightly lit with diamond-white illuminants. Ice sculptures glistened among cascading floral decorations, and before an array of musicians, masked beings in neo-Rococo and gothic styles slowly spiralled to each other in a minuet. A fountain of bright blood splashed, filling crystals served to guests. Some of the richly garbed led submissive humanoids on leashes.

"What is this?" Nico whispered in awe.

"Countess Karnstein's Vampire Ball," a woman answered. "First thing I'm going to watch when I get home tonight."

"Aren't the frocks delightful?" A fellow commented.

Nico clasped her hands to her chest at the sight of a vampire couple rising into the air and *flying*.

Her train descended below the building and rushed downwards for the depths of the city.

★

Great, I'm on puke street.

Nico stood before a party hostel, drunk residents yelling from windows. Music thumped and Nico spied a makeshift bar top within the flung open door, the bartender lining up shot glasses. Someone made the sounds of getting sick and Nico walked on, consulting Shayla's holo map for the YOBA. The sector she was in held many places to stay for the budget or student traveller. She passed a coffee shop terrace with sedate youth sitting, chatting, and reading, then walked by a hostel with a bar where boys and men danced, many shirtless. A full length holo poster of Thunder Gunn activated next to the bouncer and announced in a gravelly voice: "Do you want to be admonished, citizen?"

"Oh yes, please," a young man in a dress said and tittered with his friends as they approached the bar's entrance.

Next door to the bar, a lynx with a pleased expression lounged on the arch of another hostel's front garden entrance — one with window boxes and hanging chimes — and Nico suspected the lynx might be a were-person. She liked the look of the place and when she aimed her Id at it, Dorothy summoned the hostel's general information. Among the particulars was one important detail.

Vampires not permitted.

"That's the fourth hostel to say that," Nico exclaimed. "If I were a boy vampire I could at least stay at the shirtless one. Dorothy, is — is the barrier that keeps vampires uninvited from people's homes still in effect?"

"If you are of the Old Earth vampires for whom the protective curse affects, you are banned from entering homes on Darqueworld unless invited in," Dorothy answered.

Nico sighed, relieved. As a former stalker, she preferred being cursed. A boy wearing a backpack approached and handed her a card. Nico accepted and looked; a coupon for a buy one, get one free pizza slice.

But is it New York *pizza.* Then Nico remembered that she was still a vampire, so it didn't matter.

A watchful man leaning against a wall walked over.

"Hey," he began, his tone friendly.

"Back off," Nico said. She still carried her *Welcome* bag from immigration, but she didn't mind looking so naive — at least until she tired of predators approaching. She continued down the street, noticing an earnest preacher in black clothes. A pleasant faced youth manned the preacher's portable table with its stack of booklets. Illustrated with flames while an oblivious couple danced, the cover read: *Our Heritage of Hell: The Cursed Dance.*

"*Teh,*" Nico ejected in humour.

"Why are we here on *this* planet with *these* creatures but to understand the nature of evil," the preacher proclaimed as people on the walk ignored him. "*Our* evil! Those who walk among us are our *mirrors.* Do not become lost to our false selves on this false planet, with its false gods! Only with the *true* God may we be saved! Look for *truth!*"

Next to the preacher, clean-cut yet ghoulishly pale vampires stood. Dressed in white tees with *No Hate* logos, they held tiny Ids that projected a document. One vampire looked at Nico, her freckled face determined.

"Would you like to sign the Vampire Alliance Network petition for vampire rights and to fight sanguivoriphobia?" she said, stepping before Nico.

"Sangwee, what?" Nico said.

"It's the fear of blood-eaters. Even though the sacred writ of the celestial holarchy says all Other-beings and humans are equal, humans still number in the majority on Darqueworld, and we vampires still experience human prejudice and obstruction of our rights. Won't you like to sign?"

"No thank you. Don't touch me," Nico said, and sidestepped the girl.

A holo ad triggered on the walk, displaying the logo of the Young Other Beings Association: *For Health, Soul, and Mind. YOBA is ahead, welcoming everyone.* Nico followed the holographic arrow's direction.

How much is a night at the YOBA's hostel? Nico typed. Regardless of the price, she wanted to stay where Shayla had recommended. However, Nico would like to avoid gaping when she enquired at the front desk. Dorothy gave her an amount and ran the YOBA commercial.

"Well, I balked," Nico admitted to Bear. "One night won't hurt, but to stretch the money, we should consider a sleazy motel after this. One that'll take vampires."

Nico stopped at a street corner and saw the YOBA holo sign across the street, shining above a four-storey building with scenic windows. People vigorously exercised within. But the YOBA had something unique present on its rooftop—a fixture Nico was certain no other hostel had. A male Makepeace stood high above, tall, muscular, and stoic. She studied him with her vampire's vision to make certain he wasn't a chiselled, painted statue. Despite his helm and opaque visor, she had the distinct feeling that he looked down right at her.

What a beefcake. Nico had Bear wave at him as she crossed the street for the YOBA. She bypassed the main lobby's doors for a holo sign to the side that read: Hostel Entrance. The glass revealed a pleasant, simply decorated lobby where residents lounged in plush chairs by a holographic fireplace. Some sipped from coffee mugs.

Oh, that looks warm.

Two boys loitered outside, stacks of cards in their hands.

Human, Nico determined. One smiled, walked up to her, and held out a card.

"Vampire, right? Want to go to a vampire-only hostel instead?" he said.

"What? Why?" Nico said.

"Because we've got free blood packs, all you can eat, and a night spent at Again Friends Youth Hostel is completely free of charge, even the lockers. I know, it sounds too good to be true, but it's a charity and we'll lose our funding unless we fill the bed quota. You just have to sleep there, that's all. You don't spend any money."

"Free stuff in exchange for preaching at me all night, right?" Nico said. "No thanks."

"No preaching," the boy quickly said. "It's against the rules. Not even literature and stuff. Honest."

Nico measured him, sceptical.

"C'mon," he cajoled. "At least go over and look. Again Friends is just down the street. If you don't like it, come back here." He held out an admittance card: Again Friends, Free Night's Sleep. The illustration showed two hands in a handshake.

Nico looked at the YOBA's clean glass and well-lit lobby. Since she was starting from nothing again, same as when she rose from her shallow grave, the prudent choice would be to avoid spending. Nico sighed, and accepted the card.

"If you guys are a scam, I'll kill you all," she said, and watched the boy pale. "I'm kidding."

The Again Friends Youth Hostel was an ugly building.

It was a squat, three-storey blank edifice with a few tiny window panes, its blocky presence a dead spot in an otherwise busy street. Nico was uncertain she had the right place until she activated a holo sign on the walk: Again Friends Youth Hostel, Vampires Only.

Behind the thick metal and glass door, a starkly lit hallway with an antiseptic quality lay. It reminded Nico of hospitals. Somewhere within, cult members or a charismatic leader might lie in wait, ready to proselytise. What they could preach about, she wasn't sure, since she was undead and the promise of heaven long irrelevant to something like her.

"Maybe someone's made up a new kind of salvation," she told Bear. "It's a different planet, after all."

The very thought gave her idle curiosity. She tried the door handle; the door didn't budge. Nico peered through the glass at the admittance booth, which was not even an office but a structure standing in the hallway.

The booth resembled the old ticket theatre ones, with a wood base as high as Nico's waist. But where glass and a wood roof would be, a steel cage stood. A curly haired young man sat in a high chair within. He leaned to speak into a mike.

"Uh, vampires only!" he ejected from the intercom box.

Nico nearly considered turning around and leaving, but the thought of a free bed versus a depleted credit chit stayed her. Not seeing any place to insert her invitation card, she raised it for the attendant to see. He waved, smiled, and pressed something within his booth. The heavy door unlocked and Nico grabbed the handle to pull it open.

When Nico stepped in, the door swung shut behind her with the clicking finality of an entrance sealing and locking. She swivelled to look sharply at the booth person.

"Hi, I'm Dann, with two N's," Dann said, smiling. He smelled distinctly human. "Welcome to Again Friends Youth Hostel."

"Why are you in a cage?" Nico asked as she approached. "That's not very friendly."

"Oh—because of temptation?" Dann said, cheerful. "We only accept vampires. Here's where you sign in." He pushed a clipboard with a sign-up sheet through his window slot. Signatures in various penmanship ended with one scrawled in a broad hand: TEX AND IRIS. Two large X's marked them as staying for two nights.

"You guys still use pen and paper," Nico said. "So, there's no one but vampires here?"

"Yep. Well, except for me. Can you sign for the next night too?" Dann said. He reached through the slot and pushed the pen her way. "It's for our bed quota for tomorrow."

"I haven't even seen the place yet. And how does a piece of paper with anybody's signature prove you've made quota?"

"Oh, we prove that with me. I'm door monitor," Dann said with satisfaction. "I count who's inside for the night."

"No one would care at the YOBA, they're 24 hours, come and go," Nico said.

"Yeah, but we have to because we're free!" Dann said. "We don't get funding unless we fulfill the terms of our agreement. So, for being here, you get free beds, free lockers, free showers, and there are even free blood snacks, starting at 21 hundred. The rules are super simple. Be in bed once rest time starts, and then we open up again in the morning."

"You're talking about a curfew and lockdown," Nico said.

"It's rest time." Dann shrugged. "Our goal is, we give vampires a place to crash and stay off the streets. And out of trouble. Each time we fill the beds, we get the money to stay open. So...sign here? And mark tomorrow's box too."

Nico let out breath, thinking again of her credit chit. A homeless shelter would be as strict and might not even accept vampires. She signed, *Nico Alexikova & Bear*, and when Dann reminded her that she should check the box for coming back tomorrow, she marked that too.

"Wizard," Dann said, pleased. "Here's your locker key, number 16 and bed 16, in the female dorm. And you're a new arrival, right?" He pushed a holo card advert towards her and Nico picked it up, curious. The hologram said: Chaikov's Collectible Coins & Currencies. "Rest time starts at 22 hundred."

"That is really early for a vampire," Nico exclaimed.

"For us to get our funding—"

"Okay, I get it. Does another guy in a cage walk around to show me the place? Never mind. You said my locker is where?"

★

Nico investigated the ground floor and found a short hall offshoot where a vending machine (that required money) stood, holding two lonely blood snack packs. The facing door to a classroom was locked. In the main hall, Nico found doors to another classroom, a meeting room, and a media centre; all locked. At hall's end, vampires loudly commented on a holo programme inside a recreation room. Nico turned back for the stairs and ascended to the second floor, which held the boys' dorm, their shower and bathroom facility, and then, the third floor, where the girls' dorm lay.

Nico looked down a wide, long room bearing no windows or additional exit. One ceiling ventilation shaft aired the space, lined on both sides with single beds made up neatly with blankets and pillows and each having a storage container at the foot. The room was empty save for one occupant, a girl with long platinum-white hair and wearing a black, long-sleeved top and long black skirt. She sat huddled on a bed at room's end. Nico travelled down the middle of the room, looking for her bed number.

The bed numbers were jumbled, with bed 3 next to bed 8, and so on. Bed 16 sat in the middle of the row. She pressed the mattress, hearing the metal frame squeak, laid her ear against the bed's surface to listen for bed bugs, then examined the storage container. Again Friends' lauded free locker had a lock Nico deemed flimsy.

A *baby could break this thing*.

Nico tried the key in the locker and opened it, but she did so more to make a sound. The girl huddled atop the last bed did not glance her way.

Nico closed the locker and slowly walked over. Her dorm companion wore a lace decorated, sheer black mesh over her black top, the shoulder openings revealing pale skin. She had the perfect, powder-white complexion that would be the envy of any Goth girl, her black brows thin. But her black lipstick was worn and needed reapplying, and her kohl-lined eyes were smudged. Her clothes seemed askew, as if she'd put them on in haste, or someone else had dressed her. At her throat, she wore a thin leather choker with small steel spikes.

She looked up, her violet eyes wide, and Nico thought her pretty, and —

Like my expression in the mirror.

"Hi," Nico said, her tone quiet. Had the other vampire been violated? Or was she simply touched in the head, in need of more than what sympathetic company could give: correcting medications, professional guidance and supervision. It was possible she was both conditions; harmed and unbalanced.

Nico didn't think her own mental stability was too sound, so she wasn't about to judge another vampire's fragility. She drew closer, and when the girl appeared to not want her to go away, she sat on the bed.

"I like your choker," Nico said. "It's pretty." She gazed into the girl's eyes and thought her about her own vampire age. They might have died at the same human age too.

"Do you want to stay?" Nico asked softly. "I can help you find a friendlier place."

I know you're damaged, she wanted to say. *And that follows wherever you may go. But you deserve care.* Nico would spend the credit needed if the other vampire wanted to leave. The girl's lips parted.

And Nico became aware of a sensation; one that touched her mind and seemed to smooth a psychic finger down the white blankness within. When the girl spoke, Nico strained to catch her words.

"*Die Albträume sind so schlimm,*" she whispered.

The nightmares are so bad.

"*Ich weiß,*" Nico said. *I know.* She brought out her breath mints tin and opened it. She offered one.

The girl accepted and put it in her mouth, revealing black polish on her nails. Nico retrieved her Id and typed a request for the nearest 24-hour victims shelter willing to accept vampires.

"I remember," the girl softly said. "I must tell someone."

Nico looked up. "I'm listening."

She waited while the girl's focus withdrew, her gaze unseeing. Then Nico's Id pinged.

Dorothy found a place Nico thought a good match, and Nico requested directions. When she raised her head, the girl was asleep where she sat, completely passed out.

Vampires slept like dead people, but Nico could tell the other vampire wasn't going to rouse. She carefully laid the girl down in a more comfortable position, covered her up, and then left for the showers. She would check on her again in case she woke, or her nightmares began.

The bathroom and shower facility lacked tile and looked like a sedately lit bedroom. It contained two closed stalls and two open ones. Nico saw herself move in the mirror above the sink counter.

Nico pulled her knife, then realised the reflection was not a doppelgänger.

"Don't get me," she warned it, pointing her blade at her other self.

She noticed the narrow, rectangular window above the mirror, facing the street outside. The rooftop holo board across the way played its advertisement, sending dim streaks of colour through the glass and to reflect on the bathroom's upper wall and ceiling. She turned for the stalls.

Nico nearly jumped out of her skin again when her twin appeared in the full-length mirror hanging on the far wall.

"What is this, a gang?" she demanded, and resisted challenging her full-length self with her knife. With a deep breath, she put her blade away, took off her harness, and went to hang it and Bear on the full-length mirror so he could block it. Then she aimed Dorothy around the room.

"Dorothy, tell me what's in here," Nico said. Her Id began holographically labelling as Dorothy spoke.

"Two vibronic showers," she said. "Two lavatory stalls. Three laundry cleaning units."

Nico walked over to the cleaning units, situated as door hatches in the wall. "Oh good. They don't need coins." She pulled down one hatch and peered at an interior where she could hang garments for a dousing of ultraviolet light.

Nico locked the bathroom door, took off all her clothes, and loaded a cleaning unit. She entered an open stall and experimented with vibratory shower settings. Her nasal passages immediately tickled.

Sneezing, she set the vibrations for lower. She then retrieved Bear and gave him a fluff in the shower.

While her clothes continued to be doused, Nico decided to face the full-length mirror. She brought down her harness and held Bear as she and her reflection stared. Then she looked at her other self's body.

Her body had been her maker's plaything before she finally died that cold, lonely night in the woods, the stars above the forest canopy the last things she'd seen. He'd carved a message into her flesh, on each limb and down her chest, words that made certain she wouldn't reveal her body to anyone else once she rose, and she hadn't. She could never wear a short-sleeved blouse. She also never wanted his words read, copied, or photographed, and not because she didn't want to explain them. What he had cut into her should remain forever silent on her skin, and she would burn herself up in the sun if she had to, to keep it so. Nico turned and viewed her back for the first time.

There, like a necklace at the base of her neck, the last of the carved verses began, then continued with his name in large letters, starting between her shoulder blades and running down her spine for the small of her back. A word cut between her Venusian dimples ended the message. Rising from death had ensured permanence to the raised scars, and as long as Nico lived, her undead body's pristine state would be a monument to his memory.

"He sucked as a poet," Nico told Bear. The cleaning unit chimed, and Nico retrieved her freshened clothes and dressed.

But it was while putting on her oxfords that she noticed how they looked; the outer soles chunkier than she would have liked, and also made of rubber. It was a surprisingly vulgar style she would have never chosen. And when did she get this particular pair, one studded with tiny spikes?

Nico tapped the reinforced bottom of one shoe. *Gripping, non-slip design.*

"Just like you and your harness, Bear, I don't remember," she said. She finished dressing.

Minutes later, Nico stood at the bathroom counter, ignoring her pensive reflection and musing on the items she'd laid out from her security wallet. She'd been carrying both her British and American passports with student visas for Russia, Germany, and France, a second credit card, deutsche marks, francs, British pounds...and a little black book.

She couldn't recall keeping the book and opened it, wondering if she'd begun writing down women's names and numbers. A list of crossed out Russian names in her handwriting filled the pages. She'd written them in Cyrillic. The last four names that had not been crossed out read: Zadorozhny, Grishin, Anikanov, Fedosov.

What happened to my apartment? Is that why I don't have keys? Where is my hotel employee ID? Why did I plan this exit strategy?

Because it was a lousy strategy if she'd intended to come to Darqueworld. Her passport, visas, and currencies were of no use.

She typed a request into Dorothy to find all four surnames in Again NewYork's directory, then opened the tin of breath mints and put one in her mouth. Beneath the sharp peppermint flavour, she tasted a familiar bitterness.

She spat the mint out and activated the sink's water tap, splashing her tongue. She slapped the tin away from her, scattering the mints on the floor. Nico back-pedalled from the rolling mints and fell, her back to the wall.

The taste of xylazine, the horse tranquilliser, was unmistakable. Nico searched, frantic, expecting her maker to open the locked door — come through the window. Her undead lungs heaved as she pulled out her knife, her hands shaking.

The holo board outside played out its advertisement twelve times while Nico knelt, watching both the window and door. Her chest rose and fell.

He's dead, she reminded herself. *This is exactly his trick, but I'm the only one who duplicated it.*

Nico's lungs stilled. What if—? She might have pressed the xylazine herself. She'd obtained a steel tablet punch back when she'd stalked her maker, intending to use the same trick on him.

He's dead, she reiterated.

Nico went to her knees, her hands still shaking. She gathered up the fallen mints and put them back in the tin.

*

Immigration had done a bio-scan of her — including one where she'd been frisked. They had to have known her tin wasn't full of mints.

She could almost understand being allowed her switchblade, especially after seeing Other-beings carrying around their weapons. Disguised tranquillisers seemed a more insidious possession, but Nico knew she wouldn't have prepared them unless she'd thought having them was a good idea. She couldn't remember pressing them or for what purpose, but she would trust the Nico locked up behind the blank in her mind that for whatever reason, that Nico had thought it important to have them.

She closed the tin, deciding not to flush the tablets, repacked her passport wallet, chucked the pamphlets and her welcome bag, and squirrelled away the tissues, coupons, snack pack, and toothbrush in the back storage panel of Bear's harness. She straightened out herself and Bear in the mirror, and then exited.

Back in the girls' dorm, the girl she'd drugged was still unconscious in her bed, and if she dreamed, she would remember none of it upon waking. That was the nature of xylazine. Nico hung her head, ashamed. A young vampire would not shake the effects of a horse tranquilliser until the morning.

"I hope it brings you some peace," she said. A soft footstep sounded and Nico turned to look.

Three vampires entered, one of whom wore a black ruffled dress and silver buckled, pointy-toed boots. She was half Nico's age, while the two who followed felt younger—barely five years un-living. Nico looked at the first one's strong nose and jaw and thought her a boy transitioning to female. She carried a thick, paperback novel.

"You should hurry down, the snack bags are nearly gone," the paperback owner said in a smooth contralto as she and the others headed for different beds. Her gaze was deliberately distant, indicating no desire to provoke. One of the vampires yawned, her tongue piercing glinting, and plopped back on a bed with her Id projecting a holo star magazine. She sucked on a straw stuck in a snack pack as she read.

The free blood at 21 hundred; Nico looked at the knocked out girl once more while the third vampire approached the bed next to her. She wore a Sushi Hut uniform with nametag, and placed her ball cap, apron, and shoes on her locker top. She then laid down on the bed, crossed her arms over her chest, and closed her eyes. Nico turned to the one who'd spoken to her, the girl already seated on her bed and reading her novel. The title read: *Middlemarch*.

"Okay, thanks," Nico said.

*

The evening news blared from the holo programme playing in the rec room when Nico descended and looked in. Six vampires were present, sucking on the straws of blood packets and loitering or sitting on the couch and armchairs before the holo unit. A white translucent box with a lid sat on the coffee table. The logo on the side was of a single drop of red blood. Before the table, a thin male with craggy face, dark brows, moustache and goatee lounged on the sofa with his arm wrapped around a skinny, purple-haired girl. He wore motorcycle boots, tight black jeans, and a black work shirt with rolled up sleeves over a white tee. Nico assessed him first, for blocking her way with his long legs to the only vacant armchair and for his age, which felt a few years older than herself. She was second eldest in the room, and everyone else seemed barely five years. Nico was a little perturbed to be in the presence of so much freshness.

Like "new car smell", except with vampires.

"Introducing the latest Faering from Vahalla," a deep-voiced narrator said while a holo commercial of a sleek road vehicle played. "Fast, smooth, impenetrable, on the road and in the water. The Shearwater."

The curvy girl in the corset and black clothes seated next to the purple-haired girl turned to look at Nico as she sucked on a straw. The entirety of her eyes was light green, with pupils of black slits.

Is she wearing contacts? Nico didn't think so. Cat-eyes girl had the pallor of the undead, but Nico suspected she had been a were-cat—full or partly—when alive.

"Your shoes are diesel," cat-eyes girl said.

"Thanks," Nico said. The guy with the motorcycle boots glanced her way.

"Ay," he drawled. "Tex. Iris." He nodded to the skinny girl in his arm, and Iris smiled. "Delores." He indicated cat-eyes girl.

"Nico and Mr Bear," Nico said.

"Diesel," Tex said, and returned his attention to the holo display.

"Who wants another?" a brunette girl announced airily, and she rose from her armchair to take off the box's lid and pass out more snack bags. "They'll only go bad if we don't finish them." She wore sandals, comfortable, boyfriend jeans, and a sunny, yellow tee that made Nico think of too much time spent in sand and surf, except the girl was a vampire.

What accent is that? Nico's first thought was "Sydney." The girl handed her a snack bag. She had a pretty face, one with a benign friendliness that could easily reel in victims.

"You rocked up just in time," the girl said, smiling.

"Ta," Nico said.

"No worries," the girl said.

"You're a long way from Oz," Nico remarked.

"Aren't we all?" Ozzie girl replied. "Does your bear need a snack?" She looked at him curiously, as if expecting Bear to answer.

"No thank you. Mr Bear doesn't drink blood."

A boy as dark-browed and broody as Matt Dillon's Dally stepped up to toss the scrunched pack he'd sullenly sucked dry into a trash receptacle, accepted a new one from Ozzie girl, then returned to lurking in the shadows. Another boy with wavy, brown hair, tortoise shell glasses, and a tweed jacket over a knitted vest stood with his back against a wall. He perused immigration pamphlets in one hand as he concentrated on sucking his snack bag's last drops, his cheekbones prominent. Nico thought of Eton boys and of Britons who'd gone through wartime rationing.

Eton boy stepped forwards and also accepted a second bag from Ozzie girl. The blood was inviting, but Nico didn't feel greedy. She'd practiced fasting. Willed deprivation had been her attempt at taming an appetite that saw all humans as potential meals, and her rewards became the living blood women gifted. She'd been rewarded quite handsomely already, even if only by Shayla's kettle.

Blood is earned, Nicky, her maker said. *Go on and get it, girl.*

She stepped over Tex's legs and put her blood pack back just as Eton boy smiled and approached.

"Hello," he said, his British accent cultured. "Are you a recent arrival to Darqueworld, or?"

"I'm a chrono-immigrant," Nico said, moving to the side and out of the way of the others watching the news. "You too?"

"Oh, I'm a chrono-refugee," he said, cheerful. "I'm so glad to be here. I lost all my books, though. My only regret. I'm a poet."

"I knew a poet," Nico said. "He would always kill something or somebody when he left me a poem."

"Oh," Eton boy said. He smiled, nervous. "Well, not me."

"That's good," Nico said. "Excess is stupid."

Eton boy nodded, then went to stand by the wall again.

Darn, I wanted to ask him why he still wore glasses. Nico sat in the empty armchair by Delores and pulled out her Id.

"*Tex!* Use the straw," Iris exclaimed, then giggled. Tex had sunk his fangs into the snack pack, causing it to leak. He removed his mouth.

"Straws are for the toothless." He stifled Iris's mirth by kissing her with his messy, bloodied mouth.

Kiss me, Nicky, her maker said, his mouth bloodied. *Or I kill her.*

One of Tex's eyes remained open during the kiss, and he arched his gaze at Delores, who watched him.

Delores turned back to the news and sucked on her second pack. She smiled, smug.

Tex and Iris kissed more, and Nico unconsciously waited for arousal's signals—the escalating heartbeat, blood flow, and body heat of humans—which she sought when looking for willing girls or women. But nothing seemed to happen in the room that Nico would call "chemistry", except that the sexual energy of vampires was a different pheromonal sensation. It was mesmerism and will, exerted; it was the commingling of undead blood's power.

Vampires are just sexualised dead meat, Nico typed in her virtual journal.

Say NO to sanguivoriphobia. Stop the Hate, Dorothy responded, and played an anti-discrimination ad by the Vampire Alliance Network.

"In migration news," the holo display's newscaster announced, "the Isle welcomes fresh chrono-arrivals from the druid vessel, Galatia, and the surprise visit of a prime minister who will be returned to his time interval after a warm welcome. Galatia had sustained heavy damage from its latest voyage and will be escorted to Nuit One."

"Weren't you on that boat?" Tex said to Eton boy.

"Why yes, I was. I had to abandon it for a lifeboat that landed near here. Galatia had borne the brunt of a blitz attack," Eton boy said.

Blitz? Nico thought, looking up from her perusal of Chasca Vasquez's contact info.

"Sure you don't want any, mate? There'll be none in the morning," Ozzie girl said to Nico. She tilted the box with the remaining four snack packs within.

"I'm fine, thank you," Nico said.

"I'll have another," Delores said, and Ozzie girl handed her a pack.

Nico glanced at the holo news, which showed a large, battered space vessel orbiting a dusky planet, then cut to footage of chrono-refugees being helped out of lifeboat pods, floating in the sea. She turned to look at Eton boy.

"Don't you wish you were back home, helping with the war?" Nico asked in curiosity.

"I do," he answered, his tone heavy. "Though being a vampire has its unfortunate limits once the sun is up. I couldn't even ferry planes or be a dispatcher like the women. It became difficult explaining my able-bodied presence in London, and my... vampiric reaction to the death and blood. When the sky boat appeared, I took a chance and tried to help save it. And then I ended up here."

Nico nodded. "The Allies won the war, by the way." She acknowledged his look of gratitude before turning back to her Id.

If she had fled Earth for Darqueworld, what had been her reason? Had there been a global catastrophe? Nuclear war? How did she even learn about Darqueworld?

Dorothy, give me all the important events of the year 1998 on Old Earth, Nico typed.

Due to the existence of several variations of Old Earth in different dimensions, please specify your numerical variance, Dorothy replied.

Nico stared blankly at her Id. Had Dorothy just said, "different dimensions"?

Is it in my bio-tag? she typed. She then looked at the Russian names Dorothy had searched in Again NewYork's directory. Two belonged to men who were deceased, and their spouses too. Anikanov and Fedosov did not exist in Again NewYork.

Ozzie girl made a noise of disgust.

"I wish you'd use the general audience rating filter on this thing," she remarked.

"C'mon, we're vampires," Tex said, and Iris and Dolores giggled. Nico looked up again, expecting something provocative on the holo display. Instead, the news played footage of an Other-being confrontation and its aftermath. A fellow lay on the street, beheaded, his useless sword by his body.

The news here is really explicit. But Nico had become used to gore thanks to —

Her thoughts slid against the blank spot in her mind.

Thanks to...her *maker* hadn't revelled in gore, just the cold brutality of murder, so when had she ever experienced...?

*I don't...*Nico frowned. Her teeth ripping flesh. The thought skidded away.

She looked at the holo display and its sudden close-up of ravenous teeth flashing in the darkness.

"The world lost a prominent Other warrior today, one who'd made a name for himself in two successful encounters with the spawn," the solemn newscaster announced. "Speculation has risen, however, that his third Slaughter Spawn match was not a loss but a suicide."

Nico stared at the footage following. An onsite reporter stood dwarfed within a dark, massive tunnel, ringed with arching girders. Dead roots, broke earth and old cables hung down. The reporter, positioned before a large pit, attempted to speak. Her tense face grew frightened as a flurry of rapacious gnashing drowned her words. She abandoned the broadcast. The footage and lighting shook as her cameraman joined her in running down the tunnel, their footfalls splashing in trapped water.

"The reason you lose is because the spawn gets you *as* you're coming out of the pit," Tex said, "every single time."

"Once they have you, it's useless," Ozzie girl said, stiff.

"Did Kahu Nakahi die from one final mistake in the pit?" a voice-over said as scenes flashed of lone, furious Other-beings fighting moving darkness. "Or did he sentence himself to death?" Multitudinous teeth and claws slowly emerged from the morphing pitch-darkness, attacking from every direction. A creature's face showed, brief and screaming, and Nico's stomach froze.

"What was that?" she said.

"The spawn," Tex drawled.

"The spawn," Iris repeated, grinning.

"Diesel," Delores enthused.

"What are they?" Nico asked, even as she typed the question into Dorothy.

"From what I understand," Eton boy said, "an alchemist from ages past created a machine to harvest the evil from beings. Having nowhere to put what he captured, he cast the accumulated evil into the depths below Again NewYork."

"There's more to the story than that," broody boy remarked from the shadows.

"Well, that's how I heard it," Eton boy said. "The harvested evil spawns more of itself, hence the name, so extermination of the spawn has been made into a gladiatorial game: Slaughter Spawn. You have to last six minutes in the slaughter pit to win."

"There's prize money?" Nico said.

"The prize is getting out alive," broody boy declared.

"You bet on yourself," Tex said. "The betting boards don't care because they know what the pit's like. You can't set up the odds so you'll win."

"Therefore, winning is entirely against the odds. There's no certain way to fix a Slaughter Spawn fight," Eton boy admitted.

"Why doesn't the city just set fire to the spawn and eradicate them that way?" Nico asked.

"Because that wouldn't be fun," Tex said.

"The partial remains of a male vampire has been discovered today in North Park," the newscaster announced. "Consisting of only the upper body, arms, and head, the victim had been eviscerated of all organs, including the heart."

"It looked like whoever did it tried to cut his skull open too," an interviewed man said, his byline reading, *Eyewitness at North Park*. "But they didn't get his brain. More like they screwed up and turned it into jelly."

"Are there zombies on this world?" Nico exclaimed.

"There's no such thing," Delores scoffed. "The werewolf gangs got him."

"Werewolves eating *undead* organs? Not bloody likely," Ozzie girl said.

"Were-people are *not* interested in brains," broody boy said.

"Maybe it was the witches," Iris piped up. "For, y'know. Voodoo. Stuff nearly happened to us in New Orleans. Remember that, Tex?" She rubbed Tex's chest.

"It could have been the vampire primacy," Eton boy said. "Their having meted out a sentencing."

"The primacy would never show the world how it punishes us," Ozzie girl said. "They'd never dump vampire remains in some park."

The vampire primacy, Nico thought. So one existed on Darqueworld, too? She felt ambivalent about that. As a vampire who cared little about politics, she'd never given the primacy much thought. They had been as remote to her as the Vatican.

"People," Tex addressed with lazy authority, raising the hand around Iris, and Iris snuggled more. "It's none of those. The *spawn* got to him."

"I heard the spawn comes up through the sewer pipes and drags us from our beds," Iris said with glee.

"I heard they come out because they're searching for more evil. They're evil needing to feast on more evil," Delores said.

"I don't buy that alchemist crap; some guy with a machine sucking out people's darkness and then tossing it beneath the city," broody boy declared. "The gods put that stuff there so it could cull us."

Eton boy chuckled. "That's conspiratorial."

"Immigrants and refugees come in every day," broody boy said. "Carrying technology, secrets—gold and jewels in suitcases. But it's not like we're the rich and famous of our kind, are we? Having vampire balls and owning corporations."

"Speak for yourself," Delores said.

"Let's watch the vampire ball now," Iris suggested as Delores yawned next to her. "I want to see the dresses."

Tex activated a holo interface from his couch seat and poked at it, changing channels. The vampire ball came to the fore.

"Is that Prince Vlad?" Iris said, and then the holo blipped out. Lights dimmed and went to black. Nico's Id glowed dully. Everyone groaned, but before protests could escalate, a calm automated male voice spoke over the intercom.

"Rest time," he said, his calm voice enticing. "Please depart for the dorms. Rest time."

Delores yawned again. "I'm beat anyway."

"What if I want to stay down here?" Nico said as the others rose.

"You can't, really. The door will shut and lock in a few minutes." Ozzie girl's eyes glittered in the dark. "Dorm's not so bad when you're knackered. C'mon."

Nico put her Id away and followed, the recreation room's door closing and locking behind her. The hallway was also pitch-black, and as Nico trooped down it with the others for the stairs, she glanced into the entry hall leading to the lone exit. The formerly bright hall sat darkened except for a single light within Dann's caged booth, which stood empty. Two vampire boys ran up to the glass door and tried the handle. When it didn't budge, they waved to Nico.

"Rest time, in effect," the calm voice said. Nico looked back at the others, who had already gone upstairs. While the vampire boys banged on the door, she approached and pushed. The door stayed shut, and everywhere she touched or pressed did not activate it. The boys threw their hands up.

"Sorry," Nico said, and the boys departed.

They could sleep in a park. If a wolf gang doesn't try to get them. Or whatever had eaten the vampire with the missing heart. Nico headed for the stairs, and as she ascended, the lights dimmed in the stairwell, then went out.

When she reached the boys' dorm, the floor became dark as well. The lights faded in the dorm while the guys talked within. Nico gained the third floor with the lights dimming. Two muffled voices made enthusiastic noises behind the shut door of the bathroom. As the girls' dorm dropped into darkness, Nico's fangs emerged.

It's like hiding in a coffin or the closet...or being buried in the forest. Waiting for day to end, no light to harm us. She entered.

Delores was busy tucking herself into the bed next to Nico's, her actions neat and tidy. Her corset sat rolled up on top of her storage locker.

"Okay, I have to ask," Delores said to Nico.

"Yes?" Nico paused.

"Does your bear walk around and stuff? Once you're asleep."

"He's not a ventriloquist's dummy," Nico assured.

"Okay, good." Delores sounded relieved.

Nico continued down the room, passing tongue-pierced girl who had fallen asleep with her Id still propped up before her. The novel reader's paperback lay splayed on her chest while she slept, her silver buckled boots still on her feet. Nico checked on the girl she'd accidentally drugged.

"Something wrong?" Ozzie girl whispered as she turned down

a bed in the row across.

"Just checking on a friend," Nico said. The girl remained heavily sedated. Nico returned up the room just as Iris broke off a kiss with Tex at the entrance.

"Couldn't you two keep it down?" Delores said when Iris approached. Iris bounced on the other bed next to Nico's. Nico sat down on hers and it squeaked.

"He did just get out of prison," Iris retorted. "I can't ever get enough of him...he's so diesel. Don't you think Tex is diesel?" she said to Nico.

"Yes, he's diesel," Nico answered. She put her feet, shoes and all, on top of the bed and lay down. Delores guffawed.

"He did *make* you," Delores said. "It's not like you can think otherwise."

"I'm his girl," Iris said. She looked at Nico. "What's your maker like? He or she?"

"A 'he'," Nico said.

When Iris and Delores still looked at her, Nico took a breath.

"He was charming," she said. "A charming, Glaswegian street poet. He was like a member of the Beatles."

"The what?" Iris said.

"Your Prince Charming, huh?" Delores said.

"There's no such thing," Nico said.

"I guess he didn't come with you huh?" Iris said. "When Tex and me got here, we could not believe it—the freedom. Just being able to walk around and be vampires. We kind of lost it and did some stuff, that's why Tex had to do time. The Makepeace was nice about not shooting us right away, so I was glad. Being able to eat all the blood we can get is so diesel. What thing blows your mind about Darqueworld?" she asked, turning to Nico.

"The sun," Nico said. "I can't believe we get to walk in it."

"I got burned once, but I always wondered," Iris said. "Would we really die in the sun?"

"Yes. Yes you would," Nico said.

"No, I mean maybe we just lie there all crispy, until it's night again," Iris said. "I ended up in the ocean once, got trapped down there for almost forever. I didn't die."

"No, you don't just get crispy, you burn," Nico answered. "It's like heaven's wrath; every bit of you turns to ash."

"How do you know?" Iris asked.

"Because the last vampire I killed, I crucified him so he'd meet the sun," Nico said.

The other vampires stared at her.

"I also doused him with gasoline," she said, "to make sure."

"Are you kidding?" Iris demanded.

"About the gasoline?" Nico said, "Yes."

"With that lovely image, let's quit the yabber and go to *sleep*," Ozzie girl called from across the room. "Good night."

A round of murmured *good nights* sounded, and bodies settled down. Nico laid back with Bear still strapped to her. She held her shut switchblade to her chest.

Nicky, her maker said.

Nico exhaled. She didn't look forward to dreaming and meeting old nightmares. She listened; silence.

Weird how everyone's gone to sleep just like that. Somehow, even newly arrived night creatures had quickly acclimated to the day-to-night cycle of slumber.

Nico counted sheep to 237 and closed her eyes.

In a dorm full of vampires, she heard no breath or movement. All lay still and dead. But she still listened for the deliberate, quiet steps of an intruder.

Nicky.

Nico sat up. When she laid her feet on the floor, her bed squeaked. Iris stirred.

"Going to the bathroom," Nico murmured.

"You actually poop?" Iris's voice was thick with sleep. Nico slipped away and exited.

The hallway was still and dark. Nothing seemed to stir below in the boys' dorm either. Nico had never seen a place shut down so thoroughly, especially when right outside, Again New York teemed and beckoned with its glittering lights. Again Friends Hostel wasn't quite how she imagined a haven of vampires would be, even with its strict rules. She entered the bathroom, shut the door, then climbed on to the sink counter to open the narrow window, which swung outward. A jointed arm prevented it from opening farther.

Nico retrieved her wallet and the credit card sized multi-tool within. She applied the flathead tool and quickly unscrewed the arm free. As the pieces fell to the street below, she pushed the window to admit her and Bear through.

She thought she heard a step.

No, that was me.

Anxiety hit her. She needed to get out of there, before someone grabbed her ankle, called her name with her maker's voice and rendered her as dead and silent as those resting within, tranquillised. Nico heard the street life below and answered the yearning to be a part of the living. She worked her body out the window and hung against the outside wall by her fingertips. She let go and dropped three storeys down.

Once on the concrete, she ran herself and Bear as fast as she could down the street.

CHAPTER FIVE

Dorothy, play me Lords of the Null-Lines, Nico typed.

She put the sound-buds she bought at the newsstand into her ears and watched Again NewYork rush by. The Five back to Jifk Spaceport was moderately filled. The dimmed car interior surprised her, because brightly lit places deterred assault and biting vampires. She returned her attention to her Id.

When she had something to work on, Nico felt better. Each city she'd followed her maker to, she would engage in a project. Stalking him was something he'd expected. Trapping him—especially with her clumsy attempts—had been merely anticipated. His responses would elicit sharp, sickening agony. Nico learned to move straight to drawing him out. Newsworthy actions, especially anything that countermanded him, caught his attention.

Come get me, she seemed to say with each deed done, and in that moment of accomplishment, dread would fill her as much as the rage she needed to kill him. She had sent Chasca Vasquez and PETH the access code for her virtual locker. She would handle Grun.

Her finger moved within a holo projection of Leningrad, 1998, where she could travel down the streets and even into buildings, as if it all still existed. And perhaps it did, through the complications of time and space travel. It was easier to consider it all long gone.

She wandered Nevsky Prospekt, then found the building she had lived in. Nothing stimulated recent memory.

Nico closed the simulation and typed: *what weapons were used in Again NewYork criminal activity of the last week?*

The list Dorothy aggregated read: sword, various, knife, various, machete, halberd, cudgel, garrote, sledgehammer, walking stick, chain, Apache knuckleduster, projectile firearm, various, steel pipe, pulse rod, various, pulse pistol, various, cryptic gun, mind-scream, baseball bat—

Nico asked Dorothy to give her design and operation information for the pulse rod, pulse pistol, cryptic gun, and the mind-scream.

The witch's cryptic gun is of unknown design, Dorothy answered as she provided schematics for the pulse pistol. *The mind-scream is a psionic ability with no design parameters.*

An amazonian Makepeace entered the car from the connecting one ahead and strolled down the aisle, studying the passengers. Nico thought the Makepeace resembled Wonder Woman's sister, Nubia. Amazon Woman turned her head to regard Nico.

The scrutiny from her visor seemed to linger. The eye lens before the helm then flashed, a light pop that barely blinded. Nico felt her bio-tag itch and appreciated the consideration. She had Mr Bear wave at Amazon Woman as the female passed. Then she returned her attention to Dorothy.

What are the weapon capabilities of the Makepeace? she asked.

"Now approaching Jifk Spaceport," the male voice-over said. "Please gather all belongings and maturing progeny and take them with you."

The train came to a smooth stop at the departures terminal. It was not too late for Nico to forget about her little foray.

But that part of her—the one that wished to stay out of trouble—was the side she'd learned to ignore after her fatal mistake in 1985. After two years of stalking her maker, she had given up on killing him, and he'd noticed.

Pretending doesn't make me go away, Nicky.

The bodies of two young women ended up in the morgue she'd been working at, with Nico's name and lines of poetry carved into their flesh.

The women rose that night and tried to tear her heart out because he had told them to.

The train moved on for the arrivals terminal, and Nico rose to exit. When she disembarked, she melded into the crowd, moving with just enough speed to draw out anyone who might be following.

Jifk Spaceport's security was severely lax in Nico's estimation, but she was used to tighter measures thanks to the plane hijackings of the seventies. No one asked her for tickets or identification — and of course they wouldn't, since she had a bio-tag — and travellers carried weapons that Nico assumed were surrendered at some point during a flight. Makepeaces and what appeared to be android or automated security units (Nico wasn't certain if "robot" was an appropriate term) patrolled everywhere. She even saw a public admonition in progress with solemn travellers gathered, compliant witnesses to an inebriated were-person's admonition by a female Makepeace. He hung his head, chastened, while the Makepeace verbally disciplined him for disorderly behaviour.

Now I feel bad about lifting Grun's Id. Nico resolved not to do things like litter or jaywalk. Deadly creatures moved everywhere, yet oddly, Nico never felt safer. Or more watched. She consulted her Id and faded as much as possible into the spaceport's bustle, and looked for where Grun might be.

An hour later, Nico stood sucking on a Japanese blood snack bag called *Nude and Nice!* she'd purchased at the space terminal's noodle cart. Her other snack pack, courtesy of immigrations, already sat within a trash receptacle, half-eaten. It had had a terrible tomato paste flavouring that even her new toothbrush (with the ultraviolet light setting) could not remove the taste of, so Nico decided to indulge in another snack bag. It was probably outrageously overpriced, but she couldn't resist something both whimsical and Japanese. She wasn't certain what the *Nude* part of her snack implied, except that the blood was simply that and not wasabi or soy sauce flavoured. A snack bag called *Fire Butt Good!* was next on her list to try.

She lingered at a railing overlooking a row of exclusive bars and executive lounges. Travellers walked briskly behind her while she pretended to browse virtual lingerie shops on her Id. In reality, she watched the darkened windows of the sports lounge below. Her vampire's vision could pierce its artificial dark, and she spied Grun within, drinking at the bar top, swallowing live rodents and enjoying a badly lit, gruesome fight on the giant holo display— one with a single individual battling a ravenous horde of unseen night creatures.

Slaughter Spawn.

Nico switched from pictures of lacy satin bras and panties and the girls and muscular males who wore them to access the latest spawn battle. She couldn't get official access (without paying a sum) but an on-site spectator currently filmed the fight and was feeding a public channel. Grun stretched his mouth wide to swallow another tiny beast, dangling it by its tail.

Grun had been easy to find. Cru'k were not allowed beyond the spaceport, and Grun owned one of the last Cru'k transport vessels allowed planet-side. Nico only had to query the bartender at the captains and pilots' bar to find where Grun was not yet banned.

"He's been in the pit five minutes! He's—he's coming back!" the spectator yelled in Nico's sound-buds. "He's trying to climb out!" In the grainy dark, shotgun blasts flashed and boomed from a female figure standing at the edge of the pit. "Aw man—his second is— is trying—aw—"

If the fighter's not dead already, he'll wish he was. The spectator's filming grew erratic.

Grun hit the bar top, apparently displeased with the fight's outcome, then rose to depart. He exited, swaggering down the

corridor with his ivory-handled pulse pistol on his hip, and Nico
put Dorothy away and followed, a shadow pulled along from
above. When Grun reached the open terminal for the airfield
outside, Nico quickly descended the escalator.

Once on the field, Grun walked over to parked buggies. He
boarded one and zipped away into the darkness. Nico took off
running, keeping him in sight. A small ship activated and nearly
sucked her into an engine, and she adjusted her course to remain
within blue safety lines and clear of bright red indicators. Grun
crossed the field and passed hangars, energy depots, the traffic
controller's hub, and maintenance buildings for a far off perimeter
structure: Royal Bento Food Packaging Co. Nico spotted a
shimmer above the building and wondered if Grun noticed. The
levitation orb of a Makepeace crested and landed on the rooftop.

When Nico reached the building, a concrete bridge arched
over the dry water channel and led to Royal Bento's loading
dock. There, Grun's buggy stood, the Cru'K disappearing behind
a metal door that slammed shut behind him. Nico crossed
the bridge and skirted the well-lit dock to come alongside the
building. She wondered briefly about the hidden Makepeace
above. A large vent blew down a hot, familiar smell.

Nico paused beneath the warm blast and stuck her tongue out.
The air had a flavour; the sweaty chemical message of human
alarm and fear. She pulled out her Id.

Do the Cru'K cook humans? Nico typed into her Id.

*The Cru'K do not cook their food as it is considered a cultural
offence,* Dorothy answered. *Ingesting prey live is a religious
obligation. Once eaten, yours forever. Prochnyy Kolbasa by Fedotov.*
Nico spied a drainage pipe leading up to the rooftop.

*Dorothy, search on how trafficked humans for Cru'K consumption
are transported,* Nico typed. She put the Id away while it worked
on her request and checked her harness, then Bear. Whatever
she hoped to attempt within the building was made easier by the
marvel that was a handheld HAL 9000, despite the constant ads.
She would have appreciated a tool like it when she had been

stalk—

Her thoughts hit the blank in her head and skidded across its surface.

Nico blinked. When she had been, what? Stalking her maker? If the Id had been possible in her era, it would have been her continued death sentence, because *he* would have had the same technology. And he'd been *dead*, eleven years. Stalking what, then?

Her head having no answer to give, Nico crouched, then jumped.

Her leap surpassed one storey. She grabbed the drainage pipe and braced her feet against the wall. She climbed at a steady pace, hand over hand, stepping up. A spaceship lifted off the airfield and rose into the night sky, its lights pulsing, and Nico thought of the movie, Close Encounters of the Third Kind. The movie's iconic tune played in her head as she surmounted the rooftop's lip and stepped over. There, near the edge facing the spaceport, the Makepeace stood.

On closer scrutiny, the Makepeace appeared to be more of the third sex. All the Makepeaces wore significant codpieces (where, Nico thought, a weapon or two might be stashed) that made their gender ambiguity even more intriguing. The present Makepeace had a long, sinuous body with pectorals similar to breasts. And his—or her—mouth was as full lipped and sensual as Shayla's. It was the pretty, pert mouth European boys tended to have.

Nico straightened her cardigan and went to stand beside thon—she preferred "he" in thons case, but decided to be respectful—and looked down at what thon was viewing. At the bottom of the dry water channel, the werewolf motorcycle gang waited. Leroy was among them, carrying a length of chain. Nico looked at her Id and scanned the trafficked humans information Dorothy had retrieved. Traffickers transported human cargo by cryonic packaging, similar to Han Solo in carbonite. The warmth that had blown from the vent had been the heat lost from human bodies as they were being blast-frozen.

Nico secured her Id and looked up at the Makepeace's collar number: MP-1634. The collar number was high, indicating the Makepeace might be relatively new: a rookie.

"Hi," Nico said.

"How may I help you, potential citizen?" 1634 replied, finally turning thon's head to acknowledge her. Nico raised a brow at the word "potential", but sidled closer. Apparently, Makepeaces did not need to scan bio-tags to know to whom they were talking. 1634's voice was androgynous—and silky. Nico wouldn't mind hearing a bedtime story from thon.

"I have a conflict with an off-worlder," she said. "Can I kill him?"

"You may not inflict death on any galactic species, except in matters of self-defence," 1634 answered.

"Okay," Nico said. "His friends may be Other-beings, who may threaten me with death. Can I kill them?"

"Death is permitted in resolving conflicts between Other-beings and Other-beings and their kin," 1634 said.

"Okay. Thank you."

The rumble of arriving motorcycles rose from the channel's bottom, reclaiming 1634's scrutiny. The werewolves howled and the sound echoed. Nico went to the roof's access door.

She'd hoped when she spotted the Makepeace on the roof, that thon would take care of the Cru'K problem. But even if she'd told 1634 of what was happening within—whether Other-beings were present or not—the Makepeace would simply hold an off-worlder suspect for the regular police. And Grun would walk of course, only to return to Jifk Spaceport and to Lucy's Diner, flaunting what he got away with, and perhaps take another waitress or two to keep the intimidation in place.

She broke the door's lock and entered. Sounds from the channel seemed to indicate the confrontation was escalating. 1634 did not follow her.

✱

"Lot six," a bird-like off-worlder requested, and two vampire thugs pushed frightened and naked humans before a holo cam on a tripod, while the bird female pecked at a projected holo interface with a steel stylus. Each square in the interface represented an obscured bidder who observed the human lots via the holo cam. Nico stood on the girder above and filmed the auction with her Id.

Bidding was brisk; the bird female would describe the lot, and the vampires would make the humans turn this way and that for inspection. Two vampire thugs stacked six crying infants into a food service cart—a recently won lot for an extraordinary sum—then rolled it into a cryonics food processing machine that vented via a duct leading to the outside. The machine burst into activity and roared, the babies' cart advancing. One captive female wailed at the sight. The cart exited the machine with whitened, stiff babies suspended in a gelatinous casing.

Birdseye meals for aliens.

Cryonics was suspended animation, Nico reminded herself, not cryogenics, where food was frozen too slowly to prevent expanding, destructive ice crystals to form in bio-matter. The babies would still be alive when defrosted. The vampires who'd processed the babies then rolled the frozen cart into a shipping case and shut it. They tagged it with a security and identification lock.

Nico continued to film as another vampire, female, seated within the operating cage of a mechanical arm, picked up the packaged babies and placed it on a flatbed truck destined for Grun's ship. Grun himself stood near the auctioneer and her holo camera, participating in the lots viewing. He made bids as well. Three male vampires handled the captive humans. Two stood armed with pulse pistols on either side of the group, and one, who appeared to have no weapons, stood in the back.

That one. The guard to the left was a tall vampire in a leather coat, his pistol stuck in his belt, and his cool gaze missed nothing.

Nico sensed he was the eldest of the vampires, and possibly the leader.

She'd rarely had the chance to fight another vampire except for her maker. Facing six who all felt older than her, plus one pistol-toting Cru'K, was perhaps horrible odds. However, she only required one death; rescuing the humans was a bonus.

She counted sixteen remaining, naked shivering humans, and did not see the Sufi family among them.

I'm sorry I didn't involve the Makepeace for you, she thought to the huddled, frightened group. *But I need to get someone killed tonight.*

Nico sent the footage to her virtual locker and an update notification to Chasca Vasquez and PETH. Then she sent a message to Again NewYork's emergency contact number.

She put her Id away and patted Bear.

Okay, Bear, let's screw this up.

She stepped out and dropped down from her girder.

Her shoes clapped loudly on the concrete floor as she landed near Grun. Everyone stilled.

"Hi," she said to Grun. "Can we talk?"

"What—what is this?" Grun cried, and drew his pistol. The barrel was ornate and long, and Nico held her hands up.

"I only want to talk." She indicated the captives. "I'm looking for someone. Maybe she's in there?"

Grun aimed.

"A Lucy's Diner waitress," Nico stated clearly, looking him in the eye, and he pulled the trigger.

She turned aside as the pulse blast shot passed her, rippling along her clothes, flesh, and Bear like a jet engine blast. Nico moved. She grabbed Grun's gun hand and the nape of his coat. She spun him around to face the vampires and aimed.

"Bye toilet licker," Nico whispered to him, and squeezed down on his trigger finger.

Grun fired at the unarmed vampires near the cryonics machine. The recoil on his huge gun nearly jumped Grun's fist out of Nico's grip. The vampires flanking the screaming captives advanced and opened fire. Grun jerked as blasts exploded against his body, driving Nico back. His flesh bubbled and burned. One blast skimmed his neck, bursting a blood vessel. Green blood sprayed Nico's hair and clothes. She fired high, trying to avoid the cowering humans. No vampires fell from her volleys, and Grun's dead weight and inert gun arm sagged into her.

God, I'm such a bad shot.

She dropped Grun and pulled her knife. She sent it flying into the eldest vampire's face, driving the blade through his eye. He collapsed to the floor, and Nico dove for where the bird person cowered.

"No-no!" she cried, as Nico snatched the stylus from her hand. The remaining armed vampire fired as Nico ducked, his shots hitting the off-worlder hard enough to spin her out of Nico's way.

Nico's arm whipped. The stylus stabbed the shooter in the throat, and he clutched at it, dropping his weapon. Nico ran across the floor and reached for her switchblade, stuck in the twitching, elder vampire.

"You little—" the third guard said, pushing through the frightened captives. He grabbed Nico, swept her off her feet, and roared in her face. His fist came up just as he let go and he punched her hard into the floor. Nico bounced on the concrete.

Faster, Nicky, her maker said, hitting her. *Get faster.*

Stars sparkled before her eyes as her foot came up and she felt it contact the vampire's male member.

"*Argh,*" he uttered, doubling over and clutching himself. Nico pulled her knife out of the inert vampire's head, and spun on the ground. Her arm swept, slashing the other vampire across the throat. Blood sprayed her chest and Bear.

She heard a door slide open, the metal grating. One of the unarmed vampires scurried out the door, the others following.

I need a vampire with intact vocal cords for the police. Nico jumped to her feet and ran after the female vampire, the last to depart, who then spun to confront her. Nico skidded to a halt.

The woman snarled, her fangs bigger than Nico's. Nico bared her teeth and snarled back, her blade up.

"*Don't move!*" police suddenly shouted, barrelling swiftly through the open door. "On the ground now!"

Nico stilled.

"*Do it!* Get on the ground now!" the officers shouted again.

Nico and the other vampire put their fangs away and slowly dropped to the floor while the police rushed at them.

✱

The police cuffed Nico and made her sit with the other apprehended vampires. Even the injured ones were restrained while the police gathered the victims and inspected the cargo.

The emergency medics arrived and loaded Grun and the bird off-worlder into body bags. The pulse blast injuries had caused Grun's body to swiftly swell, his trigger finger stuck in his pistol. The medics zipped his bag up, and Nico remained impassive when they rolled the gurneys by.

Mission accomplished.

The former captives walked by next, wrapped in blankets as the police led them out.

"What are you doing?" one woman cried to the police. "The vampire with the bear saved us! Let her go!"

"Ma'am, just continue out the door and victim services will take care of you," a male detective with greying temples and curly brown hair said kindly. His blonde female partner regarded the vampires with hands on her hips, revealing the badge hung at her waistband. She was thick and tough and gave Nico a long, measuring stare.

Look at me all you want, lady. I didn't directly shoot a gun.

The captives might talk, but hidden as Nico had been by Grun's big body, she doubted any had clearly seen who was doing the shooting during the chaos.

The female detective spoke to an officer in blue. He then came over to Nico.

"We're gonna put your bear in safekeeping," he said with reassurance, reaching for Mr Bear, and she pulled back.

"You can't do that. My bio-tag says he's my conjoined twin," Nico cried.

"But he's detachable. C'mon, he'll be safer with us than in a cell with these guys, right?" The cop motioned his head to the other vampires. He then added in a lower tone. "You don't want to be tranq'ed."

Awake, Nicky? her maker said, his hand on her bare hip. *Too bad ya can't remember.*

"Okay, fine." Nico's tone was hollow. She shut her mouth tight as the officer took Bear and his harness off of her and then bagged him. The female detective looked on.

Come closer and I will break your face with my head, Nico thought at the detective as Bear and the cop walked away, but the detective never neared.

Nico sat, feeling the effects of having been punched into concrete, and tried not to think about Bear. She concentrated on healing her swollen face and eye. Already, the vampire with the hole in his throat had closed the wound, his eyes shut as he focused. The vampire with the slit throat appeared to be meditating, the slash across his throat a thin, bleeding line.

My weak diet as a vampire child is showing. She concentrated harder on diminishing her swollen eye, even as the police made the vampires regain their feet, and then walked them out to a waiting van. MP-1634 stood on the lit loading dock, watching the vampires emerge.

"We got this, Makepeace," the female detective said.

"Get in there, bloodsucker." A cop pushed Nico into the van.

Things are looking up on the new planet. Instead of misogyny I'll get bigotry now. They shut and locked the van, and it lurched as it drove away.

The other vampires sat in silence and either glowered or ignored her. The male she'd stabbed in the eye slowly regenerated, the inside of his head making squishy sounds. His mouth lifted at one corner in seeming amusement as his remaining eye looked at Nico.

Except for the business of selling humans as food and possibly other unsavoury activity, she thought she might find the elder vampire likeable outside of his "work." Then she realised: she seemed to measure all vampires against *him*.

No one, it seemed, could be worse than him.

The steel mesh over the small back window allowed the occasional light from street lamps to flash on her companions' faces. Nico looked at the window.

Come get me, she thought towards the dark.

The stone and brick precinct where the cops processed her resembled one right out of New York City, complete with worn wood interiors with peeling paint, cracked tile, and dusty, wrought iron fixtures. Nico found the place confusing to her senses. It didn't smell or feel like a recreation, but the real thing, having gone through its earned age and received the feet and noise of human presence. Below, they put her in a holding cell with the female vampire.

"I should kill you," the female said.

"Kill your alibi? Pshaw," Nico said. A jailer then returned and fetched the other vampire for questioning. Nico blinked, testing her healed eye, then became irritated by the pungent odour Grun's dried blood exuded.

"We smell like a meat eater," she complained to Bear, forgetting that he had been bagged for safekeeping. Noticing his absence, she hung her head, and her heart hurt. She told herself to forget, then slept.

She woke when the female vampire reentered the cell. The woman took a seat on the other side and ignored Nico, who blinked, disturbed by the odd, residual effects of some dark dream.

An uneasy, ugly dream, set in some facility like Royal Bento.

She remembered: the electrical plant where she'd found another of her maker's victims. Her dream had recalled a true memory. Nico had been enraged that night, because the strung, sharpened wire she'd lured her maker to had failed to take his head off. He shot Nico four times. Then he violated her.

I'm going to melt you in a nuclear reactor, she'd said, and he laughed.

The male detective took Nico's statement in an interrogation room, his partner standing over her, glowering. His manner was congenial, with an air of consideration and understanding, but his teeth, when he paused, slid against each other, reminding Nico of calculated men rolling a toothpick as they bided their time. She did her absolute best not to ask about Bear.

He queried: your reason for being at Royal Bento that night? She answered that she'd wanted words with Grun, having heard about the missing waitress at Lucy's.

"So you were working for him?"

"No."

"Why did you and your vampire gang start shooting?"

"No. I'm in no gang."

"How much was your cut, selling the humans?"

"No. I'm not a seller."

The questions continued in that manner, a fabrication designed to eventually addle her, make her admit to *something*, even hypothetical, so they'd leave her alone. It didn't matter that she'd arrived on Darqueworld only hours before. They were not going to ask the human captives or even the vampire thugs about her, and if they did, it would not be to validate her story. He asked her to tell the truth. He tried to convince her nicely. Then the detectives left the room, and Nico sat in the chair and slept.

*

BAM.

Nico started awake, the female detective leaning over the table threateningly. The detective had smacked the table hard. Nico had heard them reenter the room; she'd decided to sleep a little more rather than acknowledge their return.

"You have Cru'k blood, all over you," the detective said, menacing.

"Yes," Nico said.

"Because?"

"Grun bled all over me while I was standi—"

The detective suddenly grabbed Nico's front and hauled her up from her seat. Her blood-stiffened cardigan creaked in the detective's grip.

"Don't touch me," Nico said with calm.

"You are lying," the detective said, staring into Nico's eyes.

"You know I'm not," Nico said.

"You *killed* him." The detective's grip tightened. "We can beat you dead again, you know, until you talk, and you'll heal right up."

"Yes," Nico agreed. "But you won't."

"We won't what?"

"You won't heal right up," Nico said.

She looked into the detective's eyes and made a string of assertations: the evidence would disappear, the suspects would go free, and the victims would be charged with vagrancy, prostitution, or any other illegal whatever that could be dug up or trumped up, silencing demands for justice.

"Did they take your baby hostage?" Nico suddenly asked. "Or did you like Grun's money?"

The detective looked at her, both flabbergasted and revealing another emotion, swiftly shuttered from Nico's scrutiny.

"It must have been a real surprise seeing me there," Nico added, "a vampire you didn't know."

The detective let her go. She walked out, her partner looking at Nico with his teeth sliding, and then he departed too. As the door shut behind him, Nico nodded off and slept.

★

By the end of the night, the detectives charged her with nothing.

Nico walked through the worn precinct, escorted by a uniformed female officer in New York blue, and felt she might really be in the original New York City if not for the dawning light coming through the window blinds, falling on her without harm. Chasca Vasquez leaned with both hands on a detective's desk, too focused on the protesting detective to notice Nico passing by. Nico admired how alert and beautiful the woman looked so early in the morning, and wondered if Ms Vasquez could trace back the digital delivery to her.

"Probably," Nico said to an imaginary Bear, then yawned. She heard loud voices outside the window. When she peered out, PETH protesters were organising on the walk, signs in hand. Nico continued to follow her escort to the property clerk's window in the reception area, where the female officer then left her. Nico hoped PETH wouldn't notice the green blood on her—especially that it was Cru'k's blood.

I'm not a crusader.

She wasn't a vigilante either. Her attention was already drifting away from the trafficking of human flesh for consumption. Grun was dead, Shayla and the others at Lucy's were safe, and Ms Vasquez and PETH could follow up on the rest. But something still unnerved at the pit of Nico's soul, and she felt at the beginning of things again.

"This wasn't it," she said.

"This wasn't what?" the property clerk said as he scanned the claims voucher stored in her bio-tag.

"I don't know," Nico answered.

When the clerk returned with Mr Bear and her possessions, she gave Bear a big hug — his poor head stained with blood — checked to make sure he hadn't been tampered with, inspected the state of her blade, then pocketed all her things and put on the harness. With Bear back, she was complete again.

While situating Bear, the vampire whose throat she'd slit approached the window to have his bio-tag scanned. As the clerk retrieved his items, the vampire looked down at her.

"You're dead," he threatened in a raspy whisper.

"Not before I sleep with your wife," Nico said.

At the vampire's blank expression, she realised her error.

"Or your husband?" she asked. "Or your sheep?"

The vampire picked up his things and walked out, ignoring her.

"I'll have to come up with a new retort," Nico told Bear. She hurried, and fell in step behind the bigger vampire as he descended the steps. He pushed his way through the PETH protesters and their signs with Nico closely following.

Once passed the protesters, she let the vampire walk away. She marvelled at a street with buildings contemporary to her time except the smell of it and the smooth, crisp sound of traffic could not be mistaken for Old Earth. She paused by a young cop in blue, leaning with his back against the building, coffee cup in hand. Head raised, he looked at the hotel holo marquee across the street. The letters resembled an old-fashioned neon marquee, and reminded Nico of the Rocklyn Hotel in Los Angeles. Pigeons flew through the holo projection and disrupted it. She glanced at the cop's youthful face.

When you get tough, make it for all the right reasons. Merope emerged from between distant, sky-piercing buildings to hit the hotel's windows with bright light, dazzling the world. Nico flinched. The cop looked at her.

"Heliophobic?" he asked.

"I guess so." She pointed up to the holo marquee. "It just reminds me of the time I watched a vampire burst into flames, right up there on a hotel's neon sign."

The cop's brow knit, and because of his youth, Nico wasn't sure if he knew what a neon sign was.

"What was the vampire doing up there?" he asked.

"I put him there. Nailed him to the Y of a marquee."

The cop frowned more. "The Y, huh?"

"It was to be poetic. Because I was asking 'why'," she said.

"Why you did that?"

"No." She walked away. "Why did he pick me." She pulled out the sound-buds stored in the back of her Id and put them in her ears.

Dorothy, play me Last Exit For the Lost, she typed.

She crossed the street. A white, domed church stood, a golden cross atop. The morning sun struck, making the cross bright enough to burn.

Nico stared at it.

Her maker wept as his face blistered and smoked, and Nico felt her own face burning in the shadows, but she had to see.

Nicky, he cried, before erupting into flames.

CHAPTER SIX

"When the gods felt their twilight had come, they left Earth in their star chariots, sky boats, and sentient ships. They followed living maps for the star cluster known to all celestials, as these stars were visible from every part of Earth: the Seven Sisters. There, they found a dusk planet perfect for shaping, and established cities and settled lands destined for the Earth kin who also saw their approaching twilight times: the *Tuatha Dé*, the Dreamtime, the circumpolar peoples, and the leviathans."

The what? Nico thought in mid-suck. She was watching an educational holo film while heading back down "puke street" — a street a roaring, automated truck presently power cleaned. In the crisp morning light, the hostels, bars, and shops that had seen so much activity sat silent and shuttered. Nico tossed her scrunched snack pack, *Fire Butt Good!* in the truck's path, its vacuum sucking the litter up. The blood had the salty, red-hot flavour of sriracha sauce, which made for a nice wake-up call. Her Id then lit, indicating an incoming message. She paused the citizenship course vid, *Immigrations Holo Vid No 1: Darqueworld Beginnings*.

"A reminder from the Immigration Centre," Dorothy announced, "you are scheduled for your citizenship exam on this date and time."

"What?" Nico exclaimed. "That's four days from tomorrow."

"If you would like to appeal the scheduling, you may make an appointment to see the immigration judge presiding at circuit court—"

"No thanks. Are they rushing us so that whoever fails can be made into soylent green? Never mind. What do I have to study?" Dorothy then sent her one hundred civics questions and their answers.

A girl in a Sushi Hut uniform hurried down the walk, her gait erratic. It was the vampire from the girls' dorm. She bumped into Nico and Nico saw the dark circles under her eyes.

"I got to get to work," the vampire murmured to no one in particular, and hurried on.

"I guess she needed even more sleep," Nico said in surprise to Bear. "We better get there before Violet Eyes leaves. I want to make sure she's okay."

People were already hitting the exercise machines within the YOBA. Nico looked up at the rooftop, spying a different Makepeace silhouette from the broad V shape of the muscular Makepeace from last night. Even backlit by the rising sun, Nico recognised the long, sinuous body.

MP-1634.

Nico had Bear wave at thon while she crossed the street, the Makepeace's gaze following her.

When she reached Again Friends, two agitated boys quickly exited and the door shut behind them. Nico pulled on the door handle and her hand abruptly slipped off. The door remained locked.

"This is so rude," she said to Bear. Dann sat in the caged booth, waved, then pressed something. Nico grabbed the door handle again and pulled it open.

"In need of our free showers and laundry facilities, I see," Dann said cheerfully. "Funny, I didn't see you leave this morning."

"I didn't see you leave last night," Nico said. "Or did you turn invisible and just stay inside there? Do you even go to the bathroom?"

"I'm here until 22:30, those are the rules," Dann said. "I was in the john."

"This place has barely any windows, and no fire escape signs," Nico said. "I didn't see one emergency exit. Where do I go when there's a fire?"

"Oh—the roof?" Dann looked at her, disconcerted. "I—well, you're vampires. Can't you just jump out or something?"

"You guys actually *lock us* inside," Nico exclaimed. "How is this legal?"

"Well, you signed to the terms of agreement on the sign-up sheet." Dann lifted paper on the sign-up clipboard and revealed the bottom sheet, indicating a long, typed legal document. "Y'know. The one where you agree to be a vampire kept off the streets in exchange for free lodging, showers, lockers—"

"You never mentioned this piece of paper," Nico accused.

"I didn't?" Dann said.

Broody boy hurried down the stairs and walked quickly for the entrance. He looked at the dried green blood on her with raised brows, and then rushed out the door, pushing it open.

Oh good. Dann's not needed to get out.

"Did the girl with the choker come down already?" Nico asked instead. "Little spikes on the collar. She has violet eyes."

"There's no fraternising in the dorm rooms," Dann stated.

"I'm just asking if you've seen her," Nico exclaimed.

"I don't know. You all kinda—that vampire look? You all start to look the same." Dann shrugged.

"If we all look the same, then how do you remember me?"

"Because of your, uh, soft buddy? Want to sign for tomorrow night? We're already filling up." He pushed the sign-up sheet before Nico. Only half the spaces had signatures. One of them, a Danica Rodriguez, had checked the boxes for two nights.

"No thanks." She picked the sheet up to look for the old sheet from last night. It was missing.

"Oh? You found someplace cheaper than free?" Dann asked. He then pushed a holo card towards her from beneath his window. It said: Chaikov's Collectible Coins & Currencies.

"You gave me one of these already," Nico said.

"Have you gone yet?" He pushed the sign-up sheet in her direction again.

"I wish you guys would just proselytise and shake me down that way." Nico left to go upstairs.

Up in the girls' dorm, all the beds had been made. A new vampire stood over the last bed. Freckle-faced and with her long curly brown hair in a ponytail, she wore narrow, frameless eyeglasses (for appearances, Nico thought,) a plaid shirt over a tee, and cargo trousers. She looked at an Id with a sturdy rubber casing. The locker at the foot of the bed lay open, her red backpack with garish, green accents sitting beside it.

"Hi," Nico said. "Did you see the girl who was in this bed last night? She wears a choker, little spikes on the collar."

"No," the new girl answered. "Bed was all made up when I got here. But that stuff was in the locker, maybe it's hers." She nodded to a *Welcome to Again NewYork* bag on the bed. "I'm Danica, by the way." She held out a hand, and Nico shook it. "What type of blood is that on you, if you don't mind my asking?"

"Oh, it's Cru'k's blood. I'm Nico, and this is Bear. Mind if I claim this for the friend I'm looking for?" She pointed at the bag.

"Go right ahead."

Nico picked it up and looked inside. The Id was still sealed, its logo label on it.

"Heyy," Ozzie girl hailed as she entered the room. She walked across and smiled at Danica. "You're giving it a fair go. Fantastic."

"Yeah, this place is all right. Thanks for suggesting it," Danica said.

"Excuse me, but do you know where the girl in this bed went to?" Nico said to Ozzie girl. "The one with the spiked choker and violet eyes. I'm looking for her."

"No." Ozzie girl looked wide-eyed at Nico's bloodstained state. "I can't say I know." Her nose then wrinkled.

"Low carb diet," Danica said.

"The dead guy also liked to eat out of a toilet," Nico said, and left the room.

★

Cat-eyes girl? Paperback girl? Eton boy? She even looked in the empty boys' dorm, all its beds made. No girl with violet eyes. Nico went downstairs with the missing vampire's bag and Id and entered an equally vacant rec room. She searched the bag, looking for anything that might tell her where the girl would go next. Nothing was present that was any different from what Nico had received from immigration. She found no credit chit or social worker's card.

She knew to keep the money on herself.

"She was in shock, not stupid. I don't think she would have woken up and just left her Id," Nico said to Bear.

If her missing vampire had already hit the street, she was long gone. But to where? And what had hurt her? Did it come back? Nico looked at the new Id in her hands.

"She'd just arrived," Nico said.

She was searching in Dorothy on how to properly report the Id and its missing owner to immigration or the Makepeace when Iris appeared at the rec room's door. She hugged herself, as if cold.

"Have you seen Tex?" Iris said.

"I haven't." Nico returned her attention to her Id.

"He wasn't here when I got up this morning," Iris said. Nico looked up. Iris didn't look well.

Is she having withdrawals? "Maybe he's out scor—getting you something," Nico suggested. *With cat-eyes girl.*

"It's not like him to leave me alone. We're inseparable. What's that green stuff on you?"

"Alien stuff," Nico said.

"It smells like a dead horse." Iris laughed briefly. "Once, in the desert, me and Tex came across a horse carcass. We put it in a tree. We thought it needed to be up there, but we were high on peyote."

"I can't do psychedelics; I see demons when I do. Have you seen the girl with violet eyes?" Nico asked. "She wears a choker with tiny spikes on the collar."

"Oh, her. She's pretty," Iris said. "Me and Tex thought so. No, I haven't." She then bit her lip. "I'll—I'll see if—maybe they're outside."

Nico didn't answer right away, having found how to report the missing girl's Id by using its identification tag. Tex and her missing vampire together seemed farfetched, and not because two of his own women were around. Nico didn't think he was Violet Eyes's type. When she nodded, a delayed acknowledgement of Iris's worry, the other vampire had already left the room.

If Nico took the time to indulge in a familiar, sick feeling, she might do so. She kept busy, even if it was a desperate kind of busy. The girl's disappearance was like old times; her maker kidnapping someone she knew or had just met. Nico would then rush—rush with fear and dread escalating, to find the victim before it was too late.

"We don't do lost and found," Dann declared when Nico tried to give him the Id for safekeeping.

"This Id needs to be here when or if she comes back for it," Nico snarled. "And I've reported it to the Makepeace, so unless you want me to get one of them to talk to you, you'll keep this Id for me."

"Okay, sure." Dann accepted the Id. "What's her name again?"

Nico stared at him and then left to take a shower.

How did Violet Eyes get to Darqueworld? Nico waited for her clothes and Mr Bear to finish laundering. *If she had somewhere to be, why end up here first? What got to her between here and immigration?*

Nico did not think her missing vampire had carried traumatic history over to Darqueworld. What Nico had witnessed in the girl's eyes had been a fresh wounding, one the other vampire had called nightmares, but sometimes that was a way of coping. Nico knew. She'd seen that gaze enough in the dying girls her maker would leave for Nico to find.

Your mirror, Nicky, read one note he'd pinned through a girl's skin.

Laundry done, Nico dressed, situated Bear in his harness, and jumped at the sight of her own reflection. She did look and feel refreshed, however, and not at all like she'd been crusty with meat-stinking, Cru'k's blood all night. Out of curiosity, she hopped on to the sink counter to inspect the window she'd pried open. To her surprise, she found it bonded shut with metal sealant.

Nico tried to budge it, finding the seal too strong to give, even to a vampire's strength. She gave the glass a measured bang with her fist to see if it would crack; it didn't.

"What is this glass made out of?" Nico said to Bear. The bathroom door opened.

An African woman entered wearing a black leather car coat and her tied-back hair in long braids. Nico immediately sensed that she was older than even Tex—twice as much. The woman glanced at Nico standing on the sink counter.

"What'cha doing up there, sunshine?" she said, her accent American. "Go-go dancing?" She washed her hands beneath the sink's vibronic setting, humming as she did so, then pulled out a lipstick from her pocket.

Nico hopped down, then jumped again when she saw herself in the mirror. The woman only raised a brow and applied her plum lipstick, the shade matching her nail polish. Nico admired how she touched up the edges of her lips with a critical regard.

"Hi," Nico said. "Do I really look like sunshine?"

"Naw, you look the exact opposite."

"It's great having a reflection again," Nico remarked. "Or maybe you're used to it, if you're from here?"

The other vampire capped her lipstick and put it away. "A reflection?"

"Us." Nico nodded to the mirror. "Seeing ourselves in a mirror." The woman looked at the mirror.

"I could always see myself," she declared. "Which Earth are you from?"

Nico stared at her. "The invisible one," she deadpanned.

"Yeah? Well, welcome back to the visible world, go-go girl. I'm Re'shawn." Re'shawn smiled, and Nico saw that her fangs were evident—and bigger than Nico's. "I just got here."

"I'm Nico, and this is Mr Bear." Nico made Bear wave. "You mean you arrived from your Old Earth, not from one of the other Darqueworld cities?—that are planet-side."

"*Planet-side*," Re'shawn said, grinning. "Whuass."

Nico didn't know what *whu-assss* meant, but the way Re'shawn drew out the exclamation, she decided it was the equivalent of *cool*.

"Yeah, go-go girl, I mean from my Old Earth," Re'shawn added. She fished in her pocket and pulled out her Id, the label still on it. "Look at this thing they gave me. Is it ugly, or what? I liked my phone better."

Her phone, what? Nico wasn't sure what a phone had to do with anything, and decided to ignore the reference.

"Have you seen a girl with long platinum blonde hair, violet eyes, wears a choker with tiny spikes?" Nico asked. Re'shawn considered her question.

"Naw. I'd remember a girl like that. She your girlfriend?"

Nico's mouth quirked. "How did you know I liked girls?"

"Because of the way you said 'violet eyes', like it was really dreamy," Re'shawn answered with an exaggerated expression.

Nico's mouth quirked more.

"I have a dumb question: how did you know this world existed?" she asked. "And space travel. Aliens. Gods." Nico glanced up at the ceiling in emphasis.

Re'shawn put a hand on her hip and considered the question. She beckoned to Nico. "Let's go eat and we'll talk."

★

They sat in a hard plastic booth next to the picture window of Shivers, a fast food burger joint across from the YOBA with cheap food and workers wearing cheaper ball caps and striped uniform shirts. Even in a futuristic society with living gods, banality still existed. Her new acquaintance's fangs didn't go away; Nico wondered what that was like, always having one's fangs out. She herself had an opened paper napkin tucked over Bear's head. Not that she intended to try any of Re'shawn's food; not that Re'shawn was about to offer. Nico merely anticipated some sauce splatter. Her companion had ordered a massive blood burger with fries and blood shake, and when Re'shawn bit the burger, its patty oozed thick blood and dripped on to the foil wrapper. The patty looked injected with a load of flavoured simulated, one extra-spicy. The holo menu had called Re'shawn's burger selection the Flaming Sanguine with Cheese.

How does a dead stomach process all that? She watched as Re'shawn wolfed her burger down, sesame bun and all. If Re'shawn really was from a different Earth, Nico didn't want to chance their not having the same vampire physiologies. She had ordered only a chocolate blood shake for herself.

I hope I don't have to start using a toilet again.

"So that girl you've been asking everybody about, she just got here too?" Re'shawn asked, after wiping her mouth and hands with a fastidious air, the main portion of her meal concluded. Nico admired her deep plum nail polish again. On the way to Shivers, Nico had stopped at every building to make enquiries about her missing vampire, including the YOBA, and then the employees at Shivers.

"Yeah. I just have a bad feeling," Nico said. Re'shawn nodded.

"You reported her Id missing, right?" Re'shawn said. "Once they look up who she is, and someone starts spending her credit chit, the Makepeace'll find her."

"That's true." Nico blew breath. "I could canvas a little more, but I got nothing until someone gets back to me."

"That's right."

"So, about the gods."

"Yeah, the gods. This is how I heard it," Re'shawn said. "When the gods blasted off Old Earth in their star chariots and sky boats for a place or time they could live in, lesser gods stayed behind, and Other-beings too. Because star chariots cost money. But the story of where them elder gods went and the *planet* they found was passed down. How did Other-beings know that the bigger gods made it to somewhen? A star chariot would come *back*. If you didn't have a ship or couldn't ride on a visiting one, there were gates—portals—that could get you all the way from Old Earth to here."

"Like Stonehenge? The Bermuda Triangle? Atlantis?" Nico said.

"Yeah, maybe," Re'shawn mused. "I was thinking more people's closets, labyrinths, subway tunnels."

She is pulling my leg, Nico thought as Re'shawn sucked on her blood shake.

"So that's the short of it," Re'shawn said. "None of the other vampires told you?"

"I don't like other vampires." Nico said, and Re'shawn gave her a look. "I just don't."

"You don't need to *like* other vampires to hang out with an elder family, or a clan—you go to network, y'know? How about your local vampire club?"

"No," Nico said, emphatic.

"Takes all kinds," Re'shawn exclaimed. "You got internal sanguivoriphobia."

"I do not."

"We're on a planet where you can get help with that."

"Okay, sure. Now how did you get here, again?" Nico demanded.

"Aw, that. I knew this guy with lineage straight back to ancient times — we're talking Babylon — "

"Babylon," Nico recalled her ancient history studies. "'Gate of the Gods.'" Re'shawn nodded.

"Yeah, that. Anyway, he helped me get into Iraq and to Babylon's ruins. Okay, until then, I only half-believed. But when the *ship* came, it all became real — the star chariots, Darqueworld. The gods. The stories weren't only shared among Other-beings, humans knew 'em too; the ones who wanted to get here. Like the magic wielders. The mystics. And the Illuminati."

"But most vampires don't have a clan or lineage," Nico said. "A vampire made at random can't know all this."

"I guess not."

"I rose fifteen years ago. By myself. I was a murder," Nico said. "I had no one to talk to."

"You got lucky, then. Look at this," Re'shawn exclaimed, and Nico looked at their plastic yellow seats, the dead flies on the sill, and the big S icon peeling back from the picture window. "Blood burgers. Blood *catsup*. We've made it." Re'shawn grinned at Nico, fierce, then calmly opened a blood catsup packet and squirted it on her fries. The catsup smelled of thickened blood mixed with a touch of tomato sauce and vinegar. Nico sucked on her blood shake and wondered if she'd try French fries next. She could vomit it up again later if it didn't digest.

"All this is good. I get that. But I did okay back on Earth," Nico said. "I went to universities. I worked front desk at a hotel; night shift."

"You liked to pass. Pretend."

"It made things easier," Nico protested. "Fake ID's and black market blood weren't that hard to get."

"Naw. Too much work." Re'shawn ate more fries. "I did a short job to pay for my passage here. Got shot eight times — once in the head — but it was worth the six kilograms of plutonium I had to acquire. How did you pay for yours?"

"My what?" Nico sat back in her seat, wary that Re'shawn might be giving off radiation.

"Your passage."

"I don't know. I can't remember how it happened. I was just here."

"Huh, amnesia. Maybe you jumped through. Like into a folding portal. There's always a chance you don't reassemble right when you pop out. That's pretty cool."

"What, that my bits might be scrambled?" Nico said, alarmed.

"Hey." Re'shawn pointed at her. "No talkin' about your bits. Cool because it's so risky. Those gates like at Babylon? They get you here by celestial passages—Hecate's roads or Persephone's corridors."

"You mean a gravitational space corridor. Or an extra-dimensional corridor. Or are you really saying, 'wormhole'?"

Re'shawn gave Nico a look again. "I said *Persephone's* corridor. The chariots came that way, *I* came that way. If you need to blow a hole in reality to get into the corridor, you use sorcery. And because the one travelling isn't in a star chariot with a weird matter engine, you fold the corridor to pop that person out the other side. *Pop.*" She snapped her fingers.

"But you don't fold a corridor, you fold a—okay, never mind," Nico said. "I can see why you think that's cool...and why I might be scrambled."

"Naw, there's more. Guess what makes that kind of portal happen."

"What?" Nico said, as Re'shawn paused to suck on her shake. She put her drink down.

"Twelve innocents. Sacrificed."

"What? You mean children?" Nico's stomach dropped. "Is that how you got here?"

"I boarded a ship, remember? I'm talking about you and no ship, no spacesuit, and being pushed through—like a birthing baby. But with twelve babies dead because of it," Re'shawn said. "You need them innocents to feed the corridor demons; they're the ones who pull you through and then push you out the other side. Before you explode and stuff."

"Demons," Nico said.

"Yeah." Re'shawn sucked again on her straw, stirring last dregs. "I thought so too. But a sorcerer called Kepler wrote about it."

"You mean an astronom—never mind. Maybe I came by ship," Nico said.

With the meal done, Nico and Re'shawn parted ways, but Nico knew very well she didn't come by ship, landing like she did in that airfield. If she really remembered being content with her Old Earth life, she didn't understand why she'd kill twelve babies to leave it.

✱

"Dorothy, are you sure all hotel work requires a new arrival to be here a moon cycle before applying?" Nico said, exasperated. She'd already canvassed the hostel area for her missing vampire, checked the morning news for Chasca Vasquez's investigative reporting of the Royal Bento bust, then decided to start job-hunting. A guaranteed paycheque would mean no longer having to stay at Again Friends. She followed her Id's holo map to Chaikov's Collectible Coins & Currencies. Dull, grey clouds filled the sky and muted the sun, making Nico feel she needn't buy an umbrella to hide beneath. The neighbourhood she presently traversed was iffy; the littered street lined with pre-fabricated, makeshift tenements of precariously stacked living units. Sulphuric steam rose from grates. Bums and hustlers loitered, but Nico still preferred to walk rather than utilise her rail pass or hail a taxi. It was daylight, after all.

Wonder what got razed to put up this rubbish. I could be anywhere, rather than New York.

"Dorothy, never mind answering, I know why they have a wait period before hiring," Nico grumbled. Front desk clerks handled personal information, sensitive documents, and of course, money. She didn't exactly have references anymore, much less her Curriculum Vitae.

"Job finder suggests that you apply for ship crews for your skills set," Dorothy said. "Set sail for the job opportunity of the nebula with Star Queen's Stellar Cruise Lines—"

Nico ended the ad. "I think I'd want my new intragalactic citizenship and passport finalised before getting shanghaied into space."

"Place your bets," a holo-girl projection said next to a betting shop. She winked at Nico, and Nico glanced up at the shop sign: Winkie Bets. "Punk Monk Martial Arts Supplies and Weapons Shop sponsors the next champion for Slaughter Spawn."

"*Teh*. Punk Monk," Nico said, humoured. She crossed the street and left behind the tenements sector.

The neighbourhood she entered next contained a Jewish deli, Russian grocery store, a Russian restaurant, and a Russian bakery. She walked into the gated, faded storefront of Chaikov's Collectible Coins & Currencies.

Chaikov had a morose, worn face with tired eyes. His very conservative (or possibly utterly bored) reaction to the rubles, francs, deutsche marks, and British pounds she laid out on his glass counter made Nico want to sink into moroseness as well. He quoted a sum and Nico balked.

"We also buy passports, driver's licenses, identity cards—" Chaikov said in a sonorous voice.

"No."

"What more do you have?" he said, pointing at the security wallet she held.

"Don't touch my stuff. How about a Leningrad metro pass?"

"*Nyet*. We already have too many. We also buy those." He pointed at her second credit card that she'd laid aside while digging for the paper money.

"Too many metro passes from *Leningrad*? But my credit card is just a piece of plastic," Nico said. Her gaze narrowed. "With my signature on it."

"We buy plastic cards too. People like those. Coins, stamps, paper...anything that belonged to someone has collectible value." Chaikov shrugged. He pointed down at the contents on display within his counter.

Nico saw a 1940's charga-plate, signed "Mrs Jas N Read", a 1954 Diner's Club card, one Black Card, several identity cards, employee cards, and—

"*That* can't be Elvis's driver's lic—never mind," Nico said when she saw Chaikov's expression. "Okay, I'll sell you my credit card."

Chaikov quoted her a price that could buy a few blood servings at Lucy's. Nico slid her credit card over but continued to press on it when Chaikov tried to take the card.

"If I somehow end up with my identity stolen, I will come back and kill you," Nico said, and Chaikov stared at her in fright. "I'm kidding," she added.

✸

Nico stepped back out a few credits richer.

"I have to stop saying stuff like that," she said to Bear. "No wonder people don't want vampires around." She had nearly asked Chaikov about the four Russian names in her little black book, and then decided against it. With two of them dead and the others non-existent, whatever history she had had with the names might have remained on Old Earth. Chasing old ghosts was not what she wanted to do. A world meant for vampires beckoned.

She had the odd feeling that she was being watched.

She looked down the street. A Fedotov van with the peasant girl logo sat at the kerb and next to the grocery. She glanced back at the coin shop's window, and Chaikov abruptly turned his head.

"Humph." Nico continued on her way. If she was being followed, that someone was certain to slip up at some point. She activated Dorothy and requested a job finder search, beginning from her present location. A holo map projected, showing Nico the first place she could enquire at.

Nico decided to try four listings; the search would keep her out and about on the streets and easier to follow.

✷

Vampires not wanted. Please provide references. Citizen papers required. No Vampires need apply.

Nico put an X through another job she'd queried—a bakery that found her lack of references unappealing—on her job finder map and told Dorothy to ignore any postings that didn't want vampires and other criteria she couldn't fulfill. Green dots disappeared from her holo map.

"Well, at least we get to see some of this city," Nico said to Bear. They'd been wandering for an hour, watching the city stir from sluggishness and become more active beneath the dreary skies. She no longer felt eyes upon her nor caught anyone following, so she continued to walk and wrapped up watching another of her required citizenship class vids, *Immigrations Holo Vid No 2: Darqueworld Today.*

Weird matter engines, Nico learned, didn't just power celestial sky boats. People on Old Earth could (if they knew to plan beforehand) transport entire city blocks to a place like Again NewYork during a dire event like a bombardment or natural disaster. That explained the presence of a precinct that felt and smelled like a real precinct, but Nico wasn't sure what happened to Again NewYork itself when a transfer supposedly occurred. Did sewage pipes magically extend? What about utilities? Did the city undo another notch on its belt to accommodate a magically expanding belly?

"I have lots of questions," she told Dorothy.

"Immigrations Holo Vid No 3: Understanding the Dreaming Planet that is Darqueworld," Dorothy said, "Multi-physical Realisation From Celestial Weird Matter Engineering. Narrated by Carl Sterling, the history of harnessing Darqueworld's quantum realities is explored."

"I'll watch it later," Nico said. "But you're really saying... this planet has ways of making stuff happen for us, like ghosts appearing on the veldt." She looked around with interest. She'd entered a street with a worn, Art Deco automat complete with copper boilers on the counter within, the aroma of freshly brewed coffee wafting through the open glass doors. A woman walked out of the self-serve restaurant wearing peep toe pumps, a wide brimmed hat, and a tailored suit in the utility style, looking ready to visit Rick's Cafe Americain. The woman consulted the holo projection from her Id while holding her handbag and *Welcome To Again NewYork* bag.

Wow, Nico thought. *Which reminds me...*

"Dorothy. Any answer yet to the lost Id I reported?" The street looked like one snatched from the original New York City, complete with fire escapes, apartment stoops, and marquee signs. Despite the presence of the 1940's female chrono-immigrant (who then departed determinedly for a building with a Room For Let sign) Nico guessed the era at 1950's, if she identified the automobiles beside the walk correctly.

"No messages," Dorothy answered.

"How is it possible to have cars like this now, driving on the super flyways?" Nico said in wonder as she looked at the dash inside a green Packard. Perhaps they didn't operate and merely sat where they'd landed when transported to Darqueworld, run out of gas and time. She saw a woman's friendly reflection in the Packard's window, her hair a waved updo topped with curls. Another 1940's female. Nico turned to her and the woman smiled.

"Cute bear," the woman said with a New Yorker's accent. "Did you get him at the Woodrow's?"

"Oh, no," Nico said, straightening. "I got him—"

I got him...her thoughts hit the white spot and slid off.

"I," Nico said. *This amnesia is too much.*

"It's okay, honey," the woman comforted with a reassuring smile. "Have a nice day."

Nico stood at a loss while the woman walked away, her sturdy red sling backs clicking. But from the corner of her eye, Nico noticed the distinct figure of a woman standing across the street—a female not from a past era. Nico stepped back within the silhouette of a street lamp, and then looked.

Heloise Allen stood before the Woodrow's and its mechanical kiddies horse ride and gum ball machines, holding a hard pack of cigarettes. Her creamy blood-dark lipstick matched her pumps' outsoles. Besides the new lipstick, Heloise wore a different outfit, a dark grey two-piece with a black shirt and bright red narrow tie— red like fresh blood. Nico felt envy at Heloise's new clothes, and she straightened her cardigan and then held Bear, self-conscious.

Heloise tossed the new purchase up in the air and caught it, obviously happy. With a twist of her fingers, she tore the top part of the wrapper, and then tapped the pack in her palm, ejecting a single cigarette. Heloise put it to her red lips and brought out a silver and black lighter. Eyes squinting, her cheeks sucked while she lit the end, then exhaled into the air. As the stream of smoke left her mouth, Heloise lowered her chin and looked straight at Nico behind the car and lamppost. Her mouth curled into a smile.

Nico stiffened. She turned and continued down the walk.

She shouldn't have spotted me; I need to be more careful.

But her laxity could be forgiven; she hadn't practiced hiding from another vampire since stalking her maker.

Nicky, her maker chastised.

Nico hurried and rounded the corner. When she looked behind her, Heloise did not follow.

Nico was beyond delighted; perhaps more so than when she'd visited Tokyo's Sanrio Puroland.

"We're in England—we're in London. We're in Victorian London," she exclaimed to Bear.

She and Bear sat at The Blue Owl Tea Room's small, outdoor

table on a cobblestoned street, complete with gaslight street lamps and a row of half timbered houses, one of which bore a hanging hand-painted sign: The Pea and Cock.

Before Nico could exclaim on how rude (or clever) the pub's sign was, an open, black, horseless phaeton rolled down the cobblestones, clattering. The cloaked driver in the coachman's hat held a whip for an invisible horse. Vampires like the ones from Countess Karstein's vampire ball sat within, in hats and black outfits. One of the women held a silvery parasol made of fine gossamer and looked at Nico, her piercing, vampire's gaze stark in her pale face. Nico gawked and had Bear wave at the carriage as it drove by.

The Victorian sector consisted of several streets, and its buildings—augmented and adapted since their snatching—still bore the sooty, greasy stains of the original London's factory-polluting miasma. When Nico had entered the area, she had activated a holo historical plaque on the walk. The holo narrator explained the section's snatching of over one hundred years previous. The original occupants, Nico realised, had long since passed away, and she doubted their descendants would have kept up Victorian appearances and ways. But it made an excellent haven for time travellers of the era. A contemporary woman opened a shutter in the upper storey of a half-timbered building to air out her unit.

"I want to live here," Nico said to Bear. A goateed gentleman emerged from the tearoom's entrance: a vampire.

He stood on the walk in grey gloves and with walking stick in hand. To Nico, he felt as old as Heloise. He was dressed in the Belle Epoque style; all of hand stitched real wool, cotton, and silk fabrics, and wearing a blood red silk waistcoat and beaver fur top hat, which he tipped to her. He then presented her with a card:

Dear Miss
As I am going in your direction
Allow me to be your protection

The flirtation card was bright and new. Nico looked at it and thought of how many women he might have killed, presenting them with his charming card.

"I'm a vampire too," she said, though she was certain he knew. "And I prefer women."

He smiled and nodded in understanding, and Nico wondered: was he a killer, or a donor eater? Was he seeking her company only, or looking for a hunting partner to indulge with? He flipped the card so that the long end extended forward, a silent invitation for her to accept it, and she did.

"Then may this humble device aid ye more than it has myself, miss," he said, his accent Irish, and tipped his hat again. He then progressed down the street for a storefront called: *Absalom, Fairditch, & Vastagh, Rare and Unusual Books.*

Fairditch? Nico recalled her fellow chrono-immigrant and her two Victorian vampires. Dorothy confirmed that Livy Fairditch was indeed an owner of the bookshop.

The waitress emerged from the tearoom.

"How's your blood tea?" she asked congenially. "Would you like anything more with it? A blood custard? A pudding?"

"The blood tea is great. I'll try the custard, thank you," Nico said. "Is that gift shop over there for the United Kingdom, or— what's it for?" The gift shop across the street displayed a kind of Union Jack in the window that Nico had never seen before, one with a red dragon in the centre of the red cross. The blue background also bore stripes of gold along with the red and white.

"Oh, you're a new arrival, aren't you?" the waitress said. "That shop's for gifts from the Isle. It's not the United Kingdom, it's the Isle Kingdom, and the Queen travels back and forth from Old Earth to rule, from time to time."

"The...Queen?" Nico said when the waitress went back inside. She looked up "Isle", and the map showed an isle across the sea, settled by Scots, Irish, Welsh, British peoples, the Sidhe, and other fairy brethren. Along the coast lay Selkie territory.

"The fairies pulled a huge transfer," Nico exclaimed to Bear. "And three different British Queens helped. I should have kept my British pounds. Dorothy, search for Shayla O'Fey. Tell me if she's native to Darqueworld."

Dorothy affirmed that Shayla was a Darqueworld native, which meant Nico couldn't ask Shayla how she got to the planet. But a slew of records and news data popped up with mention of her last name.

Wow, she's a—a coven's pistol? What's that? But before Nico looked up the definition, she wanted to check if Shayla was married; according to public records, no.

Tee hee, Nico thought.

The waitress brought Nico her blood custard, and she ate it as she read what a pistol was: a coven and community peacekeeper.

But it looks like she isn't one now. Nico scanned the headlines. She opened one article titled: Promising Pistol Gives Up Badge.

"Is Shyla O'Fey a misspelling by the media?" Nico said in surprise.

"Shyla O'Fey is the elder sister of Shayla O'Fey," Dorothy answered, bringing Shyla's public record to prominence. "Death at age twenty-two. Vampire life currently at three years."

Fascinated, Nico watched news footage about Shayla and her vampire-witch sister, Shy.

Her Id chimed. Nico started out of her perusal, wondering what the alert was for.

"Oh! Maybe they found Violet Eyes." She checked the caller's identification.

It said: Specs Plonsky.

My social worker.

"Hello?" Nico answered, and Specs's face popped up, his holo reducing Shayla's data to secondary prominence. He looked exactly like his photo, from his shaved head to his thick-rimmed Wayfarers, except for the stubborn stubble that looked resistant to laser razors.

"Hey there, how's it going," he greeted.

"It's going good," Nico said.

"I'm your social worker, Specs Plonksy. You can call me Specs. Mr Plonsky would be my father." He chuckled. "It's your second day here on our fair planet, Ms Nico Alexikova! Tell me what's going on with you."

"Well, I did some job hunting and learned that vampires need not apply to nearly all of the job postings. This is great, by the way."

"The, uh, lack of jobs?"

"No. Being here; the possibilities. I'm only now appreciating it." Nico stared at him. "It's euphoric."

"You don't look or sound euphoric. But I agree, I felt the same when I got here."

"Do you mind if I bring the thing I was looking at back to prominence? I just want to finish something."

"Yeah-yeah, let me do that," Specs said. His visual blipped out, leaving only Nico's data on Shayla in view. "Great. Initiative, I like that. So, besides the disappointment that is our job market for vampires, everything else going good? I got contacted about your adventure at Royal Bento Food Packaging Co—"

"Oh?" Nico said, curious. "Who told you about that?" She thought it highly unlikely the police would want to talk about her. She typed a message to Lucy's, enquiring if Shayla was at work.

"Let's just say your friendly neighbourhood Makepeace like to keep an eye on their Other-being flock. On behalf of all fully ordinary humans having no enhancements or abilities whatsoever, I wanted to say how grateful I am for what you did last night."

"Okay," Nico said. "Can I have more money?" She typed a response to the diner's answer. Shayla had the day off.

"Not until your status evaluation at the end of the month. And now that we're back to business—how're you doing on your immigration education vids?"

"I'm halfway through viewing them."

"Excellent. And did you go over your vampire rights and rules pamphlet?"

"Um." She'd thought the pamphlet had looked boring, which civics was. She wasn't about to tell Specs that she'd chucked it. "No, last night I was too busy—vampire stuff."

"That's right! Stalking off-worlders, right? If you can refrain from doing that tonight, I suggest you read it, because better you know now than have a Makepeace blow a hole through your heart for not knowing. First thing you should be aware of, making one like you is forbidden by la—"

"I'm not interested in progeny," Nico snapped.

"Y'okay! Very good. But if you ever were," Specs said, "you would have a ton of paperwork to fill out. And a three-month wait, in case the intended progeny—or you—changes his, her, eir mind. And there would be tons of forms for the intended too. On Darqueworld, it's like having an adoption."

Nico thought about her maker beating her to death and into a shallow grave.

"Uh, you there?" Specs said.

"Yes. Shallow grave." She typed another response to Lucy's, thanking them for further info. "Just a question: what if a vampire makes another to save that person's life? I mean an on-the-spot decision. No time for consent forms."

"Ah, that. Simple answer is...well, thanks to the last time that happened in Again NewYork, there's no simple answer. But it's still considered an arbitrary act, especially when the dying person's consent is in dispute."

He's talking about Shy O'Fey. "Okay, thank you. I got another question, since you were a new arrival too. How did you learn about Darqueworld?"

"Wow, that. Well...I didn't. Back on Old Earth, I was a UFO hunter. Chased them from New Mexico to Washington. Wrote about it, blogged about it, took tons of pictures and footage—"

Blogged? Nico thought. *What kind of word is that?*

"—I wanted to believe," Specs said. "And then I got abducted." He cleared his throat. "And I guess I rode all the way here, naked and in suspended animation."

Specs ceased speaking, long enough for Nico to realise she should offer conciliatory words, but she was stuck on the reference to the X-Files. The last thing she remembered of Leningrad was that she had been looking forward to seeing the upcoming X-Files movie.

"A bunch of activists ended up liberating me," Specs continued. "I was on someone's dinner platter when PETH busted in and forced our captors to release us. Not before I saw someone else get eaten, but I was really grateful."

The Cru'k, Nico thought.

"That's why I gotta say: Nico, you are my hero," he said.

Nico didn't think she'd acted like a hero last night at Royal Bento; babies and people did end up packaged, and from their expressions, painfully. But she'd taken her time busting the operation because she'd no idea what she was doing. She'd known from the countless times she'd tried to kill her maker that even with the best care, things could go horribly wrong. Planning could become over-planning; deliberation could become over-thinking. Her maker had been an improvisor. He could make up a murder in a minute. He could do ten random murders in ten minutes, and walk away.

This is the game of chess, Nicky, where I knock all yer pieces over, he had said.

Nico hadn't planned on killing her maker the night she'd dragged him across the Rocklyn Hotel's roof. After four long years, circumstances had fallen into place. The hotel had been in the midst of marquee repairs. Nails and duct tape had been present. And the morning's dawn had started; no more escape for him.

Perhaps had she learned to emulate her maker sooner, she could have saved more lives like Spec's.

"...And I'd sing you that song, 'My Hero, Zero', except I can't remember the words right now. But about the job search," Specs said. "Bodies aren't trafficked only for food."

"Are you going to warn me about sexual slavery?" Nico said.

"Yeah, I guess I could do that too. I was more going to warn you about certain recruitments. Other-beings are valued for their physical enhancements. Like for off-world mining."

"Slave labourers," Nico said.

"You got it. Families fall for the ads because it's wages and housing. Then they're locked up behind fences, never to leave again. I wanted you to be aware. Well, if you were recruited."

"I'm not much for labour," Nico said. "I like being a clerk."

"Well." Specs coughed. "I meant more as an enforcer."

Boy, Nico thought. Vampires really had a bad rep on Darqueworld.

CHAPTER SEVEN

In lower Again NewYork, Nico entered Loch Niamh Community Centre. Lucy's robot hostess said Shayla might be found volunteering there.

The centre kids—human and Other—left their little weaving projects to gawk at Mr Bear in his harness and his toy Union Jack tucked in behind him, which Nico had bought at the Isle gift shop. Once Nico learned that Shayla had left, she departed. She walked out to a green park before a small lake, edged with trees and beyond their line, apartment buildings. Birds flew.

This isn't a real loch. It's artificial. For a tiny, manmade lake, it was still decent for walking and enjoying, and its surrounding forest was recognisable to Nico and hadn't the alien—or off-world, or First Native—quality she had come to associate with an alien—a non-Terran, or non-Sol—

"Gods, I'm so backwards," she said to Bear, and summoned a news article on her Id that she'd been reading: *Newly Risen Witch Slays Own Coven.* The photo of Shy O'Fey looked very much like Shayla, if her human soul had fled.

While she read and progressed down the walk, enjoying the breeze flowing off the lake below and to her left, she kept aware of the street on her right, separated from her walk by grass. The trees surrounding the lake opened up and ahead, she spied a young woman with hair of sunshine on the pebbled shore, tossing breadcrumbs to the ducks. Shayla wore patched jeans and a cable knit cardigan opened over a faded, powder blue tee. The pushed back cardigan sleeves revealed leather corded, cowry shell bracelets on her wrists. Nico deactivated her Id and fell into a stealthier walk.

Shayla threw more breadcrumbs, and then regarded Nico, as if she'd been aware of her long before Nico had started her approach. Shayla smiled.

Like at the diner, the expression seemed both delighted and intrigued, and right then Shayla did not temper it. The corners of Nico's own mouth crept up.

Gosh, she's pretty.

A vehicle came to a smooth stop by the kerb. The hatch popped open and a woman's legs emerged and crossed at the knee, the deep Bulgarian rose of her high heels' outsoles briefly flashing. Within the vehicle's dark interior, a woman's long-fingered hands folded over the front of a dark grey two-piece suit, unbuttoned, with a black shirt and bright red narrow tie.

Christoffel Loulain heels. Nico veered off the walk and up the grass in their direction. She told herself she only wanted a closer look. Heloise grinned and nodded to Bear's Union Jack.

"Look at you and Mr Bear, you've been to the Victorian quarter."

"Mr Bear thinks his Union Jack is very punk rock." Nico neared. "What do you want?"

Heloise held her palm up. Her middle finger's steel ring emitted a holo interface displaying Nico's mug shots.

"Do you know who you are?" Heloise asked.

"Do you know you sound like a Vorlon?" Nico said.

Heloise smiled more, her teeth perfect and white in the interior's darkness.

"You already took a picture of me in the bathroom," Nico added. "Why do you need my mug shots to stare at?"

"I took that picture in the bathroom to check if you were who

I thought you were," Heloise soothed. The holo image blipped out. She held out a black, engraved business card, *Heloise Allen, Consultant*, and Nico ignored it. Heloise arched a brow and pocketed her card.

"Fine. You seemed to have memory trouble back at immigration. But if you want to know, just ask." She moved back into the vehicle, tucking her legs in.

"Okay. I have a question: how come the lady at the spaceport called you a refugee?"

Heloise looked at her in surprise. "I forgot; you're more a tourist or an adventurer, aren't you?" Her tone turned wistful. "Looking at you is like looking at what we lost."

"How did you get here?" Nico asked.

"The hard way. A weird matter engine that opened a portal, built by Old Earth's vampire primacy."

"Not in a spaceship."

"No. Gate-to-gate connection. And no spacesuit. Very risky." Heloise grinned. "You keep looking at my dash."

"The central steering wheel is very interesting." The vehicle seated three across, just like the chopped coupe of Miss Fairditch's vampires, with a centred steering wheel having a few controls circling it and nothing else. The interior looked spacious and roomy enough for Heloise's long body and legs. "This is a Faering Shearwater, by Vahalla. Do you really know how to drive it?"

"I do. First thing I did when I got it was make reverse figure eights."

"In high heels?" Nico exclaimed.

"Of course in high heels. But all the vehicles here default to automated operation. Just speak and go. Want to hop in and try it?" Heloise smiled.

"Creep. Bye," Nico said.

Heloise glared at her. "Creepy is if I'd offered you a lollipop." She tapped her dash, activating a holographic interface, and the door shut. The vehicle zoomed away.

"I bet she's looking up 'Vorlon', right now," Nico said. She turned back for the lake, and Shayla watched her with a bemused expression.

Shayla turned and threw the rest of her breadcrumbs as Nico descended down the grass. But the quacking ducks ran waddling for the lake, as if they knew Nico's true nature. Once in the water they paddled to a safe distance.

"Verry nice legs ye were talking tae," Shayla said, her mouth quirked in humour. Her brogue rolled her R's, creating a soft, warm burr Nico gravitated towards.

Your voice is nothing like his.

"They belong to a vampire. She says she's a consultant, but I bet she's really a lawyer, or a countess," Nico declared. "Or a countess lawyer. I call them Bathorys. Because they prey on girls. I hate them."

"Is she very good looking, then?"

"Beautiful. That's why I double-hate them." Nico looked at Shayla's leather corded necklace and at the three-armed Brigid's Cross hanging from it, freshly woven from long blades of grass.

"Such luck, us meetin' here," Shayla remarked. Her tone was casual but meaningful. "Or did ya come tae see me?"

"I was more trying tae stalk ye," Nico said, imitating Shayla's accent.

Shayla raised eyebrows, but her smile was wry. "Ye should choose yer prey more carefully, love. And how did I earn this honour?"

"Ye're a braw lass, nicer and prettier than a Bathory." Shayla's eyes lit at Nico's use of Scots slang, and she did not hide her pleasure. Pleased, Nico pointed at Shayla's sealed grocery bag on the ground, with its flower pattern and wooden handles. "I can help carry your groceries."

★

Dear Miss
As I am going in your direction

Allow me to be your protection

Nico walked beside Shayla as they followed the lake's shore, the sealed groceries in no danger of spoiling, and spotted Other-beings lurking in the foliage. But Shayla paid them no heed, and Nico realised that other creatures needed to indulge tracking and hunting skills as much as a vampire did, though without the desire to add psychological threat.

Vampires: screwing with people's minds since time began.

"The hostess at Lucy's told me you had the day off," Nico said, apologetic. "And where you like to volunteer. Then the community centre told me you were here. I'm sorry. I only wanted to talk. I shouldn't have made it like stalking."

Shayla looked at her with mild surprise. "Most vampires don't apologise for stalking."

"You shouldn't even believe an apology," Nico admonished. "Most anything a vampire may say can be untrue."

Shayla made a humoured sound. "Aye, that's true." She pointed at the Union Jack tucked behind Bear. "How happy Mr Bear is. Does he want tae visit the Isle?"

"He does." Nico pulled the flag out. "This is the most amazing Union Jack I've ever seen."

"Shall I show ye its meanings?"

"Yes please." They stopped, and Nico held it out while Shayla took one end of the flag, stretching it flat between them. Nico watched Shayla's fingers trace the designs and thought each movement seemed to cause the patterns to glow.

"Here lies St George's Red Cross for Albion," Shayla said softly as she traced the cross. "St Andrew's Cross of white against blue for Skye; St Patrick's Cross of red for Éire." She traced the red X of the flag. "And here be the red dragon for Cymru, and here, the gold of *Tuatha Dé*."

"I'm surprised the faerie would accept the sovereignty of one, human queen," Nico said. "And the new Irela—uh, Éire too. Aren't the Tuatha dé Danann the Fae?"

"People may ken them as such, but *Tuatha Dé* are gods. The beings below them are the *Aos Sí*, and those ye may ken as the Fae." Shayla resumed walking down the lake's side and Nico tucked the flag behind Bear again. "But as tae the Queen, what's a union of five peoples tae do? Her sovereignty maintains our civility and we've peace these past two centuries. I'll confess tae ya; it's a strange marriage, livin' with the *Aos Sí* and they with us. Livin' in Again NewYork is easier."

"I've spent the whole day wandering the city," Nico said. "Looking for work, learning about Darqueworld, and learning about witches."

"Oh?"

"Well, only about you, but it's a start. Because magic is—well, still a mystery. But gods can do it, and I guess, you. Also, Darqueworld has whatever enhances what you have...or are."

Shayla looked over at her as they ambled. "I've never ken a different world. Darqueworld is me; it's myself and the Weird."

"That's another reason why I looked you up. I wanted to ask how you got here, but you were already here."

"Aye. I was born to our world. Is there somethin' ye need knowing?"

"I...I have memory loss," Nico admitted. "I don't know how I got here. I don't even know how I got Bear." She put a hand over Bear. "That's too much missing from my mind."

Shayla touched her. "Some crossings tae here can affect the memory. If they don't return soon, ye might try psychic therapy."

"You can't just—" Nico waved in the air. "Do some spell and poof, I can remember?"

Shayla rolled her eyes and smiled. "If I were a witch in stories, chick, maybe."

"How come at Lucy's you said you didn't think you did sorcery?" Nico asked, curious.

"Ah, that. At Lucy's, we have our wee spell-works, but our table tricks are simple weird work. We hide the objects in an unseen place, y'see, and we draw them out again by manipulating reality's matter; the weird matter. Working the weird is not the same as commanding. Commanding's the nature of sorcery."

"Commands," Nico said, her tone thoughtful.

Their path meandered away from the lake and entered a wooded area, thick with undergrowth. Shayla motioned to the trees. "For example, chick, if I made this wood walk, what would that be?"

"Your asking the dryads nicely to get up and leave? Uh, sorcery," Nico said.

"And if I darkened the sky, coverin' Merope?"

"Witchcraft," Nico said. "*If* I believed you could curdle cow's milk and cause crops to die. Now we're talking ignorance."

Shayla raised a brow. "Aye, for the most part, that is. But it's sorcery when Circe or Merlin does it."

"Merlin?" Nico made a sound of disbelief, and then regretted it. "I meant, oh."

"How's this for sorcery? Men tae swine. I could turn ye into a wee kitten," Shayla cajoled. "Such a cute one ye'd be, with those pretty grey eyes."

"Um," Nico said, her eyes wide.

"I take that as a 'no'?" Shayla smiled. Nico smiled back, happy. Then she paused.

She felt that eyes were upon them—a gaze not human. Her fangs broke out. Shayla only glanced at her, unfazed, and touched her arm again.

"Wheesht," she said, low. "Put yer chibs away and walk on, now." Shayla did so, and Nico made her fangs recede and followed. But she looked behind and discerned—by separating staring eyes from the surrounding foliage—three camouflaged, humanoid bodies within the growth. One was distinctly female, embraced by her tall, willowy companion of mixed gender, and the third— more boyish than gamine—stood wrapped in the willowy one's other arm. Nico could not tell what gender thon might be. She and Shayla stepped out of the wood and regained the lake's edge again.

"Tree people," Nico whispered. "And three of them — together!"

Shayla grinned. She held several long strands of coloured string — red, black, and white — drawn from her cardigan's pocket. "Aye, ey has two loves with em taeday, eir triad. Are you of an era or belief that favours monogamy?" She twisted and formed a tiny loop at the end of the strings, then knotted them.

"I favour what makes people happy," Nico said. Shayla offered the loop to her and Nico hooked it with a finger. "And harms no one. 'Eir'...my social worker, Specs, had said eir."

"It's a neutral way of speakin'," Shayla murmured as she began quickly braiding the three colours. Nico held the loop firmly. "Many of the Other are not simply male or female, and so are many of the galactic species. So we say: ey has legs. Eir legs. We let em in."

"You dropped the 'th'," Nico said in realisation. "I like it."

"'One' is as good tae use. An auld word is 'thon'." Shayla formed two knots to seal the braid. "Hold it now by this knot, love." When Nico did so, Shayla began weaving a pattern.

"I will try using 'one.'" Nico felt remiss in her galactic understanding. She was a cave girl in a futuristic world. "How does the rest of the galaxy see us? Or is it just me who feels I'm trying to catch up?"

"They call us the wean of our gods, for we are still so new." Shayla looked up from her weaving and smiled. "And dinnae worry about makin' mistakes. So many are here from different times, different belief systems. It's good when ye try."

They fell silent as Shayla weaved her pattern and Nico watched. She wanted to pay attention to the image slowly building as Shayla's fingers rapidly worked, but Nico's gaze kept returning to Shayla's face, which did not simply concentrate but held a deep, meditative regard, singularly focused on a silent purposing; a sacred communication.

She's praying. Awe suffused Nico's being. She parted her fingers to accept and hold firm the second set of knots Shayla made to seal the pattern. Shayla then resumed braiding again, and Nico wondered what words or sutras she silently chanted into the moving strands. Shayla ended the braid with two firm knots.

Nico let go, and at Shayla's touch, offered her wrist.

"Bless this one. Guard this one. Gods walk with this one." Shayla said, and tied the string bracelet around Nico's wrist, knotting it.

"Thank you," Nico softly said. She turned her wrist and looked at the tiny woven pattern between the two braids. The weave revealed the black head of a cat. "Oh! A kitty!"

"Aye. A lucky *neko* for Niky," Shayla said, smiling. "Ye're a young vampire alone on Darqueworld, aren't cha? And a brave wean."

Shayla resumed their walk and Nico followed, grocery bag in hand, perplexed by what Shayla had meant. Perhaps like fortunetellers, she saw something in Nico.

My wean, her maker said.

The overcast cleared when Nico and Shayla left the lake for a group of apartment buildings. A jumble of complexes stood, unlike the massive blocks at the city's farther edges. A shirtless male covered in dark, Buddhist tattoos worked at deep frying catfish on his balcony while children ran in the winding streets. Clothes flapped from lines. Nico followed Shayla and resisted the urge to avoid the bright sun and hide in the shadows.

I'm carrying groceries. I'm walking in the sun with a pretty girl. Nico indulged in marvel. Three young men leaned on a balcony railing and as Shayla and Nico passed below, they hooted.

"Yip-yip-yip."

"Aw, look at the puppy. Shayla, is that your new puppy?"

"Hey, little puppy."

"I'm *not* a were-dog," Nico yelled at them, appalled.

"Shayla's picked up another stray," a third man mocked.

"Get a job!" Nico snarled. She turned to Shayla. "Do I look like a were-dog?"

Shayla laughed, the soft sound brief. The touch she gave Nico's back was fleeting but reassuring. "No, chick. They're only teasing.

I'd a friend and lover who followed me thus, and ey was happy tae do so. Ey was a vampire. That was three years ago."

Three years ago was when Shy got killed. Whoever "ey" was, that one didn't appear to be around anymore.

"You're the first person I'm following just because I want to," Nico said in surprise. It was a strange and very new realisation, and it made her give a little skip. Shayla looked at her, intrigued.

Three little girls bounced a ball to each other on the street ahead when two little boys ran up. One snatched the ball away and then shoved the girl.

"*Stop it,*" the girl hollered. "Or I'll make Shayla *admonish* ya." She ran to Shayla and clung to her legs.

"I dinnae do nothin'," the little boy yelled.

"Callum, I witnessed what ya did," Shayla said firmly. "Come apologise now."

"Ye're not the *real* pistol, anymore!" Callum shouted, and threw down the ball. He ran away.

The little girl turned around and pointed at Callum, her hand in the form of a gun.

"Pow, pow," the girl said.

"Wissht, Lainie," Shayla said with severity. She took hold of the girl's pointing finger and put it down. "Tae yer ma, now."

The little girl went to her mother, who'd emerged from a doorway, and Nico looked at Shayla. She caught the pain in Shayla's gaze.

Nico thought about witches become vampires and witches with pistols when Shayla finally stopped before a building; they had reached her apartment complex.

"That's me, then," Shayla said, and held out a hand for her grocery bag. Nico gave it to her.

"You've been so nice," Nico said. "Don't invite me in."

Shayla grinned. "Ya follow me home and then want me tae make ya go away?"

Nico held Bear. "I just...I'm sorry about your sister," she blurted.

At Shayla's surprised expression, Nico looked down.

"I didn't simply ask around for you. I looked up stuff published about you too. I know that the news never gets the whole picture? But I'm sorry about what happened to you and her." Shayla touched her arm, and Nico met her gaze.

"Thank ye," Shayla said.

Nico played with Bear's arms. "It's creepy again, my reading about you. It's something I need to stop doing. But I had wondered why you were so okay with something like me."

"Now chick," Shayla began, her tone chastising.

Nico shook her head. "You shouldn't be so tolerant of vampires. We might mistaken it for your being passive...instead of patient with us."

Shayla smiled, bittersweet. "It's an earned patience, love. There's a reason for it."

Nico yearned to ask: what's it like, having a murdered sister rise a vampire? Do you blame yourself? Has she tried to kill you? Has she tried to make you like her?

"I'm sorry," Nico said again.

"Ah, love." Shayla put her bag down and hugged her, and Nico stiffened, overwhelmed by Shayla's softness, warmth, and golden peach-bergamot scent. Nico made her arms move and hugged back with Bear mashed between them. A grandstand of Bears waved Union Jacks within her.

When Shayla ended the hug, her gaze was mischievous.

"Now," she said. "What did ye really want tae talk about?"

Nico skipped as she left Shayla's building.

I have a date!

Shayla was not currently attached. And she hadn't really said "yes." It had really been a very gentle "no" that had made Nico want the earth to swallow her up for asking.

"I like ye, Niky, but dating's not fer me, right now," Shayla had clarified when Nico's entire being sank into the ground.

"Can we still be friends?" Nico had asked. "Because I have so many questions. When I get creepy, just shoot me."

Shayla had smiled, both amazed and humoured. "I cannae leave ye unable to ken this world, can I? I'm free early the morra… how's that?"

Yes-yes-yes.

"Yes, I want a real friend on Darqueworld," Nico babbled to Bear as they descended into an underground station. She then thought of Heloise. "And one I can *trust*. Plus, I like Shayla more than that. But the 'date' thing! I'm an amnesiac, I have Old Earth problems come over with me—that might be real, or maybe imagined. I don't even know how to explain it to her. And I'm unstable. Why am I even doing this?" The query of a date leaving her mouth had surprised her as much as it hadn't seemed to surprise Shayla. Nico could only think that she'd risked it because Shayla was worth rejection.

Shayla had to work the night, a graveyard shift, because Lucy's was a 24-hour diner. But Nico would be there in the morning, on the dot, for chatting.

Not for a sex encounter, not for a clandestine "arrangement". Nico was going to spend genuine time with a woman—in public—simply to be in her company. So far, nervousness had not yet outweighed elation.

"Later, I may throw up," Nico said to Bear, and hugged him. Her Id chimed.

She pulled it out and read the caller's identification.

Caller: *Deepika Kapoor, immigrations social worker*

Subject: *client's Id found*

Nico answered, and Deepika's holo popped up. She was an older Indian woman dressed in a purple silk sari and wearing silver-rimmed spectacles.

"May I speak to Ms Nicolette Alexikova?" Deepika said in even British tones.

"Yes, that's me," Nico quickly answered.

"Thank you for finding my client's Id," Deepika said. "Can you give me a description of her, the time and day you last saw her, and in what condition or circumstance you found my client in?"

Nico did, recalling as much detail as possible. "I think something bad happened to her," she added.

"I understand." Deepika looked off-holo and typed. "I've submitted a missing person's report. It dispatches to all police, public services, and the Makepeace. Hopefully someone will find her."

"What's her name?" Nico asked.

Deepika looked at her over her glasses. "Are you kin, spouse, maker, guardian, or champion to my client?"

"Champion," Nico answered.

"Indeed."

"Wouldn't I know her name if I were her kin or spouse?" Nico asked.

"You'd be surprised. One moment, please." Deepika glanced off-holo, and then returned her attention to Nico. "If you would affirm your champion's pledge to me, I can tell you her name. Vampire face, please."

"Oh, okay." Nico bared her teeth and her fangs grew. Her eyes changed.

Deepika peered at Nico closely, and then Nico's Id flashed her in the face. "Visual affirmation; checked." She returned her attention off-holo and began reading aloud. "As the celestial holarchy, the primacy of vampires, and this servant of the under-holarchy are your witnesses, you, Nicolette Alexikova—"

"And Bear," Nico added.

"You, Nicolette Alexikova and Bear, give this Utterance of Life, and pledge with your heart, truth, and soul that you will champion Esche Abram-Angel, giving protection and aid in her time of need, whether she be living or dead."

"I pledge it," Nico promised.

"Duly recorded. Well, there you are." Nico's Id lit up, and she saw data had been added. "Now you may go find my client."

✳

Nico reviewed Esche's immigration information while riding the Four back to the hostels sector. She'd been correct, she shared the same vampire age and age of death as Esche, who came to Darqueworld via the star chariot *Lusitani*.

"Esche means 'ash tree' in German," Nico told Bear. "I like her name."

But the next information gave her pause. She read:

Psionic ability detected.
Psychometric score is:
60% recognition in uncommon aestheses
100% recognition in empathic perception
Recommend telepathic testing
Recommend telekinetic testing

Nico recalled the mental sensation of a finger lightly touching her mind's blank spot.

"She's a sensitive," Nico whispered.

✳

She asked in the hostels sector if anyone had seen Esche, from the preacher, the medical clinic, the Shivers, to even the street hustlers, and stared into the hustlers' eyes and feigned non-committal attitudes, trying to gauge if they were kidnappers. She even enquired at the boys' hostel and bar.

"Do you want to be admonished, citizen?" the holo of Thunder Gunn said when the bouncer allowed her in. A German couple ran the hostel and bar, the bouncer had told her, and many of the hostel's guests were of the culture. If anyone came from the same ship as Esche, Nico might find such chrono-arrivals there. She put Bear's Isle flag away and moved through the boys and men gyrating to the driving techno beat. She showed people Esche's holo photo and received negatives to her enquiries about her and the *Lusitani*.

"*Wissen Sie Esche*?" she shouted up to a muscled male with blonde beard, braids, and a Thor's hammer amulet on his bared chest. "*Esche Abram-Angel*?" He scrutinised the holo, then shook his head. Nico headed to the bar counter and its bartender, who watched her.

"Where did you see her last?" he said above the music as she showed him the holo picture. He introduced himself as the hostel's co-owner, and they shook hands.

"Again Friends Youth Hostel," Nico said.

"Oh." The owner shook his head. "Vampires come and go very fast on this street. They don't hang around—have themselves a good time."

"Those vampires are having a good time," Nico said, pointing at boys wearing black. One showed off his shirtless body in a chest harness similar to hers and Bear's. With their white-blond hair, eyeliner, and piercings, Nico had thought the boys possible undead kin to Esche. Or her boyfriend type. They had not recognised her photo.

"Yah, that's because they are staying *here*," the owner said, grinning.

"I should stay here," Nico said. She bade the owner farewell, and returned to the street.

✶

"And her name is?" Dann said when Nico showed him Esche.

"Esche Abram-Angel. The vampire the Id belongs to. So you didn't see her?"

"Maybe she signed in." Dann pushed the sign-up sheet in her direction. "Want to sign for another night?"

"I already signed for this night. I checked that box yesterday." She looked at the signatures. None were for Esche.

"I mean, sign for tomorrow." He pushed a card for Chaikov's Collectible Coins & Currencies towards her. Nico pushed it back.

"And no one came to claim her Id?"

"Oh, that. Nah. Hey, the blood snacks are late, but they are coming."

"What if the snacks don't come, and lockdown happens with all these hungry vampires trapped inside? With you?"

"That can't happen," Dann said. "The snacks always come."

Nico showed him Esche's holo photo again. "Remember that face." Then she left.

The girls' dorm held three vampire girls, including the backpacker, Danica, while the boys' dorm held a scruffy group of four—boy punks who laughed and smoked, hunched together like conspirators. None recognised Esche's holo photo. Eton boy, broody boy, and Tex were not present.

Sparse night for Again Friends. Maybe they'll lose their funding. She didn't feel sympathetic. She returned to the ground floor.

She was standing before the vending machine, contemplating its emptiness, when Iris suddenly spoke to her.

"It's almost rest time," Iris said, and Nico turned, having not heard the other vampire's approach. Iris hugged herself, her eyes bearing dark circles beneath them. "I've been searching all day. Tex and Delores still aren't back."

"You have your Id, right?" Nico said. "Have you tried calling them?"

Iris smiled, brittle. "I lost mine, and I can't afford a new one. Delores helped me keep in contact with Tex's social worker so I'd know when he got out of prison. We haven't separated since."

"Here." Nico held up her Id. "Let me call them." *That way Tex and cat-eyes girl won't ignore it, thinking it's you.* "What's Tex's contact code?"

Iris showed Nico her wrist. A contact code was written on her skin. "This is Delores. Tex never got the hang of an Id." Iris laughed nervously. "I've already had people call her."

Nico nodded. She tried the contact code, and she and Iris watched as the call's icon slowly pulsed.

"I was thinking," Iris said, "what if...what if the spawn got to them?"

"I think the spawn would need to take the rail to get here," Nico said.

"Now you're making fun of me," Iris accused. "And sure the spawn can take the rail. They live underground, don't they?"

"Sorry," Nico said. "Are you okay? You haven't been looking well."

"I'll—I'll have some blood and sleep and I'll be okay." Iris hugged herself more.

"If you need a clinic, I'll take you to one." Nico ended the call attempt. "They've free ones and they don't ask questions."

"Oh, I know about them, there's one a street over and they give away free drugs! Me and Tex got a little excited about that, that's why we got into trouble." Iris smiled. "I'll be okay, especially when Tex comes back. Look! The blood is finally here."

A human deliveryman walked in carrying a white translucent box with the blood drop logo on it. He went down the hall for the rec room and Iris followed.

Nico blew breath. At some point Iris would have to make the decision to contact the Makepeace, and when they located Tex and Dolores honeymooning in neuvo wherever, Iris could then have closure.

Dorothy, where are the spawn located? Nico typed, curious. Dorothy projected a holo map. The red circle lay within a populated (and poor) sector between where Shayla lived and mid-town's business sector began. Nico requested an isometric projection to discern how far below Again NewYork the spawn's location was.

"Teh," she uttered in humour and surprise. "A ground-level commuter tunnel, seriously? I guess they can come out and get us, after all." And one easily accessed via an abandoned and over-grown surface passage. "That looks bigger than the usual tunnel. What are the specs, Dorothy?" Dorothy gave her the size, length, and materials the tunnel was made of, and stated:

"The Jotun tunnel was built to accommodate the leviathan train known as the Mammoth, which was three times the width and twice the height of the standard train. However, veldt leviathans attacked and consumed three Mammoth trains on the cross-veldt route before the project was abandoned."

"Wow." Nico made a note to look up First creatures eating trains, then put Dorothy away and went to the rec room.

When she entered, Ozzie girl was happily passing out blood packets again. The early birds were present: paperback girl with her thick book under an arm, tongue-pierced girl, and the Sushi Hut worker, still in uniform and seated, hunched with fatigue. Broody boy lurked in the room's shadows, already sucking on a bag.

"Has anyone seen Esche?" Nico asked, and displayed the holo picture. A round of *no's* answered her.

"She might've moved on, mate," Ozzy girl said.

"That'll be me too. Just one more night." Paperback girl sighed as she accepted two packs from Ozzie girl. "And then I am out of here."

"Really? To where?" Ozzie girl asked.

"Found a vampire nest that'll take me. They're in the fashion sector."

"That's great," Iris enthused.

"Really great," tongue-pierced girl said.

"Sounds bodgie," Ozzie girl said, sceptical.

"Sounds like I found home," paperback girl said coolly.

"Are these your Again Walker friends, the non-biting pacifists?" tongue-pierced girl asked, her tone teasing.

"You know I don't like to bite," paperback girl said.

"I can't wait until me and Tex and Delores find a place," Iris said. "A place to call home. On Darqueworld we can be like everyone else."

"Oh yeah, and with a white picket fence," tongue-pierced girl said lightly.

"I wouldn't mind one." Iris smiled. "But more a wrought-iron balcony, like in New Orleans. Did you know there's a New Orleans *here*? It's called Sister Orleans. That's so diesel."

"Ugh," Sushi Hut girl uttered, rubbing her eyes. "Sorry. Didn't mean to interrupt." She picked up her blood packs and rose to leave.

"Dreams keeping you up?" tongue-pierced girl asked as she turned to follow, and sucked on the straw in her bag.

"I don't really dream anymore; do you?" paperback girl remarked, also departing. Iris left with them.

"I can't remember anything," tongue-pierced girl replied.

I can't remember anything, Nico recalled thinking when she had been human, and had woken up in her own bedroom in her parents' home, her clothes feeling wrong.

Ozzie girl held a blood packet before her.

"Here you go," Ozzie girl said. "Cheers, mate."

The generic pouch reminded Nico of the awful tomato paste flavoured one from immigration.

"No thanks," Nico said.

"What a face!" Ozzie girl laughed. "It's not bad. The taste is ace. Well, you've got less than a tick to change your mind, 'cause I'm calling down the others." She smiled and left the room. Nico looked over at broody boy.

"You should be outside. Dancing at the boys' bar," she remarked. "Why are you even here?"

"Why are you?" he retorted.

"I'm waiting for someone to come back tonight. Have you seen the boy in the tweed jacket, the one who came from that druid ship?"

"Tonight? No." Broody boy tossed the pack he'd sucked dry and started his second one.

"He found somewhere to go?" Nico asked, and broody boy shrugged.

Eton boy was reading new arrival pamphlets just yesterday. And he was a splashdown refugee. He had nothing. If Eton boy had found a way to travel on for the Isle with only his Id and credit chit, she wouldn't mind learning how he'd pulled that off.

The vampires from the dorms entered, Ozzie girl leading them.

While she passed bags to the girls, the scruffy boys grabbed packs and sucked hungrily, their vampire visages present. Nico watched them scrunch down the bags and remembered when she'd first risen. She'd killed many forest animals that night.

"Saved you two," Ozzie girl said to her, and held them out.

"It's okay. Those guys seemed to need it more than me," Nico said. Ozzy girl made a humoured noise and shook her head.

"I don't know if that's being noble or just weird. Give it a burl, mates." She tossed the packs back in the box and two boys snatched them up.

"Cool, thanks," one said to Nico.

"I'm going up," a girl announced, taking her packs. Her friend followed her out. Danica tossed an empty bag she'd sucked down.

"Weird hours, but at least the place and blood is free." She shrugged, then departed, sucking on her second bag.

"Yeah. And we're leaving. Thanks for the blood, losers," a boy declared. His teeth were bloodstained and his friends laughed. They ran out.

"Oi, y'whackers, ay?" Ozzy girl cried, and followed.

"They got the right idea." Nico turned to go as well.

"There's nothing wrong with staying here," broody boy said. Nico stopped to look at him.

"Are you trying to convince me, or you?" she said.

"I'm tired of not knowing where I'm going to sleep." His face darkened. "Ha. *Sleep*, at night! I never did that before. But Jess makes it work while she's job hunting."

"Who?"

"Jess—the Canadian girl. The one who just left."

"Her? She's Australian," Nico said. "Ask her where the dunny is. You don't look like you'd have a problem finding a place—tonight or the next night."

Broody boy smiled, a cute grin that lit his eyes briefly. "Neither do you. Okay, I just want to lay low, all right? That vampire they found in the park. Too much like the Milwaukee Cannibal, you know? Or maybe you don't. Are you—were you American on Old

Earth?"

"Sort of," Nico said. "I heard of him. Aren't you the one who thought it was the spawn?"

"Well yeah, but then." He laughed, humourless. "It can be anything now, right? I get to this planet, and—it's all upside down! Everyone can *see* us. They know what we are. The underworld is the main world, and what's under that is actual hell. Darqueworld is crazy."

You mean Darqueworld is scary.

"I gotta go." Nico left the rec room.

"Wait," broody boy called. "Where are you going?"

"I don't know. The boys' bar. One of us should be go-go dancing."

She entered the entry hallway. Dann's booth sat empty again. Nico glanced at the sign-up sheet as she walked by—still no signature from Esche. She pushed the door, and she and Bear smacked into it.

"Rest time," the automated voice-over announced. "Rest time." The hall's lights dimmed, and then winked out.

"I cannot—" Nico shoved at the door again. It didn't budge. "*Believe* this!" She pushed harder, then gave up. When she pulled her Id out, the time was 21:45.

"Dorothy, is this the right time?" she demanded.

"Rest time," the voice-over repeated.

Nico looked out at the nighttime street, where people walked, oblivious.

"Rest time."

✷

When Nico ascended to the third floor, all was pitch-black. Iris chatted, seated on her bed next to Nico's while the two new girls in beds across the way politely listened. Was Re'shawn present? Nico walked the length of the dorm until the last beds. Paperback girl, tongue-pierced girl, and Sushi Hut girl appeared to be fast asleep on top of their beds. Danica lay still as well, her eyeglasses on her face. Ozzie girl, in the bed across the aisle, did not stir. Re'shawn was not in the dorm. Nico walked back to her bed.

"So I heard that there are vampires here who have *families,*" Iris said to her. "I mean, they can have babies together. Can you believe it? They're called 'living vampires' because they're warm-blooded. I kinda don't get that. But what if I could have Tex's baby? That would be so diesel."

"Look. You don't breathe, so I'm betting you can't. We're not alive," Nico said. "We're nothing but blackness inside. Nothing sprouts there, okay?"

"You're mean," Iris said.

"Okay, good night you two," a girl said. A few *good nights* answered her and then the dorm became still. Nico lay with her shut switchblade held to her chest. She touched Shayla's bracelet.

Living vampires. Rubbish. Her thoughts turned to the events of the day and especially to Shayla. But after a while of pleasant revelry, distracting herself with beauty and warmth, a part of her became uneasy, as if something could—

Something could, what?

She tried to order her thoughts again, but listened instead, for the sound of soft footfall; of one of the girls, muffled, getting murdered in her bed.

Nico swallowed, clutching her blade.

Nicky, her maker said. *What's the matter, luv?*

What's happening? Nico thought. The other girls slept on, unperturbed by the inexplicable fear assailing her. Her day's good humour fled before the cool, coffin-dark of the dorm, a sensation colder than shadows. Yet something shadow-like was growing, and Nico wasn't sure if it dwelled in her, or was outside—

Nicky, he said. *Didn't ya feel me comin'?*

She rose; Iris didn't stir. She left the dorm and went downstairs to the boy's floor to try their bathroom window. When it cracked open, she set to work on the screws, listening for a soft approach from behind.

Once loosened, she shoved the window hard enough to break the hinges. The windowpane hung, precarious, as she squeezed through.

"You're not taking me like you took Esche," she gasped.

She dropped for the walk below. Nico looked up and saw Tough Guy standing on the rooftop across the street, the holo board's advertisement lighting his armoured body.

"I can't stay," she said to him. She turned and fled.

"Where are you," she whispered as she ran down the street. "Where."

CHAPTER EIGHT

If her maker had taken Esche, he would have made her into little pieces already, left here and there for Nico to find, as if time remained to retrieve Esche alive.

But her maker was *dead*. The entire situation—her possible paranoia—it only smelled like him. She needed to go where something like him was and kill it first.

Traff—trafficking, she thought, feeling the word slide off the blank in her brain.

And perhaps she was simply grasping at something to do, somewhere to go, just to avoid remaining trapped in one place where a boogeyman could get her. She couldn't be like broody boy, trying to use darkness to disappear into, hoping the monsters wouldn't notice. Only her human self had wanted that, and it hadn't worked. Her maker had gone into her safe place anyway and snatched her.

Trafficking.

Esche.

She and Bear would get the snatchers first.

*

Employment Opportunity—Girls Only, any kind—full-time hostessing, entertaining, singing, dancing. We reward talent. Earn high pay, overseas and off-world opportunity. Work in the best clubs of the galaxy.

Either, or. Nico dismissed the ad. It could be trafficking; it could be legit. She sat on a train platform's bench and perused more such ads on her Id. The snack bag she sucked on came from an Indian food cart. It had a touch of red curry flavour, and she quite liked it. If she found an ad worth investigating, she had the perfect photo to show them.

Earlier, Nico had Dorothy search inside human social hubs for a girl similar to herself—black hair, pale, white blouse, and cardigan—preferably photographed standing on a train platform at night. The photo she presently possessed was of a girl with a casual, expectant expression, looking fresh and young and not at all like a living-dead, shell-shocked waif.

Showing up as herself would be a bait-and-switch, but the similarity in outfits and colouring would at least get her through a club door.

Esche. Trafficking. The strand of connection was faint, but she would work it until she tripped over her missing vampire, alive or dead.

She sucked on her snack bag until it scrunched. Then she saw a likely kidnapper's ad:

Human Girls Only—Needed Immediately—hostesses, dancers, servers for private engagement, immediate pay, one night's work. Ad expires 3 standard.

She continued perusing. She still found no suspicious ads asking for vampire girls. She had Dorothy give her background on three clubs downtown that catered to clients with a vampire fetish. Vampire dancers stripped there. Though sleazy, nothing rung Nico's alarm bells; a background check on the owners seemed to prove they were legit, providing work for those who needed it. Even the endorsements she found in a private discussion page for working, vampire girls did not appear to be from planted sources. However, the ad wanting *human* girls—

Nico blew breath. She returned to the likely kidnappers' ad. The timer had a few hours left.

She ran through all her choices again as a vampire looking for sex work. She could hit each place and see if Esche was at any of them, enslaved or doing legitimate work. Or—

Her attention returned to the suspicious ad again.

"Okay Bear, let's screw this up," she grumbled.

She told the ad she was a recently arrived chrono-immigrant. The ad's response was immediate.

Need your visual.

Nico sent the human girl's photo.

Are you bringing a friend?

No, I'm alone, Nico typed.

Go to Halo train station, the ad said.

Do I get the job?

Automated alerts will direct you where to go, the ad said.

I'll be there.

Nico cut communication and looked up Halo station on the route map. It wasn't in Again NewYork's nightclub sector or even in the red light section. The ad was sending her to the veldt outside the walls of the city.

She discarded her snack bag and boarded the Sixteen for Halo. While she tidied her virtual bus locker, she watched guerilla footage of duelling witches shooting cryptic guns. After the tenth amateur recording, Nico was disappointed. She didn't think women making exaggerated gestures where light beams or fireballs left their hands looked terribly authentic.

"So disco," Nico said.

Though the cryptic gun was a secret, weird matter weapon wielded only by witches, Nico wanted to see one in action. She opened a news tidbit in curiosity:

Witch Wins Slaughter Spawn Using Cryptic Gun

"Wow," Nico said, but before she could read it, the train's male voice-over spoke.

"Now approaching Halo station," he announced.

When Nico stepped on to the outdoor platform, she could smell the unseen veldt, its cool air pure and invigorating. Something primal in her responded, and she felt her fangs emerge. A cue lit her Id.

Take 167 bus to Ravineto Junction.

Nico put her vampire aspect away and descended. The cues reminded her of her maker's own notes, left in her things to prompt her to come to him. One envelope had contained her cat's collar.

Nico found the bus waiting at the deserted kerb, lit by one streetlight. She boarded, the lone passenger. No driver was present. The automated vehicle departed, its interior dark, and Nico took a seat in the middle of the bus. She looked out at the forlorn buildings of a poor, nondescript settlement, sitting in pitch-darkness.

Ravineto Junction consisted of a lit fuel station, the business closed, and the bus stopped itself behind a parked van. A man in jeans and jacket stood by the open hatch, checking his Id. He looked up at Nico within the bus, then at his Id again. Then he summoned a big grin, waved, and approached as the bus door opened.

Nico rose, and when the man boarded she could smell his sweat; hear his breath. She gripped the back of a seat, feinting anxiousness.

"Hey," the man said as he approached. "Glad you could make it. We got a trip ahead of us. Are you thirsty?" He held out a water bottle.

Nico accepted. Then she grabbed him.

She threw him to the front of the bus. He landed and struck his head. As he groaned, she walked up, kicked him down the bus steps to the walk, and when he tried to crawl away, she jumped on him, both feet planted between his shoulders. His nose smashed into the concrete. Nico flipped him over, opened the water bottle, and squeezed his mouth open.

"No—gurgh—" the man sputtered, but Nico continued to force water into his mouth until his eyes rolled back.

Guess roofies work the same here as on Old Earth. She dragged him to the van's open hatch and tossed him in. Nico drew her switchblade.

A look inside revealed no one hiding in wait. An inert girl lay on a seat, her bare legs askew in the aisle. Her slacks and underwear lay tossed on the van floor. Nico sighed and threw the unconscious man towards the driver's seat. She followed.

"Great," Nico whispered when she saw the van's single steering wheel and darkened dash. She'd forgotten that she didn't know how to drive on Darqueworld. She went to bring the hatch down. As it clicked shut, the van started and began driving.

Nico looked at the vehicle's front, where the activated holographic interface flashed of its own accord for its preprogrammed destination. Nico picked up the girl's underwear and slacks and dressed her. The girl's hand flopped, revealing well kept nails. Her clothes also seemed nice, and hardly the style of a runaway. Perhaps some lure posing as a new friend or potential boyfriend had betrayed her.

"Help," the girl slurred.

"You're going to be okay," Nico said, as she finished fastening the girl's slacks. The van's wheels hit a dirt road and Nico spied into the darkness with her vampire's vision. They'd entered a drive surrounded by the twisted veldt trees. The remote ranch house in the distance had its windows boarded shut: a stash house.

Nico counted the parked vehicles as the van rolled for the back of the house, and estimated six or more johns inside. She placed Mr Bear on the van's floor, popped the hatch open, and then pressed herself against the van's wall by the opening. When the van came to a stop, a few yards from the darkened back entrance, a man stood watching. His boots crunched in the dirt as he came to investigate.

"What's going on?" he said, as he poked his head in.

Nico took a good look at him: vampire. He reached for Mr Bear.

"You picked up another ki—"

Nico grabbed the back of the vampire's head and slammed him face first into the van's floor. She brought her switchblade down and stabbed him at the base of his skull, severing the nerves of his C-1 vertebrae. The vampire's body flopped and stilled, his ability to move destroyed.

No more words for you. Nico pulled the rest of him in, his eyes desperately blinking.

Another man stepped out the darkened door, lighting a cigarette while Nico secured Bear in his harness again. When he looked in the van's direction, she stumbled out.

"Oh my god, oh my god," Nico uttered, reeling.

"Hey," the man said sharply, walking towards her. He breathed, his scent hot and sour. "Get over he—"

She drove her fist into his jaw, breaking it, then took hold of him and rammed her knee into his groin. He rose a foot into the air. When he hit the ground, curling, he still hadn't lost consciousness.

Nico stepped on his neck and pulled a thick, short rod from his back pocket. It had one trigger button. She lifted her foot and pressed the rod into the man, activating it. He arched from a direct pulse strike, and his urine scented the air.

Pulse rod in hand, she ran for the open back entrance. A girl emerged, and Nico stepped into the house's shadow. The human girl appeared no older than sixteen and squinted, nearsighted.

Bait girl, Nico thought, spying the girl's cold regard; a broken girl used to lure more girls.

"What's going on?" the bait girl called. Behind her, far within the house, another girl cried, pleading for someone to stop.

Nico's thoughts slid against the blankness in her head.

I think I found you.

She stepped in front of the girl.

"Hi," Nico said.

She slapped her hand against the girl's mouth, silencing her. The pulse rod in her hand sounded, and Nico's fangs broke out.

Nico stood in a darkened room's deeper shadows and gazed down a row of cots where drugged human girls and wide-awake children lay, her thoughts banging against the blank spot in her mind. One of her hands clapped the mouth of a john straddling a child while she filmed the room, her Id set for nighttime recording. She waited for the tranquilliser mint she'd forced him to swallow to take effect. The little girl beneath him stared up at her. When he stopped clawing at her hand, she hauled him off the cot, dropped him to the floor, and then pressed her shoe's heel into his lower back. A loud pop sounded while the child leaned over the cot and looked on. Nico continued to record the room's activity.

Down the row, three girls held down a fourth while a john moved to get on top. The fourth girl begged them to stop. Nico put her Id away. She walked across the room and drew out the pulse rod.

Each man she passed she shot, the walloping pulse-blasts exploding. Three johns at the end of the room pulled their trousers up and ran for the entry hall and the front door. When Nico reached the girl being held down, she pulsed the bait girls and flung them away. The rod sputtered and died.

The john on top of the girl struggled to his feet and Nico lifted him. She tossed him against a post. As he moved to get up, she walked over and threw him into the post again, shaking the room, and heard the satisfying snap of bone.

Nico watched the pulsed johns fight to recover, one crawling for the back entrance. The banging against the blank spot in her mind increased.

Why is this familiar? When? Where? Don't kill, she reminded herself.

She hurled the rod at the crawling john's head, skimming the side of his skull. He collapsed at the impact, and the girl in the cot sobbed while the children stared. Nico pulled out her Id again. Footage of unknown and forgotten girls and children might not make the news; but the john before her—

She filmed him moaning on the floor with his trousers down at his ankles. He was impeccably groomed, with an expensive Id ring on one hand and perfectly manicured nails.

Smile. I hope you're as rich as you look.

She typed: Likes it dirty and illegal. The more sordid, the more he enjoys it.

Look at that one, Nicky, her maker whispered, *pointing out a man entering a sex club. The more sordid, the more he enjoys it.*

She added the note to the footage.

While she sent the recordings to her bus locker, the john reached into his coat pocket with shaky fingers.

"Are you looking for your Viagra?" Nico asked as she sent Chasca Vasquez a message. She kicked him. Tears squeezed out of the john's shut eyes, and Nico bent down to search his pocket, finding a wallet and a vehicle's crystal keyblade. She threw the wallet at the girl in the cot, glanced at the keyblade's rental holo logo, then frowned; she'd heard no vehicles departing.

Nico put away her Id and the keyblade. She rushed out the room and down the entry hall for the open front door, switchblade in hand. Makepeace 1634 stepped into view, weapon pointed.

Nico halted.

"Hello," she said.

Nico stared into a gun barrel big enough to crawl into. The Makepeace raised one's left gauntlet and spoke into it.

"Activate," one said.

The surface of Nico's skin buzzed as something electric flared to life outside. Beyond 1634, a net pattern glowed in the darkness. The Makepeace had erected a containment barrier around the ranch house, including the vehicles. One's gun remained pointed at her face.

"Your explanation, potential citizen," 1634 said.

CHAPTER NINE

Nico had read that Makepeaces did not care for prevarication. She gave as short an explanation as possible.

"Sexual trafficking," she said.

1634 continued to aim for her face.

"And I happened to answer their want ad," Nico said.

"To do what, potential citizen?"

"To serve drinks; hostess. Just quick money for the night." *Please don't think I came to join up as an enforcer.*

1634 seemed to weigh her answer, then slowly lowered one's weapon. One moved passed Nico and entered the house.

Nico let out breath and didn't follow. She stepped outside and looked at the containment field running along the ranch house's perimeter, emitted from discs embedded in the ground. She looked up, and saw the field arc overhead; she had nowhere to go. Nico appreciated 1634's effectiveness. Had she time to plan better, she would have trapped everyone in the house with her. But the temptation to beat on the johns and traffickers until they turned into mushy pulp would have been too great. Even breaking a john's back had been pushing it.

The johns who'd fled sat within another containment circle, their hands up to hide their faces. Nico filmed them, then sent the additional footage to her bus locker and for Vasquez to pick up. Children and girls who weren't too doped up to walk emerged from the ranch house with 1634's help. They were all human; none were vampires. Nico looked away and stared into the dark.

The ordeal was over for some; a few might have a home to go back to. The more ruined ones would disappear back into the sex trade, and the cold-eyed girls, especially, would make more girls like themselves. Nico glanced back and saw the bait girls mingling with the others; victims pretending they were still victims, when they were victims become predators.

This yer new friend, Nicky? Her maker held a girl down. *Now watch, luv.*

Her thoughts slid again, falling off the blank spot in her mind. The veldt's darkness beyond gave her no ghosts.

"I've got nothing," she said. The little girl she'd broken a john's back for approached. Someone had dressed her in a man's tee shirt. She walked up in her bare feet and stared at Bear, her eyes distant and dead. Nico looked elsewhere and wished she'd go away.

When the girl didn't, Nico reached down. She guided the child to her, and then helped her wrap her arms around herself and Bear. She placed a hand on the child's back while the cold-eyed girls watched.

Are my eyes like theirs? Or am I feeling something so deep, I don't know I'm feeling it?

The girl that had been held down shuffled up too, her face streaked with tears, but there was fury present within her anguish. Nico thought that was good. When Nico removed her hand, the little girl dropped her embrace. Nico put her in the girl's arms.

"Thank you," the girl said tremulously. She moved to hug Nico too.

"Don't touch me," Nico said. "Uh, you...I think you'll be okay." She turned away again. The Makepeace stood before her.

"Hi," Nico said. Her gaze was level with 1634's pectorals — or breasts. One's body armour even possessed nipples.

"The ad you answered, please," 1634 requested. Nico looked for it, then displayed it on her Id. Nico couldn't tell from 1634's visor where one's gaze truly lay, but it seemed to take in the entirety of the ad with one glance. The Makepeace's head turned, as if listening to something.

Is one sharing it with Tough Guy and the other Makepeaces? Nico wondered. *Are they having a conference call about me right now?*

"The ad is for human girls," 1634 said, turning back.

"I thought I'd try anyway," Nico admitted.

"Did you come intending harm, potential citizen?"

"I—"

Nico stopped; her teeth in someone's throat. A man's head bursting open from the tire iron she'd thrown at his skull.

But that didn't happen.

Her thoughts slipped off into the dark.

"I came...looking for something. And it wasn't here."

"You are still seeking the potential citizen, Esche Abram-Angel?"

"Yes." *Of course 1634 would know that.*

"You did not come here for her."

"No," Nico answered truthfully.

1634 merely looked at her, and then flashed her in the face.

"Oh, god—" Nico covered her eyes. She'd had her vampire's vision on. Painful spots assailed her. She expected her wrists grabbed and cuffed at any second.

When Nico's sight cleared, 1634 had turned away, by all appearances not interested in arresting, shooting, or even admonishing her. She wouldn't mind an admonition if it made 1634 feel better. Nico stood awkwardly.

"Victim services will arrive before the sheriff," the Makepeace said, and one's cold tone seemed displeased.

"Maybe the sheriff is over there?" Nico offered, indicating the group of johns who covered their faces. "One of them is wearing those kind of shoes...law enforcement shoes."

The Makepeace stood, one's pretty mouth pursed, and Nico was certain one was wishing one had werewolves to fight instead of babysitting possible dirty cops. Vehicle lights shone down the dirt road, then stopped before the containment barrier: victim services. 1634 pressed on one's gauntlet and a small opening formed in the barrier.

"They will see the children home," 1634 said, as people disembarked and walked through.

"More likely they won't," Nico said. "It's parents and relatives who sell the kids into these things."

"How do you know this?"

"I don't know." A van marked NEWS ALPHA rolled up and stopped behind the other vehicles. The hatch popped opened. "That's Chasca Vasquez," Nico noted, anxious. "Can I leave?"

"That one," 1634 said in reference to Chasca, and one's silky voice bore a touch of irritation. "You may go."

✱

The keyblade Nico took from the manicured john lit up and activated one of the parked vehicles when she neared them. It looked just like Heloise's Faering Shearwater.

"Destination," the onboard BRAI calmly asked when she entered.

"Go to Halo station," Nico said, wondering if automated driving was as simple as that. The vehicle backed out and headed for the dirt drive. Apparently it was as simple as that. Nico pulled out Dorothy for a quick driving lesson, only to find herself sinking back in the plush seat and sighing. The Makepeace opened a hole in the barrier for her to pass through. Chasca Vasquez stared hard into the tinted glass as Nico's stolen vehicle drove by, her hands on her hips, while her cameraman captured the entire vehicle.

"I hope Mr Manicured is a prominent figure." She activated Dorothy to get a brief lesson on vehicle operation.

But when the Faering approached Halo station, another thought occurred: why not save on using her rail pass?

"Go to Jifk Spaceport," she ordered. "Fastest route."

The vehicle sped ahead and accessed a flyway for the city wall and beyond. Soon, they were zooming among Again NewYork's glittering structures, and Nico closed her eyes, both to sleep and avoid the vertigo.

Her Id chimed. Nico reluctantly stirred and looked at the caller's identification. She answered, and Spec's holo popped up.

"You are one busy vampire," Specs said, and then yawned.

"I was just looking for something."

"Well, the legit girls and boys work downtown, FYI—whenever you decide to take a break from fighting crime. I got done reading the Makepeace's report. Way to go, Super Nico!"

"I am not super," Nico snapped.

"Got it. Stupid nickname. You are Lone Nico and Bear. Were you a dark avenger back on Old Earth? And if so, can I have your autograph?"

"No. I was a hotel desk clerk. Nightshift. And I was studying computer science."

"Right." Specs nodded. "Mild-mannered. Very secret identity. Are you enjoying being the scary monster now?"

"Can we have this conversation later?" Nico said. "I need to sleep."

"Gotta have it now, Nick, the Makepeace are waiting."

"Okay." *Psych evaluation.* "Me, being scary. Well, I guess," Nico said in surprise. "It is kind of nice. But I don't want to hurt anybody."

"Really? Because on Darqueworld, you get to be one hundred percent vampire. Without killing innocents and the less-than-innocent. And believe me, you're not alone in that kind of self-discovery. You should see how the werewolves celebrate when they realise they can let it all hang out. And I mean, do they. So, you don't want to glorify in bloodbaths and the sucking down of people's essence?"

"Do I look stupid? I know the rules; I want a future."

"And that's exactly what good potential citizens like you should want. But answer the question, please."

"No. I mean, the answer is no." *I hope not.* "I just—"

Blank spot. Her teeth sinking into someone; hot-hot blood spurting.

"I feel I've unfinished business," Nico said.

"Not the missing girl, Esche Abram-Angel? Who the Makepeace are looking for, too."

"Besides that."

"You were a vampire for fifteen years, right?" Specs said. "You put a lid on it, tamed it. Now it wants to come out. Whatever you're looking for, it may be that. So, when you get the more deadly urges, you talk to me. We're here to help. You like to stalk, right? There's a dating service for vampires like you. Though it's more for any Other-being with that certain itch."

"A service?" Nico said, her voice squeaking. "What itch?"

"The itch to chase something; hunt it. Okay, maybe you need to terrorise it too, before you go in for the kill. But the end result is not killing, it's sex. Human women are absolutely gaga over this kind of dating, and I cannot fathom it. You like girls, right?"

"Did immigration tell you about my—" Nico said with suspicion.

"Oh yeah. Your predilection for moon cycle worship? There's a dating service for that too." Nico's Id lit up. "Sent you the Stealth Lovers page. You can look up Womb Lovers yourself."

*

Nico arrived at Jifk Spaceport and sent the stolen Faering back to the ranch house. Inside the terminal for intragalactic flights, where many off-world species were present, Nico booked a sleep-egg nestled among other eggs overseen by an attendant. The large ovoids lay on their sides, comfortably accommodating one humanoid form on a firm, cushioned bed. She could have slept in the vehicle or at a terminal gate, but the indulgence—which took a chunk out of her credit chit—clearly stated to anyone who might be monitoring her traceable activity, where she and

Bear presently were. Makepeace or otherwise, they could come find her—and drag her out or attempt to kill her before a filled terminal lobby. Nico took advantage of the complimentary vibronic shower, and then entered her egg for the night. The attendant helped to close her hatch.

"The egg will awaken you at your designated time," she said. "Pleasant dreams."

"G'night," Nico said, arms crossed over Bear, and when the hatch closed, all sound from the terminal cut, and a soothing aural and electric wave motion ran from her head down to her toes, then up again, calming her. Thoughts of 1634 popped up, and reluctantly, those of the ranch house.

She didn't want to explain to Specs (and, by extension, to the Makepeace) that she wasn't running about in the night to sow wild vampire oats. She was trying to work out the connection of Esche and trafficking, but most of all, she was committing disruptions as if *he* could be out there, noticing.

Whatever smelled like him might then make a move.

Until then, she and Bear were refreshed, ready, and—

Safe again.

Nico triggered her switchblade, and then slept.

CHAPTER TEN

"Again Friends Youth Hostel," Dann answered, his holo projection looking as cheerful as his voice.

"Hi. This is Nico Alexikova. Did Esche Abram-Angel come back to the hostel this morning?"

"Who?"

"The vampire I *showed* you the holo picture of," Nico said, nearly snarling.

"Oh yeah-yeah. No."

"Are you sure? Will you check the sign-up sheet? Her name is E-S-C-H-E."

Paper rustled. "Nope. No Eshah. You're checking really early. She could walk in later."

"No one's claimed her Id, though, right?"

"Yeah-yeah. I mean no-no. It's still here."

"And you'll call me when Esche shows up, right?"

"I sure will Neko."

"*What* did you call me—" Nico's fangs emerged.

"Gotta go. Can I put you down for another night at Again

Friends?" Dann said pleasantly. "But I need your signature."

"Okay, sure," Nico said, and cut the connection.

She sat, grumpy, in one of the red vinyl seats of the spaceport's shoe shiner station, getting the scuffmarks expertly buffed from her oxfords. Travellers hurried by while Nico rested her feet in the iron footrests and the shiner worked.

"If you don't mind my sayin'," the shoe shiner said, dabbing polish. The strong, oily scent of blackening rose. "With your cute little fangs, you look like a *neko* to me."

"I'm a vampire, not a were-cat. I gave my name as 'Neekoh' and he calls me 'Nehkoh'. He's looking to get kicked." Nico made her vampire aspect recede.

"With these spikes?" the shoe shiner grinned, indicating the small spikes studding Nico's oxfords. "He won't make that mistake again."

While the shoe shiner buffed up the leather and then gave the studs attention, Nico summoned the cryptic gun link she'd set aside. She played the Slaughter Spawn holo footage. The recording had been taken in near darkness, the quality grainy and hard to see. But when the witch jumped into the pit and activated in midair, kinetic power warping reality around her, Nico witnessed the harnessed manifestation that was weird matter, detonating instantaneously within the spawn and bursting them apart. Slowing the footage revealed that the blinding fast shots of seeming nothingness exploded from the witch's warping body-field. Her gaze merely aimed and the shots spiralled from her, ploughing through spawn-matter. Each shot sent a lashing recoil behind the witch, impacting spawn behind her.

Her gun-self boomed. The pit's walls sprayed debris. The witch herself was the cryptic gun.

"So cool," Nico breathed.

"Like Hagler versus Hearns," the shoe shiner commented. "But one hundred times the crazy."

"She's so fast."

"She was a machine. No one knew she was coming to fight.

She had no second, nothing. She was Hagler the war machine, bringin' death poetry inside her. She out-deathed the spawn. That's how she did it."

Death poetry. Like the poem carved into her own skin.

"When was the Hagler-Hearns bout?"

"1985."

Nico made a note to view it later and then continued watching the match, reading the details that popped up. Shyla O'Fey, sister to Shayla and the vampire-witch the fight was credited to, cleared the pit of living spawn in three minutes, then entered the spawn's own tunnel, her shots exuding warping light. She emerged two minutes later and climbed out via a rope hanging down the side, the remaining spawn rushing for her. But they attacked too late; Shy gained the top, unscathed.

"Going into the spawn's tunnel was *suicide,*" the shoe shiner remarked. "Raised the odds nicely, though."

"Shyla O'Fey is one of five fighters to conclude Slaughter Spawn unharmed," Dorothy announced. "She is also one of two fighters to ever clear the pit and emerge before the six minute mark."

Nico replayed the footage that caught Shy's face briefly on camera as she departed from the pit area. Her horrified, frozen gaze held no victory.

"Her record has not been beaten," Dorothy said.

✶

"Shayla will be with you soon, honey, she has something to take care of out back," the robot hostess said to Nico above the diner's morning din. "Is she dressed pretty? Well, I'm not one for fibre clothing, but I don't think she wears that cotton fabricated dress of Pantone colour swatch 13-1020 TCX for just anyone."

Nico stood before the hostess's podium, hair freshly brushed and shoes gleaming. The thought of Shayla somewhere behind the diner made her recall the wolf gang that had stolen the ribs.

"Yeah, Shayla thinks they'll be back after spending the night in jail," the hostess said, reading more of Nico's thoughts. "First thing in the morning, once they're released. Why do you ask?"

Nico looked at her, then spun around and exited.

She sped around the diner and heard the approach of motorcycles. As she rounded the corner she saw the driver by his delivery van, the wolf gang barrelling for him. The old cook yelled at the scullery entrance. Shayla stepped past her and into the gang's path, her long skirt and hair catching wind. She turned to face them. Her bracing foot slid back just as Nico ran up from behind. The driver and cook scurried for cover.

Nico skidded, but the warping around Shayla's body had begun. Adrenalin pumped Nico into hyper-awareness. She watched in slowed time as a cryptic shot's recoil burst from Shayla's back and lashed. The oncoming blast pushed against Nico's teeth.

She collapsed backwards, the top of her head aiming for the ground, and felt the recoil's air displacement ripple across Bear and through her sternum, shaking it. The force clipped her chin.

Nico slammed into the ground and dimly heard motorcycles screech and crash. She made her head rise.

Shayla stood calmly, her warping burst having shoved the riders and their bikes aside, sprawling them. From the safety of cover, the cook and driver looked on.

"Turn yer bikes off, *now*," Shayla ordered. "Leroy, Séamas. *Stand* before me."

Nico tried to rise as the wolf boys obeyed Shayla. She promptly fell back again.

Need a moment, still rattled, she thought to Bear.

The weird matter disruption had not hit like a pulse blast's searing fist to the face. Instead, the recoil had punched past Nico, its accompanying shockwave then penetrating, exiting, and leaving her molecules shaken in its wake.

But even as Nico lay dazed, she analysed Shayla's cryptic gun blast and formed a mental diagram, that of a lightning fast corkscrew accompanied by a shockwave hard enough to shove oncoming bikes.

Leroy shambled forwards, suffering the effects of the shockwave's thrust against one side of his body. His bravado dissipated, he hung his shaggy head. Séamas glowered, but Shayla addressed them with authority.

"The Makepeace jailed ye fer brawlin'. When they released ye, ye tried tae celebrate with thievery. Dinnae justify or deny,"she added warningly when Séamas opened his mouth. "Are ye wolves, or are ye sly? Are ye hunters or *carrion* thieves?" Nico watched as even Séamas looked away. "Go earn yer licence to hunt, and then may yer mums and I respect ye!"

Shayla said no more, and the chastened wolves accepted that as their cue to leave her presence. They picked up their bikes in silence. But one who had stood by and dutifully taken the admonition then approached.

He was a well built young man with a scruffy chin and a forelock of red hair. He spoke low to Shayla, his attitude seemingly hopeful. He looked up from beneath his brows.

Shayla answered him, also low, and Nico was struck by the formality of the exchange, despite forelock boy's provocative gaze. He seemed to accept Shayla's answer with solemnity and returned to his motorcycle. The wolf boys turned their bikes around and roared off, Shayla watching them go.

Nico stood, unsteady, as the delivery man resumed his duties. When Shayla turned around, her eyes widened in alarm.

"Oh, lass, I dinnae ken yer presence!" Shayla quickly approached and held Nico by her arms. She searched Nico's eyes, as if to discern injury.

"You are 'To Sir, With Love'," Nico blurted.

"Niky, did my recoil hit yer head?" Shayla said, baffled. "Come into Lucy's and we'll put a cup of blood in ye."

"No-no, I'm okay," Nico assured. She was embarrassed to have been that shaken when she hadn't even been hit. Shayla turned to the watching cook.

"That's me, away now," Shayla bade.

"Thank you, Shayla. You have a good day." The cook turned for the scullery as Shayla returned her attention to Nico.

Nico sucked in breath and a very familiar chemical sensation touched her tongue. She then understood why the wolf boy had approached Shayla. The taste was of the heat and arousal signal from the surface of Shayla's skin, anticipating her moon cycle.

Nico's fangs emerged.

"Chick," Shayla said, both relieved and amused. "If ye can make such a face, then ye're okay."

Nico put her vampire aspect away and clasped her hands.

"I've a sudden need to get very Joycean with you," she said. "And then we can calmly go for a chat. Or, I mean, I can calmly go for a chat."

Shayla looked at her, wide-eyed.

"I'd really like to go down on you," Nico whispered.

She stilled, inwardly damning her concupiscence.

Shayla nodded.

A janitor's closet in the terminal; a utility sink. Nico topped the sink with its cover, lifted Shayla to sit atop, and placed Mr Bear where he could watch. Shayla's mouth sought hers, but Nico ran her own mouth along the soft skin of Shayla's jaw and up and down the muscles of her neck, her hands capturing Shayla's hair. And when Nico descended lower, Shayla was with her, flushed and fecund, her hands tangling in Nico's locks. Hot, hot quivering woman; Shayla's breath quickened and her grip tightened. Femoral blood thundered against Nico's pressed ears, and she buried her mouth, fingers, and mind, obliterating the memory of dead-eyed children with Shayla's cries.

When Nico stood once more, the sight of Shayla's satiated, roseate state was her second reward. Nico grinned, silly, and Shayla moved to kiss her.

Nico turned aside.

"Sorry," Nico said, contrite, but Shayla held her close, cheek to cheek, until Nico sighed. She breathed with Shayla, simulating heartbeat and blood flow, and Shayla pressed her lips to the corner of Nico's mouth, the contact long and loving.

"Thanks," Nico whispered.

After a sex encounter, Nico would usually extricate herself and disappear into the night. But once she and Shayla were back in the spaceport's terminal, Shayla kept her arm around Nico's shoulders, her manner languid, and Nico felt being thus embraced was the only place to be. Whenever she caught sight of her own reflection (and entirely mussed hair) in a shop's glass or in terminal windows, her double wore a goofy expression. Shayla glowed.

She is so rock star.

Don't get creepy, Nico then warned herself. Shayla did not mean more by her affection. It was merely appreciation, as one would express when very pleased with a puppy's trick.

Nico dismissed the hollow feeling the idea brought. Perhaps she'd invalidated her chances for being considered a person—a romantic interest—by acting the groupie. She thought of forelock boy.

"Did forelock boy proposition you?" she asked, curious.

"Forelock—? Oh, ye mean Aedan. Aye, he did. He wanted tae gie me sex. A giftie is how he meant, just as ye gi'ed tae me." Shayla sighed. "He was temptin'. But I know his mum." Her hand moved to the back of Nico's neck, and her thumb idly caressed.

"He wanted to gift you? Really?" Nico had no idea sex gifting was a thing on Darqueworld. It made her think of sacred sex worship, like for Astarte.

"I'm really glad I gifted you properly then," Nico said. "And that you chose me." She then grinned at a sudden thought. "This is another first for me. I usually give sex to women for something in return."

"Oh? Ye don't seem the devious sort, love. Dae ye mean a blood donation, now?"

"I love a woman's monthly donation," Nico whispered, and Shayla bit her lip, her gaze sparked with interest. But Shayla shuttered the reaction, and her hand fell away from Nico's neck.

"Chick," Shayla said. "I think ye had questions for me?" She then paused in their walk.

Something had caught Shayla's attention behind Nico, and Nico turned around.

A lobby's holo display played the news for waiting travellers. The dark figure of a slim girl in short skirt hurried across a parking lot before a boarded up ranch house. Mr Bear's shape against Nico's body was unmistakable.

Nico turned back.

"Now that we've seen the janitor's closet, why don't we find someplace bigger?" she quickly suggested. "For chatting." She took Shayla's arm and led her away.

*

The manicured john at the ranch house happened to be a high profile councillor of the city-state, and that breaking news played everywhere in the terminal.

Nico sat stiffly at a tiny bar table while Shayla sat across, watching yet another holo projection of the ranch house story over Nico's shoulder. The bar had been the nearest place Nico had hurried Shayla into, filled with weary travellers. Just as the server brought Shayla her orange juice and Nico an overpriced shot glass of blood, the morning program cut away to the ranch house news.

Shayla finally looked at her, and Nico stiffened more. Shayla's scrutiny expressed—in fleeting succession—disbelief, amusement, and then aroused curiosity.

"Can—can I say," Nico said. *Before I ruin things.* "As a girl to a girl? That your dress is really pretty. I love the eyelets, and the crochet pattern. And the scalloped edges. Is that Pantone colour 'apricot'?"

Shayla smiled.

"What would ye like tae talk about, Niky," Shayla said, her tone gentle.

Nico composed her thoughts, and Shayla drank her orange juice and waited.

"If I can understand how Darqueworld works—at least in some aspects," Nico began. "Then perhaps certain things will become clear to me. There's a mystery I hope you can explain, and it seems a very witch-like thing, this mystery."

"A mystery? There are many of those, love, and I'm not so wise as that."

"Heh." Nico thought of crones. Shayla was hardly that. "Well it's—like here we are, having travelled by conventional means. From Lucy's to this spot. Or, uh, from the janitor's closet to this spot. But when I first arrived on this planet and was in immigration...poof. I was moved around in places without my moving."

"Ah, veil work. That's pure magic."

"Do—do you mean magic, as in great? Or magic as in magic."

"Oh, as in great," Shayla said. "Pure quality—that's a belter, veil work, it's so subtle. When done well, it feels like no change at all."

"That's what it felt like," Nico said. "Was I passed around in dimensions? Or corridors?"

"It's dimensions, chick." Shayla smiled. She pondered a moment. "If ye don't mind makin' a wee excursion, I can show ye what I mean."

★

They left Jifk Spaceport by the Five, and with the news no longer present, Nico relaxed and chatted, while Shayla lounged and listened, her own body and attitude at ease. Nico did not talk of what happened that night, but of—

"Her name is Esche—it means Ash, for the ash tree," Nico said.

"My canvassing turned up nothing and I have no leads. But at least I've ruled out the hostel's surrounding streets."

"It was good of ye tae become her champion," Shayla said, her tone warm. Nico pulled out her Id and showed her Esche's holo photo.

"Oh, she's lovely." Shayla touched the projection.

"Hopefully she's safe somewhere, and I'm just being a paranoid goof. And when she finds out I made myself her champion, laughs at the idea, and then tells me to get lost?" Nico said. "It would be worth it. If someone had done the same for me—"

I would have wanted it. I would have wanted it so badly. Save me.

"I guess I wouldn't have minded," Nico said.

"Again Friends," Shayla mused. "I've not heard of them. Are they new?"

"Perhaps they are." Nico refrained from consulting Dorothy. "I'm sorry I didn't stay at the Y like you suggested. It was perfect. I love nice things and especially what tastes nice." Shayla smiled at her words. "But I didn't exactly arrive with a suitcase full of gold bullion," Nico added.

"Darqueworld values yer natural gifts," Shayla said. "Even more than how much ye can spend."

"I'm not sure I—" Nico thought of Esche's psionic scores and of the blinding flashes in the hologram room. "Or maybe I am good at something. At least they thought so. This may be the first countr—planet, I mean, that lets people in with their arsenal. But then I read that they had to because of the magic-wielders and psionics. Your weapon is *you*, isn't it?"

Shayla's mouth quirked, enigmatic.

Nico made a pistol with her hand. "Pow, pow." Shayla grabbed it and brought it down.

"Wissht," she admonished.

"Still," Nico said, as Shayla let go. "I could have been an awful person." *Like my maker.* "And I don't mean one with exceptional skills or knowledge that can make the under-holarchy look the other way. I mean a waste of space and DNA, murderous animal. I could be that."

"They'd have destroyed ye on entry if that were so," Shayla said casually.

"By just asking me if I was a mass murderer?" Nico said, incredulous.

"Ehm, no, there's a Po present when ye arrive. They're a telepathic race. Ye might've seen one; they appear as huge heads." She motioned around her own head.

"A *telepathic* head? Isn't that illegal?"

"I believe they've a sign up that telt ya. The telling is required by law." She squeezed Nico's arm. "The Po saw nothin' wrong with ye. Ye're okay."

"That's a matter of opinion," Nico murmured, but she smiled.

The train station let out on a business sector's street right before the building they intended to visit. Nico lost all idle speculation on whether she'd get an impression of being in some version of Manhattan, because it was nothing like Manhattan.

They exited into a great circle with an impressive central fountain, shooting high-reaching geysers. Buildings curved around the circular plaza, but it was the structure they were visiting that made Nico pause and stare up at what seemed an infinite, undulating glass edifice.

"Darqueworld's Immigration Centre, love," Shayla said, "one of three on this world." Organic steel blue framework formed a lattice and twined through the building of shining glass, reaching for the sky. Nico craned her neck and brought Bear up to look too.

"This is too beautiful for a governmental building," she softly exclaimed. It was a rocketing, beanstalk tower, and with its shooting fountains, perfectly phallic. "Heh," she added.

"Aye, and it's the tallest, for it must receive the sun, all around.

When ye take your citizenship's oath, Niky, it will be before the face of Merope and her witnesses."

"Face the sun without burning up?" Nico murmured. "That's too much to ask."

"Shall we, Niky?" Shayla asked, smiling.

"Yes," Nico answered, excited, and they climbed the great steps for the building's forecourt.

They did not enter the building, though Nico could peer past the entrance and into the busy lobby. Shayla led her around the building's forecourt and to the side. Ahead, a garden courtyard lay, cloaked in the building's shadow.

They entered the space. Again, beauty created by and for a governmental place impressed Nico; the design was of a Zen rock garden, with ordered and sculpted green growth, sand designs, and gravel paths. Even the noise of the city faded from her perceptions, muted by unseen means. A simple arch stood on one path, and it reminded Nico of the one she entered at the airfield. A plaque on a pedestal read:

> By our gift
> This temple given
> Enter
> And be lightened

The plaque was simply that, not even programmed to emit a holo message. Nico could see through the arch into the garden's other side. Shayla stopped before it.

"Here lies a veil," Shayla said. "One where you may enter a dimension, love. From one slice to another, then back again."

"Why aren't we all travelling like this?" Nico said. "Like Star Trek teleportation?"

"It's a secret used only by celestials and the under-holarchy, Niky, and even then, it's forbidden knowledge. Sacred."

"Don't tell me witches don't try it too," Nico said. "Nothing's sacred." She touched the arch itself.

"When some do, they act alone, and for purposes unkind," Shayla answered, solemn. "Wield veils, and ye can appear from any closet or beneath any bed. That's where nightmares come from."

Nico's fingers hovered before the arch's space. She slowly inserted them and watched her hand disappear. When she flexed her invisible fingers, she felt their presence within a warmer place, one of sunlight. But she could imagine her hand existing in a dimensional slice not so benign.

"I wouldn't feel the boogeyman coming," Nico said.

Die Albträume sind so schlimm, Esche had said.

Nightmares, Nico thought.

"Aye, and neither would I," Shayla said. "Ye enter the faerie realm in this manner. It's invisible travellin' within invisible places. Can ye see now how it's not weird work?"

"A little." Nico set aside thoughts of boogeymen and removed her hand. Her fingers remained whole. "I bet you'll say veil work is not sorcery, either. You have a way of narrowing witch stuff down to unbelievable things." She turned to Shayla and grinned.

"Unbelievable?" Shayla repeated, raising a brow.

"Ludicrous."

"Like turning ye into a kitten?"

Nico shut her mouth.

"Dinnae look so scared," Shayla said lightly. "I'm only teasin'."

"I'm certain you'd try it," Nico accused. "Just once."

"Only if ya'd let me." Shayla touched Nico's nose. Nico held it and grinned again. "Now, my brave Niky. Would ye like tae see what lies beyond?"

Nico nodded. "Yes. But me first. In case there are boogeymen." And Nico stepped through.

She stood on pale, veldt grass at the beginning of a labyrinth, the pattern laid on the ground with natural stones. The rich, primal scent of land, untouched by hands, brought her fangs to the fore. Shayla came beside her, and Nico looked at the bright, blue sky and warm sunlight. A butterfly fluttered by, and the wind tugged at her and Shayla's clothes and hair. Shayla lightly touched Nico's back, the gesture to soothe, and Nico put her vampire aspect away.

"The hidden kingdoms," Nico said softly. "Shouldn't a slice resemble the one we left?" Odd, twisted trees stood in the distance, and the rough grass rolled on into the horizon. She saw neither people nor animals, but at the outer perimeter of the labyrinth, metal discs lay embedded, similar to the ones used by 1634. Wherever she and Shayla were, it was intended to remain pristine.

"It does, love. This is the land before Again NewYork came to be," Shayla said. "It reminds us to honour what we've borrowed from this world. Would ye like to walk, Niky?"

Nico took a breath. A labyrinth was not simply a maze, but a tool for the soul.

"Because you're here with me...yes." Nico entered.

In 1986, Nico walked the labyrinth within Chartres cathedral, still healing from fresh stab wounds and the word "why" seemingly carved into her heart. When she reached the centre, she'd looked at the vaultings on high and thought: if martyred saints could stand such suffering, couldn't she?

Then Nico laughed, the sound rising and echoing, until the great house of God reverberated with her absurd lamentation.

Somehow she'd left despair in the middle of the labyrinth and emerged armed, if not with faith she could win against *him*, at least faith that she still had fight in her.

Nico followed the path while the breeze played with their clothes, Shayla following a short distance behind her. They walked to the inside, and then to the outer paths, and finally closer and closer to the centre, each step an unassuming meandering of the unsuspecting soul, oblivious to the key it might discover. Nico reached the centre and stepped inside.

In that moment, she knew an unburdening was possible, one released from her heart's box, a magician's dove flying. But Nico did not desire that knowledge from herself right then as much as she wanted it from someone else.

She watched Shayla enter the centre. When she looked at Nico, her regard held a depth Nico felt she could fall into. Nico held her hands out, and Shayla grasped them.

"I want to ask you something—something that may make you mad at me," Nico whispered.

"Ye're full of questions, aren't ya?" Shayla said, her tone low. "Might I ask a question or two of you, next time?"

"Yes," Nico. *Yes, to many next times.* She took a breath.

"You fought in Slaughter Spawn."

Shayla's eyes widened, then shielded, and her body seemed to draw away without moving. But she still held Nico's hands, and for that, Nico was grateful.

"I just...I saw it, and it was you," Nico said. "All the footage is misattributed. That's not your sister in the pit."

"How." Shayla briefly smiled but the expression didn't reach her eyes. "How dae ye know it's not Shy?"

"Your sister has no reason to be horrified," Nico whispered.

Shayla's gaze distanced; Nico held Shayla's warm hands tightly, wanting to will her pain away.

Perhaps I'm not so great at goodness. Perhaps I only understand what's sad.

She looked at Shayla. *But perhaps more, I want to know how a killer like you can remain good, when others choose to be so bad.*

"Shy was our most beloved," Shayla said, her tone soft. "The best of the wise kind. When she was taken and murdered, I gave more than eye for eye. I killed every vampire of the clan responsible.

"And I was the witch with the vampire lover. Shen Jin was new to Darqueworld. Ey was of no family or clan, and I trusted em; I trusted em to help me rescue Shy, and ey made Shy a vampire instead." Shayla looked at Nico, her gaze uncomprehending. "To save her life, ey said."

Make me like you, a dying girl had asked Nico. Nico had refused, and watched her die.

"When she rose," Shayla whispered.

When she rose, it was too late for you to kill her.

"I was the coven's pistol," Shayla said. "Their peacekeeper. I gave up the badge that day. And that night, while I was killin' vampires, Shy killed our coven."

Shayla's hands slackened within Nico's, and Nico understood: the stopping. It was the paralysis that came with horror given the soul. Herself, standing over the remains of dead parents until sunrise. Esche on her bed, uncomprehending. But Shayla had not remained paralysed after the coven's slaughter.

"I went into the pit tae see," Shayla said softly.

"See what?" Nico whispered.

"In there, ye can look upon the face of evil. After Shy died and rose a vampire, I needed tae know.

"If what I saw in her—in myself—was in the pit."

Shayla looked at Nico.

"That face is in their tunnel. Whenever ye wonder why I like ye, Niky, know that I don't see that face in you."

When she and Shayla exited the labyrinth, Nico felt words might tumble out, nonsensical and incoherent. Of deaths, words carved into flesh, and of a maker gone up in flames. But it was not her time for confession. There remained a blank in her mind, a hidden boogeyman, and a missing piece named Esche. The labyrinth hadn't the power to lighten the problems that hadn't yet been given their answers...or the deeds that would solve them.

Nico left the veldt with Shayla, and wondered.

Once in the Zen garden, Nico felt she should hug Shayla, especially after demanding so painful a confession from her, but she was still unused to such gestures. She paused, removed Bear from his harness, and offered him to Shayla instead.

Shayla put a hand to her mouth, her gaze mirthful, then took Nico and brought her firmly into a hug, Bear squished between them. The entire grandstand of Bears inside Nico did a somersault.

Shayla pulled back. "Come, Niky. I want tae gie ye something."

They entered the Immigration Centre's vast lobby and encountered no detectors or other security measures, reminding Nico again that she was no longer on Old Earth. Beings milled, the lobby floor exposed to the arcades above. Beneath a floating glass sculpture, a player sat at a grand piano, dressed in formal black despite the early hour. He played a familiar tune, the tinkling notes rising along with Nico and Shayla as they rode an escalator for above. He played Somewhere Over the Rainbow.

They gained the next storey with Nico belatedly noticing that her own crystal-clear reflection had been present in the mirrored wall behind her while she had watched the piano player below. Thankfully, she'd no time to be disturbed by her double. Shayla led her to the Centre's gift shop.

It was gaudily filled with Again NewYork souvenirs, complete with tee shirts and snow globes. But little bins in the back held one-inch buttons, and Shayla pointed to them.

"On Darqueworld, ye may come across our allegories," she said, "formed as idols and guardians: the goddess, the god, the fire, and the mystery. Which pin-back would ye like, Niky?"

Nico examined the buttons, intrigued. Though Shayla had said "god" and "goddess", both figures seemed of mixed gender. The black void of the mystery button drew her, its centre containing a dot of brightness that was either a star or an atom symbol.

"The mystery," Nico chose.

Outside the gift shop, Shayla pinned the button to Nico's cardigan front with as much gravity and grace as a knighting.

"Bless this one, named Nico," Shayla intoned, and completed the pinning. Nico beamed, feeling ready to take a sword to a dragon—or a very little dragon. Or to no dragon, as she doubted that Shayla would approve of dragon killing.

"Now I want to give you something," Nico said.

"Oh, but ya did already, didn't ya," Shayla said, and gave the front of Nico's cardigan a playful tweak.

"Heh," Nico said, as Shayla smoothed out her cardigan. Nico

grinned, goofy all over again. They crossed the floor and passed groups in business attire—or who had at least thrown on a suit jacket or clean, button-down shirt—waiting before a block of elevators. Some held Ids similar to Nico's, and looked at them.

"What is the highest court in Darqueworld?" one woman asked another, consulting her Id.

"The Supreme Tribunal," the second woman answered quickly, and Nico thought that if she'd had a buzzer to hit in order to answer the question, she would have struck it.

The citizenship exam. "Is it like this, every day?" Nico said as she and Shayla approached the escalator.

"I dinnae ken. Not all who arrive on Darqueworld stay," Shayla said. "I've seen many come tae Lucy's who go on tae the stars."

"The stars," Nico repeated, awed. "Have you ever gone—out there, to beyond?"

Shayla shook her head. "I followed my sister Shy from the Isle tae here. That's as far as I've come. My younger sister, Shane, enlisted, so she's servin' among the stars." Nico followed Shayla on to the downward escalator and took the step behind her.

Oh crap. Her doppelgänger stared at her from the escalator's mirrored wall, reaching for her own knife. It was either punch her double or—

Nico jumped the escalator's side and landed on the marble floor below. The clap of her shoes echoed, startling people.

When Shayla descended and reached her side, a security host had already approached Nico and was finishing a quiet conversation with her.

"Sorry," Nico said to Shayla when the host departed.

"Niky, who bothered ye?" Shayla asked, concerned.

Is this boy bothering ye, Nicky? her maker said.

"It was, um. It was me," Nico admitted. "My reflection. I have catoptrophobia. Does hypnotherapy really work?"

"Oh it does, they use the Po and psionic workers," Shayla said, "tae touch yer mind and lessen the feelings of pain and fear; the nature of bad recollections. Did yer reflection threaten ye?" she added in a gentle tone.

Nico exhaled. "Yes." She held Bear. "Every time I see her, I think I'm looking at the true Nico...my maker's Nico."

"That's not a good thing, then?" Shayla asked.

"No. I don't think she's a very nice Nico."

And she's going to catch up to me.

✶

Shayla wanted to ask. Nico could see it, but Shayla refrained long enough for Nico to start walking, unprepared to say more. She didn't want to ruin their time together with horrifying, vampire childhood tales. They exited the lobby for the forecourt and descended the front steps. But when they reached the final landing before the walk, Shayla moved across to the sweeping, latticed balustrade, bringing Nico with her. The balustrade curved with the landing to form a little lookout point, and Shayla stood, back against the railing, putting Nico before her.

"Ye're a girl of mysteries, aren't cha?" Shayla said to her, soft. "When ye're ready, ye can share with me, Niky."

Ye can share with me Nicky, her maker said.

Nico looked at her, wide-eyed.

"But we're still not dating," she clarified.

Shayla smiled.

Then Nico smelled—

Chasse Geraud Soeurs.

Nico glanced up and saw Heloise on the steps above, a cigarette at her pursed lips and the pack in her hands. Sharp brow raised, she seemed as surprised to see Nico as Nico was to see her. Nico quickly averted her gaze, but not before Shayla looked up too, curious.

Shayla brought her arm up to rest around Nico's shoulders.

Heloise's descending high heels laconically sounded on the concrete steps. She passed near enough for Nico to catch the peeking bright red, satin lining within the other vampire's black suit jacket. Heloise stopped beside Nico and Shayla and brought her cigarette down from her lips.

"Got a light?" she asked Shayla, and put the cigarette to her smirking mouth again.

Shayla kept her arm around Nico and raised the other, gesturing with two fingers—*come*—and Heloise obligingly leaned forwards. Shayla touched the side of Heloise's cigarette with the same two fingers, and both she and Heloise stilled. The cigarette's end ignited.

"Oh," Nico breathed. Heloise sucked, the end burning red. She moved back, removed the cigarette from her lips, and exhaled to the side.

"Thanks," Heloise said, her smile sardonic. She turned and continued across the landing and down the steps, the deep Bulgarian rose of her outsoles flashing behind black stiletto heels.

"Ah, such legs," Shayla whispered in Nico's ear. "That yer Countess Bathory, then?"

"Um." Nico hoped Heloise didn't eavesdrop with her vampire's hearing. Heloise finished her descent to the walk, a hand flicking back her jacket end and coming to rest on her hip. She stood with chin raised, and brought her hand with the cigarette down. She ejected a stream of smoke from her lips. Her sharp gaze, resting on nothing in particular, caused a young man to trip down the stairs. Heloise flicked her cigarette.

"Show off," Nico muttered, and Shayla laughed, low in her throat, and hugged Nico to her.

✴

The underground station was so conveniently near, and Nico wished it conveniently far. Shayla had the evening shift at Lucy's and needed her sleep. They stood outside the entrance leading down.

"Thank you for spending time with me," Nico said, "and for tolerating the questions I asked."

Shayla shook her head. "As long as what I'd telt ye helps, Niky, that's what matters. And it helped me too. I don't often get tae share about the pit."

"You are so beautiful today," Nico blurted. "You're beautiful everyday."

"Thank ye." Shayla smiled.

"I should have said that at the beginning, but I got carried away. We're still not dating, are we?"

"No, love. We're not." Shayla's eyes sparkled with mirth.

"Okay, good, because I don't want to get creepy. I hope I can gift you lots and lots of sex. It's nearly your time of month." She clapped a hand over her mouth and Shayla laughed.

"I should've known ya'd be a womb lover. Ah love, that's me, I must away," she said, wistful. She leaned to give Nico a kiss.

Nico leaned as well, her hand coming up to lay on Shayla's arm. She air kissed next to Shayla's right cheek, and then to her left.

When Nico straightened, Shayla looked at her with surprise.

"Oh. In Again NewYork, is the air kiss for four times?" Nico asked.

Shayla smiled, lightsome. She raised her hand and her thumb touched Nico's lower lip.

It was a light caress, the softest brush. Then Shayla withdrew. She turned and descended.

Nico touched her mouth. "Ohhh," she said to Bear.

Nico circled the shooting fountain and processed a similar circling within, of joy, then despair (as she already missed Shayla) back to joy again, then frustration (she really hated being poor and unable to afford fancy outings). But then she thought about giving Shayla lots of sex and was elated once more. At some point too, she would learn to welcome kissing on the mouth again. She sent Shayla a message .

Thank you for a wonderful time. Can I see you again?

She circled the fountain more, hoping the message hadn't been a mistake. Her Id chimed and Nico looked at it eagerly.

The morra? My shift's not known yet.

Aye. Yes. Yes.

Magic.

"She's pure magic," Nico said to Bear, and hugged him. Then she fetched her sound-buds and put them in.

Dorothy, play me This Corrosion, *the long version*, she typed. She wandered out of the plaza, curious to see if, like the old Manhattan, she might come across Tiffany's. She also decided to look up Shen Jin. She was certain thon was the vampire following Shayla around three years ago.

When she activated the most prominent link, it brought Shen's battered face and body to the fore.

It took Nico a moment to realise that she was looking at cryptic gun damage. A holo video played, running the words: When HATE is a crime. Fight sanguivoriphobia.

She watched the Vampire Alliance Network's video as it listed Shen's injuries and shared the long-term effects of weird matter disruption on a vampire's regenerative ability. They showed a photo of Shen before ey was harmed, a beautiful youth with a soulful gaze and wispy beard. The accompanying photo Vampire Alliance chose of Shayla looked cold and cruel. Nico cut away to search for recent photos of Shen. Ey and Shy had a gang in Shayla's sector, and judging by the recent news, they were quite active. Shen looked fully recovered, despite facial scarring.

Nico increased the sound level on her music and walked on, her repulsion at the sight of Shen's injuries giving way to another feeling as she thought of Shayla in the slaughter pit.

Death machine.

Nico's own death spirit rose and responded. Shen shouldn't have made Shayla's sister a vampire.

Nico's fangs elongated, remembering a maker killing her beneath moonlight.

*

While reading further about Shen, Nico found herself in another plaza, one Dorothy identified as having a landmark sculptural fountain. But the fountain was more unattractive than any Nico had ever seen, even more than the one in San Francisco's Embarcadero. A huge tangle of serpentine forms, it reared two storeys high in a great shallow pool. The sculpture's viperine ends formed torrential spouts, sitting low or high, spewing up or vigorously vomiting down. The air was filled with the sound of fresh, flowing roaring water. Nico thought the fountain might be an orgiastic Hydra, playing Twister with itself.

She put her Id away and walked around the fountain while office workers and visitors lounged in the surrounding eateries, and thought about carrying a brolly, because an open plaza held few shadows. She considered having one with a hidden sword like Mr Steed's. Children ran, and she ambled over to a small group of street vendors with display tables and opened blankets, hawking cheap jewellery and Again NewYork souvenirs. Vampires stood by a little table, pocket booklets in hand. An Id sat on the tabletop, projecting a holo donation jar, and more booklets plus snack blood packets were laid out for sale. Nico looked at the eclectic vampire bunch in curiosity. One male in a shabby coat smiled and handed her a little booklet. Nico accepted and looked at the cover.

The title said: *This Was Your Life, Again Walker!*

"Oh no, a Zick tract?" Nico exclaimed. If she still had a comic book box, she'd file the awful evangelical booklet away for the sake of novelty. When she flipped it open, it was indeed a black and white inked comic strip, very much in the style of Jake T Zick. A quick peek near the end showed the protagonist, a risen vampire, being held in account before the celestials of Darqueworld — who were drawn suspiciously like the angelic host. Nico looked at the cover once more.

"Again Walker," she said, recalling paperback girl's pacifist, non-biting friends.

"That's you, sister," the vampire said, grinning happily. He held out his hand for her to shake.

"Don't touch me," Nico said, and walked to the pool's edge. Vampires had entered it, splashing, and were wading to the fountain sculpture. Nico tucked the tract behind Bear and stood by a lanky African woman in tank top, bright wrap, and culottes, her natural hair tied back with a scarf. Her hands and feet were hennaed with Senegalese patterns, and Nico admired her dangling earrings. She wondered if the woman was a magic wielder; along with her necklaces and bracelets, she wore amulets and white *sai sins*. Then Nico looked to where the woman watched the wading vampires. One male with sideburns wore nineteenth century uniform trousers and a torn shirt. He and another male went to stand under fountain spouts, the water pounding on their heads, and raised their hands.

"What are they doing?" Nico asked.

"A purification," the woman said. "A renewal. You might call it baptism."

"*Teh*," Nico exhaled in humour. "Vampires getting baptised."

A vampire girl backed into a pouring spout and stood beneath, palms offered up. As the water inundated her, she shook like one sobbing, and vampires came by her sides to steady her. A fervour seemed to rise from them, the ecstasy of praise to the invisible. Nico glanced up, wondering if any gods might show.

"This New York," she said, "the spiritual intensity. Sometimes it's like Jerusalem or something."

"Jerusalem," the woman mused.

"The one god's holy city," Nico said, thinking that like Shayla, the woman might be native to Darqueworld. "Or, at least holy to his followers." The woman looked at her and smiled.

"No one city on Darqueworld is holy. All is sacred," she said.

"Even what's evil?" Nico said, sharp. The woman grew grave, then returned her attention to the ecstatic vampires.

"We can't recognise good without it," she said.

★

Nico never had patience with the holistic or spiritual, though Shayla's embodiment of such drew her like an unerring arrow, and perhaps it had to do with Shayla's amity coming from a place of loss and pain, which Nico understood. Shayla was a counterweight Nico could bear. But peace, love, beauty, acceptance; those qualities had a hard time seeding in Nico's darkness. Her intellect would water beauty down to mere aesthetics, its controllable aspects, when it wasn't meant for such confines but to suffuse, like the water pouring down on born-again vampires. Beauty had the power to prompt a heart's expansion. Nico didn't like that. An expansion meant love, which was a frightening concept when it had been killed in her and outside of her, repeatedly. Mr Bear was easier to love.

Her Id sounded, and Nico looked at it. It wasn't Shayla.

Behind you, the message said.

Nico turned around. At the plaza's end, by the kerb, Heloise's shapely legs rested outside the door of her Faering, crossed at the knee.

The lure of her outsoles' deep red reeled Nico in from across the plaza. She walked towards Heloise — who grinned — and Nico pretended she didn't want to stare more at the older vampire's shoes. Or ask if she could play in Heloise's closet.

Nico came to a stop before the vehicle and pulled the booklet from behind Bear.

"Would you like a copy of the Watchtower?" Nico said, handing it to Heloise. Heloise looked at it, rolled her eyes, and tossed the tract into the seat behind her.

"If you're stalking me, you're really bad at it," Nico added.

"I'm not stalking you." Heloise opened her hands. "Do you see me offering you candy?" Nico noticed something on one of Heloise's wrists. Red, blessed string bracelets peeped out beneath her sleeve's cuff. Heloise dropped her hands.

"I saw the news this morning," Heloise said. "That's the second trafficking operation in Again NewYork you've destroyed."

"Why do you think it's me?"

"Because it's your modus operandi," Heloise said, and Nico's interest piqued.

"I was just looking for something," Nico said.

"And you probably won't stop until you find it." Heloise's tone was wry. "Don't you sleep?"

"I don't like the hostel I'm staying at. It's creepy."

"Oh? And where's that?"

"You are a really bad stalker," Nico said.

Heloise smiled. "Let me treat you and Mr Bear to something from the hotdog stand."

★

Whenever a Bathory cajoled, Nico would walk away. She capitulated to Heloise, however, because she was curious as to what the vampire wanted. Heloise went in search of blood, striding purposefully amongst chess-playing elderly and lunching office workers dribbling shredded lettuce on themselves, while Nico sat at a Sushi Hut's patio table and waited. All the Again Walkers had emerged from beneath the fountain spouts and lingered by the pool, dripping and embracing. Nico wondered how long they'd be able to hold on to their peace and ecstasy. The regular world would still assail tomorrow.

"Faith helps, I guess," she said to Bear. Heloise returned from the Again Walker's little table of goods and gave Nico a scrutinising look.

"Are you heliophobic?" she asked. "Because we can—"

"No." Nico stilled her nervous knee. "You watch too many commercials. And did you buy blood from the religious cult?" she exclaimed. "It might be drugged."

"The way your mind works," Heloise retorted. She stuck a straw into one snack bag and handed it to her. Nico noticed Heloise's nail colour; a deep, tasty maroon that matched her tie. The straw was in Nico's mouth before she thought about it and she sucked. The blood tasted like a decent grade of simulated, warmed by the sun. Heloise then offered Mr Bear a Zick tract, one titled: *Birds and the Bees for Again Walkers*. Nico made a sound of amusement.

"I can't believe this," she said, and opened the tract and laid it flat for Bear to peruse.

She and Heloise sat and sucked on the straws of their snack bags, watching and listening to the fountain water's roar. Just when the sun's continued warmth began to make Nico nervous again, Heloise removed her sunglasses and raised her face, eyes closed. The golden heart that was the floral and woodsy sensual centre of *Chasse* Geraud Soeurs finally opened on her skin, warmed into being not by an undead body but by the sun, and Nico refrained from scooting nearer to sniff more. But she looked at Heloise's pallor, concealed by make-up, and thought direct sunlight made the aspect of death brutally clear. Heloise sighed and folded her sunglasses.

"That was a pretty young lady you were with earlier," she remarked. "Weren't you stalking her yesterday?"

Nico was about to retort when Heloise added, "Darqueworld makes it easier to be with them, doesn't it."

It does. Nico had been feeling very grateful about that. And right then, they were two vampires safely toasting themselves in the sun thanks to such a world.

"She's quite a witch," Heloise said. "It takes fine control to light a cigarette—and not have it blow up in a person's face. What's her name?"

Nico glared. She was quite certain Heloise had already found out Shayla's full name. Heloise grinned back.

"They're interesting, the witches here," she continued. "They have a quality about them I haven't seen since the seventies: unconditional faith in change. Faith in evil creatures like us," she added with an arched brow. She sucked on her straw.

"Does it bother you, my seeing a witch?" Nico said, curious. She didn't know how vampires felt about romancing "food."

"No." Heloise smiled, and Nico looked at her beautiful teeth again, wondering when she would get to see Heloise's fangs. "She's human, and you're a vampire, and that's all there is to it. How does Mr Bear like his comic?"

"It's bloody awful. And I think it's time you stopped flirting with me and told me what you wanted."

"I'm not flirting with you. This is small talk. Are you still having memory loss?"

"Yes."

"Then maybe this will help. Back on Old Earth, I ran a global vampire database. I tapped a network of hobbyist observers — like bird watchers, except they watched vampires. They wrote down everything: names, appearances, activities, movements. If a vampire appeared in Paris and the next week, popped up in Mozambique, an observer in either city would record it. I'd gather the rest of the background info, like historical data, photos, painted portraits, passport pictures. Vampires who thought they were completely undetected were recorded."

"You're a blackmailer?" Nico said, incredulous. Heloise gave her a tolerant look.

"I controlled information," she clarified.

"Exactly. Bye, blackmailer." Nico rose to leave.

"I can show you what you were up to in 1998."

Nico paused.

"Interested?" Heloise's tone held a smile. Nico turned back.

"How far into the future are you from my 1998?"

"Twenty-two years." Heloise cocked her head, her regard falling to Bear. "I never saw another vampire like you again. You were unique."

Nico made a sound of humour. "Say that last part again, but deeper." Heloise raised a surprised brow.

"You were unique," Heloise repeated, bemused, but she'd deepened her voice as requested. Nico made a mental note to find *Star Trek: Voyager* episodes on her Id. She'd really enjoyed watching the new female Borg character.

"So, this database," Nico said. "You carried it with you—when you were pushed through by the weird matter engine."

Heloise gave a rueful exhale. "Those corridor demons. One trip with them was enough for me. Yes, the database came over with me, but having it didn't speed me through immigration. I was in holding for *days*. Thank the gods someone had playing cards."

"So you and your fellow refugees didn't get processed through veils."

"Veils?"

"I want to see my data," Nico said, "but I'm not giving you any sex."

"I didn't ask." Heloise's tone was mild.

Nico gave her a look, and Heloise smiled, her straw pressed against her lower lip. The straw bore the bright imprint of lipstick.

"I like women who menstruate," Nico said. "Did your bird watchers observe that?"

"No. But I'll certainly enter that observation now."

Nico pulled out her Id.

"A time and place, please," Nico requested.

*

Heloise had another appointment to attend to, but she had time to meet Nico later—at her apartment.

"The database has been secured, so you'll have to go to it, I can't bring it to you. I could acquire a chaperone for you, if that'll make you feel safer?" Heloise's tone was wry as she and Nico walked across the plaza. Heloise put on her sunglasses.

"Can my chaperone be the Princess of Wales?"

When Heloise paused, as if searching for what to say, Nico realised why she hadn't taken the request as a joke.

"It's okay. I know she died," Nico said. "It was in 1997. I liked her a lot."

Nico left the plaza when Heloise did, zooming away in her Faering. Until her appointment with Heloise, she had something else needing her attention. Her time enjoying her good feelings was done. The thought she'd put on hold when Shayla had explained veils returned.

First Esche, then Tex and Delores; maybe Eton boy. She knew what her maker would say. She knew what was right in front of her face.

It dead ends right there, at Again Friends. No other trails to follow.

"I shouldn't have discounted Iris," she admitted to Bear.

Especially when the same dismissive attitude had been given herself when she had been alive, trying to make people believe that the charming young Scotsman pretending to be her boyfriend was really her stalker.

Nico rode the Five back to the hostel area and stared at the muted Nico in the window reflection.

"Boogeymen," she said.

She typed a request in Dorothy to suggest the strongest, over-the-counter stimulant available that she could purchase.

She was leaving a chemist located near puke street when she glanced down the cross street. Re'shawn leaned towards the window of a long-bodied, black vehicle, talking to someone inside. She did not look happy, and the vehicle's window rolled up, apparently concluding the conversation. The vehicle then sped away, and Re'shawn looked over at Nico.

"I haven't seen you at the hostel," Nico said as Re'shawn strolled towards her.

"I haven't seen you at the hostel either, cupcake," Re'shawn retorted. She activated her Id, showing Nico a news holo of the ranch house bust. "Was that you?"

"One of those traffickers shouldn't have touched Bear," Nico said.

"That is one cool bear, that is one *crazy* cool bear," Re'shawn said.

"Mr Bear says 'thank you'." Nico adjusted him and smiled. "Did you call me cupcake?"

"Yeah, because you're smaller than a cake." Re'shawn began walking in the hostel's direction, and Nico kept pace beside her. She pulled out her Id and showed Re'shawn Esche's holo-picture.

"Is that the potential girlfriend? No wonder you're obsessed. Naw, I'm sorry, I haven't seen her."

"It's okay." Nico put her Id away. "What are you up to?" She retrieved her energy stimulant purchase, pUff, from her chemist bag and tucked it behind Bear. She tossed the bag into a trash receptacle.

"Employment. Though my social worker told me about them off-world labour camps, so I'm being extra careful. Figures that you can't come to a new planet without another race enslaving you — again."

"Are you interested in construction or engineering?" Nico asked. "Because at Second Memphis, the present dynasty's building another pyramid."

Re'shawn guffawed. "I saw that ad. But they pay half their wages in beer." She paused before a Help Wanted sign in a coffee shop window. Beneath it said: No Vampires Wanted.

"I thought I left that crap behind, sixty years ago. If I could cuss right now," Re'shawn said.

Nico looked at Re'shawn with humour, wondering what was preventing her, and Re'shawn pointed skyward.

"Back when I was alive, I sang in church every Sunday. Seeing as cussing *can* make stuff reality here, I'll respect whoever's watching over this world."

Hm. Nico wondered if Re'shawn missed the prospect of heaven.

"Do you like being a vampire?" Nico asked.

Re'shawn stopped walking and reached into her back pocket. She pulled out a worn leather wallet and opened it. A small black and white photo sat in the battered insert, of a serious-looking Re'shawn in an A-line mini dress, her hair an afro, while the lean man next to her looked at the camera, trilby tipped back on his head. Re'shawn's hand rested on the head of a little boy with fists pressed to his mouth. They stood outdoors on grass, as if at a picnic, but someone in the background held placards on sticks: a preparation for protest.

"Your name's not Re'shawn," Nico lightly accused. "I love your cat eye frames."

"Naw, I took that name during the seventies. 'Harriet' wasn't cutting it anymore, though Mama named me that for Harriet Tubman. Harriet was dead, anyways. I liked those glasses too, but we don't need stuff like that once we're vampires." Re'shawn put the wallet away. "I'll tell you something; I rose, and I couldn't be there for my man and my baby anymore, but I could kick ass. I could kill ass. My mama wouldn't have been happy if she'd known, and my man would've been really unhappy. He was a pacifist; followed Reverend King and everything. But my boy grew up okay, I made sure. I decided to come here after he passed away. He had grandkids, but it was time I moved on."

"So you like being a vampire," Nico said.

"Yeah, I like being a vampire," Re'shawn said.

✷

Re'shawn and Nico entered Again Friends after Dann activated the door for them, Re'shawn going first. She continued down the hall while Nico stopped before Dann's booth. A sign at his window read: Please Don't Break The Windows.

"Do you know who's breaking our windows?" Dann asked.

"They must have thought there was a fire," Nico said. "You were lucky there wasn't one. Why is the vending machine always empty? There's nothing to eat all day. Except maybe you."

"Machine's broken. I keep calling to get it fixed," Dann said. "It's why the hostel provides free blood. That way, you guys don't eat me. Neat, huh?"

Nico activated her Id, displaying Esche's holo-photo.

"Before you ask," Dann said. "Nope." He pushed the sign-up sheet to her. "Asha, right?"

"No, Esh—never mind." Nico looked at the sheet and saw Iris's and Re'shawn's signatures, but no Esche. Tex and Delores's names were not present either.

"If you want to stay tonight, you gotta sign," Dann said, cheerful.

"Have you seen Iris? She's been here a couple of nights. Girl with purple hair?"

"You mean here right now?" Dann considered the question. "Um...she was here yesterday?"

"How can you not remember?" Nico exclaimed.

"I'm a non-discriminatory head counter," Dann said defensively. "Purple, red, orange. You're all the same to me."

"That sounds like, 'you're all the same nothing to me'. But you remember me," Nico said.

"Well, you keep talking to me. Not that I don't mind it. You're not my type, by the way."

"You are *really* lucky you're inside that booth," Nico said, and left.

She went upstairs and viewed the girls' dorm; no vampires loitered, and no Iris either. Pestering Dann about Esche had been a matter of rote. She knew her missing vampire wasn't coming back, despite the tiny hope that held out for impossibilities.

She walked the length of the dorm, feeling nothing out of the ordinary; it had normal walls, floors, and beds. She threw her shoe at the ceiling and nothing budged. She tossed one bed, revealing its wire frame, then put the bed (more or less) back together again. The dorm was a solid cell to take refuge in, a perfect Anne Frank hideaway. Except someone had betrayed Anne Frank.

Dorothy, who owns Again Friends Youth Hostel? Nico typed.

Charity Housing is the parent, non-profit organisation running Again Friends hostels in four different city-states: Again NewYork, Sister Orleans, Tokyo2, and New London, Dorothy responded.

Nico cut the YOBA commercial before it started playing.

"But who really runs *this* hostel," she murmured to Bear. She went downstairs to the boys' bathroom.

Nico was standing on the boys' bathroom sink counter, inspecting the metal sealed window when a boy walked in, smelling of beer.

"I gotta get used to the she-boys on this planet!" he exclaimed.

"Hey! Don't call me that. Use non-gendered terms," Nico barked.

"Oh. Sorry. If you're dressed like a girl, shouldn't you be in the girls' bathroom?"

Nico hopped down and pulled out her Id. She showed him the holo picture of Esche.

"No, I haven't seen her," the boy said in answer to her question. "Or him? He's pretty. Look, I gotta pee."

"If you didn't drink, you wouldn't have to pee." Nico left the boys' bathroom.

On the ground floor, she studied the seam of the locked classroom door facing the empty vending machine. The door possessed a standard doorknob and lock, unlike the rec room's automated door. Just as she was about to pull out her wallet for her remaining credit card, a click sounded in the main hallway; a door shutting. Nico looked around the corner and Jess stood in the hall with her back towards Nico, inspecting her hand.

Where did she come from?

"Have you seen Re'shawn?" Nico asked.

Jess spun around, startled. "Pardon?"

Nico's Id chimed.

"Your appointment with Ms Allen is in one hour," Dorothy's muffled voice announced from behind Bear.

"Is she the girl you were looking for, yesterday?" Jess enquired.

"Never mind," Nico said. It would take more than half her allocated time to reach Heloise's place, but Nico wanted to get ahead of rush hour.

As she moved for the entry hallway, she had the odd feeling she shouldn't leave yet, but she felt as odd lingering, with nothing left that she could think to do — especially with Jess around. Dann's booth stood empty, a little sign taped within the cage saying: Be Right Back.

Nico exited Again Friends, the door sealing shut behind her.

CHAPTER ELEVEN

Nico stood on a shining light bridge of blue-silver and looked down at Again NewYork's lower depths. Humans, Others, and vehicles milled on the byways clogged with rush hour traffic below, streaked by sunlight and shadows. The sedate upper quarter she was presently in held more calm, and the people who moved in it more confidence, as if they'd all the time in the world to merely live. The plaza was Again NewYork's version of Avenue Montaigne, with more exclusive, off-world offerings. The curvy, high-rise structures of pliable glass and metal around the shopping plaza swept up to the clouds, their sinuous frames braced by steel membranes. Nico wondered if the rooms and hallways within were also constructed unconventionally, like the organic depths of a giant–specifically, a female giant. One building's entrance had the unmistakable shape of a metallic vagina, à la H R Giger. She looked at the surrounding plaza's glowing, high fashion shop portals, embedded in the flowing thighs of the colossus, and briefly contemplated the nature of arousal and the allure of money.

The shoppers and visitors promenaded by on the bridge, and Nico stood back, hugging Bear to her, and people-watched.

Intriguingly impractical clothing, ethereal scents, biomechanical enhancements, and fashionable gaits and mannerisms—there, a long-limbed, bird-like woman with head plumes moved with a mincing stride. But was she really of the bird people, like the Royal Bento off-worlder, or an altered human affecting their genetic attributes, courtesy of Avatar? Her facial features appeared highly human. The woman bobbed her head Nico's way and stared with yellow, bird eyes. Other humans passed and Nico thought: new-rich, addict, trophy, con man. Hedonist, glutton, spoiled brat, rapist.

It was unfair of her to assume the sharply dressed politician/fascist/businesswoman crossing the bridge—a woman with impossible, cornflower blue eyes and a cruel, red mouth—might buy girls for that purpose, but Nico had run into a few humans like her.

The woman walked by Nico as if she were nothing, but passed near enough for Nico to perceive her blood's pulsation and something else: the pristine, perfect scent that Nico associated only with vampires.

How odd.

Iris's "living vampires" came to mind, but Nico knew human blood when she sensed it. The woman was neither preternatural nor "extra". The woman paused at the bridge's end, summoned a holo interface via the two Id rings she wore, and gestured behind its privacy screen. Intuition rang Nico's tiny alarm bell and she constructed a scenario: the Bathory was calling security, and once they arrived and started pressuring Nico, the Bathory would step in, rescue Nico, and offer a meal, a ride home, perhaps request Nico's help with something. That was when a girl like Nico blacked out.

The woman dallied beyond the bridge after sending her communication. Nico thought about being entirely wrong.

Never ignore it, Nicky, her maker whispered, *that's how I got ye.*

She stepped into a gaggle of strolling tourists and slipped away, rounding a store's corner while the woman's back was turned.

Nico watched as two security personnel approached the bridge and looked around. The woman looked about the plaza as well, then left.

*

Heloise's address was a few buildings away from the plaza. Nico beamed the invitation on her Id to the shut doors of the address in question and it admitted her. It was a conventional marble lobby compared to the plaza's undulating steel. When Nico walked to the back and entered the waiting elevator platform, she saw that the entire ascension tube was of glass, overlooking Again NewYork's tinier buildings as they stretched to the harbour. Nico looked to the horizon while her platform rose.

That high above, Nico was a bird flying forwards to forever. Beyond was the shining edge of a sparkling sea, folding over the lip of a seemingly flat world. By all appearances, it was a short boat ride to falling off that edge. Nico had stood in Tokyo Tower's observation deck and thought the same when viewing the Pacific, except then she had looked out at a world dropping off into night.

"It's the edge of the world, Mr Bear, and beneath, it's turtles all the way down." The platform stopped on Heloise's floor, and Nico posed Bear on the handrail. She took pictures of him at world's end.

Photo-op done, she stepped out into a circular mini-lobby with four doors leading to private living quarters. Scenic glass on the elevator's side showed the spectacular view. Nico approached the third door and looked at the lit panel she assumed was a chime. Before she could poke it, the door slid open and revealed Heloise, smiling. Her jacket and shoes were doffed, and her tie pulled from the knot. The tie's ends draped against the white of her silk shirt, where undone buttons exposed a clavicle.

"Come in," she invited, and stepped aside for Nico to enter.

The interior was cool, soft whiteness, from carpet to walls. Blue light ran along the room's edges. Heloise raised a hand to the small of Nico's back to guide her in.

"Don't touch me, please," Nico said, stepping across the entryway.

"Sure," Heloise said, her hand dropping to her side. The doors slid shut. "Would you and Mr Bear like something to drink?"

"No thank you," Nico said politely. She walked down into the sunken living area and her shoes sank into the carpet. Heloise's Loulain heels lay fallen on their sides before the white couch, the outsoles like two dark bloodstains in the carpet. Nico wondered if her own oxfords were leaving footprints.

"It won't be drugged." Heloise's tone was light.

"Still 'no thank you'."

Nico stepped further into the living area and looked at the black baby grand piano, incongruous in the room's streamlined smoothness. The handwritten sheet music, with its many creases from having been folded down into a tiny package, read: *Somewhen, music by Leopold Bergstein, adapted by H Allen.*

"All right. Then I hope you don't mind if I finish mine." Heloise went over to the low glass table before the couch and picked up a cocktail glass. The liquid was golden orange.

"A Sidecar," she said at Nico's curious stare, and sipped. She smiled. "I can make you a virgin one."

Nico headed for the doors.

"Okay, fine," Heloise said, raising a hand. "No more small talk. My interface is over here."

Nico stepped back into the living area and followed Heloise to a glass seat and tabletop. Heloise touched the table surface. Nico noticed the strands of blessed red string on Heloise's wrist again, peeping from beneath her shirt's cuff; Tibetan *sai sin*. A keyboard appeared, made of blue light, and a holo logo materialised above the table: AGAIN WALKER.

"That's the name of your database?" Nico said, incredulous.

"I didn't know the Darqueworld born-agains had co-opted the term," Heloise grumbled. "I should have trademarked it."

"I want to see me," Nico said, "before I died." She sat and

touched the light keyboard, making it brighter.

Heloise nodded slowly. "Okay. Those photos are there."

Nico quickly tapped in *Heloise Allen.*

"Hey," Heloise said, but Nico was already perusing the items that appeared. She selected a photograph and it came to the fore.

"I bet you made a mean pineapple upside-down cake," she commented, staring at Heloise in a black and white photo. The young housewife in the buttoned up, three-quarter sleeved circle dress, pearl necklace, and white gloves smiled timidly as she posed before a 1950's Lincoln Capri, holding her handbag before her. A new tract home stood behind the wife and auto, a perfect photo of a man's three possessions.

"My signature dessert was devil's food cake, actually," Heloise said.

Nico advanced to the next photo, a black and white studio portrait of a male who might have been Heloise's Mr Allen. Nico didn't think his eyes were friendly, despite his overall mild, Midwestern handsomeness.

"Okay, that's enough." Heloise reached around Nico to touch the keyboard. The photo blipped out.

"Did they ask you at immigration if you liked being a vampire?" Nico said.

"They did, and I said yes." Heloise touched the keys more. "Here's you." Folder options opened on the holo display for the entry, *Nicolette Alexikova (also 'Nike').* Three photos were marked 1983. Nico knew what they were. She selected them to look.

She was seated on the carpet by the white-curtained window at home, lit by the soft spring sun, because dad had wanted something casual of her as a birthday portrait, and the photographer had accommodated. Nico wore a long black jumper over a black top, and a long black wool skirt, her legs gathered under her. She rested on a hand, the other in her lap, and against her jumper front an aquamarine birthstone glimmered. It was the necklace mom had given her, a gift for Nico's eighteenth birthday. The Nico in the picture gently smiled, gracing the camera with an expectant, hopeful face. A simple, intelligent face.

Nico closed the photos. A week after the photo session, the stalking began. Three months later she was dead, and her parents too. She didn't want to look at more pictures in case they were in them.

"Did that help?" Heloise asked quietly.

"I was just wondering if I was the kind of girl I'd want to kill," Nico said.

*

Heloise's Again Walker database became globally accessible once the World Wide Web launched in 1994. A bird watcher had already "discovered" Nico in 1985, after the morgue incident where she had killed two risen vampires. But the watcher didn't join Heloise's database until 1996, when he uploaded his observations. By 1990, Nico had long left America to attend schools abroad. Various bird watchers entered mid-90's sightings for a vampire they named "Nike", who Heloise later affirmed to be Nico (the entry claiming to have spotted her at a Morrissey concert in Doncaster was unfortunately untrue) and she combined the folders.

"Did you ever take the name Nike?" Heloise asked curious. "Because that's a variation on your name."

"If I'd been born a boy, I'd have been Nicolas." Nico continued to scan her folder. "Dad wanted me named for victory; 'the people's victory'. But no. Nike, Neko, Nicole, Nikkita, Colette. I've only been Nico. "

"I don't see you as a Colette. More a Coco."

Nico paused in her perusal.

There, in 1998. She inexplicably went on a spree.

"For fifteen years you were quiet," Heloise said. "Then this."

Nico quickly read through Russian news clippings reporting murdered traffickers, destroyed property, and bombed cars. Nico was certain the car bombings were misattributed. She had no idea how to make a bomb. She found a Leningrad police report on a warehouse massacre and opened the photos. Several victims had throats torn out. Nico rotated the pictures, studying the wounds. She'd never torn out a throat, yet the evidence was there. The fleeting sensation of hot blood in her mouth returned, of her teeth tearing into warm flesh. Then it was gone.

Heloise lit a cigarette behind Nico, the lighter's flame flaring. She clicked the lighter shut.

"Care for a—"

"I don't smoke," Nico said. "And neither does Bear."

"Fine." Heloise exhaled, and wisps drifted into the holo display.

"How can your bird watchers be sure these were me?" Nico said.

"One watcher listened to what the underworld was saying," Heloise said. "They spoke of a terror carrying a bear, and the description of the girl fit you—perfectly."

"That's nuts," Nico said. "Do you know how tough Russian guys are? They'd never admit a girl with a teddy bear terrorised them."

"They gave you a name," Heloise said pointedly. Nico saw it:

страшная месть и медведь

Strashnaya mest' i medved, Nico read. *Fearful Vengeance and Bear.*

"Don't say it," Nico warned. "Don't say it out loud."

"Okay," Heloise said with unease. "You think it's a post-hypnotic suggestion?"

"No, I think it's stupid." Nico looked at more police photos, searching for someone she might recognise. Heloise leaned over and tapped her cigarette into a hand blown, amber glass ashtray on the holo table. Nico smelled *Chasse* Geraud Soeurs and wondered if Heloise had found a bottle on Darqueworld. Seeing nothing in the photos to spark memory, she skipped over a folder labelled *Letters from Rescued*. Had she been in Leningrad to receive them, she wouldn't have read them. Any of the letters could have been bait to draw her out for assassination.

"Just so you know," Heloise said, "quite a few of the victims wanted to meet you to say thank you."

"You're so American, Heloise."

"Huh?" Heloise said.

Nico didn't answer. She stared at the evidence of her rampage and banged against the steel vault her blanked memory had become.

What was I after? What did I want to kill?

"We have no idea what set you off," Heloise said, as if answering Nico's unspoken question. "You weren't only liberating victims, you were slaughtering traffickers, setting fires. Destroying it all, really. You were quite an accomplished arsonist. Then, after three months, you vanished."

For three months I terrorised, Nico thought. *Like him.* But did she achieve the final kill, like he would have? She saw the date beginning her spree: one week after her birthday.

"You killed buyers, bosses, corrupt officials. My discussion boards could not stop talking about you. If you'd gone all the way to assassinating a minister, I would have won a very nice wager."

"I killed profit." Nico looked at Heloise. "What did the vampires of the Leningrad Oblast think of my activity? Didn't they run some of these operations?" She indicated the news articles.

"I don't know." Heloise raised her eyebrows in thought. "Back then, I was too *American* to form a relationship with the ex-Soviets. Maybe you created a convenient power vacuum. Maybe you were working for one of the vampires, getting rid of the competition. No one could make sense of your pattern, if you had one. You were so random about it."

Just like him. Nico pulled out her security wallet from her shirt and fetched the little black book. She handed it to Heloise, then touched the light keyboard, activating it. She typed an entry for 1987.

Crucified maker on the letter Y of the Rocklyn Hotel's marquee, Los Angeles. Watched him burn at sunrise.

"Well, that explains things," Heloise said over Nico's shoulder as she read. She then straightened and thumbed through the black book, her cigarette between her fingers.

"I'm sure you had a better vampire childhood."

"Oh, the usual murderous sort. I wasn't chosen for my ninja abilities."

"I'm not a ninja." Nico flagged the Morrissey concert entry as *untrue*. "And I'm not some highly trained Nikita. I learned how to stalk and murder from my own murder, and I used what I learned to stalk and murder my maker. That's all." She closed her file.

"Really?"

"Yes."

"This is all in Cyrillic."

"Can you match the names in it to the ones in police reports and the news articles?"

Heloise frowned. "Well, if I apply a formula to scan these pages, then transla—"

"Thank you," Nico said. She had a sudden thought. "Can I borrow your lighter?"

The lighter Heloise handed her was of black lacquer and silver, looking more like a cosmetic case than a lighter. It was a vintage, feminine tool, meant for evenings dancing with Sinatra types and listening to chanteuses. Nico raised her foot, activated the lighter, then applied the flame to the bottom of her shoe. She and Heloise watched while the thick rubber sole resisted the flame. After a while of attempting to set her shoe on fire, Nico clicked the lighter shut and gave it back to Heloise.

Well, that explains my ugly shoes.

"Not a ninja, huh?" Heloise said.

An alert chimed from the table and a hologram superseded the Again Walkers database. Two male faces materialised, one thick and small-eyed with a horn growing from his forehead, the other of an elvish, slim lad with a mop of hair and pointed ears.

The logo above the faces said: SLAUGHTER SPAWN. A tinier logo in the corner said, *Winkie Bets.*

"Sorry about that. Let me just—" Heloise tapped the keyboard. A three-figure sum appeared beneath the elvish boy.

"You're *betting* on the spawn fights?" Nico exclaimed. She swivelled in the seat. "That's so—what vice *don't* you indulge in?"

Heloise stood holding her cocktail glass and cigarette and looked at her, perplexed.

"Can't you just go out and cha-cha? You don't do smack, do you?"

"Nooo," Heloise answered, dismissive. "That stuff will ruin you. And so would the crap tables." She sipped her Sidecar and smiled.

Nico rose and headed for the doors.

"I'll get to work on your little black book posthaste, Miss Alexikova," Heloise bade, laying down her drink. She followed. "What will you and Bear do now?"

"Oh, the usual; stroll by the lake, read poetry. Stalk something." Nico stopped.

Looking at you is like looking at what we lost, Heloise had said.

She turned to Heloise. "A lot can happen in twenty years. I have a question about when I was gone."

Heloise grinned. "We can have dinner if you'd like to talk more."

A smile nearly turned up the corner of Nico's mouth. Heloise never seemed to quit.

"No thank you. I just want to know: why did you say at the lake that I was something you all had lost?"

"Ah. That." Heloise's face lost levity. "Well, to put it simply, darling, we lost the protection of being a myth. And we were outed in the worst way possible. A bioweapon was launched against us as a result. A plague."

Heloise drew on her cigarette, then snuffed it out in an ashtray resting on the balustrade. "You're lucky to have not seen it happen. The primacy directed an exodus, because the cure was here. Every vampire who could reach the weird matter engine came through. And should still be crossing over, if the machine's still working."

"That's why you were held in immigration. Quarantine." Nico doubted she would have survived a plague herself. As a lone vampire, she most likely would have died, uncomprehending. "Were you ill?"

"No." A brief, haunted look escaped before Heloise hid it.

Nico nodded.

No wonder you're celebrating.

"Do you use a service to order live meals?" she asked, curious. "Which one?" She continued to the doors and touched the control that opened them. Heloise hesitated and Nico looked at her.

"Willing Kittens," Heloise answered, walking to the door.

"So how many girls are you having for dinner tonight?" Nico queried as she stepped out. "And which one are you going to dress up like me?"

Heloise stood, one hand against the entryway frame and the other at her hip, and looked at Nico, exasperated. The doors slid shut. Nico ran for the elevator platform before Heloise had time to consider a retort and open her doors again.

Night fell. Nico whiled the hours away at a coffeehouse's sidewalk table on puke street, where the service didn't mind that she only drank two cups of blood with a slice of blood sponge cake. The cake had been a bit much, since she was still not used to eating food, so she'd given it to a backpacking vampire. Nico studied her hundred civic questions for the citizenship exam and watched the street.

So I'm a mass murderer in a different sense. Did the Po in immigration see behind the blank in her head and learn that? Though the Nico of Old Earth seemed to have had her reasons, massacring traffickers, it was still vengeance killing.

Which I guess is okay on this planet, so I needn't worry? She preferred to focus on a different and more present problem:

Esche.

Nico watched the street and easily recognised young people and frugal backpackers she'd seen since coming to the hostels sector. But none who walked or enjoyed themselves were vampires from Again Friends.

Her Id chimed; Shayla. Nico felt the corners of her mouth lift, and then her smile broadened, reading the message. Shayla's shift began in the afternoon, tomorrow. What would Nico like to do?

Elevenses? Nico typed, *at the Blue Owl.*

Magic, Shayla typed back.

Nico left the coffeehouse and recognised a rarity. She had had a beautiful day. A monsterless day, one worthy of a new beginning for a new arrival on a new planet, with new romantic prospects. She even liked Heloise's attentions, though Nico preferred to not admit that. But at the end of the day, the question of who she had been on Old Earth, or who she'd forgotten she had been on Old Earth, still remained. And she was still Esche's champion, whether Esche was living or dead.

Nico touched the mystery button pinned to her cardigan front. *Night is when bad things begin.*

"Okay Bear, let's screw this up," she said. She stood outside Again Friends' entrance until Dann noticed her and buzzed her in.

"I haven't seen her," Dann immediately said when Nico entered. "Isn't it about time you, uh, moved on to a new obsession?"

"No. You keep leaving your booth. How do you do that?"

"Oh, I got a private exit," Dann said, cheerful. He pushed the sign-up sheet towards her.

"Really." Nico picked up the pen. "Like a backdoor?"

"Eh...it's a secret."

"No one's backdoor is a secret."

"Hey, are you implying something?" Dann said, indignant.

Nico signed her and Bear's name while staring at Dann. Then she departed down the entry hall for the adjoining ground floor hallway.

The rec room blared some holo show, and Nico turned for the short hallway where the empty vending machine stood. She pulled out her remaining credit card from her wallet and slipped it into the door seam of the shut classroom, right next to the doorknob. She pushed the card, and it slid against the lock's short bolt, disengaging it from the doorframe. The door clicked open.

In the darkness, piles of possessions lay by stacked chairs and desks: coats, garments, shoes, books, bags, and packs. A bright red backpack with garish green accents lay nearest the door, as if casually tossed in.

Nico quietly shut the door.

Nico entered the rec room, recognising only broody boy and Ozzie girl among the vampires present. The new vampires barely glanced at her and returned their attention to the holo show. She did not see paperback girl, tongue-pierced girl, Danica, or the Sushi Hut worker. No Iris or Re'shawn.

Ozzie girl smiled and made a presentation gesture to the box with the blood packs.

"Still some left," she said.

"For once, I'm hungry," Nico said.

"Ace! Give it a burl." She handed Nico two warm packs and Nico accepted, removing the straw of one pack and piercing it. Then she sucked.

"Mm," she said, and beneath the metallic flavour of simulated blood, she tasted traces of a heavy sedative. She took a seat in an empty armchair, stored the remaining pack behind Bear, and activated Dorothy. She read while she sucked on her bag. After a few minutes, Nico rose and walked out, still eating and reading. Once on the stairwell, she ran quickly for the boys' bathroom.

Nico locked the door and vomited up as much of the ingested blood as she could into a lavatory receptacle. After she washed her mouth out, she fetched her dose of pUff and put the applicator to her nose. She released the dose and inhaled deeply through her nostrils.

PUFF

Nico tried to keep her mouth shut but coughed anyway. The stimulant spiked, elevating her senses until she was a floating balloon. Nico plopped on the bathroom floor. She giggled.

"Shhhh," she shushed to Bear. When she glanced at the full-length mirror, her doppelgänger's eyes were too bright.

"Don't look high," she ordered her reflection.

*

"Rest time," the voice-over calmly announced.

Nico lay atop her bed with eyes shut, Bear strapped to her and her Id resting on her chest, as if she'd fallen asleep reading it. The room dropped to blackness when the new girls entered, talking. One eased into the bed that had been Iris's. Nico envisioned paint drying and grass growing to keep herself from jumping up and running laps around the room. If she had a beating heart, pUff would have had it pounding a mile a minute.

"It's way earlier than 22 hundred," one girl said, and someone yawned.

"It is," the yawner replied. "But I'm ready to turn in."

The last, whispered conversation died, and when the room fell to complete silence, Nico opened her eyes. She carefully turned her head, and everyone to her vampire's sight lay as still as dead people in the blackness.

She tucked her Id behind Bear. Right then, she only had to wait until the anxiety began. She stared at the ceiling and started counting shee—

The darkness compressed, pressing her into the bed, and the hand she raised in alarm fell towards her, sinking—

Nico heaved herself out of her bed. She landed face first on the floor. When she looked up, the girl in Iris's bed raised her arms and legs high, her body sinking. Nico jumped up.

The girl disappeared into the bed. Nico looked at everyone. They all sank, bodies, legs, and arms vanishing, eaten by their beds.

Nico ran for the door.

She pounded up the steps for the rooftop exit, feeling ghost fingers might catch up and drag her into the vanishing place. The door to the roof stood bolted. Nico threw herself against it, making it rattle. She kicked hard, and the metal surface dented. She kicked again and again, her blows echoing in the stairwell.

The door's metal suddenly screamed as it twisted from the pull of an outside force. Nico stepped back down the steps when the door jerked. Gloved fingers appeared in the gap created between the stubborn door and the doorframe. Another hand joined it and slowly peeled back the protesting metal, revealing the Makepeace, Amazon Woman.

Nico looked up at the moonlit Makepeace as she created an opening big enough for her armoured body to step through.

"Come down, hurry," Nico cried.

Nico led Amazon Woman quickly down to the girls' dorm. She ran in, and then stopped.

Vampire girls lay in the beds, still and asleep. Nico turned around. Everyone seemed present. She looked at the Makepeace, who surveyed the room, apparently having no trouble with visibility in the darkness.

"They were all gone," Nico said. "Sucked into their beds. I was nearly one of them, but I jumped out in time."

"Oi, what's going on?" Jess said slowly, rousing at the end of the room. She then sat up. "What's a Makepeace doing here?" Other vampires stirred at the sound of Jess's voice.

"These girls were not here when I ran to get you," Nico insisted to Amazon Woman.

"We were what?" a girl said in drowsy confusion. She looked around. "We were where?" Jess got out of bed.

The Makepeace raised her arm and pointed her gauntlet. Jess put her hands up.

A beam emitted from the gauntlet, and Amazon Woman scanned Jess, then widened her beam and ran it along the room, floor, and each bed's occupant, some stirring awake while others slept. The Makepeace cut her beam and said nothing.

"They were not here," Nico repeated.

Jess approached, a concerned look on her face. "Are...are we in trouble, officer?"

"Were you dreaming?" the vampire in Iris's bed said to Nico, rubbing her eyes.

"Or did you make a mistake in the dark?" Jess suggested.

"I don't have a problem with seeing in the dark," Nico shouted.

"What's happening?" another girl murmured.

"They were *gone*," Nico said to the Makepeace. "Every one of them. Veils took them."

"This is a bit naff," Jess said under her breath and laughed a little.

"It is *not*," Nico said.

"Okay!" Jess held up her hands. "Wrong choice of words! Sorry, mate. Let's find this—whatever's gone wrong."

"It was *abduction*, that's what's wrong. The free blood is drugged with a sedative, making everyone pass out and become easier to take. Here." Nico pulled out her second blood pack from behind Bear, still uneaten. Amazon Woman took it from her and pricked it with a needle from her gloved finger.

"This blood contains tranquilisers," the Makepeace stated.

"But isn't taking a sleeping aide in that agreement we signed?" Jess said, confused.

✱

Nico descended quickly for the ground floor, the Makepeace and Jess following. Some vampires emerged from the dorms, drowsy and curious, but others could not be bothered and returned to sleep.

Dann sat in his caged booth, the only light lit in the hostel.

A holo programme loudly played from his Id, of an anime with singing cat girls. He nodded to the sugary beat, then turned his head at Nico's entry.

At the sight of the Makepeace behind Nico, Dann stood abruptly.

"Where-where did, uh—I still have that Id you gave me," he announced to Nico. "For Asha, right?"

"Shut up," Nico said. She brought the sign-up sheet towards Amazon Woman. "Here. The terms are on the last sheet."

Dann quickly lowered the volume on his programme as the Makepeace flipped the pages and then scanned the terms of agreement.

"This agreement is in order," she said, lowering the sheets of paper.

"If we're supposed to be doped up, why are you wide awake?" Nico accused Jess. Jess looked at her, bewildered, and shrugged.

"I—I may be getting used to the sedative. I have been here a few nights, mate," she said.

Nico turned to Amazon Woman. "There's a room, come on."

She led the Makepeace to the locked classroom, Jess following. When Nico opened it with her credit card, the black interior held nothing but piled chairs and desks.

"No," Nico said in bewilderment and stepped into the space.

"This was full of stuff from the missing vampires," she cried. "Backpacks and things. One from a girl who had stayed here *last* night, and there's no way she would have left a backpack behind." She looked at the Makepeace. *I should have taken photos.* "They used veils here too," Nico then stated. "Look." She pointed at the floor. Even in the darkness, she could see the dust outlines where objects had rested.

The Makepeace raised her gauntlet, scanning the floor, then the room. When she was done, Nico looked at her expectantly.

"We must exit, potential citizen," she said. "We have found nothing unordinary."

*

Nothing unordinary.

Nico understood. Dust outlines were hardly evidence. She had screwed up, and the Makepeace had nothing. Nico felt rage build.

Amazon Woman scooped her up, placed Nico over one shoulder in a fireman's carry, and walked out of the room.

"Are you leaving?" Dann called from his booth when Amazon Woman turned for the stairs. "Did you want to sign for another night?"

The Makepeace ascended and passed the boys' dorm, then the girls' dorm. Sleepy vampires trailed and looked at Nico curiously, who clenched her fists, fangs to the fore, wanting to bite something—anything.

"No worries, mate," Jess called to her in a concerned tone as the Makepeace climbed the steps for the broken roof exit. "We know how nightmares are."

Amazon Woman stepped over the bent door and on to the rooftop, walked towards the edge, and put Nico down. The night breeze touched Nico's hair and face, and she heard the traffic, people, and sounds of the nighttime city. The holo board across the way played its advertisement. Amazon Woman stood as still as a statue, possibly in communication with something.

"I *know* what I saw. Somehow the kidnappers knew to put them all back. I wish I had something you could shoot," Nico said in frustration.

Amazon Woman then scooped Nico up again, cradling her in her arms. A levitation bubble blipped into being around them. They took off and flew over the rooftops, Nico suppressing a shriek of astonishment. The Makepeace travelled a block's length, then descended slowly for the street. She put Nico down and the levitation bubble blipped from view.

"Proceed down the street and continue for two blocks. Do you understand, potential citizen?"

"Yes—yes ma'am," Nico said, wide-eyed.

"Good night."

"Uh. Good night." Nico started walking. She wanted to look behind her, but wasn't sure if that was allowed per the instructions.

"Is she sending us to Tough Guy?" she asked Bear. "Maybe she'll buy us ice cream later?"

When she crossed the street for the second block, memories of what she'd seen in the dorm returned.

A trick that a witch like Shayla or a Makepeace's equipment can't detect.

And they still want me to come back, like nothing's wrong.

A long-bodied, black vehicle stopped beside her. A male vampire in a mod-cut suit stepped out the back—tall, with mature features, pursed mouth, and a cool, blue-eyed regard. He wore thick-rimmed frames and stood with relaxed confidence. Inclining his head, he indicated that Nico step inside the vehicle.

"Don't touch me, please," Nico requested when he moved to place a hand at her back. He paused, unperturbed, and she sensed no aggression from him.

I like him, Nico thought in surprise. *I bet he has a harem.*

A small, round-faced Asian woman sat within the vehicle and leaned to look at her. She smiled and held up a silver shield illustrated with a blindfolded angel bearing a sword and scales. It said:

Other Being Mischief
Investigative Division
in service to the
Tribunate

"Helloo Ms Alexikova," she said, her voice bearing a singsong lilt.

"Hi. Do we know each other?" The woman appeared to be human. Nico stepped in, intrigued, and the male vampire followed. He sat beside the little woman in the seat facing Nico. The hatch closed and the vehicle sped away.

"Nooo, but we do now. I'm Special Agent Yoo, this is Special

Agent Rotherhithe. We're with the Other-beings Mischief Investigative Division." Yoo pronounced her lilting words as if each had special meaning.

"You're the OMID?" Nico said.

"No, we're the OI."

"But you said—"

"It's the OI," Yoo interrupted.

"Why are you called misch—"

"Because the division is 700 years old."

"Well, what's happening inside Again Friends is not some *prank*," Nico said.

"Aaand the original meaning of mischief is not pranking," Yoo said lightly.

"Why are we talking?" Nico said.

"Ms Alexikova," Yoo began, smiling.

"And Mr Bear."

"Ms Alexikova and Mr Bear. Again Friends has been under our surveillance for eight weeks now. We're very close to cracking this case."

"Sure you are. What's happening? Why are vampires disappearing?"

"That's for us to know, and for you to not worry about any longer. This is a whole new world for you—both of you," Yoo said to Bear, "and we're trying to keep you safe."

Nico suppressed the roll of her eyes. "Special Agent Woo."

"No, Yoo."

"Who, me? I mean you."

"That's right."

"All it takes is one predator, *one*, to hurt everyone, and then no one's safe. You really don't know what's going on, do you? You need to be *inside*," Nico said. "You have someone on the inside," she added in realisation, suspecting Re'shawn. "Is Ozzy girl one of you? Because she's trying too hard."

"You're a recent arrival, Ms Alexikova," Yoo said, smiling. "We appreciate that you are a concerned potential citizen, but we ask that you not return to Again Friends Youth Hostel and further jeopardise matters."

"They're using veils. I saw it."

The vehicle stopped and the hatch popped open. "Good niiight, Ms Alexikova," Yoo said pleasantly.

Nico stepped out. But before the hatch closed, she looked at Rotherhithe.

"You don't need glasses," she said. Rotherhithe smirked. The hatch shut, and the vehicle drove away.

The agents left Nico on a cross street by a teeming, open air market, bright with hung lanterns, neon-lit food carts, and fiery, little portable stoves on which flat bread, kebabs, and noodle broth cooked and hot tea brewed. Scents, steam, and smoke rose. People wandered, ate, sat around portable glow-tables, and played luminescent mah-jongg, the tiles clacking.

"If you wanted to distract me from my big failure at Again Friends, it worked," Nico said to the vehicle that had already disappeared into traffic.

Her dose of pUff was wearing off, leaving her feeling even lower than she already felt. A stall behind a butcher's shop served fresh, slaughtered blood in cups to vampires in spiky mohawks. Nico gravitated towards the scent of true animal's blood, her fangs emerging.

She hoped the stall accepted credit chits. Once she drank her fill, she needed to find a place to burrow, one where vice did not dwell and what haunted her could not pursue.

"We just need a place to sleep," she said to Bear.

CHAPTER TWELVE

"The Makepeace and police have made an arrest in the North Park vampire murder, where the upper torso of a male vampire had been found, his organs and his heart missing. Three humans are now charged.

"Their identities have not yet been released to prevent retaliation by the vampire primacy, but we do know that one is a holo film producer, and his accomplices, the owners of a small film studio. The three had been seen with the victim, allegedly lured the vampire to the producer's home and held him captive. Over the course of several days, they removed and ate his organs, saving the heart for last. Police say this may have been a ritualistic killing, where the kidnappers hoped to gain youth and immortality by eating living—or in this case, un-living—vampire flesh."

Nico unbuttoned the cuffs of her long sleeved shirt, and then swung a bamboo stick at a hung futon airing in the bright morning light while Dorothy played the news. Her cardigan and Mr Bear hung from another laundry pole, enjoying cleansing sunshine. She stood on the rooftop of a narrow building sandwiched between other crowded structures in Again NewYork's Japanese neighbourhood. Nico had wandered into it off the night market proper, and found patrons cooking sizzling *okonomiyaki* over open grills and sitting within busy noodle shops and sake bars. In a closed sundries store displaying stationary, Hello Kitty, manga, household products, and colourful vinyl Makepeace figures, a vintage 1960's wood and plastic television set had stood. It had played a kaiju film with a monster-battling, giant Makepeace, and Nico had lingered in the television's light, watching in fascination.

At that very late hour, a little old lady had appeared on the walk, bowing to a young Indian couple that had apparently dined with her. The couple had the rosy scent of the contented. But the old lady did not stand before a doorway leading to a shop; instead, it was a very narrow, residential building. When she saw Nico, she beckoned.

"*Kite kudasai*," she cajoled.

"Mama-san, I'm a vampire," Nico said.

"*Hai-hai*." The little old lady beckoned more.

She led Nico a storey up to a tiny room with tatami mats and a futon, Nico obligingly having left her shoes in the tinier *genkan*. The futon filled the room. The scents of a cooked meal lingered on the ground floor, in a room that probably served as living area as well. The old lady bowed, slid the door closed, and ascended to the next floor to retire for the night. Nico understood then that she was in a public area of the house—one that did not require a formal invitation for Nico to cross the threshold. The little old lady liked to let her extra room out to those she extended hospitality to.

"I wouldn't be surprised if we're meant to be her rottweiler for the night, too," Nico told Bear.

Nico enjoyed a deep, undisturbed rest, then rose with Mama-san at the break of dawn to help with her chores. While Mama-san diligently tackled her portion of the walk with her broom, Nico carried the futons, coverlets, blankets, and pillows to the roof for an airing. For good measure, she decided to beat the dust out of them too.

She was proceeding to the second futon with her bamboo stick when the morning news concluded. The failed bust at Again Friends had not been mentioned.

"Don't think about it," she told herself, but then she did think about it; of all the girls she'd failed to rescue from *him*.

Nicky, her maker chastised, *game over.*

She switched Dorothy to the hundred civics questions that might be asked on the citizenship exam and practiced answering them.

✴

"Hello?" Nico said to her Id.

She had left Mama-san behind after finishing the morning chores and was proceeding to the Victorian sector. Hair brushed, outfit laundered, and Bear refreshed with sunshine, Nico had felt the effects of failure recede—until Specs's call.

"Ronin Nico," Specs greeted as his holo popped into view. "Some nights you can't win, huh?"

"Something *is* wrong at that hostel," Nico said. "I know it. But I guess I ruined it for the OI. Now they'll need to back off if whatever I was trying to bust hasn't already folded, moved, or gone underground. I never heard of the OI before now."

"The OI likes a low profile, is why," Specs said. "The Makepeace are the ones front and centre because the public loves 'em. Think of the OI as the colonel behind the Elvis."

"This is why there are Makepeace toys," Nico realised. "And television shows. And porn."

"Have you listened to the Makepeace 5 album? They sound kinda like the Bee Gees. I like it. Hey, since the OI warned you off laying siege to castles, what village are you defending today, Nico and Bear?"

"Nothing really. I'm studying for the citizen's exam, and I'm having elevenses with someone I've met." Nico skipped as she said that.

"Sounds like a date."

"It's not a date."

"Y'okay. Mind if I ask what fair lass caught your bushido eye?"

"Lass is correct. I bet you've heard of her. It's Shayla O'Fey."

"Well now. Well-o-well. I have heard of Ms O'Fey. She has quite the reputation with vampires."

"Vampire Alliance has been running a smear campaign against her," Nico exclaimed. "With photos of Shen Jin that are three years old."

"Yeah, that. Like I said, El Nico, the last time an unauthorised vampire-making happened in this fair city, it got complicated. I assume you're not in support of the grey issues?"

"What grey issues? If it had been me there and Shy had *asked*, I wouldn't have done it."

Specs grinned. "The surviving Ms O'Fey would have appreciated that."

"They call her the Gunslinger," Nico said. "I didn't tell her that I knew that."

"Ah yes." Specs's tone was pleased. "There's a *certain* Slaughter Spawn fight you may want to see."

"I've watched it twenty times. Then my social worker approves?" Nico asked, curious. "My spending time with a vampire killer?"

"Lone Nico, far be it for me to tell you who you get to see. Only a vampire like you would see nothing wrong in being with Ms O'Fey."

"Ye're quiet taeday, Niky," Shayla said.

Nico sat with Shayla outside the Blue Owl Tea Room, looking out upon the cobblestoned street. Since it was a very tiny table, Bear remained strapped to Nico. Shayla had chosen to only have tea with a few cakes, while Nico simply had her blood tea. Her thoughts kept returning to what Specs had said.

You'd think I was trying to be Ted Bundy's wife. Rubbish.

"I   guess   I'm   working   out   my   complicated   internal sanguivoriphobia," Nico answered.

Shayla's mouth quirked. "How was yer night?"

Nico paused, considering how much to share. "That was complicated too."

"As complicated as yer previous night?" Shayla's tone was casual as she sipped her tea.

"You could say that." *Without saying it was the ranch house.* "Something happened, and I screwed up in trying to solve it. But the more I've thought about it, the more I see what the only solution can be. I know you'd agree, if you were in the same situation."

Shayla raised a brow. "I dinnae ken the situation, love."

"That's okay, I think I know what you'd say."

Shayla looked at her, perplexed. "Are ye comfortable at yer hostel, Niky?"

Nico almost laughed. "Again Friends is part of the problem. I lucked out finding a very sweet, little old lady to take me in for the night."

"Ye should've come tae me," Shayla said with concern.

"But you were at work," Nico said. "And for me and Bear to show up at your doorstep in the middle of the night like a lost—"

"Kitten."

"Frog. That's quite an imposition, I think."

"Ye're no imposition, love." Shayla's tone was meaningful. "Especially when ye saved myself and PETH the task of takin' down Grun."

"Who?" Nico said. Shayla's words at the lake and the gift of her blessed bracelet then made sense.

"Such an innocent face." Shayla smiled, and reached over to tap Bear's nose, which made Nico squirm as if tickled. "Nothin' happens at the spaceport, Niky, that Lucy's doesn't hear about. I dinnae bring it up earlier because ye like yer secrets, don't cha? Know that ye have my gratitude."

Nico nodded, allowing herself to feel pleased, then returned to solemnity. "The next thing I'm going to say, you may not thank me for. But I feel I must. It's something I've been thinking about, since reading about Shen Jin."

The good humour fled Shayla's face.

"And I apologise for doing the creepy thing again, reading up on you," Nico added hastily.

"What words have ye, love," Shayla asked quietly.

I'm sorry to make you remember. "When you shot Shen…" Shayla looked away. "As ey went down," Nico added more gently. "I bet ey looked at you, surprised. I bet ey looked at you like a kicked puppy, betrayed. But no matter how much he thought he was helping you—doing good, saving Shy. He was not. Deep, deep down, he knows that's not what he was trying to do.

"Making another is a selfish act. A vampire who says it's not is a liar. Shen owns Shy's soul.

"And after three years, if he still hasn't told you this, he's a jerk, letting you suffer so."

A tear left Shayla's eye, and Nico knew more would come. She reached behind Bear and found her tissue pack. She handed it to Shayla.

"Ey doesn't blame me for shooting em. Ey telt me so," Shayla said, hoarse. She accepted the tissues.

"He's a jerk still. That wasn't what he was supposed to say. And I forgot my pronouns," Niky added in a whisper.

Shayla laughed briefly, sad. "Dear Niky."

Nico could guess why she lost her gender neutral pronouns, besides the fact that Shen favoured facial hair and looked too much like a boy. Nico had been thinking of her own maker. She was projecting onto Shen and perhaps being unfair. However, Shen making a surrogate Shayla ey could control and Nico's maker raising a sick puppet he could pull the strings of seemed the same to her.

I really shouldn't be thinking about my being a sick puppet or working so hard to make women cry. I should have started this tea by recalling where I saw the local police box last so I can give Shayla sex.

Shayla wore another pretty dress, of embroidered white, with a scoop necked, sea green cardigan, and Nico's gaze fell to Shayla's exposed throat and esculent clavicles.

Shayla wiped another tear away.

Elevenses ruined. The grandstand of Bears booed.

Shayla scrunched the tissue in her hand, her tears done.

"I appreciate yer words," she said. "And so strong are they. After what ye telt me of yer reflection, I assumed yer rising was not a gift, Niky."

"No," Nico answered, and she felt it was her turn to become a shadow, fleeing emotion's touch. "I was a murder. I thought that was normal, too, until I met other vampires. You can tell when a vampire rose from a bestowed making, because they're so well adjusted.

"When I rose, I had to rob blood banks; clinics. I broke into animal shelters. I practiced on animals, how to suck enough not to kill. And then I sucked on people and dumped them at hospitals. If I was going to kill, I wanted the first one to be my maker. I'm really sorry about the animals."

"Sweet Niky."

"No, I'm not that."

"How can ye not ken yer good heart?" Shayla softly said.

"A good heart?" Nico repeated.

"Ye are what he was not. I dinnae have tae ken the man tae see it." Shayla picked up her napkin from her lap and set it on the table.

"Come, love," she said firmly. "My account here will cover the tea. Let's visit the Isle shop."

Nico stood with Shayla, unsure what motivated her companion's sudden determination. She was about to protest who would pay for tea when her Id chimed.

"Excuse me," Nico whispered, and pulled out Dorothy. Heloise had messaged. It read:

Found a name match.

Heloise gave her a time she was available. Nico held her Id against herself and Bear.

"Is something the matter, Niky?" Shayla said. Nico then noticed something behind Shayla.

A black vehicle sat farther down the cobblestoned street, parked up on the kerb. The windshield was dark.

Huh. She doubted the OI would be watching her. She turned with Shayla for the Isle shop.

"That amnesia I have? I finally have a possible lead to learn who I was," Nico said. She sent Heloise back a confirmation, but turned down her dinner invitation. "I just don't want to find out I'm a bonafide, nut-job mass murderer." Shayla put an arm around Nico's shoulders and hugged her as they crossed the street.

"If ye are one, Niky, we've ways of handlin' ye." Shayla gently teased. She turned her head at the sound of a vehicle advancing towards them, rubber wheels crunching on paving stone. Nico peered around Shayla and saw that it was a slow-moving Fedotov Kolbasa van. Despite its snail-like pace, it steadfastly approached. Shayla looked at it, as if considering whether to admonish the driver for not stopping. She and Nico completed their crossing as the van passed behind them, and Nico put her Id away.

"Here's a random question," she said. *But one I've been meaning to ask.* "When you call me 'Nicky', how do you spell it?"

"N-I-K-Y?" Shayla said, and Nico's face broke into a broad smile. "How would ye like it spelt, love?"

"Just like that. It's perfect." They entered the Isle Shop.

Within, Shayla pointed at the sweets jars holding one-inch buttons.

"Would you like another pin-back, love?"

"I would love the Saltire of Skye."

Shayla directed her to pick one, and Nico did, the image on the button of the white X on azure blue: the Saltire of Scotland. Shayla went to the register to purchase it for her.

"Getting buttons is so punk rock. It's a pure stoater," Nico said happily as they stood outside the shop. Shayla laughed, pin in hand.

"Have ye Scots history, Niky? Ya know the speech well."

"I do." Nico swallowed. "You don't know it, but your voice replaces his."

Shayla paused, her hand by the mystery button on Nico's chest. The question *whose voice?* seemed to die on Shayla's lips as realisation dawned.

"Bless Niky. Bless this one, who is loved," Shayla intoned. She pinned the button on Nico's chest, then hugged her. Nico inhaled peach-bergamot and—

Oh my gods its nearly her time.

Shayla moved back in the embrace to hold Nico's face, and her mouth descended.

"Sorry," Nico squeaked, when she turned her face at the last second, and Shayla's lips contacted the corner of Nico's mouth. Shayla laughed self-consciously against Nico's cheek.

"Oh love, I'm the sorry one," she said, and moved back. "Here I am, molestin' ye."

"Oh no," Nico quickly said. "Never you."

Her Id chimed, a tiny, unfamiliar jingle. Nico excused herself again and pulled out Dorothy from behind Bear. No message was present. When she looked up, Shayla had a holo interface activated from the Id ring on her middle finger, the privacy screen obscuring what she read.

Those rings are so cool. Shayla bit her lip, apparently not liking what she was reading. She tapped rapidly on her interface. When she deactivated it, Nico tried to keep the disappointment out of her voice.

"Is that you, then?" she said, using Scots speech.

"Aye, that's me, love," Shayla said apologetically. "Ah Niky, I want tae stay, but I've a matter tae handle, in my sector."

The gunslinger must ride.

"Thank you for everything," Nico said, and leaned awkwardly

towards Shayla.

Shayla smiled and kissed her.

I'll learn to like kissing again. Nico skipped towards the Pea and Cock, enjoying the tingly remnants of Shayla's lips on hers. They'd parted at the gift shop, Shayla walking towards the underground station with a determination that indicated the gravity of whatever situation had called her away. Nico had wanted to tag along, though her inexperience dealing with Others was a handicap. She had lucked out in her vampire fight at Royal Bento—her first real, Other-being battle. A cryptic gun shootout might see her and Bear cowering behind an upturned table until it was over.

Plus, she had to stay behind thanks to the black vehicle, which had moved and parked at the other end of the street while she and Shayla had been in the gift shop. Nico could no longer ignore its presence.

She was halfway down the block when the vehicle backed out of view and into the cross street. Nico took off at a run and turned the corner, in time to see the vehicle spin out of full reverse and zoom away, too fast for her to follow.

"That can't be the OI," Nico said to Bear. Agents would have no reason to act furtive—like criminals. Who else needed to keep an eye on her?

Found a name match, Heloise had written.

Nico's Id chimed. *Shayla? Or Heloise?* She pulled out Dorothy and looked.

The message was from Esche's social worker, Deepika.

Deepika: *Esche Abram-Angel's husband has contacted me. He had been off-planet and missed her arrival by two days. As the Makepeace have not made progress, have you learned anything?*

Nico typed: *Nothing yet. How did Esche's spouse know she arrived?*

Deepika: *All arrivals' names are published daily in the public immigrant manifest. One subscribes to the alert. I will update him.*

Nico: *I'll keep you posted.*

Nico closed the message and looked up. She stood before the shop window for Absalom, Fairditch & Vastagh, Rare and Unusual Books.

Miss Fairditch's vampires had known to meet her at the spaceport, even though Miss Fairditch herself had no idea they'd be there.

"Immigrant manifest," Nico repeated.

Someone had been alerted when she'd arrived in Again NewYork.

CHAPTER THIRTEEN

What do you mean Chaikov's is closed? Nico typed to Dorothy, peeved. She was riding the train, having so far spotted no one else shadowing her, and thought to follow up on the names of the two dead men in her little black book. After the incident with the black vehicle, she didn't want to wait until her meeting with Heloise to learn more. She'd asked for directions to Chaikov's Collectible Coins & Currencies, only to find out that it had ceased operations.

The business you wish to visit is listed as no longer active, Dorothy answered. Nico blew breath. With Chaikov's suspiciously closed, enquiring at the other Russian businesses if they knew about the two dead men would only tip off whoever was watching her. It would be prudent to wait for Heloise.

Why does that woman have to work? Isn't she rich enough, already? Nico put her feet up on the seat, then put them down again when a security robot entered the train car, rolling down the aisle.

She sent Shayla a message enquiring if all was well, and Shayla affirmed that things were and that she was headed for her shift at Lucy's. Would Nico like to stay with her that night, since she didn't like her hostel?

"Wow, we didn't blow it," Nico exclaimed to Bear. The grandstand within shot off fireworks.

If it's no bother, she typed back. Shayla said it wasn't. She would be back home late that night.

Nico sat awhile, contemplating her extraordinary good fortune. Things were looking up in Darqueworld. She departed the train at the next stop.

It was time she made herself a visible lure again.

She ended up in a tiny square within the Japanese neighbourhood, where a cauldron of burning incense stood before a small temple. An outdoor holo theatre had been set up, and Nico joined the after-school children seated on benches to watch cartoons and a kaiju film of Ultrapeace (the super-enlarging Makepeace) fighting giant space beasts. At dusk, the children disappeared, the holo films ended, and the bars, restaurants, and food carts opened. Nico saw no one who might be watching her, not even a Makepeace. She ambled, worked in Dorothy, and studied her civic questions. The night market roused to activity.

"C'mon, someone, make a move," she muttered, and drank down a cup of warm, freshly slaughtered pig's blood from the butcher's while watching couples, families, and workers gather. The vampire punks arrived, buying their own cups of blood. They sat on empty crates—a regular hangout for them, judging by the number of snuffed cigarette butts on the ground—and drank and smoked in companionable silence. Nico envied their social unit.

"We need to start collecting people's contact codes," she told Bear. "This isn't like on Old Earth, where we had to be alone all the time." A solitary existence thanks to her being a vampire. And thanks to—

Is he bothering ya, luv?

Nico gritted her teeth. She surveyed the market area without appearing to be scrutinising it, then tossed her cup. She walked away.

Come get me.

★

The fact that no one appeared to be following her right then did not stop familiar feelings of unease from escalating. During such anxiety, she would expect a phone call, an envelope, a message taped to her door, or even a graffiti. One time, he had spelt out his clue in stones laid out charmingly in a garden. Then she'd find his handiwork, always timed to be dying the moment she'd come to save the person.

Nico went directly to the wealthy sector and quickly ascended to the high fashion plaza near Heloise's building.

Once in the building's lobby, Nico calmed. The old fear that she would find death simply because she was visiting someone was, in the present situation, implausible. On this planet, she knew vampires and extra-humans. They were harder to hurt, even harder to kill. Not only was Heloise older than Nico's maker, but slitting her throat would just make her angry.

Nico stepped on to the elevator platform, only for it to ascend two more storeys before slowing. The floor it stopped on appeared to be the recreational facility, with people exercising behind its glass. Two older men waited for the platform, wearing tennis outfits and holding rackets. Towels rested around their necks as they wiped sweat from their faces, and Nico thought their tanned physiques looked well paid for—tight-skinned, polished, and pampered.

The platform's doors opened and the men entered, moving past Nico to stand behind her. The platform continued up.

"I tell you, today I outdid my personal best from when I was thirty," one said to the other. "And I still feel like I could have gone a few matches more."

"If we didn't have to be somewhere tonight, I would have beaten you," the other man said.

"Let's play again tomorrow, and we'll see," the first man

exclaimed.

The men fell silent and their fresh perspiration scented. But there was a cleanliness to their human odour; a touch of perfection, like—

Vampires?

Nico glanced surreptitiously behind her. Neither of the men seemed to be looking her way, but she sensed that they focused on her.

She stepped off the platform at Heloise's floor. The silent men rode on, and Nico watched them disappear from view.

When she continued for Heloise's unit, her vampire's hearing picked up a faint piano melody. Heloise—or someone—was playing the sheet music on her piano's music rack.

Somewhen a place for us, Nico mentally sang. Her hand crept behind for her blade. She pushed the chime. After a moment, the doors slid open, revealing Heloise with a hand resting against the doorframe, and Nico's shoulders relaxed. Heloise wore no tie and her shirt had several top buttons unfastened. She smirked.

"Hullo, doll," Heloise greeted. "Can I call you that?"

"No." Nico entered. The apartment smelled of Heloise's perfume, the lingering, fruity-pink scents of human girls, and fresh cigarette smoke. Heloise had had dinner. "You look rosy."

"Why, thank you. I would have saved you a bite but you seem the self-denying type."

"Why do you say that?" Nico turned back to Heloise and her open door.

"Because you'd rather stay at—now what did you call it?—a *creepy* little hostel like Again Friends than the perfectly nice and respectable Y."

"Creep," Nico exclaimed. "You are stalking me."

"Pot calling the kettle." Heloise leaned out the door as a man approached another unit. "Hi neighbour," she called to him. "I happened to sign for one of your packages."

Nico watched as Heloise plucked a box from the side table and presented it to the smiling, dark-haired man who came to accept it. He had a sparkling grin, and Heloise's easy charm with him seemed to harken back to days when men and women understood how to interact with each other—a confidence borne of established social parameters. The man was tall, well built, and (Nico felt) significantly older, but his appearance didn't seem so. She suspected his pectorals' heft of artificial shaping, and his strange, smooth looks of having enjoyed one surgical adjustment too many. Nico stood near enough that all she smelled was his natural scent and cologne, and when he left, Heloise closed the door and turned to her with a wistful smile.

"Saw some of his swashbucklers at the cinema when I was alive," she said. "Wish he'd let himself age naturally."

"With that much plastic in him, he probably tastes weird. While I was coming up, I saw two humans who had to have been using Mircalla products."

Heloise chuckled, the sound throaty. "That woman is a *genius*." She sauntered down to the living area in her stockinged feet, and Nico followed.

"Does her stuff really bestow youth? Is it possible?" Nico asked.

"Considering that we're undead, anything is possible. Personally, I think it's pure advertising. The vampire primacy would flay her alive for an eternity if she were really making products from our bodies."

"I think her beauty products do have something," Nico said. "Those humans smelled like us."

Heloise looked at her, intrigued. "You mean like our undead state? Maybe it was a fragrance? Synthesised."

"I guess so." Nico went to the piano. The fallboard was up, the bench pushed back, and the creased music sheets sat spread out. The keyboard smelled of Heloise.

"A fragrance for luring a vampire lover." Heloise picked up her dwindling cigarette from the amber ashtray on the coffee table and inhaled, her gaze mirthful.

"Or for passing as vampires so we don't bite them. Not everything has to be about getting laid."

"Not everyone is sanguivoriphobic," Heloise said, exhaling smoke.

"Why does—you watch one commercial and then you think you're a shrink," Nico exclaimed. "Can you show me what I came here for?"

"Right away, Miss Alexikova," Heloise quipped in a false British accent. She moved for the holo table and activated it. Nico joined her.

"I ran all the names in your little book. Anyone mentioned in a news article or police report was a crossed off name on your list," Heloise said. An icon appeared, labelled *Nic's Little Black Book.* "Don't open that yet." She waved Nico's hands away from the light keyboard. "Not until I explain something about a certain name—from the four you didn't get to cross out. It showed up in an unlikely place: the letters written to you from the rescued." Heloise snuffed her cigarette in the ashtray on the holo table. "And the letter happened to be written on black paper."

"Black paper?" Nico repeated.

"Black is the colour used for banishment spells," Heloise said. "The scanned envelope that was archived revealed no return address. When I'd gotten hold of your mail, I hadn't taken the time to translate the letter itself. Until now." She walked over to the bar top and retrieved something. She held up two blue, glass amulets painted with eyes and hung from silver chains—one chain sized for a small child.

"One nazar for you and one for Bear," Heloise said. "Put them on, and they'll deflect any evil intention aimed at you. Then you can read the letter." When Nico didn't move, Heloise let out breath.

"For crying out loud, they're not—what, poisoned? I had a witch bless them for extra protection. I'd tell you what's in the letter, but my *American* mind might misinterpret the message. Now put these on."

Nico looked at Shayla's woven bracelet on her wrist.

"In *addition* to your blessed bracelet," Heloise said.

"Okay. Thank you," Nico said, and accepted the amulets. After she put the littler one on Bear and the other on herself, Heloise summoned the letter on the holo display. Nico held Bear and read it.

Fearful Vengeance and Bear,

You are the ghost that will not stop, even after death. You are the voice of all souls who cry for vengeance. You are Nemesis, and you will pursue us to the last child and beyond that, to anything we have touched and will touch. We must not destroy you, for that would bind your wrath forever to us. We must send you away. We will send you away. We must make you as unreachable as the stars. I write this to you, to the memory of you, knowing nothing can be forgiven or appeased. We who you slaughter—we have no guilt. We are beasts, and would harm ones like yourself all over again. I recognise this. But I am only one, and my sorrow is not enough to answer you. I will summon that which can exile you. May you forget us. May you ascend to the stars and forget us. May you journey as the vampire you were before you met us and forget us. And when it is done, and you are so far away, may you find peace.

Vasili Fedosov

"Written like a spell," Heloise said. She lit another cigarette behind Nico, her lighter clicking, then deliberately blew smoke into the holo, disrupting the image. "Triple repetitions; they named you, then what they wanted done to you, try to absolve themselves, and then curse you some more. It opens and closes, spell done. A guilt confession plus incantation to reinforce keeping you away, in one pen stroke." She blew twice more into the holo image, and then deactivated it.

"Do you think they had access to a weird matter engine?" Nico said quietly.

"If the Soviets had been working on one? Maybe. That's technology we've had and lost repeatedly, since ancient times. The last one known to exist before your period was destroyed in London, around 1880. And it's highly unlikely you were shoved on to a visiting ship in the M-Triangle. I think this Fedotov used—"

"Fedosov," Nico murmured.

"Right. Not the sausage maker."

"He used twelve babies."

Heloise rested her hand on the back of Nico's chair and placed her cigarette in the ashtray.

"Whatever he did," Heloise said, her tone low. "I think you've already made up for it by your actions on Darqueworld."

"The dead babies are still dead."

"You are the cheeriest little vampire I've ever met." Heloise's tone was droll. She walked over to the bar and began mixing a drink.

"So my memory loss is deliberate, not because of my trip to here," Nico said.

"A Baba Yaga or three can do that to you."

Nico touched the amulet against her chest. The glass eye held a large crack from having deflected the letter's bad intention, and Bear's did as well. Nico removed the protective charms and laid them on the holo table, their work done. Jewellery was something she hadn't worn since...she recalled Heloise's photograph as a young wife.

"Did Mr Allen give you pearls?" Nico asked.

"No, my pearls were passed down to me from my mother," Heloise said from the bar. "Her gift for my sixteenth birthday. She said it was for my becoming a woman, but I think she was apologising for my being tall."

Mom, Nico thought.

She remembered—

Her own fingers, dusted with white particles, dangling the aquamarine stone; mom's gift to her.

That wasn't on my birthday. Her stomach lurched, the blank spot in her mind becoming *glass*—she could recall—

"Nico?" Heloise said.

Nico typed rapidly on the keyboard. She accessed the Again Walkers database and then her own folder. She called up the picture of her living self, smiling and wearing the necklace on her birthday. The aquamarine stone on her jumper front.

I don't want to remember. Her chest heaved. *I don't want to*—

Her mail; her Leningrad apartment. She'd just gotten home after her shift at the hotel. The white envelope she'd opened contained a necklace. It had dangled from her fingers; the gold chain flashing the aquamarine stone mom had given her.

Powder within the envelope had gotten all over her hands.

The paralytic sent her falling to the floor, body numb, as men broke down her apartment door.

They held her down and made her watch a videotape inserted into her own VHS player. Her maker appeared, standing in Leningrad's Nevsky Prospekt.

"Happy Belated, Nicky.

"If yer watchin' this, then ya killed me, Nicky. Aw, ya ended me, luv. But ye should know by now, I can't let ye be the one tae decide the end.

"So much planning I did, all bettin' on the day ye'd come tae yer daddy's auld town. D'ya like Leningrad, Nicky?

"Ya must be feelin' it. That sick, sick feelin'. Oh, my wean. Ya made a mistake now, Nicky. What'd I telt ya about mistakes."

Nico stood, the chair falling. She turned to Heloise.

"Did you sell me to them. Did you sell me to the traffickers?" she cried, her voice rising.

"Nico." Heloise's tone held warning.

"You had data on all of us!" Nico shouted.

"Data that was for the *primacy*, Nico; I used techno-shamans to protect everything," Heloise said. "There's no way."

"Then *what* did you sell to get *here*—" Nico saw red.

When she became aware again, her hand gripped Heloise's

throat. Heloise slowly squeezed Nico's wrist to force her fingers to loosen. Her other hand held Nico's that clutched her knife, the blade red. Nico was pressing forwards but Heloise remained firm, her strength greater. Bright red bloomed and spread on Heloise's white shirt from a gash—fresh, spilt elder's blood. A scent Nico hadn't smelled since lying broken in a shallow grave. Nico's fangs grew.

You'll drink, Nicky.

Because ye can't stand dying like this.

Nico tore away. She flung her switchblade against the far wall, burying the blade deep. She swung back and socked Heloise in the chin.

CHAPTER FOURTEEN

Nico ran from Heloise's building; she ran down, down, down. Elder vampires recovered quickly. Nico knew to run as if she could forever. A train waited at the platform she found herself on. She ran inside a car and the train departed. Flashes of memory assailed: her apartment, paralytic on her hands, mom's present. Men breaking in.

They *took* her from her apartment—Nico knew that was *true*—they did things to h—

"No more," she whispered, clutching Bear. "I'll find you. I'll find you."

What did I telt ya about mistakes, Nicky.

The men couldn't wait; they never waited. They violated her in the van. They violated her at the warehouse. Then they opened her veins for customers who drank vampire's blood.

"Okay, that's enough," Nico said, and got off the train, leaving the memory behind in a car boarded by more passengers. The train left and hurtled into the tunnel. Nico walked the platform.

"Conquer® by One Mind," a holo ad said calmly to her. "For all of life's traumas, whether from war, disasters, illness, injury, abuse, or personal violence. Mind and memory adjustment healing to protect *you*. Take control."

"It's too late for that," Nico whispered.

How long had she been held by the traffickers? Long enough. Stored in a slaughterhouse and fed pig's blood with other enslaved vampires. Sold and resold to take extreme punishment from sadistic customers and then heal right up again. Rich women especially liked to drink blood from Nico; they chatted about the bouquet, the flavour.

"She tastes like crushed flowers," one said. Then they poked her with sharp straws and kept them in her bruising flesh, sucking.

I only showed them how tae make more money, Nicky, her maker said, his image playing like some vacation tape of a Scots lad visiting Leningrad.

The sellin' of vampire bodies tae other monkeys wantin' immortality.

Our blood. Our flesh.

Our hearts.

Our sex.

Then...

I telt them tae go get ya.

"You're still dead," Nico said, abrupt and distant.

Ye're not facin' me, Nicky.

"Shut up," she said.

Come get me.

Come get me. Come get me.

Nico boarded another train.

She brought out Dorothy, her hands trembling, and opened a non-visual connection to Shayla.

"Niky?" Shayla answered, and the diner's activity sounded in the background.

"Hi. I'm sorry to bother you at work. But I need to ask you something important."

"What is it, love?"

Nico saw a path to beauty fragment before her.

"If the boogeyman were to snatch you from your bedroom and

into his dimension, how would you find your way back? Or—or lead people to find you."

"I'd use a string, chick. One tied tae my bed, and the other end tae me. It would be a very long string."

"Thank you. I'll talk to you later, when—at your place, if that's okay?"

"Always." Shayla's voice held concern. "Niky—"

"I like you lots."

"I like ye too, Niky. The moment I saw ye."

The moment I saw ye, her maker said.

'Thank you," Nico whispered. *Good bye.* She ended the call.

"Dorothy," she said, when her voice could work again. "Find me the nearest hardware store selling 250-foot electrical cord spools, please."

✳

The store, Zrysxplx's Tools & Materials, was located near the hostels sector. When Nico arrived, her spool order was waiting for her. She happened to spy another useful item.

"I would like the super self-adhesive rubber safety mat with tread surface, please," Nico requested at the hardware store's service counter. "Yes, the twelve by twelve will do." When she received the item, she checked the sticky backing; the super glue was fresh.

I'm not making a bomb, but I hope these purchases got your attention, OI and Makepeace.

Nico went to the register, watched the amount flash at the credit chit reader, and then gathered up her purchases.

Right when she stepped out of the store, she realised that one other knew to track her credit chit's activity too. Heloise's Faering Shearwater nearly jumped the kerb as it came to a screeching stop. Heloise stepped out.

She still wore her bloodstained shirt. Her jaw bore no bruise, and Nico hoped the cut across her chest was healed too. Heloise exhaled cigarette smoke, an anxious, angry cloud. She stepped to approach.

"Not now, Bathory," Nico said warningly, and Heloise stopped.

"I—I'm not Countess Bathory," Heloise said in confusion. "Nico, what—"

"You shouldn't smoke," Nico said. "You should've broken my arm." *He would have.* "Here, have a mint." Nico fetched her tin, opened it, and offered two to Heloise.

Heloise glanced at the mints as she dropped her cigarette and stepped on it. She accepted and put them in her mouth. Then she pulled Nico's switchblade out of her pocket, and Nico stilled.

Heloise held it out, the blade closed. Nico's insides turned cold and bleak. She reached for it, hesitant, then looked away as she took the blade.

"Nico," Heloise said. "The vampire primacy was destroyed. Yes, I sold the database for passage, but the under-holarchy was my buyer."

Nico nodded.

"Look," Heloise continued. She shook her head, as if shrugging off something. "I don't know what you're planning, but—"

"I don't know what I'm planning either," Nico said. "But I'm *meant* to do something, aren't I? It's here. Something came over with me from Old Earth."

"What?"

"Do you know who my maker is? Isn't he in your database?"

Heloise blinked rapidly. "Yes."

"I stalked him for four years," Nico said quietly, "and the whole time, he was remaking me."

"Nic—don't..." Heloise suddenly slumped against her vehicle, her back sliding. Nico caught her. Heloise blinked more, her gaze glassy, and Nico felt it in Heloise's grip; the trust that Nico wouldn't let her fall.

Heloise spat out the remaining mints in her mouth. "You... little..."

How many times had she seen a woman's will removed from

her—had the same done to herself? Nico opened the vehicle's door and helped Heloise into the seat. She tucked Heloise's legs in, and Heloise's hand slackened and slid off her arm.

"You're not him," Heloise uttered.

"I'll make certain," Nico promised.

She opened the tin and spilled the mints into the street while Heloise fought to keep her eyes open.

"I will never, ever, disrespect you like this, ever again." She dropped the tin, then reached in and secured Heloise's seatbelt. "This is a new world, and you're going to have a future." Nico activated the dash's holographic interface and touched the word *Home*. "Take Ms Allen home," she commanded. "And seal the car door."

Heloise had known to look for her at Again Friends; Nico guessed that was why the older vampire had reached the hardware store so fast. But that also meant Shayla would soon come to the hostel too. Nico had shut off Id alerts to ignore Shayla's communications. When the messages stopped, Nico knew she was coming.

"We are so lucky to know these women," Nico said to Bear as she quickly walked down puke street. She'd cut a length of cord, run it through the spool holes, tied it off, and then hung the spool across her body. She cut another length off, about five feet long. "My meeting Heloise or Shayla would have never happened on Old Earth. And if it had…" *If it had, he would have been so dead.*

Nicky, her maker said from the VCR in her apartment. *Ya understand why I sold ya, don'cha?*

I telt them not to use yer mouth, cuz ya bite.

"Stop," Nico said, her switchblade in hand. People scurried away from her on the walk. She put her knife away, having reached the intersection where the YOBA stood. She made a noose with the cord while waiting for the light to change. No Makepeace stood upon the roof. She looked at every rooftop while she walked: still no Makepeace. When she reached Again Friends, she didn't see any vehicle or loitering person who might be OI. She gathered the noose and held it against her rubber mat, concealing it.

"I guess it's just us," Nico said to Bear. She stood outside the door until Dann noticed her. He waved and buzzed her in.

"Uh, are you here to do repairs?" Dann said, looking at her cable spool and the mat she carried.

"No, I'm here to sign your sheet again." She walked up and put her rubber mat aside.

"That's great." Dann pushed the sign-up sheet towards her. "Hey, are you friends with holo stars? Because this hot vampire came in and asked about yo—"

She grabbed his hand and pulled his arm through the slot. Dann's face collided with the cage.

"Oh gods, oh gods," he uttered, cheek pressed against the steel. Nico trapped his arm.

"How does a coin collectors shop on another planet end up with *too* many Leningrad metro passes?" Nico asked.

"If—if this is about that rejection earlier?" Dann gasped. "I'll go out with you."

Nico shoved his arm and body back into the booth, then pulled him into the cage again.

"*Ow!* Oh gods."

"*Why* did you want me to sign in every night," she demanded. "Why did you want me to go to Chaikov's?"

"I don't know—I swear—I don't know why! They wanted you to stay here, so badly—"

"*Who* wants me."

"I don't know! I don't—I get messages from Charity Housing. That's all. Just my messages."

"Can your booth's intercom page the entire building?"

"Yeah-yeah, it can do that." Nico banged his face again. "*Ow!* Cripes, I'm not lying, yes it can! The booth can lock every room, too! Gawds, Neko, I don't know why the controls are like that, I just work here."

"Can you keep the front door unlocked?"

"No-no, I got nothing here that can do that."

"Page Jess and tell her to get her ass here."

"Righ—uh, Jess, um, which one's—"

"*Do it*," Nico ordered. She loosened her hold on Dann's arm, allowing him to grab the microphone with his free one. He pressed the mike's button.

"Testing," he said, the building-wide intercom blaring. "Vampire Jess, can you report to Dann's booth please? Thank you." He released the button and looked at Nico, his lip bloodied. "Can I have my arm back?"

"No. Now lockdown the bathrooms and the rec room."

"Oh, like right n—? Yeah-yeah, on it." He flipped switches. Nico heard the echo above of doors shutting.

"What?" Jess said as she entered the entry hall. "Did you lock the rec room, Dann? There are people still—what's going on?" she added in alarm. Nico pulled Dann's arm to her, bumping him against the cage.

"Ow," he cried.

"I'm going to kill him," Nico said.

"Oh gods, no," Dann whimpered.

"Just let him go," Jess said. She approached cautiously with her hands out. "We can talk this out, ay?"

"Do you see what he did to me?" Nico demanded.

"Wha—" Jess said.

"Look what he did!" Nico said tearfully.

"I don't know, uh, what I did," Dann mumbled against the cage. Jess looked at her and Dann, bewildered, and came closer.

Nico tossed her noose and snagged Jess around the head, then neck.

"*Oi!* Whacke—" Jess's face collided with the cage as Nico pulled hard, the younger vampire spraying blood at the impact. Her knees gave out.

"Oh my ga—you busted her face!" Dann cried. "Did you have

to do that?"

"Don't worry," Nico said. "She's a bad vampire." She tugged at the leash, putting the knot to the nape of Jess's neck, then pulled her back, the vampire too dazed to do more than clutch at the cord tight around her throat. "Now grab the mike and give it to me."

"How do I—there's only room for one of my arms."

"Bring it over, and I'll let go of your arm."

"Oh, I get it. Here you go, Neko—ow!" Dann cried as Nico released his arm and grabbed the one that held the microphone. She pulled his arm through, trapped it beneath her armpit, then pressed the button on the mike.

"Vampires in the dorms," Nico announced. "This is Nico and Bear. You have five seconds to get out before I *kill* all of you. And I will. I'm having a *really* bad night."

Jess coughed and Nico banged Jess's head against the booth.

"Don't let me find you up there," Nico warned as vampires ran down the stairs. "I'll cut your head off. I'll punch your heart organ out. What are you looking at? You want your eyes poked out?" she snarled when one guy looked at her. He ran out the front door with the others. "If I see anyone left in the dorms I will stick my knife in your brain and wiggle the blade all around. Here I come." She turned off the mike. No one else ran down the stairs.

"Now tell Charity Housing I'm coming," Nico said. She let go, and Dann pulled his arm away. He looked at her in bewilderment.

"This switch," he said. "I'm s-supposed to throw this switch every time you're here."

"Do it," Nico said. "Then use your backdoor and get out of here."

Dann flipped the switch. He grabbed his jacket and stepped back. The air seemed to envelope him, obscuring him from view. Dann disappeared.

Nico heard the shuffle of sneakers outside the entrance. Dann struggled into his jacket, watching Nico. He then turned and hurried down the walk, his harried gait like one eager to achieve normality and a distance from crazy girl vampires.

"Another veil," Nico said to Bear, and knotted Jess's noose to the cage.

"You freaky little—" Jess hoarsely sputtered as she clutched at the noose. "What do you want?!"

Nico didn't answer and approached the front door with her rubber mat. She kicked the door open while Jess struggled.

Nico ripped the adhesive protection from the mat and stuck the rubber's sticky side over the doorframe's locking mechanism. She slashed the rubber with her knife to bend it, then secured the end pieces firmly over the frame. When she stepped back inside, the heavy door slid to shut and bumped against the thick rubber.

That should give lockdown trouble.

"*Argh*," Jess uttered in frustration.

"C'mon, OI." Nico looked out into the night; no one came into view. "Fine. I'll get the proof you need." She walked back to the booth. She held Jess by the hair and ran her blade behind Jess's neck to cut the cord. Jess lunged away, staring at Nico. Blood dripped from her nose to her yellow tee.

"Hi, bait girl," Nico said.

CHAPTER FIFTEEN

Jess did not run for the front door; she ran back for the ground floor hallway.

Nico ran faster and shoved Jess into the stairs. The vampires locked in the rec room yelled and banged on the door.

"We're not leaving here through the classroom," Nico said. She took hold of Jess and flung her up the staircase, sending the vampire flying. Jess smacked the landing and groaned.

"Are they holding your baby hostage, or do you just like the money?" Nico asked as she ascended.

"Oi!" Jess cried as she painfully regained her feet. "You crazy—" She grabbed Nico by the shoulders.

"Why keep pretending you're not bait?" Nico resisted Jess's attempt to throw her. She wrestled the other vampire up the next flight of stairs for the second floor.

"*Uff,*" Jess uttered when she tripped back and fell. "I'm not a—" She jumped up and swung. Nico slipped under the swing and punched her. While the other vampire staggered, Nico turned her around and took hold of Jess's nape and the waistband of her jeans. She marched Jess across the floor and tossed her up to hit the next landing. Jess landed with a bang.

"All right, listen!" Jess gasped from where she lay. "I'm not—I—I work for the OI! I work with them!"

"Really?" Nico walked up. "Why do you never sign in on the sheet, then, mate?" She pulled Jess up and dragged her up the remaining steps. "Why are you always playing the hostel's game, ay?

"I don't care if you're a deep cover," Nico added, sending Jess stumbling. "You're too good at being their lure. You're too good at doing *nothing* a cop would do."

"Rack off," Jess yelled, swinging around. "You cold bitch! You don't know!" She threw a wild punch for Nico's face. Nico thrust her foot out and kicked Jess low, striking her knee. Off-balanced, Jess stumbled, her fist hitting nothing. Nico shoved her.

"*I'm* a cold bitch? I'm not the one letting others become—what?" She moved swiftly and grabbed Jess up by the front of her tee shirt.

She hurled Jess into the room, the vampire landing and skidding for bed number 16. Jess slapped the floor, enraged. At Nico's approach, Jess leapt for her. Nico met her in midair and punched her into the floor.

Nico brushed sprayed blood off of Bear as Jess lay, dazed. She hauled Jess up.

"Who's doing this?" Nico asked. "Are they really so scary?"

"You don't understand," Jesse gasped. "This is an intragalactic society." She laughed harshly. "These people can cross dimensions. We can't *escape*."

"You mean *they* can't escape." She spun Jess around and pressed her knife into Jess's back. "You'll have to take my place." She stabbed Jess in the base of her neck, severing the nerves of her C-5 vertebrae.

"No!" Jess shouted as her body collapsed. Nico hauled her into bed number 16, chest down and her head sideways. "I—I can't move!"

"But you can still talk," Nico said. "Scream when you get there, okay?"

"Rest time," the voice-over announced, and the echo of lights shutting off sounded below. "Rest time."

Nico moved quickly for the door.

"You don't want to know what they do to us there," Jess screamed.

"Too late." Nico crossed the hall and descended down the stairs. "I think I've been there. I just need to know whose kingdom it is." She hit the landing just as a sudden realisation did.

"Rest time." The lights went out. Nico descended to the boys' floor and pulled out Dorothy.

"Dorothy, my location; find out what's been built on it in the past one hundred years," she said. "Hurry."

"Working," Dorothy said. In the pitch-darkness of the boys' dorm, an abandoned Id's face still shone brightly, not yet powered down. Nico went to the bed and tossed the Id and the half-eaten blood pack. She knotted her electrical cord to the bed frame, let out line, made certain her spool spun freely, then quickly lay down with Bear.

"I don't think they'll wait for 22 hundred." She looked at Dorothy as the list built.

A dentist office. A club. A bar. A disco. A record store. A Baha'i centre. A hospice. A meatpacking facility.

"The meatpacker. I need pictures," Nico said.

The photos showed: an abandoned plant, covering half the block. Four storeys high. Dorothy captioned it: Brown's Meatpacking, closed forty years ago.

Nicky, her maker said, *how dae ya like yer new —*

Prison.

A man on top of her. A man who was supposed to be watching the customers who came to use her. He was carving his initials into her chest, emulating her maker's handiwork. Old meat hooks swayed on chains from the ceiling. A teddy bear hung, a kidnapped child's lost possession, placed there by an abductor for absurdity, for mockery. Nico felt the digging knife sink too deep — deep enough to pierce her heart.

She pulled her chains' fixture out of the wall.

His neck, wound with steel links; Nico pulling, the chain's straining tension manifesting a truth in glinting metal.

You are the first soul—

You are the first soul I am sending to hell.

The man's head popped off. Blood rose, champagne-like, and Nico drank down ugliness, mercilessness, and fury. She rose, shaky as a foal, and brought Bear down.

No one will ever touch you, ever again, she told him.

Nico stared at the hostel's ceiling, her Id shining in her face.

"So that's how I got you, Bear." The darkness thickened. She activated Dorothy's location beacon and sent it to the Makepeace Emergency Assistance Hotline.

Help, her message said.

The cold closed in. Nico triggered her switchblade.

The dark snatched her away, her spool rattling.

Nico lay in a bed inside a brightly lit room lined with empty beds, a man standing over her.

"*Strashnaya mest' i medved'*!" he yelled, and his pulse rod flared.

Pain ripped through Nico. Her blade came up.

You are the first soul—

You are the first soul I send to hell, Nico had thought, popping off the man's head.

She sliced through his throat as pulse fire from three different directions exploded against the bed. Her left arm seized, and the man's body jerked from being hit. She cut the neck cord of her spool and flung her knife at the nearest shooter, hitting him in the throat. He dropped his pulse gun.

She grabbed the man's pulse rod and hurled it at another shooter, bursting his nose like red fruit. The last shooter shouted into his Id ring. Nico flung the spool at the remaining gunman, hitting him in the face. He staggered and turned to run.

Nico leapt from the bed and came behind him, lassoing his neck with the spool's cord and winding it. She tossed the spool up to the rafters, looping it over a beam, then caught it on the way down. She pulled on the cord hard with her one hand. The lassoed man rose into the air, kicking desperately. She ran around a column with the cord, then knotted it. The hanged man ceased moving, and Nico shook out the arm that had taken the brunt of the pulse rod blast. She picked up two pulse guns lying on the floor.

Jess screamed somewhere outside. Nico walked to the man gurgling from the blade in his throat. She pulled it out and approached the doorway.

The hallway outside was a dead end, with Jess shrieking from the last room. At the open end, a containment field shimmered, cutting off her section from the rest of the corridor.

Keep screaming, bait girl.

Nico put her switchblade's handle to her mouth and stepped back into the room with the hanged man.

A minute later, she shoved the man with the busted nose into the room Jess screamed from. Hands tied behind his back, he stumbled across the floor, his cries muffled by the pulse rod stuffed into his mouth. It whined, high-pitched.

His head exploded. Nico stepped in and shot the men hiding on each side of the doorway, then brought her pistols together and fired at the remaining four gunmen as she advanced. The man farthest dropped when she aimed at the ones nearest her.

Gods, I'm such a bad shot.

Tossing the guns, she took hold of the blade in her mouth and ran with a vampire's speed. She slit the throats of two. But when she reached the last man standing, he held Jess up by the hair, his gun at her temple.

"I'll kill her!" he shouted.

Nico pointed imperiously to a spot over his shoulder.

"No!" he shouted, refusing to look.

She continued to point, and her gaze went to the spot.

The man's eyes darted to the side.

Nico's left hand whipped, and her blade struck him between the eyes. He dropped Jess and slumped over her on the bed. Nico walked up, pulled her knife out of his head, and heard his pierced skull crack apart. She moved for the doorway.

"Don't leave me like this!" Jess shouted. "Don't!"

The hallway remained empty. Jess continued to shriek and Nico approached the containment barrier. Beyond it lay more rooms on either side, and she heard nothing more as Jess became hoarse. She knelt to touch a button on the disc. The barrier winked from view.

The cries of tormented captives hit, echoing in the hall. She took a breath and the scent of fresh, young vampire bodies overwhelmed—pristine, clean, and bleeding.

Herself, in chains.

"Shhhh," she hushed to herself and Bear. "Shhhh."

Two rows of rooms; Nico walked down the hall and saw through the open doors where customers used the drugged and restrained vampires. A male yelled loudest from the room at hall's end, crying out against a gag while others taunted him. A whip sounded.

Her maker grinned from her VCR, a happy Scots lad in Leningrad.

Aye, happy belated, my wean!

Here's yer reminder.

One last, gentle lesson.

That all these sick little monkeys ya like to defend—

The male screamed again as the whip came down, the sounds echoing out into the hall.

Well, they're all like me, Nicky.

All of them.

Nico went back to the rooms at the beginning and entered one. Delores lay, restrained, and Nico took hold of the man atop her by the back of his neck.

I made all a' this fer ya, her maker said, sweeping his arm before Leningrad. He looked on, contemplative. *How dae ya like it.*

She cut the gag from Delores's mouth and Delores's cat eyes shone.

Kill them, Nicky.
Kill them.
Kill them.
Kill them.
Kill for me, Nicky.

"Weesht," she whispered, and she forced the man's throat down to Delores's fanged mouth.

Nico exited after the man's screams had stopped. She did not know how to unlock the restraints, and she hadn't time to find out. The next room held tongue-pierced girl, unconscious, while two men used her body. Nico slit their throats and forced one into the mouth of tongue-pierced girl until her fangs instinctively responded and she sucked, still unconscious. Nico walked into each room, killing or maiming customers. None of the captive vampires was Esche. She moved for the last one, drawn to the blood-scent of a vampire older than she.

Within, a bent over and chained Tex raged against his gag as one man whipped him and another stood behind him. Tex's legs were crooked, broken at the knees, and a bloody bat lay on the floor. A third man taunted him to his face, holding up the keyblade to his restraints. Nico entered and slid the door shut behind her.

✴

When she opened the door again, the three men lay dead, Tex ripping out the throat of the last man Nico had given him. He drank down ravenously, shaking the corpse in his mouth as he did so.

Follow, Nico thought to Tex, willing him to bring death in her wake while she moved ahead. She turned the corner and entered the next hallway. Somewhere beyond it, an industrial machine worked, emitting a high-pitched whir.

Blood; the blood of vampires was pristine, perfect, and clean. The hall smelled of too much spilt vampires' blood. Voices spoke, male and female, taunting and jeering. A pulse rod sounded and a woman cried out in pain. Another cried, too, weeping. Nico entered the double doors of a brightly lit meat storage room, vampires hanging upside down from meat hooks in the ceiling, their throats slit. Blood ran down into waiting jars, and paperback girl lay chained to the floor, sobbing, as two women smelling of expensive perfume stuck sharp straws into her neck and arms and sucked. A gaggle of humans cornered Re'shawn, who crouched, the chains from her wrists snapped apart. She raised her arms as a human, one of the tennis men from Heloise's building, shot her with a pulse rod. Re'shawn jumped from the pulse and cried out.

Re'shawn was nearly as old as Heloise. Nico was not surprised she'd attempted an escape or to fight back, but in her drained state, the humans had taken control.

Distract them for a little more. Nico walked over and punched one of the women sucking on paperback girl, making the woman's face bounce on the floor.

The second woman scrambled away and ran out the doors. Nico moved quickly, blocking the other humans from exiting. The group turned instead for another room with a heavy metal door. They ran inside it, slamming it shut right before tennis man. He pawed at the door.

"No! Don't—" he cried to the people inside, but Nico punched him in the kidney, dropping him. The humans looked out through the door's porthole. It was a non-functioning meat freezer, one that locked from the inside. Nico tried to pull it open.

"A safe room," she said, and kicked the door.

"Help," paperback girl cried. Tennis man was scrambling away, and paperback girl cringed as he passed. Nico caught him and hauled him up by his neck. She brought over a meat hook on a low chain, and ran it on its ceiling rail to hang before the freezer door. The humans behind the porthole stared. She punched tennis man in the face, then hung him from the hook by the back of his shirt.

"You can't do this," he yelled. "I'm—"

"A monster," Nico finished for him. "And—" She punched him in the back, fast and hard, her fists pummelling until he was a fish flopping on a line.

"Monsters," she said as she punched, "must learn—that there are—monster killers." She stopped, and tennis man hung, his body broken.

"Ahhg—ahhg," he moaned, his mouth wide open to draw breath. Nico pushed his body closer to the glass. When she turned around, paperback girl stared with pleading eyes.

"No more," she begged.

"They won't come out to hurt you again." Nico punched tennis man once more in his burst organs, making him attempt another wheezing breath. "Unless what I did only turned them on. In which case." She shoved tennis man's face into the porthole, then slit his throat against the glass. His blood ran down it as he gurgled. When she let go, his head remained stuck. "See? They got the message."

Paperback girl's eyes filled with tears.

"Oh," Nico said. "I forgot. You're a pacifist."

"Go-go girl," Re'shawn said, hoarse. Nico went to kneel before her.

"Get the...glasses...shortcake. They record." Nico looked to where she pointed. Danica hung upside down and insensate with her glasses on her face.

Nico nodded. She went to Danica, took her glasses off, but did not put them on. Sushi Hut girl and Iris hung beside Danica, grey-faced and their lips, colourless. Nico could not smell their life's suspension; their pure scent had fled.

When she looked at the other hung vampires, she did not see Esche among them. Nico returned to Re'shawn and put the glasses on her, then dragged the unconscious human female over by her hair, her obscene, expensive perfume lifting. She offered the woman's throat, and Re'shawn feebly shook her head.

"Naw...rather starve." Her eyes rolled back and she slumped.

Nico dropped the woman. She removed the glasses from

Re'shawn's face and went over to paperback girl to put them on her face. Then she pulled hard on paperback girl's chains.

She pulled her chains' fixture out of the wall and wound the links around the man's neck.

The fixture burst out of the floor.

"No one's going to touch you like that, ever again," Nico told paperback girl.

She and Bear left the room.

Outside, Tex had brought down the woman who'd fled the draining room and was sucking on her torn throat. His legs no longer appeared broken. The machine ahead continued to whir, and Nico walked on, glancing into empty rooms and searching for Esche. Fast gasps emitted from one. She looked in the doorway.

Broody boy was on his knees before someone.

He wore no restraints, and his body, covered with small, deliberate cuts and simple bruises, held no major injury. The second tennis man from the elevator stood before broody boy, an autoerotic strangulation device hanging from a frame and secured around the man's neck.

Nico stepped inside and stood behind second-tennis man.

Bye, tennis bitch.

She tripped the mechanism on the apparatus, causing it to constrict, then stepped around the man as he choked, his body jerking. Nico looked down at broody boy while the man asphyxiated, her switchblade in hand.

"Hi, bait boy," Nico said. Broody boy looked up at her and burst into tears.

"Where's the boss," she said.

"He's past the—there's a room...a room." He sobbed. "You can hear it."

Nico held her knife out a moment more, then lowered it.

Carve TRAITOR in him, Nicky, her maker said.

"Shut up," Nico said.

"*Iris,*" Tex howled suddenly from the draining room.

Nico left broody boy weeping before the hanged man. In the

hallway, the industrial machine's whir grew louder. She turned the corner.

"*IRIS,*" Tex wailed.

The hall was deserted, and beyond the ending doors lay a warehouse space. The clean and bloody scent of vampire bodies wafted. She stepped to where the whirring noise grew louder.

Chop.

Nico turned at the sound of a cleaver hitting a block, and smelled blood strongest from the darkened doorway the sound travelled from. But when she stepped for the door, a ghastly sensation chilled her gut and sickened. A sound filled her mind. It was the faint, then escalating resonance of a ghost screaming.

Nico stepped back, unsteady. She turned her head and saw into the room with the whirring machine.

An assembly line of men in bouffant caps and aprons worked at butchering and processing meat. The first man in the line filleted a hindquarter with his knife. But it was not the leg of a four-legged animal. In the tray next to him, a girl's hand protruded, the nails painted black.

Nico blinked. Boxes behind the man bore golden labels that said: Prochnyy Kolbasa.

Monkeys wantin' immortality, her maker said from the VCR.

The man picked up the slender forearm, chopped off the hand with the black painted fingernails, and stripped the limb of skin. The one beside him fed the filleted meat into the whirring meat grinder and added a spoonful of flakes that sparkled. A third man loaded the sausage casings.

The Prochnyy, Dorothy said, *hand-raised, highly cultured rare meats rejuvenated via a secret, ritualistic process and stuffed with precious gold flakes and sacred herbs.*

Nico heard the dull roar of a cryonics machine, flash-freezing the sausages.

I made all a' this fer ya, her maker said from the VCR.

The man pulled another limb from the tray; Esche's left forearm. He chopped off her hand.

Ye're so late, Nicky.
Was she yer friend, Nicky?
What did I telt ya about—
"You stupid man," she whispered.
She stepped in and shut the door behind her, and the man with
the hand looked up.

CHAPTER SIXTEEN

When Nico left the room, the meat grinder sat silent.

She held up her bloodstained knife. No sound came from the darkened room across except of heavy breathing and the scuffles of a struggle. She took a step, and a gruesome sensation seized her gut once more. Fear stained the air, permeated her mind, and mounted. Her knife hand shook.

I'm sorry. Nico crept closer. *I'm sorry I'm too lat—*

The mind-scream is a psionic ability with no design parameters, Dorothy said.

Esche's mind-scream slammed into Nico's head, a psychic explosion expanding, and Nico collapsed. A film reel played behind her eyes, turning her into Esche. A man was killing her in a dark room, his eyes emotionally lobotomised. No mental touch reached him. He raised his meat cleaver as Esche clawed his face.

Chop.

Esche screamed, projecting her cry across dimensions.

Chop.

She slowly died, aware of every limb lopped off and every organ forcibly removed from what was left of her body until—

CHOP.

The C-1 vertebrae, permanently severed.

Her maker carved into Nico's chest, humming, and Nico smelled the earth of her shallow grave before dying.

"Enough," Nico uttered. She stood up.

Esche's psychic imprint pounded as Nico stepped into the dimly lit room and smelled the death that Esche had. A chopping block where two figures wrestled and grunted in the dark; sawdust on the floor to absorb the spilt blood. Knives and saws neatly hung; a pile of discarded clothing on the floor. Esche's choker with the tiny spikes lay atop. Nico brought up her knife.

Eton boy struggled on the butcher's block, his shirtless body pinned down by a hand at his throat from a human male in leather apron and with corded muscles. Eton boy's trousers hung low, his braces swinging. One of his arms was chopped off at the elbow, the other desperately holding back Chop Man's upraised fist that held aloft his bloodstained cleaver. Chop Man's dull face, clawed by desperate nails, held no expression. He wore Eton boy's tortoise shell glasses.

Nico walked up and stuck her knife into Chop Man's C-5 vertebrae.

The cleaver fell from his deadened hand. The man collapsed, and when Nico pulled him off Eton boy, Eton boy tried to punch her. She saw the tattoo on Eton boy's pale chest. Over his left pectoral muscle was inked: GAIL.

"It's me," she said, her voice faint and strange as Esche's scream echoed inside her skull. She stilled Eton boy's remaining arm so he could look at her. "I got him. I'll get all of them."

"The glasses," Eton boy gasped. "The lenses record."

Nico kicked Chop Man over, his slack mouth drooling as he tried to breathe. She pulled the glasses off his face and put them on Eton boy. She picked up a limb.

"They can reattach it," she said, putting it in Eton boy's remaining hand.

"That's not...my hand."

"Oh." Nico took it back and dropped it on the floor. Esche's scream grew louder. Nico dragged Eton boy out the door.

"The girl?" he said, head swivelling.

"We'll save her," Nico said.

"So—horrible. We must stop...." Eton boy's eyelids fluttered.

"We got him," Nico said.

"Jerry's not bested us," he uttered.

"That's right, Tommy." Nico pulled him down the hall and as far away from Esche's mind-scream as she could. She set him down against the wall. "The Nazis won't win." Eton boy shut his eyes and went still.

Nico straightened Eton boy's glasses, then walked to the end of the hallway for the warehouse floor.

She stood in the shadows of the hall and peered into a warehouse space measuring two thousand square feet and two storeys high. At the end was a metal staircase leading to a balcony and an office unit, its windows protected by steel, rolling shutters. A man knelt at the balcony's railing with a machine gun aimed. Six other men were positioned around the space and behind boxes and crates, their weapons pointed.

You don't lure Vengeance and Bear into another dimension to end it like this.

She looked up. A giant bubble hung above with wires connected to it. Suspended in the liquid that trembled from electrical currents, a female Po shuddered. She floated upside down.

A tortured Po. A Po gone mad.

Nico withdrew back down the hall and returned to the chopping room. Esche's continuous scream made her stumble. Tex's distant cries echoed, incoherent. Nico straightened and entered.

When she returned to the hall's end, she pushed the wheeled butcher's block with one of the dead meat packers seated atop. The wheels squeaked, echoing, and her vampire's hearing detected the sounds of weapons being readied. She pushed hard and sent the block rolling into the centre of the warehouse floor.

The men opened fire with pulse blasts and bullets, decimating the meat packer's body. Nico stepped in and threw a butcher's knife for one shooter to the left, hitting his throat. She flung another far across the room and the man on the balcony dropped down with the blade deep in his chest. The third knife flew to the right and found a man's eye socket. Something burst through the mental door inside Nico's head.

FORGET, the Po shouted into Nico's mind, and Nico replayed the memory of Esche's death-scream back, a mental tape recorder clenched in psychic fists.

I am her champion, and I am not done.

The command *FORGET* fragmented inside Nico's head. Nico threw the cleaver at the Po's bubble. It smashed, spilling liquid as the Po resonated, a mind-scream greater than Esche's. Somewhere unseen, four other women shrieked, their twisted psychic faces flying at Nico's mind.

Four Baba Yagas and a captive Po.

Nico fell to her knees as the Po plummeted to her death, impacting the warehouse floor. The four unseen women went silent and the men dropped their weapons and writhed.

Don't pass out now, Nicky, her maker said, sticking his knife into her.

Stop it, Nico said when he stabbed her again, and she saw the night stars above the treetops as she lay dying.

Nico swayed, then stiffly regained her feet. She walked, wooden, and continued to replay Esche's death to push back the Po's. Nico walked by cowering men and mounted the stairs to the office, one step at a time. Once she reached the door, she pressed the chime and waited.

When the door did not slide open, she pressed the chime again.

The door slid open, and Nico stepped in.

Her feet touched thick carpeting, and antique clocks ticked. A table with silver candlesticks and a meal of kolbasa laid on fine china sat abandoned. The slices glittered from the precious gold flakes mixed in the pale meat. The wine glass did not exude the scent of wine, but of undead blood. Nico looked at the great oak desk at the end of the room and at the bearded, grey-haired man who stood behind it, dressed in a tailored black suit.

Fedotov. Who is Fedosov.

Vasili was small, only a little bigger than Nico, and he shook with a fear similar to that of the smitten upon sight of his idol, or of the doubter, witnessing his god for the first time.

Do we know each other?

Nico walked slowly forwards and stared, thinking him dry and colourless, nondescript and unmemorable. He seemed someone who was simply nothing unless he possessed something. He raised a trembling hand as if to ward her off, and it held something.

Two torn strips of paper; her and Bear's signed name on the Again Friends' sign-in sheet. Her credit card with her signature on the back. All three pieces sealed together by an iron nail, driven through the centre. Wound with black string, thirteen times. Nicolette Alexikova and Bear, in triplicate.

Nico raised her wrist, displaying Shayla's blessed bracelet.

"All that you hurt," she said as she approached, "for money?"

Fedosov only looked at her, frightened and seemingly uncomprehending. He backed away.

"Money," she repeated. Fedosov backed into the wall.

"Bear and me, on your label," she said. "Like a pooka."

She stepped closer.

"How many vampires did you kill, wanting it to be me?"

Why do you look like you're dreaming?

"You're not him." *Those aren't his eyes.* "You're just...."

She stepped again, and Fedosov's hands went up, as if in surrender.

"Ahhhhh," he screamed when she stabbed his hand that held his talisman, pinning it and his hand to the wall. She waited, but no blood exited the hand to bloom on the paper with her signature.

"Ahhhhhhhhh," he continued to cry.

Nico stared, wondering at his pain.

When Fedosov's cry faded away, Nico heard a heavy step on the carpet. She turned her head.

Tough Guy stood within the room.

"Desist, potential citizen," the Makepeace said.

Special Agent Yoo rushed in with agents, filling the space with moving bodies and noise. The agents hurried past Nico to secure the room and see to Fedosov. Nico looked at the Makepeace, who stood statue-like as agents passed between them. An agent wearing a medical insignia came to her side, carrying a tagger.

"Ms Alexikova, we're going to administer a dose of Conquer," the agent began.

"Don't touch me," Nico said, turning to keep her arm away from him. Someone laid a firm, but reassuring hand on her shoulder and she looked up. Tough Guy had crossed the room and towered above her. "I don't want any," she said to the Makepeace.

"Ms Alexikova, you've been exposed to the death of a captive Po and the residue effects of a psionic's mind-scream," Yoo said, approaching, and Nico listened, feeling the agent were a thousand miles away. "Conquer does not affect your memories, only the fear and pain that comes with them."

"No." *This isn't him. I can't find him if you give me drugs.*

"She has said no," Tough Guy said. He turned Nico and walked her to the door.

Medics rushed in, and Yoo barked commands about getting Nico's switchblade out of Fedosov. Tough Guy walked beside her with his hand on her shoulder, a big brother with a big gun who, like in the movies, was supposed to nod his approval because she won the karate fight, girl in high school, or secret kingdom, and then take her for ice cream. But the peace of some storybook victory was just that, a story. *He* still eluded her, causing her to quake within, an eruption building. As they descended the steps and proceeded down the floor, Fedosov's dazed thugs sat in the custody of OI agents, exhibiting no fear or suffering at all.

Why did you give them Conquer? Shoot that one. And that one.

And that one. Beat them up for me.

"I had to do this all by myself," she accused, her voice hoarse.

"You did well," Tough Guy said, and they walked.

When Nico and the Makepeace entered the hall with the chopping room, the hallway was empty, Eton boy no longer present. But Nico heard agents investigating the meat grinding room. They swiftly tagged and inventoried.

One piece of Esche, two pieces of Esche, three pieces, four.

Nico abruptly turned for the chopping room and Tough Guy let her go. She entered, Esche's scream amplifying, and she snatched up Esche's choker from the discard pile. Her hands shook as she fastened it around Bear's neck.

"Tell me I did okay," Nico said, turning to the Makepeace.

"You have destroyed a monster," Tough Guy said from the doorway.

Nico's gaze fell to where Chop Man lay. He blinked.

When she looked up, Special Agent Rotherhithe stood hidden in the shadows, his vampire visage to the fore. His lip curled and he held a meat cleaver.

Tough Guy offered his hand.

Nico left the room and the last vestiges of Esche behind.

They turned for the hall with the draining room, and the surviving human suckers and sex customers sat, cuffed, while the agents processed them. They appeared unharmed, and therefore, untouched by Tex. Nico stared at their inviolate state.

Kill them all, Nicky.

Kill them.

Kill them.

"Shut up," Nico said, and Tough Guy laid a hand once again on her shoulder.

The draining room: straws lay scattered, one of them glittering with encrusted jewels. The hooks hung empty while agents moved, attending to victims, and the freezer door stood open, its porthole smeared with blood. Tex huddled, holding someone, and his scourged back bled streaking, bloody tears. Paperback girl sat outside with a medic who fed her blood packs. She watched dazedly as Nico passed by with the Makepeace.

"Don't—arrest her," paperback girl ejected, and blood dripped from her mouth. "She helped."

"It's okay," Nico said. "He has wings."

They walked on and turned for where the duplicate dorms lay.

Within the boys' dorm, the man still hung from the rafters. A silver metal arch stood by the bed where her taut electrical cord emerged, a disappearing rope trick leading to nothing. An agent documented the dead with an Id while another conversed with him. The agents then chuckled with each other, but to Nico, their mirth amplified into grotesque laughter.

Look at them.

They're all me, Nicky.

"No, I will not let you tell me," Nico said.

She and the Makepeace walked through the gate.

They stepped out into the boys' dorm in Again Friends, her electrical cord tied to the bed frame. She walked with Tough Guy out of the room and down the steps, ignoring the investigating agents moving about. When they stepped into the entry hallway, Dann's caged booth stood empty, and Tough Guy removed his hand. Nico continued walking and did not hear him follow. She did not look back.

Outside the entry door that she had jammed, hydraulic jaws had been set between the door and the frame, bending metal. It left a gap to squeeze through. The dark outside was well lit with spotlights, and a curious crowd gathered, marked off by strung tape and an erected barricade.

Before she reached the door, Nico saw her. Shayla stood on the inside of the barricade with a three-quarter length corduroy coat over her waitress uniform, talking to an officer in blue who blocked her from entering. Nico passed through the door's gap and stepped outside.

"Niky," Shayla called. She bypassed the officer and quickly approached.

"Niky," she repeated, and Shayla embraced her. Nico felt cold; too cold, even to feel Shayla's touch. She was too far away to smell her.

"I'm not going to make it," Nico uttered in her arms. "He's here."

"Who is?" Shayla moved back to look at her.

"I won't let him out, so he has nowhere else to be."

"Where." Shayla's gaze searched hers. "Where is he?"

My wean, he laughed.

A Makepeace watching. A witch with a gun. They should kill her that instant.

"He's me," Nico whispered.

She broke away from Shayla's grasp.

"Nik—"

Nico pushed through the barrier, the crowd, and out into the street, running low and fast—out of range, out of reach—of Shayla's touch and a Makepeace's gaze.

"*Niky!*" Shayla shouted.

Shayla's voice could not drown his.

I am without angels.

And the truer hell is waiting.

Nico ran into the night.

CHAPTER SEVENTEEN

If you are me, I have one thing I can control, and that's my death.

When her maker burned atop the Rocklyn Hotel, Nico nearly burned up with him. She had needed to witness, with her own eyes, his passing. It had taken her a week to fully heal from her injuries, but his finality had been assured.

If he had resurrected within her, a mirror could not tell her. She would not wait for *him* to act, harming Heloise or Shayla and leaving a Makepeace to make the decision of death for her.

If I am you, I will take you with me to my death.

Nico walked a littered street with closed storefronts and found what she was looking for.

Punk Monk Martial Arts Supplies and Weapons Shop was still lit. Men and boys loitered within, dressed as if they'd ended practice at the dojo next door. Nico opened the door with its *Closed* sign and walked in.

"This is a stick-up," she said. "Just kidding." Nico walked to the counter and the young man with the street-wise stare standing behind it. He looked like a dojo minion, a possible were-mix of doubtful Other strength, but Nico decided she would speak to him anyway.

"I heard you'd supply a Slaughter Spawn fighter in exchange for some guaranteed odds. The fighter would be me," she said.

Dojo boy looked at her, incredulous, and laughed, the guys around the store joining him. He then struck the glass counter with both palms and stared hard.

"Punk Monk picks the fighter, not the other way around."

Nico put her hand on the counter, shortening the distance between her grasp, his head, and the glass.

"If you don't give me what I want, I will take it," she said, her voice calm and slow. "And then I'll give this place the name of someone who can pay for what I've taken, once I'm done."

Kill them, Nicky.

She grabbed dojo boy's head by the hair right when an African man stepped into view from the back room. She looked at him.

"*Argh,*" dojo boy said as Nico twisted, torquing his neck.

The man was long and wiry, and a calm radiated from his centre. His bald head and skin bore leopard marks. He looked at Nico, his placid face inscrutable, and Nico decided the only reason she would win in a fight with him was because her death spirit was greater than his.

"What'll you need," Leopard Man said.

"A kukri, please. And a lighter." She shook dojo boy when he tried to move. "And lighter fluid. Two aerosol cans of lubricant. Three flash-bangs. One grenade. No, three grenades. A pair of goggles. Duct tape. Half-mask. I'll wear your logo if you want. And if you'll let me use your tub, I'll need 88 pounds of sodium borate and 38 pounds of boric acid."

She let dojo boy go and he scrambled back, holding his neck.

"And I need a car," she said. She looked at the men standing around the store.

I'll put ya in the trunk and set it on fire, her maker said.

"One you don't plan on seeing, ever again," she added.

★

A big, bearded Polynesian man fetched what Nico needed, filling a cardboard box, while dojo boy pulled out kukris and laid them on the counter for Nico to choose. She balked.

"What is this?" she exclaimed. "You don't need eighteen inches to cut off heads. Get me Gurkha British service issue, Sarkhuri Khukuri."

"But that's only ten inch—"

"It's ten and a half and can dispatch you to Kali before you realise you're severed from your neck," Nico barked. "And hurry up, I need to sharpen it." Another boy approached Nico while dojo boy found the requested kukri and put it on the counter.

"Uh, sensei wants to know what the boric acid and stuff is for?" the second boy said.

"Fire retardant," she answered, pulling the blade from its scabbard and examining it.

"What era are you from?" Bearded Man exclaimed and placed a small canister on the counter. "We got your fire retardant right here."

Nico looked at the little can, sceptical. "Set dojo boy on fire, and I'll believe you."

To Nico's surprise, they did set dojo boy on fire, and when Nico saw that he didn't light up, she consented to being sprayed. Bearded Man pulled out a firefighter's canister, the size of an oxygen tank, and Nico stood in the store's practice yard while he applied the hose. She had Bear doused too. Getting sprayed by the contents tickled, especially when Bearded Man asked her to lift her arms. To her surprise, a giggle broke from her lips. When he suggested she spray up her skirt herself, Nico nearly laughed again.

"You can change your mind," Bearded Man said, and she knew he meant about the pit.

Nicky.

She shook her head. "I need to end something tonight."
Kill him.
"I'm going to kill you," Nico said.
"Huh?" Bearded Man said.
"Sorry. I was talking to my demon."

Bearded Man left her with the cardboard box and kukri, and Nico pulled out the *chakmak* from the scabbard and began sharpening the blade. Each stroke made her mind more still, and she finally remembered.

The Leningrad traffickers, their throats torn apart by her own teeth, and the hot blood given up because she had reaped it, as easily as the ghosts from their eyes. The spines she'd severed, the bodies she'd shot, cut, maimed, and burned. A piling body count that had sated nothing. All that had been *him*, his poetry, his words, had become personified in her. She had become his mirror, magnifying his romantic self-image: the death hero. But even when manifested as his death angel at last, Nico was still Nico. She stalked and killed every trafficker she could find because she thought she was killing him.

Nico stopped sharpening.

She rose, kukri in hand, and picked up a wooden karate breaking board. She tossed it and lashed out.

Air whistled, and nothing gave resistance to her blade. When two pieces hit the ground, she understood then that she hadn't missed.

"This time," she said to Bear, "we end him."

★

Someone played Queen's *We Are the Champions* within the shop while Nico secured grenades and flash-bangs to her harness. She packed Bear, papoose-like, into a utility pouch with only his head showing. Then she tied a little half mask on him using a black bandana with the Punk Monk logo and tightened a pair of child's goggles over his eyes.

"Esche comes too," she said, and refastened the choker around Bear's neck. She tied up her hair.

She was pinning Shayla's buttons to her harness when a small old man with long, grey hair woven with falcon feathers stepped into the yard. His left hand lacked three fingers.

"Hau, I am Chaytan. Leopard sent for me. I fought the spawn in '78," he said.

"Hau, Chaytan. I'm Nico and Bear."

Falcon man nodded, then yawned mightily. "And I am damn sleepy. You eyasses should do your fighting in the daytime."

"Sorry."

He laid a piece of paper and a pencil on the table. "Show me your plan."

She drew it for him, drawing a huge circle for the pit and a burning car in the middle. He took the pencil from her.

"The hanging rope to get out is over here. A blue light in the wall marks it." He made an X, then pointed at the spawn tunnel she drew. It lay directly across the pit from the X representing the rope's position.

"A red light marks the entrance to their burrow. You'll die here."

"I need to see him," she said. He looked at her. "My maker is in there. Will you let Leopard Man know the odds?"

"Yes," he said. He drew four more circles, each positioned twenty feet from the pit. "The pit guardians are towers. They deactivate the shield over the pit for a fighter to get through. They also film the fights. Nothing lives in the tunnel. No one is on duty. No one watches except the towers. You will be alone.

"The sound from the pit sickens. Those exposed to the sound always flee. It is why seconds abandon their fighters.

"They *know* you—not hear, smell, taste, or see you. They don't need senses to find you. You are what they are not. And they'll devour you for it."

Ye are what he was not, Shayla said.

"Light, fire, and smoke confuse them. But they won't stop because of it. Never stop when you're in the pit. Stop, and you die. You kill one, and they multiply. You must outlast the spawn."

She out-deathed the spawn, the shoe shiner said.

"Fight true. May the gods walk with you."

✱

One hour after entering Punk Monk, Nico stood on the walk with goggles pushed up to her forehead, mask at her throat, loaded harness strapped on, and kukri scabbard at her side. Chaytan had already left to make a bet on her at Winkie Bets, and only Leopard Man stood near while the others hung back.

No one offered to be her second, and she knew why. They were scared of the pit, and they also needed her to lose.

I should bet on myself and take all their money.

But there was no time for that, and Nico did not want to be distracted. She thought of who would have seconded her if given the chance—Heloise, who lay unconscious somewhere, and Shayla, who still searched for her. Nico continued to ignore Shayla's messages. She could not risk both women figuring out her final solution, once Nico viewed the truth in the pit.

If I'm him, I have to leave, she told them in her mind.

A worn, little vehicle drove up, its engine emitting a little rattle, but the windows and hatches were all present and the body and interior intact, per Nico's request. When it stopped before Nico, its holo interface played Queen. Bearded Man disembarked, humming.

"Wished there'd been time to make napalm, but this'll do." She turned to Leopard Man. "Okay, thanks."

He looked at Nico. "You gonna kill yourself?"

"I don't want to," Nico said.

"Whatever tried to kill you before you came to me, forget what it did to you. Come back to life. The pit needs your heart, not cold eyes," Leopard Man said.

"Okay," She straightened. "I'm here."

"The pit guardians know to let you through," he said. "May the gods walk with you."

Nico boarded the vehicle. "Let's go," she told the BRAI, and the vehicle advanced. She didn't bother to look back at the men and boys of Punk Monk. They had served their purpose.

The streetlights streaked past as the vehicle zoomed. She left all the windows down to admit the city's sounds and night's cool air. She spotted Makepeaces, positioned on buildings like marble sentinels, but none stopped her, and the vehicle drove on. Nico pulled out Dorothy and typed a simple message to Specs.

Thanks for looking out for me.

She typed two more messages, one to Shayla and one to Heloise, timed to release in the morning. Then she secured Dorothy behind Bear.

"Dorothy, play me 'Lords of the Null-Lines'." Nico put in her sound-buds.

The vehicle approached a deserted overpass, then turned into the chain-linked fence beside it. The gate was open, and the vehicle passed through and descended down a ramp for an overgrown open passageway strewn with debris, the train rail in the centre long disused. The vehicle lumbered over it, then sped along, following the rail between its wheels. Nico watched the buildings, trees, and street lights above that they passed, then looked at the concrete walls on either side as huge graffiti art appeared.

KAHU NAKAHI, one said, displaying the great figure of a noble Maori man, a mass of flowers and flickering candles before it. Art monuments of other celebrated fighters decorated the passageway's sides, and Nico saw nimble figures ahead, moving with spray cans in hand, intent on the concrete wall before them. Two more figures held lights for them. Goggled and wearing gas masks, the artists worked rapidly on a fresh graffiti, their spray cans spelling:

страшная месть и медведь

Nico held up Bear to see as their vehicle passed, and the artists paused to solemnly watch her drive by.

"That's us, Bear," Nico said, securing him again. "We're vampires, all the way down."

She opened the lighter fluid can and began squirting the backseat with its contents. More names came into view on either side, some spray-painted over old names, and Nico paid them no heed, knowing they were of the many who were dead.

But a massive graffiti of glow-paint came into view that gave her pause, one that had obliterated many names on the wall. Flowers bloomed in the concrete's cracks and pressed gold leaf gleamed in the artwork. The name rose, luminescent, a night-sun rising out of sucking darkness:

SHYLA O'FEY

"*Jaya Mahakali*," Nico said, raising her fist. She turned back to the dash and pulled down her goggles. The cavernous mouth of Jotun tunnel loomed. "Okay, Bear, let's screw this up."

Her little vehicle entered, splashing through trapped water.

Steel girders ribbed the cavern's throat, stretching to infinity. The tunnel stood three trucks high and four across.

"Plenty of space and oxygen," she told Bear. "I don't think we're going to cause a sucking inferno." *Or melt down most of the spawn with this small car.*

"Raise the windows to a one-fourth opening, please," she requested of the onboard BRAI, then activated the lighter. She locked the flame and tossed it into the back seat. Flames immediately licked, crackling. Nico deactivated Dorothy but left her sound-buds in. The faint sound of gnashing teeth and screams rose, an ascending, echoing cacophony that seeped into her dampened hearing. A glowing graffiti marker on the tunnel wall said:

YOU AR HAV WAY TO HELL

She slowed the vehicle and hopped out.

"Accelerate, don't stop," she ordered, and the hatch clicked shut as smoke filled the interior. Nico ran alongside, applying duct tape over her nose and mouth. She pulled up her half-mask with the Punk Monk logo. The vehicle sped up, pulling away. Thick, black chemical smoke spiralled from the vehicle's windows and rose to cushion the tunnel's top, then expand. The vehicle's interior flared, yellow and white, its fire roaring, and Nico pursued its light.

The screaming of the spawn pierced through the fire's noise and reverberated, chilling Nico to her bones, and had sense not fled her soul she would have turned around right then. But something more ran with her as she watched the vehicle roll, her wild, flaming chariot to hell. Her passageway became a tunnel of ghosts, from her parents to Fedosov's victims, and she was Anubis's herald, leading the souls to their common murderer at last.

The vehicle's fire cast light upon the four towers surrounding the pit, then abruptly dropped from view. Its smash resounded amid frenzied screaming. Black smoke billowed, evidence of plastic, metal, foam, and polymer burning and melting. The pit's sides lit, a giant's hellish campfire. Four booms sounded from rubber tires blowing and launching—Nico hoped—melted goo to take out spawn. The hatches blasted open as pressurised struts flew. Nico reached the pit's edge and the blinding heat hit. She leapt.

FOR ESCHE ABRAM-ANGEL, her mind shouted.

A frenzied infestation of grey and pink raw flesh swarmed below, exposed by the conflagration's light. Burning, screaming, they flailed, half-formed and malformed, erupting in limbs, claws, and teeth. Those not crushed by the vehicle surged, furiously clawing and biting as they burned.

Her feet hit the vehicle's hot roof. She pulled a grenade's pin and launched it towards the red light embedded in the pit's side. Nico leapt again, hurling through smoke and fire as the pit thundered from the grenade's explosion.

She landed at the blackened impact site amid raining spawn parts and before the mouth of their tunnel, an aerosol can in each hand. A flaming spawn hurtled for her and Nico pressed the nozzles.

FOOOOSH

A single streak of white-hot fire ignited from the spawn's flame, the streams of lubricant fuelling a three-foot long blowtorch. Nico sidestepped the burning spawn and pointed her flamethrower into the tunnel. She had only seconds before the cans ran out. The spawn within ignited, raking the air. Smaller than the spawn outside, they screamed, stretching from bio-matter clinging to the cave's sides.

Nico threw the cans deep within the tunnel. She sent a flash-bang down with the cans. The explosion ignited the cans and fire spread. She drew her kukri.

I'm coming for you, she mentally shouted, jumping in, and her arm whipped, slicing death.

Nico advanced, cutting spawn down that reached for her from above, the ground, and the cave's sides, their limbs stretching from the bio-matter birthing them. Spawn detached and flung themselves. More clawed for her legs and she swept, a scythe to mow them down. The screaming ascended. She sent down another flash-bang to anger them further. She was deep in evil's maw that made tinier maws, all come into the world killing.

I am *the servant of your victims*—

I am the Death *greater than you*—

His home, his hell. She would cut his heart out even if that heart were her own. Nico nearly slipped on spawn and looked down. Spuds with teeth grew out of the bio-matter.

Babies.

The little spawn wriggled, mewling and their mouths gaping. Nico saw their faces in the darkness, enraged, impotent, and weeping. Tears squeezed because—

Because?

The Rocklyn.

Her maker wept.

Nicky, he cried, before erupting into flames.

Nico dropped the lighter fluid can on the baby spawn. She ran back down the tunnel as spawn clawed, and tossed her last flash-bang behind her.

The blast sent flames flying from the exploding fuel can. The mewling spawn erupted into roaring fire that silenced them, but the mature spawn at the mouth of the cave screamed. Nico pulled the pin on a grenade and threw it towards the entrance.

The cave trembled from the explosion and earth rained down. A flying spawn limb smacked Nico in the face. She leapt through the grenade's smoke, slashing. Soot swirled in the open pit and spawn flailed, the vehicle still smoking and burning bright. Nico sliced through the spawn around her and jumped.

She landed on the rooftop without it collapsing and kept her feet moving before her fireproofed soles melted. She threw her last grenade for the blue light marking the hanging rope. In the thumping flash that illuminated, spawn bodies jumped, popcorn-like, in the air. Nico leapt across the pit.

Claws whipped for her. Nico landed at the blast site with her kukri in hand and began slashing towards the dangling rope.

Jaya Mahakali, she screamed.

Spawn bodies opened up from her blade. Limbs dropped as she whirled and lopped, slicing through everything her furious knife could reach. She saw the rope and jumped high.

Nico grabbed the rope with one hand, and claws raked. A swipe seared her back. Nico's hand slipped off the rope.

She hit the ground and the spawn inundated. Her knife whipped up, slashing through gnashing jaws. She chopped and chopped, each strike sending reaching claws and limbs flying. But each step she took moved her in an unknown direction. When she saw the blue light again, it bobbed in and out of view from a mass of spawn lunging before it. Nico moved faster and a screaming mouth descended from behind.

She swung around. The air rippled, a sudden displacement from—

Weird energ—

WHOMP

A hole erupted in the mouth, the shot ploughing through and into more spawn. Nico slashed through its body and kept her blade moving.

WHOMP WHOMP

Spawn splattered Nico's goggles, and she heard the high-pitched—whirl of—

Five air displacements—

Five spawn exploded before her from scatter-shot, splattering her and Bear. One spiralling shot brushed Nico's side and shoved her, a blow to her ribs. Nico slashed with the motion and advanced, the blue light bobbing near once more. She stuck her kukri behind Bear and leapt high for the wall. Spawn hurled themselves up as she grabbed the rope and held on. The air expanded behind Nico, shoving her into the wall. She smacked her face.

WAMWAM

Flying limbs and broken teeth struck the wall, and Nico looked up.

Shayla stood above in goggles and a graffiti artist's paint-stained gas mask, the ends of her corduroy coat pushed back as weird matter warped over her body. With hands by her sides and fingers flexed, Shayla opened fire.

WAMWAMWAMWAMWAM

Strafed spawn splattered Nico as she climbed, hand over hand, her soles slipping as the pit's side became slick with landing bio-matter. But even above the weird matter explosions and the roar of a car fire, the spawn screamed, the sound arcing through the air. Something landed on Nico's back and sank teeth into her shoulder. She yelled, ripping her lips on the duct tape, and pulled out the kukri. She stabbed at the biting mouth, sticking the blade in herself instead. Claws hooked her legs and dragged her down. Shayla pointed.

The explosion next to Nico's left ear shattered her eardrum and rattled her teeth and vision. The kukri flipped from her numbed fingers. Shayla reached down and grabbed Nico's empty hand. She pulled Nico up, made a fist with her free hand, and aimed.

Warping weird matter rippled along Shayla's arm and exploded, the recoil flaring out her shoulder. The spawn clinging to Nico's legs burst and fell away. Nico clambered over the pit's lip with Shayla pulling hard.

I am out. She stumbled into Shayla and then held Shayla before herself. She tore off her duct tape and mask, inhaling soot and smoke. *I am free.*

Screams heightened in Nico's one ear and a hot scent filled her mouth and nostrils beneath the sharpness of chemical particles.

Rich, *uterine*—

Nico lunged for Shayla's throat.

—*whoonk*—

Nico's chest burst and blood sprayed. Her left side spun back and she thought: what an odd sound. Like—

A—*projec*—*tile*—

MP-1634 stood in the billowing smoke, gun raised.

Nico became dead weight, sound and sense of touch leaving. The tunnel tilted and her vision vanished. She still tasted Shayla's scent on her tongue.

She wanted to say: *thanks for saving Shayla.*

She wanted to say: *thanks for not shooting Bear.*

She landed, her body thundering, and felt herself die again.

✳

A sharp ringing intensified in her left ear and pulled Nico awake.

Her eyes remained closed but her face scrunched at the escalating pain. Something cold and hard pressed against the suffering ear and the acute noise lessened. Then the object moved away and someone placed something soft that muffled and adhered: a bandage.

A woman spoke with a New Yorker's accent, and Nico smelled

smoke and Shayla. A case clicked shut near Nico's tender ear.

Ow. Not so loud.

"Fifteen years old?" the woman remarked. "Her ear will be good as new in an hour."

"Uhh," Nico whispered.

"Well, look who's awake," the woman said. "Can you tell me your name, young lady who's waking up?"

"Nico." She swallowed, her croaking throat dry. "Alexikova. And Bear."

"Can you tell me where you are right now, Nico?"

"I'm...on some crazy planet...with beautiful women."

"That sounds about right," the woman said, and a straw pressed to Nico's lips; blood. She sucked hard, scrunching the snack pack. Someone caressed her forehead, smelling of peaches and fresh blood.

"Niky, this is medic Bobienski," Shayla said. "She's patched yer heart, chest, and back, and pumped a few pints into yer stomach. Yer shoulder has a bad bite in it, love, but the wounds like it are healin' already."

"Okay," Nico said, her voice shaky. She pried open her eyes and saw the night sky. They were outside the tunnel and in the open passageway, the breeze rustling the treetops. Wisps of black smoke rose. She moved her eyes and saw Shayla, cheeks still flushed from the pit's heat. She no longer wore the goggles and mask. "How is Bear?"

"Mr Bear's safe and happy, chick, only needin' a bath." Shayla held him up; he still sat in his pouch and harness, unharmed. Esche's choker remained around his neck and Shayla had pushed his goggles up. Bear also looked like he'd been dipped in freshly ground spawn.

"Yay," Nico said feebly. Bobienski shut another case and Nico winced.

"Didn't even need the organ-regenerator," Bobienski said. "That heart will be good as new by tomorrow. Okay, I need my stretcher." She and Shayla helped Nico to sit up. Nico had been lying on a rolling stretcher, mucked up with her bloodstains and spawn residue. Bobienski and Shayla lifted her off and set her down on the ground.

"Thank ye for comin', Jane," Shayla said as the medic expanded the stretcher, then rolled it away with the cases atop it. Shayla turned back to Nico while Jane loaded a medic van.

"If ye'd lost organs, ye'd be needing that regenerator," Shayla said. "Ye got spawn teeth and claws in ye, love, besides their bio-matter. But vampires don't sicken from their touch."

"Wha-what about you?" Nico said. Bear's own sullied state soiled Shayla's coat. Shayla smiled.

"Since my own fight in the pit, chick, I've become resistant." She smoothed Nico's hair and Nico inhaled through her mouth, tasting Shayla's blood in the smoke-tinged air. The hatch shut on the medic van. Jane drove away, crunching debris.

Medical bills. She'll worry about them later.

"I'm sorry I attacked you," Nico said. "It's no excuse, your smelling so edible. Please say you would have shot me."

"Aye, I would've shot ye."

"You're just saying that because I asked," Nico complained.

"Attack me again, and I'll shoot ya," Shayla said, her oestral-rich scent lifting.

Nico's fangs emerged.

"Wissht." Shayla rubbed Nico's bottom lip, and to Nico's surprise, her fangs receded. "We need ya walkin' now for the healing."

A patched heart. She rose shakily with Shayla's help. The still organ within felt like a burst grapefruit, mashed back together, and Nico rubbed at the tender, new skin on her chest. It itched. She was surprised to still be alive; 1634 had decided to only partially destroy her heart. When she looked down at her bared, white chest she saw how Bobienski had slashed her clothes. Her cardigan and shirt hung open, ruined.

"This was my only outfit," Nico exclaimed.

"It's a bonnie look when not manky, and oh, ye've sweet breasts,"

Shayla said, grinning. Nico gaped and crossed her arms over her chest. Then she realised—

She pulled her shirt remnants aside. Bobienski's patching had obliterated the I and L in the word KILL carved over her heart. Below, where her abdomen started, her maker had cut the word FOR, and right at her belly button, the word ME. One more word lay far below her skirt's waistband, unseen and incised across her mons pubis: NICKY. She looked up and saw Shayla's eyes, filled with tears. Shayla wiped at the ones that fell, frustrated.

"I *telt* myself I wouldn't do this tae ye," Shayla said in self-admonishment. She smiled. "Ye're beautiful, Niky. Marks and all. Never have I seen a girl so brave and true. Ye're pure magic."

Nico's own eyes stung.

"Oh. Ow. That hurt!" she said as a tear fell. "Can we hug when I'm clean?"

"Aye, and more. Let's get ye washed." Shayla took Nico's hand, her other holding Bear, and they walked together.

"You haven't asked—why—what happened at the hostel. And then this," Nico said, her stride unsteady. "You should be mad."

"Aye, I was mad. If not for the Makepeace, I wouldn't have reached the pit in time, and I suspected ya of an intention I should wring yer ear for," Shayla said with force, and Nico put her hand to her bandaged ear in alarm. "But we've plenty of time now for ye tae gie me yer whole tale, love," Shayla added softly.

"Thank you," Nico whispered. No one else was present in the open passageway except for tiny creatures in the weeds and debris, their eyes shining. Even the furtive graffiti artists were absent. The night sky, full of stars, was evident beyond the city lights on the street level above. A winged creature flew across, its body like a lion's.

Shayla's Id ring chimed and Shayla summoned a small interface. She read, brow knitted, then tapped a brief message.

"Oh no, are you in trouble?" Nico exclaimed as Shayla deactivated her interface.

"I'm in trouble?" Shayla said in mild surprise. "No, chick, it was Lucy's, asking if I were okay. They telt me about the fight. My uniform advertised the diner durin' the Slaughter Spawn broadcast," she added, wry. "Now they've more customers than they can handle."

"I made you leave work...fight in your waitress uniform! You look beautiful in it, but it's just not—I think I ruined your gunslinger reputation," Nico bemoaned, and Shayla laughed, low. She pointed at the monumental Shyla O'Fey graffiti on the concrete wall. Its paints glowed in the dark, and the gold leaf glimmered. Shayla's face softened.

"No one's supposed to know I fought in the pit, love."

Nico's insides warmed from a sudden realisation and she squeezed Shayla's hand, wishing her own hand wasn't so cold and undead.

You earned a monument for the sister you love and mourn, and... and maybe for the creature she is. Nico felt her repairing heart might re-burst at the thought.

"You should have shot me. I'm glad I only wanted to eat you and not mur—" Nico stopped walking.

"Niky?" Shayla said.

"I di—I didn't want to murd—a ha-ha-ha," Nico said, the sound hurting her, but elation bloomed, leaving her mouth as painful joy. She no longer wanted to murder. Those she loved were in no danger.

"Ha-ha-ha," Nico cried, the sound echoing against the sides of the passageway, and she held her aching chest, her repairing heart bleeding.

★

"Niky?" Shayla repeated with gentle concern. Nico had ceased her strange laughter, but she still held her heart with both hands, unable to fathom her good fortune.

My demons have fled.

"I—I'm okay." Nico resumed walking, Shayla watching beside

her. "It's such an odd feeling, being free. I'll—you'll understand when I tell you everything."

"I'll be listening, chick."

"What happened to MP-1634?"

"The Makepeace? Oh, once she saw you were patched up, love, she left."

"She?" Nico said. "*She?*"

"Aye," Shayla said, smiling. "Couldn't ya tell?"

"Not with such a...a big codpiece. Are the Makepeace okay with me?" *Especially when I became primal and wanted to bite you.*

"Since she's not here, chick, I think they've concluded yer case."

"I hope so," Nico said, and her regenerating heart felt lighter.

"Ye haven't asked me yet how ye did in the pit," Shayla then said. "Lucy's telt me the results."

"Oh?" Nico said, picking her way over debris. "But I cheated at the game. I used a burning car and grenades. And you came and saved me." She took Shayla's hand and held it in both of hers. "Thank you." *I will thank you with so much sex.*

"Aye, but ye went into their tunnel, chick, and no fighter dares tae do that. That makes up for burning up half the spawn before ye jumped in. But ye were in their lair fer nearly three minutes," Shayla added with severity.

"Sorry," Nico said meekly.

"Ye were ruled as havin' won, for ye stayed in the pit, six minutes. Dae ye want tae know how much ye made on yer fight?" Shayla asked, her tone casual.

"My—? Oh, I didn't bet."

"I thought so! Ya bad girl, Niky, ya had no intention of comin' back out!"

"I thought I had time to tell you my story?" Nico squeaked.

"Aye, ye do." Shayla rubbed Nico's forehead with her thumb. "Ya ough' tae be spanked."

"Heh," Nico said. She'd like that. They walked past the Cyrillic graffiti.

"Tell me what it says, Niky."

"*Strashnaya mest' i medved'*. It means, 'Fearful vengeance and bear'. People gave me the name on Old Earth, when I was after something." She hung her head. "Killing everything."

"Did ye find it?" Shayla asked, her tone soft.

"Yes. I saw it in the tunnel."

Nico recalled the little mouths, shrieking.

"I saw his face," she said. "His pitiful, awful face. And that face wasn't me."

The plaza of the ugly, roaring fountain was empty, devoid of life except for the stir of litter by the night breeze. Shayla helped Nico out of her oxfords and ruined stockings and took the bandages from Nico's ear and shoulder. Nico stepped into the shallow pool. She waded to the pouring spout of a fountain's head.

"Is it okay to put evil muck in the fountain's water?" she'd asked Shayla earlier.

"Aye, the fountain's called Purity," Shayla had assured. "It cleanses everything."

Nico's slashed shirt and cardigan slipped off her shoulders, and she pulled the rest down, the remnants hanging from her wrists and skirt's waistband. She stepped beneath pounding, freezing water and held her arms out, palms up, to reveal the messages incised on her forearms. The plaza's lone lights wavered through the sheets of sharp water that might cut away the intentions carved into her flesh — drown the words forced so long ago into her mind and body.

Obliterate me.

Nico emptied, and wings and gold rushed in.

Shayla was washing Bear in the shallow pool, dipping him with a reverence that seemed a baptism, when Nico finally stepped out from beneath the pouring water. Shayla squeezed Bear, the water falling clear, and sat him down by Nico's shoes. She rose and took off her corduroy coat, then held it open for Nico.

A warm coat—warmed by true body heat. Woodsy peach and bergamot beneath chemical smoke hugged Nico as Shayla knelt and unbuttoned Nico's cuffs, and if Shayla noticed and read the raised scars on Nico's forearms, she chose to make no mention. Shayla removed the slashed clothing. Nico did not shiver; she was an undead thing—cold and with a heart unbeating—but gladness stirred within, a radiance of gratitude, as she looked down at Shayla's shining hair.

Your Prince Charming, huh? Delores had said.

Shayla rose and hugged Nico tightly.

*

Nico had put her arms into the coat's long sleeves and was wiggling out of her wet skirt at Shayla's insistence when Dorothy chimed from the harness's pocket.

Shayla buttoned Nico up, then sat down with her by the shallow pool, wringing out Nico's skirt while Nico checked the caller's identity. She blanked out holo viewing. She wasn't ready to look Heloise in the eye.

"I'm sorry about the tranquilliser," she answered.

"I swear, I'm *not* Elisabeth Bathory," Heloise said.

"Sure you're not. Are you drunk?"

"I—I can *see* stuff...even with my eyes closed! You didn't have to drug me." A thud sounded—a body impacting carpet. "I've never bathed in blood, ever."

"You could have fooled me. You should sit down."

"I am *lying* down. My betting board—it activated, and *there* you were. Did you find your answer?"

"Yes." *Yes, I found him.*

"I cheated with a car set on fire, though," she added.

"Didn't matter. You're little, and the boards like that. Nico, I would have—"

"Mrs Allen," Nico interrupted, "when you were a housewife, did you wear a frilly white apron?"

"Did I—? Sure I did, and they were *ruffled*, not frilly."

"You should get one, and only wear that. With your heels. And a string of pearls."

"Is this your way of saying you're feeling frisky?" Heloise said. "Because if I'm going to do that, you have to dress up as Mr Allen."

"Frisky, like the cat. I like that. Okay, bye."

"Wait!" Heloise said, exasperated. "You are—when I'm not *stuck* on the ceiling—you are annoying, do you know that? I wanted you to win. I *knew* you'd win."

"Did you place a bet?"

"Yes. Where would you like the money?"

"Put all of it on animal shelters. Wait. And a victim's shelter. And a shelter for trafficking survivors. And then give the girls at the strip club really big tips. For me." *And thank you.*

"Thank you," she said, heartfelt, and cut the communication. Then she gasped. She retrieved the messages she had scheduled to release in the morning and deleted them.

"I could make ye such a cute kitten," Shayla said, her tone wistful, and she touched Nico's wet strands of hair. Nico looked at her, wide-eyed. "Who is it ye'd like in a ruffled apron?"

"Oh. I guess...I guess I'm getting over a prejudice. That was the Bathory with legs."

"Don't ye feel bad 'bout flirting," Shayla said. "She's very nice legs."

"But—I shouldn't have. I'm supposed to be da—not dating you."

"Aye, me and you." Shayla grinned and gripped Nico by the coat lapels. Shayla bared her teeth playfully. "But I'm not the bad, countess lawyer vampire, am I? Who ye want walking 'round mostly naked for ye?"

"Oh, gosh, you, in only an apron. I need you both." Nico clapped a hand over her mouth for such an arrogant demand, but Shayla smiled, apparently intrigued.

When had Nico lingered long enough to know a woman beyond the brief encounter? In the past, she'd none of the cunning or deception required to hide a vampire nature from an interested human. But on Darqueworld, deception wasn't needed. She could know women. She could have *two* loves.

"Oh," Nico said, dismayed. "I've never done anything like this. Real—real girlfriends." She gulped. "Real relationships? I'm so bad at this."

"No, don't ye say that." Shayla scooted close and gently pecked Nico on the lips. "There'll be me, and Mrs Allen. Wearin' a frilly apron. Do ye still want tae do tawdry Joycean things tae me?"

"Oh yes." Nico smiled, broader than she'd ever smiled, and the expression hurt her face.

"That's a start," Shayla said, and kissed her.

The kiss Nico returned was still too tentative, but Nico held Shayla with a preciousness she'd thought no longer possible.

My hands aren't his.

"Ye look so happy," Shayla said softly.

"A future," Nico simply said, and she couldn't breathe, even though she didn't need to. Something sprouted inside her, the seed of something.

CHAPTER EIGHTEEN

Her Id chimed.

Nico opened her eyes. She was inside a sleep-egg for two, Bear on her chest and her switchblade in hand. The hatch surface woke and displayed a time: 09:30. Last night she hadn't gone home with Shayla, as much as she had wanted to.

"I tried to kill you," she had said. "And I tried to kill Heloise. I think I need a night to—to make sure I'm not a jerk anymore."

"Dinnae wait too long tae accept ye're not a jerk," Shayla had said, and because there hadn't been much of the night left, she returned with Nico to Jifk airport. There, Shayla joined her in a sleep-egg for two, filling the tiny space with the comforting, delicious scent of female fertility. Nico slept, exhausted, and only stirred briefly when Shayla roused later and kissed her good bye.

"I forgot to gie ye this, love," Shayla had whispered, and pressed Nico's shut switchblade into her hand.

Her Id chimed again, and she looked at the caller's identity.

"Hi," she answered. "I'm in an egg."

"Lone Nico and Bear," Specs hailed, his holo projecting. "That was a *close* one. Feeling better?"

"Yes," Nico said. "Are the Makepeace okay with me?" She

figured that if they gave Shayla her blade, they had to be, but she wanted to make sure.

"They will be, on one condition. Okay, this is more my condition, which I urge you to accept. Because I don't think you'd want mind or memory adjustment—"

"No. My memories are hell, but they're me."

"Got it. That's why I have a—and I wouldn't recommend this unless I thought it a good fit for you. With your kind of no-nonsense, samurai approach. I like that, by the way."

"What are we talking about?"

"Dialectal behavioural therapy," Specs said. "Very direct, very methodical. No nonsense. Let's try that first, to help you put a leash on that chronic behaviour. The terrifying one. Whaddaya say?"

"Yes," Nico said. She had two women to think of.

"Aces." Her Id lit up. "Sent you the page to an excellent outpatient group. And hey, you worried the bejaysus out of me last night."

"Sorry."

"You don't get to do that again—I'm not sure what I'm telling you *not* to do, since you do good things. You have a scary way of doing good things, you know that?"

"I didn't even arrive here to do what I did. I just...what if I'd been set up?" She thought of how she'd been allowed to keep her mints tin, of the Po in immigration. Of the way Tough Guy had simply watched her—how all the Makepeace had watched her. "What if I was meant to take down Fedotov Kolbasa?"

"That is so—where's my team of computer hacking conspiracy geeks? Guess there's just me. Whether you think this or that led you to whatever, I don't think we'll ever know the final answer. How about celebrating that it's over! Because as much as I commend your lack of quips or zero desire to charm, you went a little bat guano crazy there, Lone Nico. Your trip down *meifumado*—it's done, right? Let's get you that mild-mannered life you want."

"Okay."

"We got a few more weeks together, you and me. I want to be able to release you into the wild, born free. As free as the wind blows. As free as the—"

"Okay, I get it," Nico said.

"Another suggestion. Future Fits." Her Id lit again. "They're a non-profit that clothes the newly arrived in business attire. For the citizenship exams and for job interviews."

"Thanks. But how did you know I needed clothes?"

"Well, that tee shirt you're wearing is really cute, but it's not quite you."

Nico looked down. She wore a girl's red tee with the logo, *I Love Again NewYork*, except the love part was a big pink heart with baby hearts. Her bared forearms revealed a message in raised scars that her maker had carved. One said, *My Love*, the other, *Your Death*.

"I'll go right away," she said. "By the way, what do you know about cosmetic surgery for vampires?"

★

After ending her conversation with Specs, Nico thought about popping out of her egg, but she didn't feel ready yet to face the bustle of the terminal. Shayla would be at Lucy's already, serving up pancakes and pies.

Good morning, chick, Shayla's message said. *Come for a cup when you can.*

Nico grinned, then opened a message from Heloise. It simply contained a list.

Heloise had divided her winnings among a large number of rescues and shelters. Nico scrolled through the names, each one having four figures listed next to it.

"Wow, people really didn't think we were going to get out alive," Nico said to Bear.

Heloise had sent only the list. Nico bit her lip, remembering the scent of Heloise's blood and the blossoming red that had spread on her shirt.

"I'm not him," she said. "But I am his daughter."

She contacted the therapy treatment centre Specs recommended and made an appointment.

Nico had no one to discuss the whole of what happened, with Shayla working and Heloise—well, Nico couldn't face Heloise yet—so she talked it out with Bear. She sat Bear and his harness down on the small garment bag containing her new dress jacket from Future Fits, loosened the cuffs of her new white, button-down dress shirt, and placed Dorothy where her Id could record her words and film the diagrams she drew with chalk (bought at the Japanese sundries shop) on the rooftop of the YOBA. Tough Guy wasn't present, but Amazon Woman was, and perhaps she listened while surveying the streets below.

"My maker makes me slave-bait, knowing I'd snap and become the killer he wanted," Nico said. She drew a spawn-bud to signify him. "Then Fedosov, who later became Fedotov, sends me away." She drew a sausage for Fedosov, and an arcing line away from the spawn-spud, sausage, and the circle representing Old Earth for her journey to the Pleiades. She drew seven stars. She then drew Bear in the stars. "And I guess he got obsessed, trying to protect himself from me. Putting me and Bear on his kolbasa label. Eating vampires to gain powers. But twenty years later, the vampire exodus happened, so he sent his people and his greedy little self over here." Nico drew a large circle for Darqueworld. She paused.

"Twenty years is a long time to suck on vampires without the primacy noticing," she pondered. "The vampires of the Leningrad Oblast should have found out, especially after my spree. Fedosov might've been forced to flee to Darqueworld soon after exiling me. Unless...."

The Makepeace turned her head, her face in profile. She seemed to wait for Nico to voice her suspicion. Nico became aware of the chalk in her hand, her Id recording, and of the words, sitting on her lips that could create a new hell for her.

This isn't done, is it? She thought towards Amazon Woman. But Nico had decided: her part was done.

"Unless someone on Old Earth helped hide his activity," she finished vaguely. She returned her attention to her drawings.

"He needed to be here *before* I got here, so he timed his arrival several years previous, renamed his kolbasa business, and waited. Then, two of his henchmen died in that time." She drew two stick men on Darqueworld and crossed them out. "He also figured out a way to trap me, using Baba Yagas to make veils and a Po to mind-wipe vampires. Except Esche remembered." Nico drew spikes. "And maybe he hoped to eat me and make my skull his drinking cup." Nico drew half of a skull with bubbles rising from it, and then sat back on her heels, viewing her handiwork.

"But how long had he been manufacturing Prochnyy Kolbasa?" Nico solemnly asked the Makepeace.

"The product, Prochnyy, made its debut nine months before your arrival," Amazon Woman answered, her gaze returned to the streets below.

"And when did you figure out what it was made of?" Nico retrieved Bear from where he sat in the sun and hugged him.

"The Autocratress of New Byzantium alerted us to Prochnyy's qualities five months ago. The vampire primacy agreed to delay retribution while we determined Fedotov's methods and whereabouts."

"You didn't know where he was. And then I showed up in immigration, and maybe the Po saw something in my head. You let me be the lure to draw Fedosov out."

"You did well," Amazon Woman said.

"I let Fedosov live. What will happen to him now?"

After some silence, Nico understood. The vampire primacy had Fedosov, and they would not be kind.

Nico picked up Dorothy and made a note to look up New Byzantium. If it was Christian, she wanted to see if they were like the obscure, Jewish sect of ancient times.

After putting on her harness, polishing the mystery and Skye buttons, and then situating Bear, she went to the Makepeace. Nico hugged her from behind. When she let go, Amazon Woman turned her head again.

"Have a good day, potential citizen," she said.

★

Her unfinished business had been concluded. She was a cork shooting to the top, then bobbing. Nico moved through the rush hour crowds, float-floating, adrift on waves that kept pushing her towards a comforting shore. It was a shore Shayla happened to be on.

Shayla crouched in patched jeans at Loch Niamh's shore, watching the waves lap. No longer in her waitress uniform, she did not look like a woman who had to blast spawn apart and babysit a homeless, injured, and mostly naked vampire last night. When Nico approached, Shayla rose and smiled.

"Are ye ready, love?" she asked.

Nico reached for Shayla's hand, unable to say anything, and Shayla held it, firm and strong.

They took the train to the city's wall, and then descended down to the veldt. From the wall's edge, they walked towards a sheltered rest area. The sun was dipping, lighting the world with orange and blue, while beneath, the black shadows stretched and grew. Beyond the rest area, small memorials of flowers, candles, and gifts sat on the earth and rough grass, some emitting holo-photographs. A balloon drifted from one. At the perimeter of the scattered memorials, small cairns sat stacked. Nico laid her garment bag down on a picnic table and joined Shayla, who surveyed the veldt, thumbs in her woven belt. The last of the sunlight illuminated her calm face. Nico held Shayla's belt, her fingers in the waistband, and Shayla looked at her, her gaze kind.

"Ye saw yer maker once, love, so he'll not appear again."

Shayla put a hand against Nico's neck. They waited, watching the sun disappear beneath the horizon. Darkness moved in and enveloped. Shayla caressed Nico's nape and gestured to the veldt.

"Walk to the cairns, chick, but no farther."

Nico nodded. She straightened Bear and his choker, and walked past the memorials, the wind tugging at her hair and clothes. She stopped at the last of the cairns and stared into the dark.

In the distance, a girl stood, with long, platinum-white hair and black clothes that remained still in the veldt's wind. She wore a leather choker, but she stood too far away for Nico to discern if it had little spikes.

Nico's apology died on her lips. Somehow, she knew that Esche had travelled beyond what words could convey. One more step, and Nico might follow Esche to the wordless world.

Nico blinked, and Esche disappeared.

"Good-bye," Nico whispered.

She went home with Shayla and spent the night being sexually solicitous. Bright and early in the morning, Nico jumped up the steps of the Immigration Centre, ready to take her citizenship exam.

I'm full of witch's blood, me! Nico leaped six steps in a single bound.

She wore her new (used) black blazer, originally intended for a high school uniform. Shayla had brushed Nico's back and shoulders, then pecked her on the lips like a mum sending her child to school. Shayla had the evening shift at Lucy's, and intended to pick Nico up when the exam was done. A school insignia patch had been unstitched from the blazer's left breast, and Nico had placed Shayla's buttons to distract from any indication of the former patch. She also wore a grey and pink striped necktie, and so did Bear.

She entered the great lobby, the piano's keys tinkling. Music echoed, a beautiful, familiar melody, and a crowd gathered around the piano and its player.

There's a place for us, Nico sang in her head as she boarded the escalator. She saw herself in the escalator's mirrored wall, and noticed that her black blazer did not match the black of her skirt, nor did her black stockings. The escalator ascended and the piano's pure sounds flowed; smooth, light, and nuanced beneath strong, assured strokes. Nico glanced over the side and saw Heloise seated at the piano. Nico's still heart jumped.

Heloise concentrated on her playing, her sharp brows intent. One hand danced over the other to lightly touch the higher octaves and then returned. The music rose in the space that stretched above, following Nico up the escalator.

"Somewhen a place for us," a man sang softly behind her.

Nico's chest tightened. When she reached the floor, she walked quickly to the women's restroom. Her vision blurred. Heloise's music ended, the last, soft keystroke echoing, and in the stillness, no applause followed. The bathroom door shut behind Nico. She saw herself in the mirror, and the painful tears fell.

Our heart's opening, she thought to Bear, because her throat refused to work.

She approached the sink counter. Her mirror-double hadn't the face of the new arrival of days ago but her waif countenance remained, pointing to some great sadness within that might become more ghostlike, someday. And perhaps fade just a little away.

It's not like you can get over violation, imprisonment, torture, and mind games in one move to a new planet, she told herself, and wiped her cheeks. But immigrants and refugees had done so through the ages, fleeing wars, concentration camps, famines, and disasters. Life began again.

The bathroom door opened, and Heloise walked in.

She started at the sight of Nico, then gave her a look of

exasperation.

"I am not stalking you," Heloise said. "And I'm not going to touch you. So don't you dare scream."

Nico swallowed. "You're way over there, how can you molest me?" Heloise approached the far sink, then washed her hands beneath the vibrations.

"I don't know. Maybe with my thoughts," Heloise said with sarcasm. She looked in the mirror and pulled her black, narrow leather tie out of its knot. "The girls at the Pussy Lounge said thanks."

"How many lap dances was that?"

"Six." Heloise undid her tie's knot and adjusted the ends, bringing the wider end to hang lower.

"I was serious about the frilly apron," Nico said.

"Oh?"

"And the pearls."

"Oh?"

Heloise made a four-in-hand knot, her long, slender fingers working, then pulled it apart again. Nico walked over to her.

"Here, let me. I used to do it for my dad."

Heloise lifted her chin, put her hands behind her back, and averted her gaze. Nico held the tie's ends. She carefully folded them over, pulled them through, and formed the small, slightly elongated shape that was the four-in-hand. When she tightened the knot at Heloise's throat, she smoothed the points of Heloise's collar, then followed the tie down to tuck the long end into Heloise's waistband.

There. Her countess lawyer vampire. Beautiful piano player. Nico let her fingers linger within the waistband and took a breath. Heloise had been in the sun recently, and her warmed fragrance bloomed.

"Thought you might assume next that I *helped* turn us into sausages," Heloise grumbled.

"I made a mistake," Nico said. "I'm sorry." She held Heloise's waistband and sensed her perfumed body's stillness; cool, pristine, and clean. Nothing pulsed in Heloise's perfection, her death's suspension. But Nico felt her own undead state drawn to such perfection, and perhaps Shayla had known that would happen.

Be my maker.

Heloise looked at her. She slowly reached into her jacket's inner pocket and pulled out a small, bright red, translucent lollipop, wrapped in flat cellophane.

Nico made a sound of humour and swallowed, unable to meet Heloise's gaze. She accepted the treat.

"I hate to see a little girl unhappy," Heloise softly said.

Nico hooked Heloise's waistband with both of her hands, the lollipop pressing.

"Show me your fangs," Nico whispered.

Heloise bared her teeth, snarling. Her blue eyes changed.

Nico snarled back.

Nico hurried into her testing room dead last, her hair entirely mussed, and received her paper test booklet, two wooden pencils, her answer sheet, and a blank sheet of scratch paper. She didn't think she needed scratch paper because it was a civics test, not a math test, but she accepted it anyway. The ballroom-sized testing room was filled with small desks, all occupied by a variety of humanoids and last century chrono-immigrants who might find paper and pencil easier to handle than a holo interface. She found a desk to sit at, and the introduction to the test commenced.

Half an hour later, Nico was done, the vast room gravely silent as people coughed, sighed, chirped, or hissed, working on their questions. The test monitors walked down the aisles, and Nico decided to sit and while away the rest of the hour rather than rise early and hand her sheet in. A tree person rustled in the seat behind her.

Mr Bear sat beneath her seat, and she didn't think he minded being stored away as he'd had the pleasure of sitting on the bathroom counter and witnessing a spot of carnality, half an hour before.

Nico licked her lips, and still tasted Heloise.

Heloise had beautiful, big fangs. Nico drew fangs on her scratch paper.

She still couldn't kiss properly on the mouth, but she could always do the other kind of kissing, and that had made Heloise swagger out of the bathroom, once more the owner of the world.

"How about I take you for ice cream later," Heloise had whispered, and rubbed away her lipstick mark from the corner of Nico's mouth. "Is that the pretty witch I smell on you?"

Nico would need to message Shayla about Heloise. This nascent triad—and she hoped she could make it work—required reading a book or watching a holo, and she made a note of that on her scratch paper. She drew more fangs and then a pistol for Shayla. Shayla might not approve—a pie or coffee mug might be nicer—but to Nico, Shayla was her secret gun, and she blew holes in evil.

Nico wrote: *Nico loves*—she drew a heart—drew a pistol—and then drew a set of fangs.

She looked at what she'd drawn and thought a kind of perfection had been attained. It would be necessary to draw the combination often, in several different formulas that proved the same result over and over. It was a spell to annihilate the one carved into her body.

If Heloise had been Scots too...I don't know if I could have dealt with that. Or Shayla, a vampire.

She was certain her psyche would have blown up. No, their aspects had to be separate. Two defeated one. Slowly but surely, Heloise and Shayla invalidated her maker's memory, one particle at a time, with sheer numbers.

THE END, monster, she wrote on her scratch paper.

★

When test time ended, Nico was busy drawing pictures of spawn-spud makers getting ground into sausage. The monitors gathered booklets, test sheets, and pencils, and Nico shuffled out with the rest of the potential citizens into the hallway. Doors opened across the way and sunlight spilled, the light so bright it made Nico jump back. Grinning people exited, their companions photographing and congratulating them.

New citizens, Nico thought.

"That's gonna be us," a woman who'd exited the exam room declared. Re'shawn, dressed in a blouse and blazer, filed out of a second exam room that had also opened its doors. She looked completely healed from her ordeal.

"Hey, sugarplum," Re'shawn said.

"I'm glad you're okay. But now I'm a fairy?" Nico exclaimed.

"Yeah, if fairies were sugarcoated almond balls."

"You're a cop," Nico accused.

"Naw, more like I got deputised," Re'shawn drawled. "Was recruited to get in on that sting operation at my immigration interview. Didn't you?" She walked to the side of the corridor as it became crowded, and Nico joined her. Nico recalled the series of flashes she'd experienced in the hologram room.

"You stood out like a sore thumb at the hostel," Nico pointed out instead.

"Didn't I know it," Re'shawn said, wry. "The moment I went back there with you, Aussie Girl got the drop on me. I'm still ashamed about that."

"Ozzie."

"Huh?"

"But you weren't the only one working for the OI."

"Naw, two others had gone in before, and both didn't come out. They wore glasses to record what happened." Re'shawn pointed at her own eyes. "Wearing those probably gave them away. I didn't do any better—when I first walked into that hostel? Shee—I mean, pardon me, Lord, shoot. I knew the bad guys had made me."

"But the OI told you to go back. What made you qualified for the sting?" Nico recalled Eton boy's altruism.

"I dunno." Re'shawn shrugged. "My last kills were vampires who tried taking over the ship bringing us here. I wasn't cool with mutiny. Not down with the meat grinding of our kind, either. So, they didn't ask you to investigate this?"

"No," Nico said. "I was the vigilante."

Re'shawn held out her palm. "Five, go-go girl."

Nico slapped her palm awkwardly.

Nico didn't have a chance to ask Re'shawn what she got in return for nearly being made into sausage. She also wanted to ask if Eton boy was okay. But she received a summons on her Id that told her to report to another room and had to scuttle plans of lunching with her friend. Re'shawn departed and Nico ascended to another floor—one high enough to cause nosebleeds—to sit outside a closed door.

I hope I'm not in trouble for that car I set on fire.

She and Bear watched Patrick Stewart as Capt Jean Luc Picard in "Drumhead" on her Id when a clerk emerged.

"Ms Alexikova and Mr Bear? Follow me please," she said.

Nico put Dorothy away and followed the clerk into the room's front entry, then through the inner doors for a low-lit, great chamber. Shield doors blocked the scenic windows, and a marble fount stood in the middle. But what gave Nico pause were the people present, standing to the side of the fount.

Shayla? Shayla smiled, dressed in moss green and wearing an amber necklace. MP-1634 stood beside her, the helm removed, revealing an impassive face with eyes of mirrored silver. When Nico neared, she saw who waited beside the Makepeace.

Specs sat within an enclosed mobilised unit, his head against a cushioned rest. His chest and one arm were visible, dressed in a button-down with blue striped tie. An exo-skeleton device covered his resting hand. The bottom half of his body was not apparent.

He gestured with the control device and turned his unit to face her.

"Got out my best tie for you, Nico," he grinned. Nico raised both of Bear's arms in celebration, though she still didn't know what was happening. A pedestal next to the fount and waiting clerk emitted a holo projection, lighting the surrounding area. Nico's mouth dropped.

Sabella Peck looked twenty years older than the one Nico knew from her photographs. Fine lines edged her mouth and warm eyes, and her face bore the broadened aspect that came with age.

She is so beautiful.

"Hello Nico," Sabella's hologram said. "I am Immigration Judge Peck. For your service to Darqueworld, we express our heartfelt gratitude and wish to grant you citizenship. Are you ready to take your oath?"

Nico breathed. "I am."

"You will act as proxy for Mr Bear, yes?"

"Yes."

"Step forwards and hold Darqueworld in your hands," the hologram said.

Nico looked within the fount's bowl and smelled the ocean. Pure seawater sat, a glistening mirror. Nico glanced at Shayla and Shayla cupped her hands.

Nico dipped her hands, cupping water. She held it up, and the shield doors rumbled and parted, letting the first beam of Merope fall upon her. She blinked, dazzled.

"As Merope is our witness and as three who know you will witness, please repeat after me, Nico," the Sabella hologram said, the opening widening, and Nico did.

"I, Nicolette Alexikova, do solemnly, sincerely and truly affirm and declare that, on becoming a citizen of Darqueworld, I will be faithful and bear true allegiance to its holarchy, respect and observe the Basic Laws and laws of Darqueworld, and refrain from acts which might cause it harm."

Light flooded the room, and water sparkled in Nico's hands. Merope's face illuminated and the Makepeace's armour shone.

Congratulations, Nico and Bear," the hologram said, and Shayla and the clerk applauded.

Nico let the water fall from her fingers and into the fount, her body hot from pure sunlight. She looked at the hologram.

"I have to say it," she said. "I love you."

"I love you too, Nico," the hologram said. "Welcome the sun."

Nico opened her arms.

The end.

"It's
vampires,
all the way
down."

A DARQUEPUNK
NOVEL

BLOODY
NIKE

ELIZABETH WATASIN

More from Elizabeth:

The Dark Victorian: Risen Vol 1
The Dark Victorian: Bones Vol 2

Ice Demon: A Dark Victorian Penny Dread Vol 1
Medusa: A Dark Victorian Penny Dread Vol 2

Sundark: An Elle Black Penny Dread Vol 1
Poison Garden: An Elle Black Penny Dread Vol 2

Monster Stalker: A Darquepunk Novel Vol 1
Bloody Nike: A Darquepunk Novel Vol 2
Gunslinger: A Darquepunk Novel Vol 3

The Wrecking Faerie: A Charm School Novella Vol 1
Hot Roddin' To Hell: A Charm School Novella Vol 2
Body Chase: A Charm School Novella Vol 3

AUTHOR'S NOTES

Leningrad:
Nico is a 90's vampire, but Leningrad still exists where she is (which in our timeline, returned to the name St Petersburg in 1991). Therefore, she's from an Earth alternate from our own.

Food made from blood:
Lucy's Diner menu of foods cooked from blood was made possible by the Nordic Food Lab research of Elisabeth Paul:
http://magazine.good.is/features/the-nordic-food-lab-cooks-with-blood

Shayla's Scots dialect and slang:
I used this young woman's laid-back brogue to guide me (but less on the 'creaky voice' touch):
https://youtu.be/rBaB-7Jf5SI
I kept it really light, to avoid reader unfamiliarity and caricature (as I'm no native speaker). Scots slang—in this case, possibly the Glaswegian sort—is considered working class, but

I think Shayla's background on Darqueworld is equivalent to that background. I do have her pronounce 'you' and 'your', for example, rather than 'ye' or 'ya' at times (Scots casual speech) for the sake of her having to communicate universally. Otherwise, 'I' would be more like 'ah', 'was' more like 'wis', and so on. True Scots voices, when written with great naturalism, is a pleasure. Read samples here: http://www.ayecan.com/read_scots.html

Words and phrases Shayla may use:

auld = old
bairn = infant
belter = great
blootered = very drunk
bonnie = pretty
braw = (compliment on looks and merit) very nice, great
brither = brother
cannae = cannot
chib = knife or razor used as a weapon
dinnae = did not
ehm = um
fash = fuss
fayther, or paw = father
gie = give
gi'ed (more correctly, *gied*) = (gived) gave
hen = term of endearment; though Shayla says "chick" where Nico is concerned.
Is that you? = Are you done?
ken = know
magic = great
manky = dirty
mither, or mum, or ma (maw—"mahw"—is presently more an insult) = mother
pure = very (as in, "that book was pure quality")
quality = great
shairp = sharp

skelp = hit or smack someone or thing
skunnurt = disgusted
stoater = really exceptional
tae = to
telt = told
that's me = I'm done
the morra = tomorrow
wean = child
wee = little
wheesht/wissht = be quiet, hush
ya = you (informal when addressing someone, as in, "ya idiot")
ye = you (common use)

Gender:

Gender perception is rapidly changing presently, mostly because general culture is becoming aware (again) of identities beyond the usual two. Historically, some cultures already understood gender outside of the two accepted ones. There are several gender-neutral pronoun sets, and I chose the Elverson pronouns (1975) *ey, eir, em*, where dropping the *th* makes writing easier.

https://en.wikipedia.org/wiki/Gender-specific_and_gender-neutral_pronouns

https://en.wikipedia.org/wiki/Spivak_pronoun

Nico's music:

"Last Exit for the Lost," by Fields of the Nephilim, 1988.

"This Corrosion," by Sisters of Mercy, the long version, 1987.

"Lords of the Null-Lines" by Hyper On Experience (Alex Banks, Danny Demierre). The original 1993 version is what Nico listens to, with the entire original sampling intact. https://youtu.be/tbLCAIkunL4

Symbolism of the null-line:

For an explanation of the null line, you can refer to p390 of *The Einstein Equations and the Large Scale Behavior of Gravitational*

Fields: 50 Years of the Cauchy Problem in General Relativity, by Piotr T. Chrusciel and Helmut Felix Friedrich, published by Birkhäuser, 2004 (view the book at Google Books: http://bit.ly/1dFODYQ) quote:

"...a null line in space-time is defined to be an inextendible null geodesic which is globally achronal, *i.e.*, for which no two points can be joined by a timelike curve."

It then goes on to say:

"All of the null geodesics in Minkowski space, de Sitter space and anti-de Sitter space are null lines. The null generators of the event horizon in extended Schwarzschild space-time are null lines."

Or, you can refer to Alex Banks's proto-mystical explanation here: http://www.discogs.com/Hyper-On-Experience-Lords-Of-The-Null-Lines-The-Extremely-Bootlegged-Remixes/release/31712

Which begins:

"A Null Line is the path of a light ray or other massless object through space-time.

The consequences of this statement are both fascinating and frightening. To understand why, we must first consider what happens to a particle at light speed.

Albert Einstein said in his theory of relativity that an object travelling at the speed of light is not effected [sic] by time, that is to say it does not experience time. Something that does not experience time takes no time to travel any distance. Although we may observe a particle of light (called a photon) travelling a set distance in a measured time, the particle itself has not aged."

It then goes on to give a metaphysical explanation of the universe.

The corridor demons:

This is in reference to Johannes Kepler's book, *Somnium*, published 1634.

Lone Nico and Bear:
When Specs calls Nico, "Lone Nico and Bear", he's referring to *Lone Wolf and Cub*, a manga created by writer Kazuo Koike and artist Goseki Kojima.

"Okay, let's screw this up":
When Jacqueline Kim performed at Xena Con 2015, she would say this before each song. An audience member asked if her saying it was akin to "break a leg", which was possibly the spirit of the line.
https://en.wikipedia.org/wiki/Jacqueline_Kim

Sexual Trafficking:
I hope the following resources will help inform and give an understanding of how sexual trafficking works, and why justice often does not protect victims or persecute those who hurt them.
My first understanding of sexual trafficking came from reading an article a long time ago, which opened with a scene of a shack available to migrant workers, where children who'd been sold by their families lay in cots. It was an image that stayed with me for years, and I've now resolved my feelings about it, however inadequately, with Nico and Bear.
http://www.traffickingresourcecenter.org/what-human-trafficking/human-trafficking/traffickers
http://www.thenoproject.org/english/slavery/the-traffickers/
http://facts.randomhistory.com/human-trafficking-facts.html
http://www.bethejam.org/tactics

"She tastes like crushed flowers," one said:
I wrote this line in reference to a certain metaphor (not the cut sandal-tree or the crushed violet flower metaphor, though they are the same idea). Quote:
In 1855 a metaphor employing trampled flowers appeared in a journal called "The Sacred Circle" which contained articles about spiritualism:
Forgiveness is the perfume which flowers give when trampled

upon.
http://quoteinvestigator.com/2013/09/30/violet-forgive/

Brown's Meatpacking:
The name is in reference to Upton Sinclair's *The Jungle*.

"Jerry" and "Tommy":
When Eton boy says, "Jerry's not bested us," he's using WWI British slang for the Germans. Nico responds by calling him "Tommy", which was British slang, dating from Victorian times, for common soldiers in the British Army. Since Eton boy was under duress and possibly confused, Nico did not correct him about who his captors were.

Gurkha Service No 1 (Sarkhuri Khukuri):
Happens to be this knife from Khukuri House, and the perfect size for Nico. http://www.thekhukurihouse.com/catalog/product.php?id=3935fc5113

How to set a car on fire:
And no, they do not explode like in the movies.
http://www.slate.com/articles/news_and_politics/explainer/2005/11/so_you_wanna_torch_a_peugeot.html
http://truckyeah.jalopnik.com/i-set-two-cars-on-fire-last-night-heres-what-i-learne-1540984020
Watch how a car burns and see how much I embellished, https://youtu.be/9MklETU3DyM

Heloise's piano playing:
This very enjoyable and lovely performance of a certain Broadway song was my reference. https://youtu.be/q3IBWKgj6WY

When Re'shawn refers to a sugarplum:
She really means a sugar-coated almond, or comfit, not a dried plum. An in-depth history of the true sugar-plum (British)

is given at this site, http://www.historicfood.com/Comfits.htm

Quote: "When C. T. Onions composed the definition of sugar-plum for the OED some time after 1914, the original meaning of sugar-plum was still extant -

'Sugar-plum - A small round or oval sweetmeat, made of boiled sugar and variously flavoured and coloured; a comfit'."

Possible Resemblances:

Again NewYork may resemble New York City

Jifk Spaceport may resemble JFK Airport

Count Ulock may resemble Count Orlock

Sabella Peck may resemble Isabella Rosellini

Beckensdale coats may resemble Burberry coats

The parfum Chasse Geraud Soeurs may resemble Chamade Guerlain

The shoe brand Christoffel Loulain may resemble Christian Louboutin

Pantone colour Bulgarian Rose Red may serve the function of Chinese Red

The Rocklyn Hotel may resemble the Rosslyn Hotel

Paperback versions contain
illustration galleries.

ELIZABETH WATASIN

The DARK VICTORIAN
SERIES

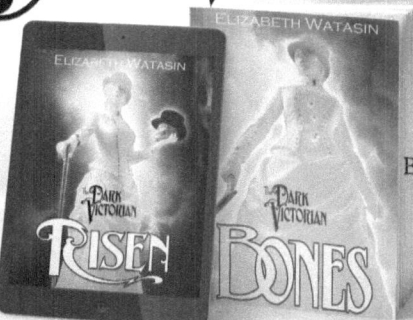

Amazon
Barnes & Noble
iBookstore

Learn more at
A-girlstudio.com.

Bringing you uncanny heroines in shilling shocker mysteries,
paranormal romance, and Steampunk adventuress tales.

ELIZABETH WATASIN

The DARK
VICTORIAN

BONES

About The Author

Elizabeth Watasin is the author of the Gothic steampunk series *The Dark Victorian*, the *Elle Black Penny Dreads*, the *Darquepunk* series, and is the creator/artist of the indie comics series Charm School, which was nominated for a Gaylactic Spectrum award. After twenty years working in animated films and comic books, she lives in Los Angeles with her black cat named Draw, busy bringing readers uncanny heroines in shilling shockers and adventuress tales.

Follow the news of her latest projects at A-Girl Studio.

www.a-girlstudio.com

Visit her online at:

https://www.facebook.com/groups/ElizabethWatasinsClubHecate

twitter.com/ewatasin

www.ingramcontent.com/pod-product-compliance
Lightning Source LLC
Chambersburg PA
CBHW032146190626
46814CB00005BA/1855